The Abyss line of cutting-edge psychological horror is committed to publishing the best, most innovative works of dark fiction available. ABYSS is horror unlike anything you've ever read before. It's not about haunted houses or evil children or ancient Indian burial grounds. We've all read those books, and we all know their plots by heart.

ABYSS is for the seeker of truth, no matter how disturbing or twisted it may be. It's about people, and the darkness we all carry within us. ABYSS is the new horror from the dark frontier. And in that place, where we come face-to-face with terror, what we find is ourselves.

"Thank you for introducing me to the remarkable line of novels currently being issued under Dell's Abyss imprint. I have given a great many blurbs over the last twelve years or so, but this one marks two firsts: first *unsolicited* blurb (*I* called *you*) and the first time I have blurbed a whole *line* of books. In terms of quality, production, and plain old storytelling reliability (that's the bottom line, isn't it?), Dell's new line is amazingly satisfying . . . a rare and wonderful bargain for readers. I hope to be looking into the Abyss for a long time to come."

—Stephen King

Please turn the page for more extraordinary acclaim . . .

death's door

door

JOHN WOOLEY
AND RON WOLFE

A DELL BOOK

Published by
Dell Publishing
a division of
Bantam Doubleday Dell Publishing Group, Inc.
666 Fifth Avenue
New York, New York 10103

Copyright © 1992 by John Wooley and Ron Wolfe

ISBN: 0-440-21196-4

Printed in the United States of America

Published simultaneously in Canada

October 1992

10 9 8 7 6 5 4 3 2 1

OPM

To our friend and agent, Harold Schmidt,
for knocking on the right door,
and to Jeanne Cavelos for answering.

—J.W., R.W.

PROLOGUE

November, 1990

The woman screamed as the bullet exploded in his chest, and the shrill noise buzzed through his head like a hornet as he crumpled, thinking *Damn this life!*

Case Hamilton saw only a blur of the mayhem in the corner of his eye. He heard the far-off report of Frank's .38, and he knew that Frank had dropped the punk in the ski mask, the one with the chrome-plated automatic.

Case still could see the white flash from the muzzle of the gun that might have killed him—a dancing light, red on the edges. Pretty in a way. Like blood on marble.

He hoped that Frank had shot to kill.

Case hoped that he would be keeping company on the bloodied floor with two dead niggers, instead of just the one he'd dropped himself: three shots to the head.

He tried to lever himself up. His big hands slipped against the buckled linoleum in the aisle of the liquor store, and he didn't have the strength to try again.

His hands explored the floor around him, finding shards of broken glass. They came back to him smelling of thick wine.

DAMN THIS LIFE!

Thunder cracked, and a hard flash of lightning etched the

store's shelves of wine bottles in blue-white. The storm would have no mercy.

He felt hands on him, heard voices. The meaningless words sounded small, tinny and intense, as though they were coming from a TV set someone had just turned on in another room.

Maybe a cop show. Case tried to laugh at the sardonic thought, but he couldn't.

He was inside himself, in a place where the hands weren't touching, and the lifeblood spurting from his chest had nothing to do with him anymore.

He wasn't afraid, but he hated. God, how he hated. Hatred was his blood now, swirling hot and viscous inside him, and he let it flow, washing in and out of his consciousness the accumulated residue of a lifetime of bitterness. The spics, the niggers—the blight of the inner city. The drugs. The drunks. The street crazies. The Bloods, the Crips. The syndicate. The rich scum, and the money monkeys with their long, soft fingers into the city government, swelled with the arrogance of having skipped away clean with whatever they wanted. The fat-ass lawyers gotten always-and-always fatter, and their drug-dealer clients, pleased as punch, grinning as they waltzed out of the courtroom. The squishy-soft judges who emptied their crawling cages full of human vermin onto the street. The punks who laughed at him, knowing they were going to be cut loose quicker than a cop could fill out the arrest reports, the paperwork that kept him shackled to a desk.

And women—the women who threw him over. Took his time, took his money, took his love. Took a walk.

The women who laughed at him. All red lips and sharp teeth, those women, and their bodies for sale, and their dark eyes welling with contempt for him as a cop who wouldn't bend.

Daring him. Calling to him. To reach out to them—out from the depths of his loneliness, and only to be taught again, and again, and again they were all liars. They were all whores. They were all Beverly.

In a final, desperate search of reason, Case knew that he'd begun to die a long time ago, from the night that he'd caught her with another man.

In *their* bed, with her tanned legs locked around her Lover Boy, and her eyes seeing Case in a moment of dreaminess—just before the terror.

And even then, if she'd only tried a little, cared a little, he thought he could have stayed married to her. They could have had a home together, and he wouldn't have come to *this* . . . this ebbing away of his life in red rivulets, the color of all that he hated.

And it all came together, rolling like thunder into a white-hot core of hatred, and he knew what he hated the most.

Hated. The man who'd betrayed every dream in his life. Hated. The man who'd forsaken his beautiful daughter. Hated. The big, bad cop.

Hated the man who was dying with nothing to cling to . . .

He felt himself caught in a whirlpool, flying down through darkness. His fingertips found a sharp-edged rip in the linoleum, and he caught hold, anchoring himself to the floor. But he couldn't stop falling.

The store's fluorescent ceiling lights seemed as far away, as dim as guttering candles, and he was falling away from the light, from the last of the light.

Into silence. Into absolute darkness.

Only then, he heard the ringing of the bells. Bells! Bells! Without song, without rhythm. The bells rang out with cries and moans, with screams and curses in the night.

He couldn't see, but he felt the air itself seem to shudder at the pounding of the bells. And he turned cold.

With every groaning strike of every bell, his heart turned colder.

It was the cold of the tomb, the bottom of the ocean, of a meat locker full of carcasses, and *he* was one of them. It was the dead cold of the bowels of a lonely cave, a place of no light, no life, no hope.

Abruptly he knew also it was a place of forever.

He screamed then, or seemed to, feeling a depth and breadth of chill, of hopeless terror. He grew even colder as the darkness grew deeper around him, as if someone were slowly turning down the last feeble rays of a great light. He felt himself being—

Extinguished. There was no other word for it. His struggling spark was going out forever, surrendering to an infinity of cold and darkness. He thought he felt a webbing around him, and cold, wet clods of rich earth seemed to wall up just beyond his reach.

The atoms of his body began to separate, flecking out one by one into the infinite darkness, floating away like the smoke from burning trash. But he wasn't burning. There was no heat, no light. He was simply disintegrating. The darkness was taking him, and his screams were cold ashes, expelled and flickering away with the rest of him.

Dimly, he became aware of a horrible, accelerating pain, coupled with a sense of movement and a sudden *whoosh!* as though he were being sucked backward through a tunnel. He felt himself tumbling, spasms of agony shooting through him. He heard the voices again. Frank's voice.

Blessed light burst around him, but no one else seemed aware of the blinding explosion.

They were carrying him somewhere, lifting him. A bottle hung over him, swinging, a tube snaking down from it that ended in the soft hollow of his arm. He squirmed a little, saw the red-haired woman from the liquor store, heard her say to a man beside her, ". . . so cold. His skin's like ice. Why is he so *cold?*"

But he wasn't. He could feel a spot of warmth in his hand.

She was holding his hand, her flesh warm and alive against his. When she started to slip her hand from his, he frantically grabbed at it, squeezing it, holding to it as though it were a lifeline.

She looked down into his face, her eyes wide with surprise. Green eyes, red hair, miracle touch.

"Please," he said, in a voice that sounded like someone else's. "What's your name?"

Her eyes flickered away for a moment, and then he saw that she was looking at Frank and the other two men, the men in white, ghost-white. Paramedics.

She looked back to him, her face weighted with compassion and confusion. "It—it's Gwen."

Someone else—Frank?—told him not to try to talk.

"Gwen . . . will you hold me, Gwen? Will you hold my hand?"

"I'll hold your hand."

"Please don't let go."

"I won't. I promise."

Another voice, a man's, said, "Ready?" and Case felt himself being rolled and lifted into the night. He allowed himself to close his eyes, Gwen's hand pulsing against his, full of the little twitches and movements of life itself.

He heard her climb over something and sit down beside him. Again, she asked someone, "Why is he so *cold?*"

He could have told her, but he didn't. He didn't say anything else for a long time. And later, it took two nurses and an intern to pry her hand out of his so they could take him into surgery.

the windup

Oh, somewhere in this favored land
the sun is shining bright;
The band is playing somewhere,
and somewhere hearts are light . . .

—E. L. Thayer, "Casey at the Bat"

1

July, 1993

The Man With No Name endured another sip of tepid coffee and flipped ahead in his Max Brand paperback, counting the pages to the end of the chapter. He yawned the kind of openmouthed groaner that made his ears pop against the silence.

He glanced at his watch: 9:53. Late night for the emptied lobby of the Cedar Ridge Medical Center.

In seven minutes, he could look forward to the canned music being cut off in mid-chorus of meandering violins, always a highlight of the night's festivities. In thirty-seven minutes, he would be treated to seeing the janitorial crew give the floor a going-over with mops that smelled of jail cells and astringent memories. In two hours and seven minutes, he would be able to call it quits, and maybe stop for a cherry-frosted donut on the way home. Maybe not. Probably not.

He tried twisting his head back and forth to wake up. He fooled with the squelch control on his walkie-talkie, mostly just to hear the static, to break the quiet.

But the radio wasn't working. No static—no response to the talk button. He made a note to have it fixed. He knew he ought to report the trouble by phone, but writing a note gave him something to do with his big hands.

He heard every scratching mark of the felt-tip pen on the yellow pad of Post-It notes. So quiet. The note made no sound when he pulled it loose from the pad, but he thought he could hear the glue popping.

He fastened the yellow note onto the top page of a clipboard full of unblemished report sheets. He dropped the pen, just to hear it clatter onto the desktop.

The pen rolled to a stop next to the telephone, and the silence enveloped him so tightly that he couldn't breathe— when the phone rang.

"Case? . . . You didn't answer the radio."

"Sorry, I didn't hear you, Mabel," he said, crumpling the Post-It note he'd written. "The radio's gone dead."

His heartbeat steadied, recovering from the jump-start of the phone's intrusion. He counted the beats.

Mabel answered, "Dead, is it? Why didn't you tell me?" She had a voice turned to loose gravel by a lifetime of chain-smoking Camels. He could see her in his mind's eye: Mabel in the basement, keeping a mother hen's watch over a half-dozen security monitors through a swirling blue haze of carcinogens.

Case said, "I've been waitin' for the coroner to check it out, just to be sure."

"Oh, for the . . . !" Mabel caught herself just in time. She might have said, "for the love of Pete," which would have been strong talk for the security supervisor. Case knew something was wrong.

"Okay, I'll get the radio taken care of," Mabel said. "Meantime, I need for you to cover E.R. for Spaulding again."

The emergency room was assigned to Larry Spaulding—a

kid with a wispy blond mustache, soft-mannered but serious. He'd been missing too many nights work. Mabel was worried he might have an ulcer, maybe worse.

"Same trouble?" Case asked.

"Stomach pains. He's going home."

"What a business," Case said. "Man gets sick at the hospital, he goes home."

"Well, you know. He's scared of doctors."

"He should be," Case said, then, "Sure, I'll cover," acknowledging the unspoken agreement between him and Mabel. They would do all they could to protect Spaulding's job, so he wouldn't be cut loose without health care.

Mabel said, "I need for you to double up—lobby and the E.R., back and forth. Any problems?"

"No problems," Case said. None that he could talk about. He was caught in the push-pull of being glad for a break in the numbing routine, but with a prickly sense of edginess. He would have to leave the desk. Something might happen to him.

Mabel coughed. "And keep an eye across the street, okay? I've got Mellon out there, but he's gotta watch the parking lots, too. I guess we're all gonna be stretched a little thin tonight."

"Well, I could use a good stretch."

"Thanks, Case," Mabel said. "Let's keep this place as quiet as a hospital."

The phone clicked to silence.

From his desk, he could see across a flatland of green-and-white checkered tile, out the two-story glass at the front of the building into the dead of night.

He guessed seventy-five, maybe a hundred people were clustered as a mass of dim shapes across the street from the hospital's entrance. Twice as many as last night.

They were just standing in place, though, trying to keep candles lit against a gathering wind. They didn't look like trouble. Anyway, they weren't going to be holding much of a candlelight vigil.

Lightning flashed far to the north. But Case already knew there would be a thunderstorm coming; he could feel it as a tiny ache in the small, round, still-indented scar that he bore on his chest.

He'd been shot three years ago. And still, every day, he seemed to find some way of reminding himself of the shooting—because he might have felt a touch of the old pain, or because he felt cold, or because he might have driven past a liquor store.

A thunderstorm nearly always drove him to remember *everything*, and all of it etched in lightning, like the fire in the sky on the night of the shooting—like the blue-white flash of a chrome-plated automatic.

He remembered the report sheet that told of the shots fired, written in Frank Morrow's terse way. It listed the deaths of the two suspects shot and killed during a robbery of Foster's Liquor Mart.

The report told that homicide detectives Frank Morrow and Case Hamilton, off-duty, were driving by the liquor store. They witnessed the robbery in progress, and they intervened.

But Frank hadn't mentioned the dollhouse in the backseat of his station wagon, Case thought, remembering.

The house was a three-floor Victorian, gingerbread trim, a jillion pieces of wood. They were going to be up all night assembling it. It was going to be ready for Frank's girl, Jennifer, the moment she opened her eyes Sunday morning. It was going to have a card that read, "Happy 7th Birthday, Jenny. Love, Dad . . . and your pal, Casey."

So far as Case knew, the dollhouse was still in pieces in its

box in Frank's basement, although he didn't see much of
Frank anymore.

He tried calling Gwen, just a quick call, but the line was
busy. He wondered who could be on the phone with her this
time of night. But he tried not to wonder too much.

She didn't have a lot of women friends.

He sucked at the coffee again, remembering the last of
Frank's report: the part that said Case had been admitted to
Cedar Ridge.

Condition critical. Intensive care. Gunshot wound to the
chest, the bullet having missed his heart by less than an inch.

There were other reports, follow-ups. Firearms review
records. Official clearances from the firearms review board.
Statements of citation, praise for the officers' bravery.

None of them mentioned the only part of the incident that
mattered to Case—the fact that he'd died.

His heart stopped in surgery, and he'd flat-lined for twelve
seconds.

Not very long, twelve seconds. Not long enough to light a
good cigar, or to feed a handful of change into a parking
meter. Not long enough to chew the flavor out of a stick of
spearmint gum—just long enough for him to find out what it
meant to die.

But they hadn't let him go. There were medical experts,
machines brought to bear.

The Glasser heart-lung resuscitator. It was state of the art,
and it kept him alive almost three hours through the rest of
the surgery.

They assured him it was a wonderful machine. They told
him how it worked to keep his blood pumping, to prevent
brain damage.

They told him all about the wonderful Dr. Glasser who'd

designed the resuscitator, and who'd performed the surgery, and how Case had been lucky.

Case only knew that he'd died.

They told him that he could expect to keep feeling pain from the bullet wound, no one knew for how long.

The old wound still gave him a jab now and then, but he took it as a reassurance. He was alive. Nothing else mattered.

When the pain dulled, he began the rite of his prayers in the secret cathedral of the Church of Hamilton, and every prayer sounded the same.

Don't let me die. Not again, never again.

He caught himself straightening the badge that was pinned to his rumpled beige shirt just above the scar, as if it mattered if a rent-a-cop's badge hung a little out of line. The badge read Diligent Security Service.

He yawned again, diligently. He was yawning the moment that something hard thrust against his spine with the hiss of a warning. "Freeze!"

In that moment, he surprised himself. He felt the sudden closing of his right hand around the checkered grip of his holstered revolver—felt the cold weight of the Smith & Wesson.

The voice behind him whispered with a rush of pizza breath, heavy on the oregano. "Freeze, Terminator."

They called him the Terminator. They called him the Man With No Name. Almost no one ever called him the name that was pinned to his shirt, below the badge.

C. Hamilton.

He told himself he didn't care what they called him, they didn't mean any harm. He couldn't allow himself anger. Not at the risk of a stroke.

The voice behind him said, "If you don't want this place

painted with your ancient guts, you'd better come through with a dozen eggs—and I mean quick!"

Case recognized the voice. The joke was a ritual.

All the same, he didn't like that kind of talk. It made him think about a certain wall he'd seen *painted* with the flesh and blood of a man he'd killed with a twelve-gauge shotgun on a fugitive track-down.

His stomach roiled at the slaughterhouse smell he remembered from ten, maybe twelve years ago, and he remembered the glint of a bone fragment that stuck to the wall.

"All right, Jake," he said. "Y'got me."

He let go of the revolver, chilled at the touch of it.

Sometimes, he tried to think of death as a frozen eternity that awaited everyone the same. But he didn't believe it.

Case thought of his Grandmother Hamilton, a God-fearing woman who seemed to have spent her every waking moment concerned with helping other people. He thought of the flower beds she tended in front of her house—a treasure of roses, freely given to the eyes of anyone passing by, just to show in one small way that life could be such a good thing.

He could not believe that Grandmother Hamilton had been consigned to darkness and oblivion when she'd passed away in her sleep at the age of ninety-three, after a full day of volunteer work in a nursing home.

He still had the blue of his grandmother's eyes, but there was nothing of the woman's boundless love of life to be found inside of him. And he'd come to believe in a personal hell.

He'd tended his gardens of hatred and vengeance, and he'd been punished for his sins.

Damned.

Condemned.

Extinguished.

*   *   *

He felt the trickle of a bead of sweat along his neck—felt the jab in his back.

"Yeah, I suppose you've got the drop on me," he said. "You want those eggs to go, Jake, or you want to suck 'em right here?"

The pressure left his spine then, replaced by a slap on the shoulder as the black orderly named Jake grinned down at him.

Jake held his right hand with the forefinger straight out, thumb cocked back, to make it a pistol. He acted out blowing the smoke from the barrel.

"Just trying to keep you on your toes, man," Jake said. "Who knows? Some desperado might come in here some night to shoot the place up, and you'd need to be ready."

Case wondered how funny Jake would be with a flashlight cracked over his head. There had been a time when Case Hamilton couldn't have questioned a black suspect on the street at night without it costing him another flashlight.

But now, the memory came to him with a shudder. He prayed for atonement in secret, even as he rummaged into the lower desk drawer where he kept his cartons of farm-fresh eggs.

His prayer echoed into the cathedral of the Church of Hamilton, saying he was sorry for the evil, racist things he'd done, praying not to be punished again for his sins.

As always, too, he prayed that he might be told exactly what his sins were. Certainly, there were some as plain, as repellent in hindsight as a broken, bloodied flashlight. But he feared that he still might be doing wrong. He might be transgressing in some way that he couldn't see—committing sins he wouldn't recognize until they were totaled against him on yet another day of judgment.

He prayed for answers that never came. Meantime, young Jake was expecting a laugh from the Terminator.

"Shootin' the place up gets to be a chore this time of night," Case said. "Any desperado with any brains at all is at home asleep, not out looking for work."

"I'm not interested in anything that looks like work, either," Jake said. He shook his head, and his earring glittered gold.

"It figures. You're no desperado," Case said. "You're just desperate to get what these eggs got, Jake—laid for a dollar."

Jake snorted a laugh in response, even though it meant dropping the veneer of his well-practiced cool. He slapped a dollar bill onto Case's desktop to pay for taking the eggs.

"Just for that, I'm haulin' my ass outta here," Jake said. He winked. "I still might get lucky tonight."

Jake zipped up the red satin jacket that, on top of his white pants, made him look like a drum major.

"Hey. Wait a minute." Case remembered the sack under the desk. "I forgot the shopper's special."

Jake turned. "Say what?"

With an effort, Case bent from his sitting position to feel around for the paper grocery sack at his feet. He reached into the crinkling sack to find a couple of baseball-sized tomatoes.

"Here," he said. "Catch!" He tossed the tomatoes to Jake —the first one underhanded and easy, the second with a bit of the wrist action that might have taken him all the way to the majors.

He flexed the stiffness from his throwing arm, remembering that summer, just out of high school, when he'd never imagined that he would be anything in life but a baseball player.

Jake seemed genuinely proud of himself for having caught the second tomato that smacked into his hand.

"I've got more'n I can say grace over, and more on the way." Case topped him off with a grin. "Besides . . . if you don't get lucky, well, kid, you can squeeze those instead."

Jake barked a second laugh that almost toppled the two tomatoes off the top of the egg carton.

Case watched him go, listening as Jake's footsteps faded down the hallway past the closed cafeteria to the building's side exit.

He dialed Gwen Foster's phone number again, thinking he would ask her to go to the lake with him over the weekend.

Case owned a wooded half acre at Lake Tenkiller an hour's drive outside the city, nestled into a cove that a bloodhound wouldn't have been able to find without written directions.

It didn't amount to much as a place to stay, just a tin-can trailer set on concrete blocks. But his spot at the lake had become everything Case Hamilton knew of serenity.

He went there alone, telling no one else that he owned the land, as if telling might corrupt it—except for telling Gwen.

Gwen with her red hair. Her brilliant green eyes. There were times he yearned to touch her, just to clasp her hand.

Waking up with her, with the warmth of her, he could believe that he might live forever, or that death might treat him kindly.

But the line stayed busy. Case slammed the receiver, realizing too late that he wasn't alone in the lobby.

Someone walked past him—someone who might have seen him slam the phone. Someone who might complain about him. He didn't want trouble.

Case looked to the side. He saw the darkened gift shop across the lobby, the shelves lined with silk flowers and teddy bears. He caught a glimpse of gray.

Ash-gray, a man's suit of immaculate tailoring. It more than fit the man. The fabric seemed a part of the man's natural grace, the quick strides of the long legs. The gray was a match to the traces of steel-gray in the man's dark hair, just at the temples. A red tie almost pulsated under it, a perfect accessory to the powder-blue shirt underneath.

Dr. Stephen Glasser walked past without a word to Case, not a glance, not the smallest acknowledgment to the man whose life he'd saved.

The doctor stood a moment, waiting for the elevator. Case saw there was a peppermint-striped bag in the doctor's hand —a bag with the florid face of a laughing clown.

Clowns. Bears.

More fun than a circus, Case thought.

The elevator came for Glasser. The tall doctor stepped into the car, and the doors began to close.

At the last moment, Glasser looked straight at Case. The doctor smiled at Case as if they shared some secret pleasure. The doors closed to a flash of white teeth.

Case allowed himself to breathe. His big hand slid from the phone, and he warned himself there would be no more phone calls to Gwen this night.

He had no right to feel jealous in regard to Gwen—no claim to her, no reason to slam phones because of her. He couldn't give in to the cold fire of jealousy. Never again.

Never again like he'd done with his wife.

From the time that he'd married her on a Sunday in June, 1965, he'd been jealous of Beverly—Barbie-doll Beverly, always showing something more of herself than could have happened by accident, a peek of lace, a glimpse of cleavage, a look of all too much willingness to the perfect face.

His arm had been broken the last season he played baseball. It kept him out of the military on a 1-Y draft status, and it probably should have kept him off the police force, too.

But the city needed patrol officers with a desperation that counted for more than upholding the rules of recruitment.

Beverly was good for him those first years. She told him how handsome he looked in his blues, and she didn't care that he'd fallen short of the major leagues as a baseball pitcher. She didn't like baseball. She liked cops.

She liked men.

Case knew she could have had any number of other men, and he began to wonder why she'd chosen just him—or maybe she hadn't. He began to have doubts.

His darkening suspicion of his pretty wife had tainted the last of their eight years of marriage, ending the indelible night that he found her with another man. And he'd beaten the man senseless, turning Lover Boy into red meat, spattering the bed sheets, Beverly screaming.

You called me a whore! Over and over, every way that you could, every self-righteous way. Whore! See, you got what you wanted.

It hadn't been just a divorce; it had been a bloodletting, mopped up by a judge who saw Beverly's admitted infidelity as the lesser of two evils.

Beverly had won custody of the Hamiltons' seven-year-old daughter, Diana.

Case had been afforded weekend visiting rights in spite of his court-proven penchant for mental cruelty, but his visits became more and more infrequent as the years went by, and he invented a thousand good reasons to abandon his daughter.

All but the truth.

He had come to think of all women as faithless variations of Beverly, no matter what they did, no matter how they looked.

Diana, though . . . *looked* like Beverly.

* * *

Case tried to read his book some more. He liked to read the old-time westerns that Max Brand and Zane Grey wrote. He liked those books because they weren't messy and mean, and they didn't remind him of anything in real life.

Men were shot to death in Max Brand's world, but they didn't experience what Case Hamilton knew to be the truth about dying.

They didn't hear the crushing ring of the bells. They didn't feel the eternal cold. They didn't die only to come back. They didn't blight their lives with the dread, always the fear of death's door.

Case read about a gang of rustlers, but he couldn't keep his mind on what they were planning.

Instead, he thought about the smart-ass doctor who'd starting calling him the Man With No Name. The doctor was a radiologist. He had thick, pouty lips that thinned to pale lines when he laughed.

The doctor liked old movies, and he liked cruel jokes. He liked Clint Eastwood in *A Fistful of Dollars,* too, and all of those interests came together in the hilarity of calling Case the name of Eastwood's character.

What could be funnier than to make a joke of Security Officer Case Hamilton, a man whose belly was starting to overhang his belt as if to fit the cartoon stereotype of the dumb deputy?

Officer Hamilton—whose job consisted mostly of showing people where they were on a laminated map of the hospital, explaining how to find the maternity ward to see the babies, sometimes helping to navigate a wheelchair patient out the door.

What could be more of a hoot than to call him the Man With No Name?

Sometime later, Jake had started the business about the

Terminator, probably because Jake was too young to remember any of Eastwood's spaghetti westerns.

The Terminator—just the name for a man assigned to keeping the peace in the quietest place in the world.

Case listened. He could hear the humming of a fluorescent light that was going bad in the hallway. The singing of blood in his ears.

The soft, scraping sound of a snake's scales, sliding through the darkness.

More often than not, there were nights like this when Case had absolutely nothing to do in his role as one of the hospital's six night-shift security guards.

His usual post was the lobby. Spaulding watched the E.R. Another guard was stationed in the parking garage, and a fourth man stayed close by the drug dispensary.

Mabel Holden rarely left the basement. Mabel was doing all she could to wedge her wide bottom into the chair where she sat all night, but nobody had any funny names for her.

Case rarely saw much of the hospital's other guards. When he thought of them at all, it was mostly to wonder about Duane Hardage, assigned to the fifteenth floor, top of the building.

Hardage seemed decent enough. Case wondered what kept Hardage from showing the renowned Dr. Glasser the quick way out a window.

Case found himself scratching a rough picture of a cat on the top sheet of his Post-It notes, thinking of the hospital's top floor. The cages. The animal cries.

The top floor, given over to Dr. Glasser's experiments that were the hospital's last claim to authority.

Cedar Ridge was a forty-three-year-old lady of light brick, trying to hide her true age behind a facade of plants and pastels, sandblastings and widened entranceways. It didn't work.

Not even the best of makeup could disguise that she was keeping disreputable company these days—surrounded by an area of failing businesses that gave way to streets of ill-kept houses, all caught in the widening blight that spread from the inner city.

But she still had Glasser. She still had her name in the news, spelled out as "Dr. Stephen Glasser of Cedar Ridge Medical Center."

She would give him whatever he wanted to stay, and he'd wanted the top floor. Staffing. Equipment. Renovations. He'd wanted the best.

It was Frankenstein's Lab up there—so called by the funny radiologist, amused to such an extreme that his lips stretched to nothing.

Case began to draw wires that led to the top of the cat's head.

He'd pulled a couple shifts on the fifteenth floor: enough to know that he'd been treated the same as one of the doctor's lab animals, except that he'd gotten off easy in comparison to some of them.

The straps are loose. Hold him down. Hold him! I need to finish—

He blacked out the cat's eyes, giving the eyes a flat, dead look, although the mouth was wide open, full of zigzag teeth.

He tore the top sheet loose from the notepad, wadding the paper into a tight ball, warning himself to forget about Glasser. He tried to think of something else.

Case thumbed to the end of his book. As he'd suspected from the first, the rustlers were in cahoots with the ranch foreman, and there were bullets flying over the sagebrush.

* * *

He dialed Gwen Foster's phone number a third time. She answered.

"Hi, Gwen, it's—"

"Case!" she said. "I'm so glad you called. I've been worried about you."

He could see her in his mind. There were deep lines in her face around the mouth and eyes, but she still had some of the freckles that she must have had as a twelve-year-old, redheaded tomboy, and a soft voice that made everything sound like a secret.

"Worried?" he said.

"About the news, Case. I've been seeing all those angry-looking people marching around on TV, right in front of the hospital."

Cedar Ridge had become the focus of an abortion protest that seemed likely to escalate into a large-scale rally.

The antiabortionists were calling for national support, and their calls were being answered by the busload. But Case hadn't seen more than a few of the sign-carriers, and the candles had flickered out across the street.

"Not a whole lot of marching gets done at night," he said. "The light's bad for the TV cameras."

"I think you ought to be more concerned, Case, really."

He didn't tell her he'd asked for a change to the graveyard shift when the abortion protests started to gain momentum at Cedar Ridge almost six months ago.

If he caught the slightest inkling there would be trouble at night, he would be home with a "stomachache"—kicked back with a beer. He wasn't taking chances.

"Here's what concerns me," he said. "I think we ought to head up to Tenkiller for the weekend."

There was a moment's silence from her that seemed deafening.

"I, uh . . . I'm sorry, I can't this weekend, Case."

"Other plans?"

"Yes, and I'd rather be with you, Case, you know that, but I'm . . . well, sort of stuck."

He imagined the way she would be biting her lower lip a little, the way she did when she felt embarrassed.

"Aw, that's all right, babe. We'll make it another time," he said, hardly aware of the pen that he snapped in his hands.

"Case? . . . I have an idea. You might not like it. I wish you'd listen, though."

"Sure." He saw the ink on his hands. He took a long, slow breath, reading from the secret scriptures that sustained him in the cathedral of the Church of Hamilton.

Thou shalt hang on.

"Call Diana," Gwen said. "Just call her. Ask if she wouldn't like to take a drive up to the lake with you. No big deal, no heavy talk, just a drive to the lake."

He was caught with a half-spoken sound in his throat—his daughter's name.

"She might be . . . well, surprised, but I know she'll say yes. I know her better than you do, Case, and that's not right, is it?"

Gwen spoke with the too-quick sound of a nervous recitation, as if she'd been practicing.

"She's a fine person, Case, and she's a daughter you ought to be proud of, and there—I've said it. Think about it."

"I'll think about it," Case said.

They wound up with promises of a trip to the lake in two weeks, even as Case heard the clank of the janitor's bucket, telling him it was ten thirty, past time for him to give a nod to the emergency room.

Case shoved back his chair, trying to look forward to the prospect of a night spent on his feet for a change.

His feet tingled. He shifted the weight of the holster.

The desk had a circular water stain in the corner, probably the mark of a flowerpot that somebody had kept there. He thought of how different his life might be if it included the small pleasure of keeping a plant on the desk.

A plant—and a photo alongside of it. A family photo. A photo of his daughter.

How different his life would be if he could look at Diana, just once, without feeling at such a loss.

It's after ten o'clock, he thought. *Do you know where your children are?*

Hell, no.

2

The woman's eyes welled with tears, and she already seemed to have been crying a lifetime.

Looking at her, Diana Hamilton tried to imagine this same, streaked face in a moment's expression of happiness, or innocence, or even sleep; but she couldn't.

It was a thin, pale face. It was a face shaped by tears—etched by the flowing of tears over a long time, just as surely as the force of trickling water will cut away at solid rock.

And she wasn't made of rock, this woman. She looked woefully thin—a small, frail figure, lost in the misfit cheeriness of the yellow-and-orange uniform she'd worn to work.

The tears spilled out, and she wiped at her eyes with the backs of her hands, leaving a wet sheen over the darkening purple-and-red of the bruise under her left eye.

"Arrest?" she said. "Oh, no. I don't want him arrested. Oh, no."

Diana sat beside her on the camel-backed, floral-patterned sofa, ignoring the stained cushion that appeared to have been baptized with beer. There were cigarette burns in the fabric along the arm of the sofa—black-edged holes that exposed the wooden framework under the faded upholstery.

The bare wooden floor was scattered with baby toys, broken cookie, a smear of crumbs.

"I don't want him arrested," the woman said. "I just want him to quit hitting me."

Diana said, "I know. But the best thing would be for you to press charges, Mrs. Katzeff, so we can start the procedure to have him . . . where he can't hurt you."

"In jail," the woman said. "You mean in jail."

Diana nodded. "I mean in jail." She touched the woman's hand. "Mrs. Katzeff, this man has hurt you before, and I think you know he is going to hurt you again, and he is going to keep on hurting you."

"But . . . he's my husband." The woman's eyes widened, as if she couldn't believe such an all-encompassing truth would have to be pointed out. "He's my Anthony. I call him Tony-toes. He's like a little boy sometimes, I love him so. And he'd never hurt the baby."

Diana Hamilton glanced toward her partner across the living room in the Katzeff house. He returned the look, but there was no spark of communication between them.

Det. Sgt. Douglas Bloch. She still didn't know what to call him for short. He wasn't the call-me-Doug type, but nothing else sounded right to her, either.

They'd been assigned together not quite a month, but Diana had come to understand that no amount of time was going to make any difference. She could respect the sergeant's experience, and she could trust him—but she wasn't going to know him.

When he moved into the conversation, Diana wasn't sure if he simply intended to help, or if he meant to signal to her that she wasn't handling the situation.

Bloch said, "Let me clarify what Detective Hamilton is telling you, Mrs. Katzeff. If you agree to press charges, we can arrest your husband on a complaint of aggravated assault. If you don't, there's no point to our being involved in this."

He shook his head in a gesture of impatience better left to thinner men with longer necks.

"Sure, I'll have a talk with him, for all the good it's going to do," Bloch said. "But he knows, and I know, and you know—it's not going to make any difference."

He turned as if to leave. He'd taken off his coat—thrown it over his shoulder. His cream-colored shirt made no statement, but the back of it was blotched with a sweat stain that stuck to his skin like wet paper.

Diana thought he was being too quick to give up with nothing accomplished, but he might have been right.

She ran a mental check on what she knew. The case had begun as a 911 call, an anonymous complaint of screaming in the Katzeff house.

The woman squeezed Diana's hand. "Please," she said. "Can I think it over, just a moment? Can I be alone? I just . . . I want to make the right decision."

Diana clasped the woman's hand in hers. "I know," she said. "Sergeant Bloch and I will step outside for a few minutes, Mrs. Katzeff, and you can—"

"I wish you'd call me Sarah," the woman said.

"Sarah."

"Other times the police have been here, they've always had uniforms. They've always had guns . . . and those clubs they wear hooked to their belts. I couldn't ever talk to them, I felt so ashamed, and they never even tried to help. But you . . . it's different."

Diana felt the dry touch of the woman's hand. She stole a glance. She saw that Sarah's hand was red-knuckled, and it was crisscrossed with veins like blue worms.

Diana's hand was smooth, and her nails were even, and it

seemed incredible to her that she and Sarah Katzeff could be the same age, both twenty-seven.

"What do they call the kind of clothes you're wearing?" the woman asked. "Such a pretty blue . . . not like a uniform. I had a dress that color."

Diana smoothed the fabric of her skirt. She decided a quick smile might help her to gain Sarah's confidence.

Diana said, "I guess they call this being a plainclothes officer. But I try not to make it too plain."

"I had a dress that color," the woman said, almost childlike, almost wistfully. "Anthony . . . tore it. Anthony has such strong hands."

For the first time, Diana was aware of the sound from the TV set in the living room, and the rattle of canned laughter in response to some comic predicament that bore no relationship to anyone's life in the real world.

She stood. She touched Sarah's shoulder.

Just a touch, but it helped her to connect with Sarah. Diana felt the weariness that was soaked into the yellow blouse.

Sarah had worked a double shift in an all-night donut shop called Long John's. She had come home smelling of donuts and grease and cigarette smoke, carrying her baby, probably having paid most of her day's wages for childcare. And now the perfect ending for a perfect day: cops and questions.

"We'll leave you for a few minutes to think it over, Sarah," Diana said. "We'll be right outside."

Bloch knocked a cigarette out of a crumpled pack. He lit it with a World War II–vintage Zippo with a Marine emblem nearly worn smooth on one side.

Diana had taken note of the lighter before, always trying to piece together some kind of personality profile to help her understand the sergeant. It wasn't much help.

Just before he slapped the lighter shut, Diana noticed the peeling white paint on the siding of the Katzeff house. She caught just a glimpse of the torn, sagging wire in the screen door that creaked shut behind her.

Bloch stood on the wooden-floored porch. He looked past their car that was parked at the curb—an unmarked car about as nondescript as a two-ton porcupine on wheels with its prickling of radio antennas. The houses across the street were mostly dark.

"Listen to her. Crying again," he said. "Tell you what, this well and truly sucks."

Diana caught her breath. The comment surprised her. It was the first time that Bloch had voiced any feeling about any of the cases they'd worked together.

She remembered when she'd been assigned to the headquarters division's Rape and Domestic Violence Unit. The lieutenant in charge of the section had warned her it was going to be a tough assignment—that families could turn into war camps, and that plenty of hard-seasoned officers would sooner walk naked into an armed robbery.

The lieutenant had told her she could learn a wealth from the way that Douglas Bloch handled himself on the job.

Until this moment, though, Bloch's lesson to her seemed to be that it was best not to have any feelings at all. Until this *well and truly sucks.*

Diana accepted the sergeant's complaint as the opening to a conversation, although she wasn't sure where it was headed.

She said, "I think I know Mrs. Katzeff—how she feels. I think she's hurt, she's confused . . . but she'll sign the complaint."

Bloch took a drag that made the tip of the cigarette flare to orange.

"And she'll cry every night that her Tony-toes is gone," he said. "And he'll whack her again on the first day he's out."

"We're just the law, we're not the answer," Diana said.

"Well, that's cute," Bloch said. "But I was hoping that you would be asking some of the same questions that were bothering me, without me just laying it all out for you. But here's a clue—

"Dispatch logs in thirty, forty calls a day on wife beatings. More tonight. Miserable, hot night like this . . . they play 'The Star-Spangled Banner' behind those closed doors, and they throw out the first wife of the season.

"And don't look at me that way, sister, you know damned well I don't think it's funny," he said.

Bloch stubbed out his cigarette. He kicked the still-glowing remains off the porch.

"It's hard enough to answer maybe half the calls, let alone to make an arrest stick, let alone to convince the D.A. to give a rat's ass, let alone to haul a case through court," Bloch said. "But here we are, assigned to worry like weeping angels over Sarah Katzeff being poked in the eye."

Bloch cupped a meaty hand behind one ear. "Don't detectives ask questions?" he said.

Diana resented the game that he seemed to be playing, but it was better than no communication at all.

"Detectives ask why," she said.

"Ah! My question exactly," Bloch said. "I did some nosing around the division, and I wound up asking why to Frank Morrow in robbery-homicide. I guess you know the lieutenant."

Diana said "Yes" with a deliberate lack of elaboration.

She knew him simply as Frank, almost an uncle. She tried not to let the relationship show on duty, and she'd received no special favors from Frank's office. But the few times she had referred to him as Lieutenant Morrow because of other people being around, he'd invariably called her aside later to say, "Now, what's with this friggin' 'Lieutenant Morrow' shit?"

He'd been her father's longtime partner. Her father's best friend. Her assurance that her father had to be a good man, otherwise Frank Morrow wouldn't have thought so much of him.

But, Daddy, won't you hold me? Don't you miss me?

Diana felt jarred to have made the unwelcome thought connection. And with it came a brand-new truth she didn't like at all.

She realized there were qualities to Douglas Bloch that reminded her of her father at Bloch's age, about forty. A certain weariness of the years, not to be confused with weakness. A certain edge to his temper. A taunting quality. A certain gruffness. A way of talking, a way of not talking.

She realized that if they had trouble communicating, maybe it wasn't Bloch's fault—it was hers.

Bloch was looking away from her, watching the moon give way to thunderheads.

Bloch said, "Near as I can tell, Frank Morrow knows everything that's going on, his department, our department, no difference.

"He had a good-sized file on Anthony Katzeff I hadn't seen before. Way he described the guy, our Tony's no genius any way that shows up on a test, but he's smart like a weasel. Upstairs, they think he's cleared a half-dozen holdups where people got hurt, and they want to say that he's bought his way into the drug trade."

"Nice guy," Diana said. The moon seemed to have died, and the darkness clung to her.

"Trouble is, they can't prove it, so the idea is to burn his feet a little," Bloch said, "make him uncomfortable, see what he does."

"Frank's idea?"

Bloch went to the trouble to shake his head. "Nah, Frank took a risk when he showed me the file. I'd guess it came out of the captain's office, maybe higher."

"But why not just tell us?"

"The courts don't like harassment. It's too effective. But if we honestly don't know that we're out here to yank on the guy's dick—"

Diana caught herself twisting her foot on the heel of her right shoe, a motion of anger she'd picked up as a kid. "One: I should have been told of all this from the time that you found out." Her voice clipped the words. "Two: It doesn't bother me a bit to be causing Anthony Katzeff some measure of grief, and I only wish he'd been here—"

Bloch cut her off. "One: I'm in a sour mood. I get sour, I don't talk, and I've got no excuse. Two: It sure as hell oughtta bother you when a man's rights get slapped around—"

"*His* rights?"

Bloch nodded, teeth clenched as if he might have liked to growl like a bulldog. "Innocent until proven guilty," he said. "What would *you* call it, Officer? The man's right to be left alone for lack of evidence, or a fucking nuisance?"

Diana felt a hot rush of anger. But the feeling gave way to an impulse to laugh.

"The fucking F-word doesn't shock me, and it doesn't hide the shameful truth of what you really are," she said. She couldn't resist it. The whole night's emotional pressure seemed to break all of a sudden, and she had to give in. She touched him on the chin, twisting with her finger. "You are a liberal," she said. "And you're the worst kind. You're a mean ol' *wounded* liberal."

Bloch caught her hand. He was a moment slow to let go of it, and he was still holding on to her when the door opened.

"Thank you for waiting. I know what I have to do," Mrs. Katzeff said. Her eyes were rimmed with red.

"I'll . . . whatever, press charges. I know it has to be done," she said.

She held open the door. Bloch released Diana's hand, and she led the way into the somber house with embarrassment, as if she'd been caught passing notes at a funeral.

A look at Sarah's swollen face, and Diana felt the push-pull of another confusion. She wanted with all her heart to see Anthony Katzeff behind bars. But she knew that Bloch was right, too—and they were going after Katzeff for the wrong reason, in a way that wasn't going to help Sarah Katzeff at all.

Sarah Katzeff didn't need a cop, she needed a divorce.

But Diana forced herself to simply get the job done. She reached for the clipboard of half-finished paperwork she'd left on a straight-back chair.

Sarah went back to her place on the sofa. Bloch stood, shifting from one foot to the other. A baby cried from somewhere in the back of the house.

Diana uncapped a ballpoint pen. She'd bought it because of its thick plastic barrel that felt easy to hold, but she regretted that it was decorated with a cheery rainbow.

"You said that your husband was here about ten yesterday morning, and that's when he hit you," Diana said. Half question, half statement.

"Yes," Sarah said. "He said he didn't like the way my hair looked, but I only cut it because he'd said he didn't like it long."

"Afterward, he left the house, and you said you haven't seen him since then."

"He likes to say he doesn't have to have Mama's permission every time he goes out, so I never know—"

The baby cried louder. A silence. A shriek.

"I'd better go see to him," Sarah said, standing.

"I imagine so," Diana said.

Bloch looked out the front door. He didn't seem to find anything worth a second look.

The baby was still crying from somewhere down a hallway that was papered with yellow flowers.

But Sarah came back into the front room with pinched steps, her face white.

"I . . . I've changed my mind, and I wish you would leave," she said.

Diana set the clipboard aside. She reached toward Sarah. The dread of nothing certain brought a fragment of ice to her throat.

"Sarah?"

"Please! Leave." Sarah's small hands were bunched into fists, pressed into the sides of her face.

Bloch said, "All right, Mrs. Katzeff. We'll be going, if you say so." But he was pulling her close to him at the same time, a hand on her shoulder.

Bloch eased the woman's left arm away from her face, holding the arm outstretched.

When he did, Diana could see the skin was red around the underside of Sarah's forearm. She saw a row of four cuts wet with fresh blood. Fingernail marks.

Bloch whispered so closely to Sarah's ear that Diana barely heard him. "Is it Anthony? Just nod."

Fresh tears welling, Sarah nodded yes.

"All right. I want you to come out of the house with us, Sarah—" Bloch said, hushed.

"I can't." She tried to keep a low voice, but the tears

swept it out of control. "I can't, he's got the baby, I can't, he's got Amanda. He came in the window. Tony—he'll hurt the baby!"

Bloch glanced to Diana. "Get her out of here," he said. "Be ready, we might need a backup."

But the last of his words were lost to the deep-chested thunder of a man's voice from the hallway that led to the baby's room. "*Sarah!* You don't leave this house."

Diana guessed his height at about six feet five, weight about 250. He was wearing faded denims over a pair of blunt-toed boots, and a sleeveless undershirt torn off at the hem to show the world he was proud of the black hair that plastered his belly.

He wasn't doing so well for hair on top. He had a bald patch near the front that left a spiked fringe of hair like a broken farm fence across his forehead.

He held a blank-eyed, wriggling baby in the crook of one arm.

His gray eyes found Bloch.

"I don't like cops in my house," he said.

"I don't much care what you like," Bloch said.

The man looked toward Sarah. He said, "It's time for you to tell Batman and Robin that you don't need 'em around anymore, Sarah."

Diana kept a grip on Sarah's arm. She could feel the arm tighten.

"Please," Sarah said. "Anthony, don't make trouble."

"No trouble," Anthony said. "Just wave bye-bye t' the nice cop-sies." He made the baby's arm wave up and down. "Bye-bye, bye-bye."

The baby cried, but Anthony kept waving the arm, making the hand snap like a flag at the wrist.

"Bye-bye."

Sarah screamed, and it was like nothing Diana had ever

heard before. It was inhuman. It was high-pitched, and it lasted until Sarah was out of breath.

But just when she expected that Sarah would go slack in exhaustion, she felt the wrenching movement of Sarah breaking loose from her—Sarah hurtling toward her husband, hands outstretched like claws.

The flash of a smile disappeared from Anthony's face, replaced by a dumbfounded look. But he wasn't lost for long.

Bloch wedged himself between them, trying to keep them apart, just in time to catch the backhanded slap that Anthony Katzeff must have intended to reshape his wife's face.

Bloch reeled, and Katzeff made up for his error. He swung a hard-fisted blow that caught Bloch on the side of the head with the sound of smashed melon, and the baby fell out of his grasp at the same time. Bloch caught himself on the sofa.

Sarah knelt to the baby, leaving herself open to Anthony's gift of a kick in the midsection that sent her rolling.

Even then, she snared his leg, pulling him off balance, clawing at him, screaming at him.

Diana yelled, "Stop!" But she might as well have mailed the order on a postcard for all the effect it had, and her other options weren't much better.

She couldn't hope to subdue the big man by hand. She touched the cold grip of the .38 LadySmith in its pocket of her holster-purse, telling herself she could justify using it to protect Sarah. Anthony Katzeff meant to kill his wife.

Anthony entangled the fist of his left hand in Sarah's hair. His right fist found her mouth in a spray of red, and Sarah's eyes rolled to white.

The revolver. But Sarah might be hit if Diana fired into the struggle. Worse, the baby—

Do something. Do it! Now!

Diana saw the rainbow-colored pen on the clipboard she'd left on the chair.

Cursing, Anthony shoved Sarah away from him. He rose to his feet, grasping toward Diana with the bloodied fingers of his right hand. And he would hold her by the hair, and he would hit her until things broke loose in her face. She could see in the madness of Anthony's eyes all the pain that he intended for her.

He reached with splayed fingers, and Diana jammed the pen barrel between Anthony Katzeff's index and forefinger.

She caught his hand in a way that enabled her to squeeze his fingers against the pen barrel, like working a nutcracker. She introduced him to a pressure point that seemed to strike him as brand-new.

Tony-toes howled in surprise.

But there was more than surprise to it. Diana knew the pain could be intolerable, and she brought both of her hands to bear on making him feel the worst of it.

He tried to shake her loose, he tried to force her back against the wall, but he couldn't.

They hit the end table next to the sofa, knocking it sideways, scattering the table's accumulated mess of *TV Guide* magazines. Diana heard the lamp smash. Wood splintered. A plastic rattle cracked beneath her foot.

Anthony screamed at her to let go of him until the words had no more meaning, and the sounds that were left to him came out as strangled yowls of anguish.

He dropped to his knees.

She saw the glint of a tear in his eye. His free hand slapped the floor, and he rolled to the side, but she wouldn't let go.

He was crying. Blubbering.

Diana thought he must have been faking, but he wasn't. He was bawling at her. Begging her.

She felt sickened beyond words.

A flash of gunmetal blue, and Diana saw that Bloch was

standing just behind her. Bloch had his revolver drawn. Bloch's left eye was on its way to swelling shut, but he had a rock-steady grip on the revolver.

He showed Anthony how the muzzle of a .38 looks.

"Flat on your stomach," Bloch said. "I want your hands behind your back. I think you know the routine."

Diana could feel Anthony's hand go as limp as a dead snake.

She loosened her grip.

Anthony said, "I'll kill you, bitch. I swear it—I'll kill you."

Diana thought she'd never seen an uglier face, red and wet, slick like a blister.

"Tough guy," Bloch said. "Put the cuffs on him. If he's nice, we might give him a cookie."

The handcuffs made a sweet sound closing.

Diana held the baby, cooing to it, feeling the wet touch of the baby's questing fingers on her face, thinking.

She wondered how it would have felt to hold a baby of her own.

She wished she had said no to Stephen's call. But she never said no to Stephen.

3

Bloch called for a black-and-white unit to transport Anthony Katzeff to the headquarters jail.

The patrol car arrived with the dry scrape of a tire against the curb. The two uniformed officers who emerged from the car were both men of broad shoulders and thick, bristling arms, and Diana almost hoped to see Katzeff decide to give them a fight. But he didn't.

Instead, he walked between them in silence. He walked with a heavy, crouching shuffle, feet scraping the cracked walk, head bowed, eyes to the ground, hands cuffed behind him.

Diana knew that he must have been making a show of this whipped-dog behavior. His hand might still be throbbing, but he wasn't really hurt.

She guessed that he wanted to demonstrate how terribly the police had abused him. But the cops weren't impressed, and the night didn't care.

Bloch settled into the driver's seat of their own car with a grunt that seemed to punctuate the whole experience.

Diana knew he must have been suffering a pile driver of a

headache from the blow Katzeff had landed on him, and she tried not to think about the purpling around his right eye.

He never talked about his home life, but she knew he had a family—he had a wife who was going to be distressed at the ugliness of the bruise.

Diana could remember her dad coming home with cuts and bruises, and her mother sometimes running into the bedroom to cry, or into the bathroom to be sick.

Her dad never showed that he hurt, though. He never asked for anything more than a beer and the ice bag, and Diana had learned to fetch both those requirements for him by the time she had turned five.

She knew that Bloch probably shouldn't have been driving. But he was enough like her dad in temperament that she also knew he would appreciate being left alone.

Bloch reached across the dashboard to click open the glove box in front of Diana.

She'd been expecting this. Bloch had one habit she knew of, or it might have been a superstition. It wasn't just a sweet tooth.

He pulled a Snickers bar out of the glove box. Every arrest: another Snickers bar.

"Want one?" he asked her. The compartment was crammed full of candy.

Diana shook her head. "I don't think so." She had begun to unwind from the tension of her struggle with Katzeff. She felt shaky, and there was a stirring of queasiness she was determined to keep to herself.

"Sure?" Bloch tore off the end of the candy-bar wrapper, sweetening the hot air inside the car with a smell of soft, melted chocolate, a scent as clinging as syrup.

He took a bite. "Mmmm, hmm. Can't beat a Snickers bar that's been slow-cooked in the glove box," he said.

He chased his tongue across the streaks of chocolate that stuck to his front teeth.

Diana's stomach roiled. But something else inside her *wanted* the candy—the reward, the sharing, the bonding of equals. She knew there was something more than chocolate being offered to her.

She reached toward the glove box.

Bloch encouraged her with a *mmumph* sound, and her tentative fingers enclosed a bar of chocolate goo that felt almost liquid inside the crinkly wrapper. She imagined how she would look with chocolate on her face, booking Tony-toes Katzeff into jail. She couldn't help laughing.

Bloch nodded, seeming to share in the joke.

She tore open the wrapper. She bit half the shapeless bar at once. Her teeth clicked, and the candy tasted like a mousse gone bad.

She bit the other half, watching the red wink of a turn signal from the patrol car at the end of the street.

She licked the chocolate from her fingers, thinking she wouldn't have traded the taste of it for a box of gold-wrapped Godivas.

Bloch thumbed the two-way radio to report they were 10-98, assignment completed.

Diana looked one last time at the Katzeff house. She wished she hadn't. Sarah Katzeff was standing in the front window, baby Jessica cradled in both her arms, watching them leave.

Sarah had refused to be transported for medical treatment, although her lower lip was bleeding with a cut that needed stitches. She'd promised to drive herself to an emergency clinic. But there she was, framed like a Renaissance painting: the martyr with child.

Diana felt a flash of resentment toward Sarah. The woman seemed determined to make the worst of her life. Diana caught herself wondering if Sarah *liked* to suffer—wondering how much Sarah might have been the willing cause of her own misery.

The idea was uncomfortable. And it came attached to something worse.

She thought of the baby's touch on her own face, and of the damp, doughy fingers. But the image blurred, and she thought of the stroke of Stephen Glasser's hand against her cheek.

Again, she brought the baby to mind, but the baby's fingers had turned cold, like wet tendrils, like dead seaweed, washed up on a barren shore, tickling her cheek as if with some mocking semblance of life.

Not a baby to hold, just a dead thing, created by some diseased union, some pathological codependency . . .

And who was *she* to fix the blame on Sarah Katzeff?

Weren't they just sisters under the skin? Diana thought— the cool cop and the long-suffering, bruised and bleeding wife, both willing to dance when a man pulled the strings.

Considering that she had said yes to Stephen's call, and that she would be going to meet him this same night when she couldn't say why; considering that she seemed to be helpless to break free of him, or even to know in her heart what she wanted—

Who was she?

Diana listened to the drone of the police radio—to the crackle of monotoned voices, of coded communications, the sound of business as usual for another night in the city.

Code 10: bomb threat; 211: robbery; 10-70: prowler.

Bloch hunched over the wheel, again a cipher, but Diana fit words to her roiling self-doubt.

"Is it true that people can become addicted to other people? Is that what's wrong with me? Am I addicted to Stephen Glasser?"

Bloch kept his eyes on the street. "Glasser? You mean the big shot, the neuro-whoosis . . . doctor. The guy on the top floor at the hospital."

"Dr. Stephen Glasser."

"Yeah, well. Happens all the time, doesn't it? Lady cop meets the world-famous Dr. Wonderful."

"He saved my father's life—"

"He lays the pipe to her, and she goes off wondering why the relationship never seems to have, ah . . . blossomed."

"He's lost in his work. It would be hard for him to reach a commitment in this sort of relationship."

"Yeah. What a shame he's been ever so busy. But you? Sister, I think you've reached all the commitment there is."

Diana looked toward Bloch, never expecting he would notice, but he must have been able to feel the heat from her eyes.

"What's the matter?" Bloch asked.

She felt suddenly guilty, as though he had been able to hear the made-up conversation in her mind—as if she had been talking out loud, not just in her thoughts, imagining what he might say to her.

"I'm just . . . I'm tired is all," she said, demanding of herself to know the real answer.

What's wrong with me?

And, wholly unbidden, the answer took shape from the sound of Katzeff's hissing threats and curses, still in her mind.

Think you're something special? You're a dumb bitch, just like Sarah, lady, no better than Sarah. Women like to be hurtttttt—

* * *

Diana snapped to the here and now, already aware of what the radio was saying. Robbery in progress, robbery in progress. They were close to the address of the all-night convenience store, and all kinds of hell was breaking loose.

Code 30: officer in need of help. Emergency. Officer down. Code 30, code 30.

Bloch whapped the side of his fist against the steering wheel. "I'll be damned!" he said. "This whole night's got the runs."

He cranked the wheel, grinding the car onto a side street that would lead to the scene of the robbery.

Reaching out the driver's side window, he slapped the magnetic bubble light onto the roof of the car in a pulsing splash of red. He hit the siren, and they were banshees in the night.

They took the corner in a squall of tires and pavement, suddenly out of residential zoning, onto a street of chunky buildings of brick and plate glass, past the dark, forsaken ruins of a movie theater called the Palace that might have been the centerpiece of a thriving neighborhood fifty years ago.

"There!" Bloch pointed. The corner. A glass-fronted store. Jiffy Bob's #2.

It was ablaze in light, an almost surreal overkill of mercury vapor, fluorescence and neon, like a nuclear-generated campfire that was meant to protect against the wolves of the city.

It had six-packs of beer on sale that were stacked like a waist-high wall of loose bricks just inside the sheen of the plate window, blocking most of the view into the fluorescent-white interior.

Diana saw the black-and-white patrol car that was parked

diagonally toward the front of the store. The driver's side door was open.

Closer, and she was able to see into the shadow behind the car door—the gleam of a blue-steel revolver.

Bloch swung in just to the side of the black-and-white. He brought the detectives' car yowling to a stop where the car's length could be used for cover, in case of gunfire from the front of the store.

Diana realized he'd chosen the angle of approach that made himself the closest target, but there weren't any shots.

She spilled from the car, Bloch behind her—a push on her back—and the uniformed officer scrambled to meet them.

The fear in his face gave Diana a glimpse of how he must have looked as a boy—a blond-haired, blue-eyed winner of Scout badges and good-citizenship awards, too scared to pretend to be anything tougher.

"S. Field" was the name pinned to his shirt. He pointed with the barrel of the revolver as an extended finger.

"My partner's in there," he said. "You can see her . . . she's in front of the counter, she's there on the floor, and she . . . oh, jeez, she hasn't moved—"

Diana risked a glance over the hood. The light stung her eyes, and the air seemed alive with swarming motes of silver and gold, moths and mayflies.

She could see the blue of a police uniform through the glass of the front doors: an officer sprawled on the floor. The motionless figure lay facedown in the wet clutter of what appeared to be a catastrophe of spilled groceries.

Broken bottles of mustard and pickle relish splashed the floor, and there were red-and-white cans of Campbell's soup, and pork-and-beans, motor oil, cans of Hawaiian punch and dog food, all in a froth of beer with glints of amber glass.

At the same time, Diana could hear Bloch asking questions to fill in the blanks in the story.

Field said his partner had gone into the store to bring back a couple of cups of coffee. She'd been talking to the night clerk.

"I saw the Prophet go in, too," Field said. "I should have considered—"

"The Prophet?" Bloch said.

"It's what everybody calls him. Any other name, he won't respond, and he's got no ID. We've checked him. He's never been trouble."

"Description."

Field swallowed. "About six feet seven—wild eyes, wild hair, thin build, all rags and bones. You couldn't miss him at a glance."

Bloch squinted toward the store.

"He's there, but he's taken to cover," Field said. "I think behind the potato chips—"

Bloch gleaned the rest of what happened, leading Field into a summary of the essentials.

Officer Donna Morrison had been at the counter, her back turned to the Prophet, when the Prophet had started yelling "Jezebel!" so loud the whine of his voice carried outside the store.

She turned, and the Prophet lobbed a can of soup off the shelf with a limber-legged windup and throw. He pitched a zinger.

The can struck Officer Morrison in the side of the head, and the Prophet began to scream about stoning the Jezebel, stoning the whore, death to the wicked—all the time throwing everything else he could reach off the store shelves.

Bloch said, "What about the store clerk?"

"Behind the counter, I think—hit in the face," Field said.

'I tried to go in, but . . . it set him off, the Prophet, worse than before, and he hit her again."

Sirens wailed in the distance. Diana heard them as the prospect of a standoff, the sound of tear gas and rifles with night scopes. There had to be a better way.

Stoning. Something about stoning.

The lesson began to come back to her. It was something from the Southern Baptist Sunday school classes of her childhood, the classes her mother had insisted she attend, although Diana had never known her mother to have darkened a church door.

Diana had left the church at the same time she'd left her mother's home for good, but she still remembered some of the lessons, and she still found herself thinking about them at odd moments.

Especially, odd moments.

The one that came back to her was the story of Jesus, coming upon a group of people who were about to stone a woman to death for adultery. And Jesus had stopped them with one sentence.

He that is without sin—

Stones, cans of food, bottles of beer, it was all the same thing. Stoning the whore. And Jesus said . . .

"HE THAT IS WITHOUT SIN AMONG YOU, LET HIM CAST A STONE!"

She hadn't meant to yell it, but the words had found a voice of their own, leveled toward the store.

She yelled it again, and the words echoed into a silence as dark as the sky.

Bloch looked at her as if she'd mooned him, and Diana couldn't bring herself to say anything that might explain.

But the door to Jiffy Bob's pushed open.

The Prophet stood there, a specter in loose jeans and a ragged T-shirt, eyes as wide as fried eggs. He was every bit of Field's description of him, except that Field had neglected to mention the salt-and-pepper tangle of the man's beard.

Lifting his arms in surrender, the Prophet dropped a can of Del Monte green beans.

4

He'd done it. He'd really done it.

He'd done it for Vincent, and now Vincent would like him, and Vincent would punch him on the arm. And Vincent would tell the rest of the Cobras.

Vincent would say, "Look! Goldie did this, he did what I told him. You don't think so? You don't think he could? Well, look!"

And Vincent would tell them, "You're going to leave Goldie Wagner alone after this, he's a friend of mine."

Goldie could hear Vincent's voice, a soft voice, almost a whisper, but everyone listened. He felt swelled up to imagine that Vincent would be his friend. He felt a tightness in his throat.

He looked again to make sure he'd done it. He was fourteen, but he knew things. He knew that he had to be careful. He knew that his head sometimes played tricks on him.

Sometimes, it showed him butterflies that weren't real—butterflies that had glittery wings, silver and gold, that filled the air like the sparkles in the magic snow globe on Grandma Wagner's knickknack shelf.

She never would have let him touch the snow globe, even though she knew how much he wanted it. Goldie knew she didn't like him, she didn't trust him. But after she'd died, Grandpa Wagner didn't seem to care about much of anything, and Goldie dragged Grandma's step stool from the kitchen to stand on to reach the high shelf.

He'd solved the mystery and the magic of the snow globe. It had a plastic plug on the bottom. He pried loose the plug, and all the water ran out of the snow globe, and the sparkles turned out to be flecks of nothing that clung in wet clumps to the sides of the globe, and to the roof of Santa's plastic workshop.

Also, Goldie found a yellowed and brittle strip of cellophane tape that fastened a little gift card to the bottom of the snow globe. The card read, "Merry Christmas, Mom. 1984. Love, Bryan."

The card made him think of his dad for the first time in so long, it was like a new idea. Goldie's dad had been a highway patrolman, shot and killed on the day after Christmas, 1984; and Grandma Wagner had kept the stupid snow globe on her stupid shelf ever since, and she wouldn't let Goldie have it.

He'd smashed it with a brick in the alley behind the house, and he hoped that Grandma Wagner was a ghost; he hoped she saw what he did. He hoped that ghosts could feel sorry.

Anyway, he liked these other sparkles better, the ones that winked in snaps of light in front of his eyes when he stood up.

Goldie stood up too quickly. The living room swirled around him, and he dropped to his knees, giggling, gagging, giggling. He thought of how it felt to step off a Tilt-A-Whirl ride at the carnival with his feet gone crazy, and the ground rolling, and the loopy-doop sky turning circles.

He got to his feet again, warning himself there was more to do.

He liked to think about the snow globe, about breaking

the snow globe. He liked to play the memory of it over and over like a song on the radio, but he couldn't. He didn't dare.

Goldie knew he didn't dare to mess up, or Vincent wouldn't like it.

Vincent.

It was time to call Vincent. Vincent was waiting.

Goldie shuffled out of the living room with its old, dark furniture that seemed to suck in all the light. His bare feet brushed the carpet, feeling where the carpet was worn smooth.

The carpet was another mystery. It was gray in the middle, and there were holes with frayed edges that snagged his toes. But Goldie had discovered that if he moved the stiff-backed sofa, he could see the cushy carpet beneath it was patterned with pink roses against a leafy green.

Sometimes, he could see other things, too, in the hidden part of the carpet. He could see eyes—jungle eyes, watching him. And one time he saw the carpet rise up, and the flash of white teeth, and he smelled the rotted meat on the lion's breath.

It scared him, but it was better than television.

Goldie picked up the receiver from the wall phone in the kitchen. Call Vincent, he thought.

He dialed Vincent's number. But his head was full of sparkles, and he wondered if he'd done it, really done it, even as the phone rang.

Goldie stretched the phone cord to carry the receiver with him into the living room, as if Vincent could *see* through the phone. Goldie snickered at the silliness of the idea. There were times when he tickled himself.

The phone rang, and Goldie felt important to be calling Vincent at home. Nobody ever called Vincent at home, none of the big guys, none of the Cobras, not ever. Vincent didn't allow it.

He thought again of Vincent being able to see through the phone. If he *could*, and Goldie didn't doubt it . . . then maybe Goldie could see through the telephone, too.

He squinted one eye, then the other, staring at a spot on the wall until Grandma Wagner's yellow-flowered wallpaper began to dissolve into ripples of gold.

The phone rang again, as Goldie saw, or thought he saw, the shimmering spot on the wall come to life, as though he were peering into a golden telescope that wasn't quite in focus. Something moved.

Yes! There was Vincent, walking toward the phone. Was the phone on a table? On the floor? Goldie couldn't tell. It was too far away, and Vincent was just a black-and-white ghost shape, moving.

The phone rang a third time. Goldie wondered what Vincent's house looked like. Big? Rich? Beautiful? He hadn't ever been to Vincent's house.

He squeezed both eyes together until he barely could see. His vision blurred and streaked with gold, the streaks like infected cuts.

Fourth ring, and Goldie had an awful thought. Vincent was always joking with people. Maybe he'd only been joking with Goldie, maybe he never meant for Goldie to go through with it, maybe—

The phone clicked. Goldie heard a lot of hollering in the background, cussing, some man's bellowing in a drunken slur. He heard a woman's voice winding through the din, crying. He couldn't make out what they were saying, but for a moment, he thought they were screaming at him.

Goldie's heartbeat echoed in his ears, and he swallowed. Hard.

Then . . . from out of the noise came a voice so soft he wasn't sure he'd heard it.

"H'lo."

It was a child's voice, muffled with a smacking mouthful of something wet. Goldie thought for a cold moment he'd gotten a wrong number. He couldn't see into the wall anymore.

"H'lo! You better say 'lo to me, I'll hang up, g'bye—"

Goldie thought the snippy, bratty voice must have belonged to a girl, a dumb little girl. But she couldn't be dumb, not if she had anything to do with Vincent. Vincent's sister? He didn't know anything about Vincent's family.

For all that Goldie knew, she could have been Vincent's own carpet weasel, and he'd better be nice to her.

"H'lo," he said. "Is Vincent there?"

The argument in the background died to guttural noises, the only reason that Goldie heard the girl's reply.

"He . . . pizzen . . ."

"Huh?"

"Pissin'! Vincent goin' to the baf'um."

"He's in the . . . bathroom?" Goldie hadn't ever thought of Vincent in terms of bodily functions. It didn't seem possible. All of a sudden, Goldie had to revise his image of Vincent to include the reality of a torso, of guts, of coarse hair, of—

Goldie's hand cupped his crotch.

A pause, and the girl said, "No. Vincent, he pizzen in th' hall."

Goldie heard another explosion of words in the background. He almost *felt* the phone being grabbed away from the kid. He tried to look at the wall to see what was happening, but he couldn't see anything real—just shimmers of movement, yellow eyes, golden demons.

"Yeah. Who the hell is this?" came the voice. Vincent's voice. Goldie was so thrilled to hear him, the words spilled in a rush.

"I did it man I did it for you Vincent you gotta see—"

"Shut *up!*" Vincent shouted with such ferocity that Goldie jerked the receiver away from his ear.

He'd done wrong. Biting his tongue, Goldie slapped himself in the face with his free hand. He tasted a trickle of salty warmth, a rivulet of blood from his nose.

Vincent called him a name. When Goldie put the receiver back to his ear, Vincent said it again, and the next thing was silence.

Goldie sniffed, collecting a mouthful of blood. He swallowed.

He thought of his mom. His mom would have told him to sit with his head down, and to pinch his nose until the bleeding stopped. But his mom wasn't there, and she hadn't been there for a long time—hadn't been there since the day that Goldie saw her get into a station wagon with a man whose face he didn't recognize.

He'd been sent home from school for fighting. Otherwise, he wouldn't have seen the station wagon when it pulled up at the curb with a crunching of tires on the snow. He wouldn't have seen his mom as she left the house with a suitcase.

She had her long coat buttoned all the way to the top, and her face was wrapped in a scarf, like a secret.

When she saw him, all she said was, "Good-bye, Raymond. Be a good boy. Mind your father."

Mind your father. Mind your grandma. Mind your grandpa. Mind the doctor, the doctor is trying to help you.

Goldie flinched, realizing that Vincent was talking to him. He didn't know how much he'd missed.

"—everything? *Did* you?" Vincent demanded, and Goldie wiped at his nose and at his cheeks, where his tears were making the blood all watery.

Goldie wasn't sure how to answer. He didn't dare to answer wrong.

"Yeah, I did it," he said, trying to make his cracked voice

sound gruff. "With a baseball bat, I clonked the ol' fugger. Easy."

"Yeah?"

Goldie imagined the gleam of a smile on Vincent's face— imagined Vincent's face breaking into laughter, although he didn't hear laughter.

Vincent had a face that wasn't quite black, wasn't quite white, wasn't brown, but it was all those things.

Vincent wasn't anything, but he was everything. And he had teeth like a movie star's, all white and even, and blue eyes like fire, and black hair with the shine of polished metal.

Vincent's voice lowered, a feathery whisper. "You *sure* you did everything right, shithead? Everything?"

Goldie looked at the baseball bat in the middle of the living-room floor. The blunt end of the bat still looked wet.

Goldie said, "Everything you told me."

He waited forever. Butterflies danced in the corners of Goldie's eyes, but the wall was just a wall, after all, and Goldie realized he'd never been able to see through it. He still didn't know if Vincent was happy with him.

Leaves rustled under the sofa.

Vincent said, finally, "Okay. Wait there."

The phone clacked to silence. Only then, Goldie realized that he'd lied to Vincent, and his breath caught.

Everything *wasn't* done. But he still had time.

Goldie hung up the phone in a rush. He clattered through the cans and bottles under the kitchen sink, Windex and oven cleaner, to find the rectangular can of paint thinner in the back.

He ran with the paint thinner into the bathroom, almost slipping on the fuzzy pink rug in front of the sink.

He glanced in the mirror. Goldie didn't like mirrors. Sometimes, he saw other people in the mirror, his dad, his mom, Grandma Wagner.

He thought Grandpa Wagner might be in the mirror this time, but Grandpa wasn't there, not yet—just Goldie himself.

He had the look of a clown, Goldie thought. He was a cartoon clown. His eyes were red-rimmed, and his bloody nose had dribbled down his chin. And his nose—what a clown's nose, all painted gold!

Some of the gold paint was smeared onto his cheeks, too. It made him giggle.

Goldie found the can of gold paint where he'd left it, in the laundry hamper, wrapped in a towel splotched with gold.

It was special paint. It was the best. It was the first and best thing that Vincent ever gave him, but Goldie knew it wouldn't be the last.

He sprayed a circle of gold onto the towel. He held the towel to his face, breathing in the giddiness of the paint vapor.

Again, and the butterflies sparkled. They caught fire.

Again, and he could still see them, even with his eyes closed, even as the bathroom wheeled around him.

But Vincent was coming, and so he had to be cleaned up. He stripped off the mess of his shirt.

He splashed the towel with paint thinner, thinking of what a roo-rah Vincent was going to make over him, and not just Vincent.

He thought of himself in the center of a Cobra gig, and Concho and Terry were grinning at him, and Jermell, and he wasn't even afraid of Wart.

Wart gave him a punch on the arm—a solid punch with a fist the size of a basketball, but Goldie could take it, and Wart backed away.

And B.J. was there, B.J. black as night, with a long arm wrapped around his lady's middle, where the white skin showed, his fingers tucked into the waistband of her jeans.

B.J. telling her, "Cyan, I want you to be good to m'man Goldie from now on. Goldie's done it."

Goldie looked around at all of them, all of his good friends, seeing how sorry they were for how they'd treated him before.

Vincent, especially.

All the others drifted off, out of sight, but Vincent was still there, watching him out of the mirror.

Watching him scrub at himself with the towel, helping him breathe in the sharp smell of paint that still clung to the air.

The paint began to rub off his face, though, thanks to Grandpa Wagner's can of thinner from K mart.

Vincent faded off to just his eyes. Eyes in the mirror. Eyes of deep-dark approval.

Goldie kept scrubbing.

The stuff worked on blood, too.

5

Case planned his patrol on a route that encompassed parts of the hospital's first and second floors, looping through the E.R., back to the lobby.

He tucked his paperback book into the desk drawer, along with the clipboard.

He swallowed the last of the cold coffee, grimacing, unaware of when the lobby door had hummed open—hearing only the staccato tap of a woman's footsteps on the tile floor, coming closer.

He turned to meet the woman's eyes.

He thought her a striking sight—a twenty-seven-year-old accomplishment. He liked the erect walk, and the trim figure. Fitness and confidence. He liked the no-nonsense style about her.

He liked the crisp lines of the powder-blue jacket and skirt she wore, and the sharp white of her blouse, and the accent of the single-strand gold necklace, although it wasn't the one he had given her.

Her dark, curly hair framed a face with turquoise-colored eyes that might have glowed in the dark, they seemed so luminous. Her mother's eyes.

As she clipped toward him, the corners of her mouth

turned up, causing the dimple to show in her left cheek whether she liked it or not, and she nodded to greet him.

"Hello, Dad," she said, stopping.

"Hello, Diana." He almost lost his voice. He feigned a cough to hide the uneasiness he felt at talking with her, wondering why his daughter had come to see him. He risked a moment of hope that she might have wanted some kind of reconciliation with him.

Diana said, "I . . . I didn't realize this was one of your work nights."

No, I don't suppose you did, Case thought, knowing he'd played himself for a fool. *Reconciliation, hell.* He was twenty years too late to be claiming some part of her life.

She must not have recognized him when she came in the door, or she would have turned around. She must have been thinking about something else.

Someone else.

Glasser.

But he could hide the sudden anger that welled inside of him, and he could hide the foolishness, and he could care just as little as she did.

He said, "Yep. I shifted to Wednesday through Saturday a couple of weeks ago." Then, he couldn't help saying it, "You're out late, Diana."

"I know. I got off duty late."

Lady cop, Case thought. Lady. Cop. There was a time when he couldn't have fit those two words together without a laugh that wasn't funny. But she was every inch a lady, and she was a damned fine cop. He should have told her so when he had the chance, when it would have mattered to her what he thought.

"You look tired," he said.

"Uh-huh."

The silence between them was all too familiar. It brought

out the faint humming of the fluorescent ceiling lights. The building groaned somewhere deep inside of itself.

"So—" Case reached for the sack under his desk again. "I guess you heard I have some tomatoes to give away."

She forced a smile. However she might have meant it, it came off looking tolerant.

"Not right now, Dad," she said.

"Date tonight?"

"Yeah, well, not exactly. Sort of."

Case knew the word *date* didn't apply to whatever Diana had going with Stephen Glasser. They weren't going to the movies, or to dinner, or even parking up on Scratch Mountain. She wasn't "dating" like a kid anymore. He knew he'd used the word to embarrass her, possibly even to hurt her a little. He couldn't seem to stop hurting people.

"Dad . . . you're sweating." She touched her own forehead. "I don't think it's hot in here, is it? You don't look so well. Are you doing all right?"

"Top of the world," he said. "Top of the world."

She hesitated. "If you say so."

"I say so."

"Good, Dad. I'll . . . see you later."

She walked past him. Case thought he could smell her mother's perfume in the air that she stirred, a smell of musk and cigarettes, and of bed sheets soiled by other men. But Diana didn't like perfume, she didn't wear it, and she wasn't Beverly.

Case took a second deep breath of the hospital's sting of floor polish, to punish himself for what he'd thought about his daughter.

Diana punched the button for an elevator.

Case hoped she might stop there. She might decide to leave Glasser waiting. She might say, "Dad, I miss you."

But the elevator door slid open immediately at Diana's call, and she stepped inside.

Case called to her almost before he realized that he was going to fill the empty lobby with the sound of her name.

As the elevator doors began to close, Diana thrust her foot between them. The doors sprang back. She stood in the opening, eyebrows arched, waiting to listen to him.

He could have said anything. A lifetime's regrets needed saying.

He said, "I, uh . . . don't forget, I want to send some of these tomatoes home with you. I've got more'n I can say grace over, and more on the way."

"Sure, Dad," she said, and stepped back as the doors closed.

He looks so old, Diana thought.

She tapped the fifteenth-floor button. The button failed to light, and she realized Stephen must have shut off access to the top floor. She reached into her purse for the silver pass key that would activate the elevator.

She fit the key into a slot beneath the button, and the elevator whined to life. It seemed to be full of the larger-than-life sounds of machinery at night.

He can't be an old man. But he is.

Stephen had told her that most people could look forward to active lives well after retirement age with the right care, and that medicine someday would eradicate the aging process as nothing more than a weak disease.

Her father was just fifty-three. Fifty-three wasn't old. But *he* was—turning to dust on his feet.

He'd recovered from the bullet that nearly killed him. But he seemed never to have stopped bleeding somewhere deep in his soul, and the reason was a mystery to her.

The elevator stopped for a nurse carrying an armload of

bed sheets. It stopped again for a doctor with a sour look, biting the ends of his droopy mustache with a clicking noise.

By the eleventh floor, a series of other passengers had gotten on and off the elevator, and Diana had the car to herself again—and to her unwelcomed thoughts about Case. She leaned against the rumbling side of the car, still recovering from the scare that he'd given her.

He'd said something about a "date," and then he had looked as though he'd been struck in the chest. The way his hand had clenched the front of his shirt—

Now or later, the man is going to die, and you're going to have to deal with it, Diana. You're going to have to come to terms with what you feel about him, and you are nowhere close to ready.

She remembered him the way he had been before the shooting. Lean, hard-muscled, good-looking, a man given to explosive angers, explosive laughter, a man who could cut you cold with only a stare.

She had grown up with her mother after the bitterness of her parents' divorce, and she had grown up learning to hate Case as the cause of it—because of the man's flash temper. Because of his cruel accusations. Because of all the violence in his life.

But at least, she had been able to *feel* toward him.

Right or wrong, Case Hamilton had been a fighter for what he believed. He could be stubborn, and mean and bitter, but he'd demanded her respect. And he'd shown her what it meant to carry a detective's shield—that nothing counted more.

Her mother had opened a picture-frame shop after the divorce, but Diana never thought of growing up to be a picture-framer. She didn't want to be a secretary, either, or a stewardess, or a dental assistant, or any other of the *nice, well-chosen* jobs for women that her mother suggested.

All she ever wanted was to be a cop. Like her dad.

Dusting away.

What would he have done if Stephen hadn't pulled some strings to get him a job on the hospital's security force? She supposed he would have sat around home, tending to his chickens and to his squawking peacocks, and picking weeds out of his garden.

The elevator climbed with a shudder, lighted numbers flashing over the door. Twelfth floor, thirteenth, fourteenth . . .

Diana tried to blank out the confusion that she felt from seeing her father. She couldn't help him. She didn't owe him. She couldn't remember any time of being happy to be around him, but there was a hole in her life—something missing, something *he* should have been to her.

She thought of a touchy-feely psychologist she'd seen on one of those TV talk shows, *Donahue,* maybe, saying it's never too late to rebuild a relationship. It's never too late to say, "I love you."

No, but there is such a thing as too soon, if not too late, and she wasn't up for any major sort of emotional overhaul this night.

She found she was anxious to see Stephen. He wasn't offering her any promises, but, after all, she hadn't asked for any.

She thought of how she had tormented herself with doubts about seeing Stephen again. *Lady cop meets the world-famous Dr. Wonderful.*

But the closer she came to him, the more she found herself glad that he'd called—glad that she had agreed to this late-night meeting with him in the laboratory.

The elevator clanked to a stop, and the door swished open to the distinctive, opulent red of the carpeting that bled over the fifteenth floor, Stephen's floor.

He'd sounded secretive. He'd said he had something to show her, something that science could not explain, whatever that meant.

Diana guessed she was about to find out, but the truth was, she didn't care.

The closer she came to him, the more she realized how much she lived for a chance to be with him.

She had dated three other men in the long weeks since the last time Stephen had called her, but they weren't serious dates, they were fill-ins. They were something to do, waiting for Stephen to call.

Diana stepped off the elevator—away from her father, away from the night's madness.

Into the red realm of her own Dr. Wonderful.

Case set the four tomatoes in a row on his desktop as if to force them to mean something, thinking of what he should have told his daughter.

He should have told her that she was a better cop than he ever was, or ever could have been, because she was cooler, smarter. Except with Glasser.

Dad, you don't understand him.

He should have told her, he understood all that mattered. He knew.

Diana had brought him a science magazine that ran a profile on Glasser, printed on slick paper with a color photo of the handsome doctor, telling of his new work in electrical brain stimulation. The article hinted that Glasser was on the verge of yet another breakthrough—something important. Secret. Wondrous. Bigger than Clip/Chip.

Written in the breathless tone of techno-pop, the article read as if all of the lesser lights of medical science had come to a standstill, everyone hushed to hear what discovery Glasser was about to announce.

But Case had seen dead animals carried out of Glasser's laboratory in full-sized garbage cans, their heads cut open, sometimes with bits of metal glinting from inside the exposed brains.

Somehow, the magazine missed showcasing a photo of the dead animals that wouldn't be waiting for Glasser's discovery.

The monkeys bothered him, especially the way they looked human, their eyes opened wide, their mouths gaping, locked in a rictus of pain.

Stephen is . . . so complex.

Complex. So far as Case could see, it meant three years of an on-and-off affair, entirely at Glasser's convenience.

Glasser had been the surgeon who saved his life three years ago, but Case would sooner have died than to think of Diana and—

The darkness. The cold. The bells.

Case swallowed through the tightness of his throat. No, he wouldn't sooner have died.

Not for Diana.

Not for anything.

Case almost unconsciously picked up the brown paper bag from beneath his desk. He sacked the tomatoes, twisting the bag closed.

He carried it with him, letting the bag dangle beside his leg, crinkling, as he began to walk the silent hallways.

6

They were running hot—the lights, the siren, the whole circus, up the ramp onto the crosstown expressway.

The siren whooped and howled its warning to the traffic around them. *AMMMM-bulance coming!* it said. *AMMMM-bulance coming! WOW, WOW, WOW!"*

Ambulance driver Benny Bishop liked to imagine the voice of the siren that way. He fit his own thoughts to the rhythm and pitch of the siren, and then he could scream into the night like the world's loudest head-banger.

Look out! Look out, Mr. Big-ass Buick! What's wrong with you, man? Can't you see? There's an AMMMM-bulance coming, AMMMM-bulance coming!"

Here it was, almost half past midnight, and still there were cars puttering along all three lanes of the expressway—just the sort of traffic that rankled Benny the worst. Nobody was in a hurry, nobody had a home to go to, nobody had a girl-friend waiting up for him with a tingle in her tits, nobody had a dog to feed; no, but just try to get these brain-dead bozos to move out of the way.

It was time for the Equalizer.

With a practiced hand, Benny reached under the dashboard to thumb the small black box he kept taped there. The box flashed a sequence of tiny lights.

It was a game now. Benny's special Me-or-Them Game. He *played* the traffic, pulsing with the same fierce intensity that he felt when he played his Nintendo game, when he really got into it. The cars were the obstacles, and the idea was to get around them—or to eliminate them.

Five points for the Chevy, cut left, another five for whizzing by the foreign scooter, whatever it was. No points for the blue battleship that swung to the right to clear the lane for him, obeying the law.

Don't shoot the friendly blue one, Benny thought. *But the red Fiero . . . the enemy red Fiero in the way. Lock on target. Twenty-five points for the Fiero that won't yield the way.*

Benny pressed one of the little buttons on the black box, steering with his other hand.

The box came to life with a warble and wail. *BWEEEP-BWEEEP-BWEEEP!*

"Die, you Klingon clunkhead," Benny said.

In his mind, a crackling bolt of red fire shot from the front of the ambulance to vaporize the Fiero.

On the other side of the ambulance cab, paramedic Mike Sturdivant sighed in resignation, feeling the weight of his forty-three years.

He wished their mobile display terminal worked half as well as Benny's toy noise-maker.

Mike gave another knuckle rap to the MDT—the computer that was built into a console in the center of the cab, between him and Benny. The MDT's screen rewarded him with a flicker of garbled letters, but then something went wrong with an audible snap inside the monitor. The amber screen blanked out, once and for all.

Terminal is the word for it, Mike thought. *For all the won-*

ders and breakthroughs he'd seen evolve in ambulance technology, the idea of an on-board computer wouldn't ever be foolproof. They might as well try to keep an MDT working on a roller coaster.

Benny sent the Equalizer into a spasm of wails.

Mike tried his headset again, as if it somehow might have fixed itself in the last couple of minutes. It hadn't. Whatever had gone wrong with the vehicle's communications system would have to wait, and Mike would have to listen to the radio speaker the old-time way—with a bent ear.

Benny didn't like wearing a headset, talking into a microphone. He'd told Mike that headsets were for old guys, like bifocals, which he still hadn't noticed that Mike had been wearing for two weeks.

But now, Mike longed for a headset. He'd forgotten how much racket there was to an ambulance. The siren, the radio that linked them to central dispatch, the motor, the traffic, the creaking of the vinyl seat, the annoying clatter of a Coke can under the seat—and now, oh, yes, the Equalizer.

Only Benny would have appreciated something to make the ambulance a little noisier, Mike thought.

Mike knew he had no one but himself to blame for the Equalizer.

He remembered the night that he gave it to Benny—the night Benny had gotten his general equivalency diploma in a junior college classroom.

You could be an EMT and drive an ambulance without that diploma. But you couldn't go much further than that. You couldn't even be a paramedic.

As soon as Mike had discovered that Benny was a high school dropout, he began to badger the kid to finish school.

—because you're not going to want to drive an ambulance all your life, hotshot.

Over and over, they'd fought each other to a verbal stand-off in the cab of this ambulance.

Yeah, Mike, but I do. I mean, why not? . . .

Over and over, through the dark hours, in convenience store parking lots all over the city.

You want a reason? Because I say so, there's a reason. Mike Sturdivant says so! And you're going to find out, kid, that's reason enough.

Mike remembered Benny's graduation night with more pride than he remembered any of his own graduations. He savored this memory as the payoff to endless hours of firing questions to Benny out of a GED prep book.

He remembered the line of students in street clothes, standing awkwardly in front of a blackboard. And then, Benny thumping toward him with his coyote grin.

The Equalizer had been a gag gift, picked up cheap in some discount store long after the fad for such gimmicks had passed. Mike also had given him a good wristwatch.

Of these two graduation presents, it was the Equalizer that Benny had loved from the moment that Mike gave it to him, from the first punch of the "atomic grenade" button that scared the hell out of the rest of the people in the classroom.

Benny's Equalizer had been installed in the ambulance ever since. And if it violated some company rule—which it probably did—in six months, nobody had ever said so.

Another sound filled the cab: this time, a whistling, twisting noise that ended in the rattle of an explosion.

Mike looked at Benny's intense profile. He saw the reddish-blond hair that spilled across Benny's forehead, and he thought for a moment that Benny looked sort of like the sheepdog that used to pound on the coyote in those old

Warner Bros. cartoons. Only Benny was built more like the coyote.

Benny grinned a little like the coyote, too, showing a wall of teeth every time they shot past another vehicle.

He was a kid playing spaceman, Mike thought—a raw-boned twenty-two-year-old, and twenty-two was a good age to be driving an ambulance.

But forty-three was old for these long nights of boredom, of bone-numbing tedium, maybe now and then a transfer call to handle, and then all of a sudden a Code 31.

Code 31: external bleeding.

They were posted to UDN, the police department's Uniform Division North substation, a priority-two post. It was one of the city's poorest, most crime-ridden areas.

Had they been posted to UDS—assigned to playing nursemaid to the high-dollar neighborhoods that rimmed the southern edge of the city—he wouldn't have felt such a dread of a Code 31. It probably would have meant that some Junior League fluffhead had stuck her hand in the food processor or, for an even trendier injury, the pasta-maker.

But UDN meant it probably was going to turn out to be a shooting, a stabbing, a slashing, maybe a beating, that happened someplace dark and dirty.

Whatever it was, Mike assured himself it was going to be a nasty bit of business.

And then, afterward, they would go park in the lot to the side of the 7-Eleven again, and they would go buy some more coffee that would give Mike another hour's worth of heartburn. Benny would play video games some more. And Mike would paw through a bunch more illiterate magazines that were of no interest to him.

A special purgatory had been built on earth for those who failed to finish med school, and that was to read the *National Enquirer* in a 7-Eleven at midnight.

* * *

Benny caught himself edging the speedometer close to seventy-five. The limit was fifty-five on the expressway, so he was allowed sixty-five as an emergency driver. But seventy-five could have gotten him into trouble.

He couldn't afford to find another speeding ticket in the mail. People didn't know it, but ambulance drivers could be nailed for speeding the same as anybody else.

He slowed to seventy-two, to seventy, to sixty-eight . . . until it felt like a crawl. They had four minutes left to reach the address of the call, 1548 N. Cumberland. They were supposed to clock an eight-minute response time, and it was a point of pride with Benny that he always made the run on time.

He remembered what Mike had told him the one time they'd clocked a twelve-minute run six months ago, even though it had turned out to be a false alarm.

People are dying out here, remember that, Mike had said. *If twelve minutes is the best we can do, hotshot, we might as well not show up at all.*

Now, Benny glanced toward Mike. He saw that Mike's mouth was set in a straight line—saw the way that Mike just stared ahead, as if Mike couldn't have cared less if they ever got to the scene.

He realized that Mike hadn't said a word to him since they took the call, and hardly a word before that.

Benny swung right onto the Fifteenth Street exit that would take them to Cumberland. He saw Mike's face lit white by the here-and-gone illumination of a mercury-vapor light.

Mike was a big guy, thick but not fat through the middle, but he was going to be fat, Benny thought. *Mike is going to be a fat, sad old man.*

Benny flushed with shame at what he'd thought about Mike, as if he'd said it out loud behind Mike's back.

The dispatcher's voice from the radio broke into Benny's thoughts. They had an update on the call.

"—elderly white male. Took a fall at home, sustained head injury. Grandson will be there, watch for him: Thomas Wagner, he's fourteen."

The police had been notified, but they had no reason to be involved. It was a routine ambulance run.

Benny groaned in disappointment. He liked the drama that enveloped any situation where the police showed up. It was better than a cop show on TV.

But when he glanced toward his partner again, Benny felt relieved to see that Mike looked all right. It must have been just the weird light that had screwed around with Benny's thinking for a second.

Ahead of them, a pickup truck swerved to get out of the way of the ambulance, but Benny let him have it just for being slow.

He jabbed at the black box, and the Equalizer went into a spasm of *BWEEP! BWEEP! BWEEP!*

Mike said, "You're leaning on that death ray awfully hard tonight, hotshot. Girlfriend troubles? Molly cut you off?"

"Nah—" Benny answered with grin. "I'm just trying to conserve on the atomic grenades."

"Oh, sure. Good idea."

Benny brightened to find that Mike had something to say to him. It didn't have to be any big conversation to keep Benny going.

He cranked the ambulance onto Cumberland with a rattle and clank in the back end, thinking it would be hard to beat this job. In Benny's mind, here was a job that combined the closest friendship he'd ever known with being turned loose to rip down the streets at night.

It was a job that tossed in all the lights and bells and whistles of Ringling Bros., Barnum and Bailey, and on top of that, a job that meant something. It was a job that offered the honest-and-true opportunity to save people's lives.

Seven minutes, forty-seven seconds response time. Benny felt pleased with himself.

Mike regarded the neighborhood that surrounded them. There were light poles at either end of the block, neither one lit. The darkness settled onto him.

Mike welcomed the glitter of small bits of glass in the street that caught the garish light of the ambulance's flashers.

Houses and cracked pavement, low-hanging tree branches, cars that were parked along the curb like a row of dead beetles: now, everything pulsed red and blue, red and blue, in a surreal dance of colored shadows to the rhythm of the lights.

Here and there, a darkened window blinked to life, but no one ventured outside for a better look.

In a moment, Mike's eyes adjusted to see the one-level, white frame house that shrank into the lot that was numbered 1548 at the curb. He saw the weedy lawn was mown, and there were flowers in the window box.

Mike took stock of all this at the same time that Benny killed the siren and radioed dispatch a 10-97 to confirm they'd arrived on the scene.

He was out of the cab, already carrying the orange canvas bag of emergency medical gear that Benny called Ole Doc Sturdivant's Bag O' Miracle Potions and Cure-Alls . . . when he saw the pale shape of the boy with no shirt.

The front door burst open, and the boy came scrambling

toward them, waving his pipe-stemmed arms at them. And now, Benny and Mike were both running.

The boy met them halfway. To Mike, he looked all eyes— nothing but gleaming eyes like saucers—set into a skintight face that looked a lot older than fourteen. He looked like he'd probably been doing serious drugs for at least that long.

"It's my gran'pa! . . . Grandpa Wagner," the boy told him. "He fell, man. Hurt his head, man, y'know, hurt . . ."

The boy slapped himself on the side of the head to finish telling what happened.

Benny was up the four steps, into the door just ahead of Mike, holding the door open to the sight of the white-haired man in striped pajamas, sprawled facedown on the floor.

Mike knelt beside the man, setting Ole Doc Sturdivant's Bag onto the long-faded, rose-patterned carpet. He knew from the blood loss it was going to be a bad injury.

Blood pooled around the man's head, turning the carpet black.

Benny helped him to roll the man faceup quickly and smoothly. Mike held the man's head, keeping it cushioned, while Benny caught hold of the man's pajamas for leverage to roll him over.

The old man's face was a mask of glistening red. Mike saw the ugly, sunken wound to the side of the man's head, right where the damned kid had indicated.

Mike felt the room tilt a little, as if he'd never seen blood before. He shook off the queasiness.

He felt for the pulse that he knew wasn't there. He listened for the breathing that he knew he wouldn't hear.

Then, Mike began to understand what was wrong—what it was that made him feel sick.

It was murder.

Here was a papery-skinned old guy, fallen into the center

of the room. And it was the kind of room that seemed to have been arranged with a stick of dynamite: all the furniture, what little there was of it, blown flat against the walls.

The man couldn't have hit anything but the carpet by falling, couldn't have—

Benny got up. He said, "Mike, I'm going to go bring in the stretcher," but with a flatness to his voice that made Mike look toward him.

He saw the wall behind Benny—the yellowed white wall that was spattered red at Benny's shoulder level.

Mike stood, so that he loomed over the wide-eyed kid. "Tell me again what happened to your grandpa," Mike said.

He gave a nod to Benny to get out of there, to go call for the police in a way that wouldn't alert the boy.

Only then, Mike heard the laughter. Only then, he knew they weren't alone in the house.

All too late, he saw the rest of the boys when they came out of hiding from the kitchen. One of them bit into an apple with a wet crunch.

Mike saw denim and leather, chains, studs, an incongruous flash of white—a pair of high-dollar Nikes—all in a blur.

He focused on the kid at the front of the pack—a dark-haired, tall kid of Benny's size, maybe of Benny's age, only stronger-looking, with something hidden behind his back.

The boy grinned in a pretty way, a truly handsome way, that froze Mike's heart.

"Tell him again, Goldie," the pretty boy said. "Hey! The man wants to hear all about it."

Goldie nodded. "I'll tell 'im, Vincent."

But Mike wasn't listening. He watched as Vincent's long arm snaked gracefully from behind his back, holding something that wasn't right.

Mike heard it rattle—just a heartbeat before he saw what it was.

7

The lean man was older than her father by perhaps five or ten years, but his uniform was stiff and knife-edged at the creases, and he wore it with the pride of a Marine Corps lifer. He was standing to greet her.

He was, as always, Diana's first impression when she stepped off the elevator on the fifteenth floor.

"Hello, *Detective* Hamilton," he said, his hands folded against the small of his back. He nodded, smiling.

Diana wondered how he'd learned about her promotion from uniformed patrol to the detective division. It wasn't earthshaking news. He seemed to be enormously proud of her, as if he'd arranged for the transfer himself.

As if he'd somehow found out that she had caused Anthony Katzeff to howl—

"Hello, Duane," she said, smiling back.

She wondered if he ever sat behind the immaculate top of his guard desk. He was always standing, rocking back and forth on the balls of his feet, whenever she saw him. And he was always smiling.

Tonight, he must have had other plans than to work into a double shift, but he always seemed agreeable to the whims of Stephen's unpredictable schedule.

"It's awfully late to be working, isn't it?" Diana said, feeling some call to acknowledge the obvious. Duane seemed so much the opposite of Stephen's intensity.

"The doc almost always wants a guard on duty if he's in the lab," Duane said, rocking. "I'm it."

She looked for secret meanings in Duane's smile—for the smile of a secret joke, a leer at her being there to see Stephen so late at night.

Date tonight?

Instead, what she saw was a man smiling with pride at his job, a man content with what life had dealt him.

In many ways, Duane Hardage was like her father, Diana thought. He was an ex–military man; her father was ex-police. Duane had been wounded seriously in action in Korea; her father had nearly died of a gunshot injury in the war zone of the city.

Both had put in years of service with their lives on the line, winding up in a place that demanded little.

But the differences between them were greater. Duane never left the fifteenth floor during his guard shift, but he always looked as though he had just heard something interesting. He seemed *alive* inside, not the shuffling shell of a man that her father had become.

Diana felt an urgency to know more about him.

"Duane," she said. "Do you mind if I ask you a question?"

His smile broadened, extending into the gold of a series of tooth fillings. "Of course not, Detective, as long as you aren't gonna take me downtown for a workout with a rubber hose."

"We don't do that anymore. We're a lot more psychological these days. It hurts more."

"So I've heard." Duane nodded. His hair was full and wavy, still brown more than silver, held in shape a little unfashionably with a slick sheen of hair cream. He smelled of a slap of Old Spice.

Diana wondered how her father's steel-gray hair would look if he let it grow just a little for the sake of appearance, instead of shearing it off as a nuisance.

"What can I do for you?" Duane prompted.

"Well . . ." She felt awkward, searching for a way to phrase a question that she knew was highly personal, all the more so to be coming out of nowhere.

Diana said, "I guess what I want to know is what you *do* up here for eight hours, five days a week."

"Eight hours—that'd be a short day for the doc," Duane said, considering the question. "And there's lots to do, why . . . people get on and off the elevator, and I have to check their IDs."

He pulled a clipboard from the top drawer of his desk. "See?" He pointed to her name—*Detective* (underlined three times) Diana Hamilton—written in Duane's neat hand on the top sheet under the clip on a form that specified her time of arrival at 11:21 P.M.

"The doc's got a lot of important stuff in that lab, and not just anyone can traipse in. And sometimes he needs something, and I have to make calls—"

"No," Diana interrupted. "I mean, when there's nothing to do . . . what do you do?"

He chuckled, cocking his head. "Huh?" It took him a moment to think over what she meant.

Duane reached to a black box on his desk, turning the big knob that brought up the volume. Diana heard the all-too-familiar crackle of voices talking in radio code.

"Police scanner," Duane said. "I su'pose you might call it foolishness, Detective, but I like to listen in. I was on the force ten years, you know. I still like to follow the calls."

He turned the sound off. "That nut case at the Jiffy Bob's —I was glad to hear you got things settled."

Diana was startled to realize just how closely Duane paid

attention. But, now, he looked a little sheepish, as if he'd been caught eavesdropping with a jelly glass pressed to the wall.

She laughed to let him off the hook. "The reason I asked, Duane—my dad always seems to be nosed into a book, and I'm not sure he ought to be reading so much on the job."

"I only read one book in my life," Duane said. "It was after I got shot through th' gizzard in Korea—Inchon, proud to say it—and I was there in the base hospital.

"Thought I was going to die, I don't mind telling you, and somebody brought me this book out of the library. I remember the title—"

He made a clacking sound with his tongue at the memory.

"*Sink the Bismarck*," Duane said. "Good book, too." He shook his head. "But, naw, I don't read or nap like some of 'em do—no names, now. I just think about things."

He nodded, rocking, a man of action.

Diana asked, "What kinds of things? I know that's private, but—"

"Oh, I don't mind telling you," he said. If anything, he seemed to be warming up.

"It's not very interesting, really," he added. "Like right before you got off the elevator, well, I was thinking about where I wanted to go fishing this weekend, and what I wanted to fish for. A buddy of mine told me how rotten bananas are good for catfish bait, and I was thinking that it might be better than blood bait or stink bait either one—and whether I could just go out and buy some rotten bananas, or if I'd have to set some fresh ones out until they got rotten. And I was thinking that if I went bass or crappie fishing, instead, I wouldn't have to worry about any of that—"

Diana wasn't listening to the words, but to the flow of the words, the easiness, the genuine enthusiasm Duane held for his plan of fishing.

She thought of a still lake, the water sparkling with ripples of gold and silver at daybreak. She thought of a boat in the water. The boat rocked a little as the fisherman made the day's first cast.

In the bottom of the boat, she could see a thermos of hot chocolate and a paper bag that held ham sandwiches wrapped in wax paper.

They were going to be out on the lake all day, just her and her dad. He was going to teach her how to fish. He promised. If not this weekend, then next. If not this year, then next.

If not in this life—

So many times, she'd seen her father charmed by other people's little girls, reduced to a sentimentality that was wholly out of character for him. He'd turned into a laughing, lovable Pal Casey when it came to Frank Morrow's girl, Jenny, calling her "Button Nose"; and Diana had ached for years with a secret jealousy.

Only with time had she come to realize what Case must have been feeling about Jenny, although he never said it.

Jenny had no connection to Diana's mother—no connection to the midnight shouting matches and the clothes flung into suitcases, no connection to the body that Diana had grown from and that big Case Hamilton had been unable to control.

He'd lost his wife. In Case's mind, that must have meant he could lose his daughter, too, and it was better to let go than to lose.

But Jenny? Jenny was just a friend, a happy little friend who couldn't really hurt Case no matter what she did. The stone man didn't have to be afraid.

At Jenny's age, Diana had thought of her father as being hammered out of stone. Only later, she realized that he must have felt *something* in his heart of hearts—something so powerful that it forced him to let his own daughter slide right through his life.

Maybe it was not wanting her to have power over him. Maybe it was something darker, even more complex. Whatever it was, Diana knew it was wrong, and she knew that her father's rejection had shaped her adult life, even though she had fought hard to rise above it.

She didn't think Duane Hardage would have let the same thing happen to any girl of his.

And she didn't think it should have been so damned hard to take a kid fishing.

Duane's voice filtered through to her. "—not very interesting, like I said, but that's the kind of things you can mull over."

She was afraid her eyes might be wet. Maybe not. Duane didn't seem to notice.

"Thank you, Duane," she said.

A few steps down the hallway, she turned. "Duane—" She tried to stop herself, but she couldn't. "Are you happy, or what?"

He didn't hesitate a beat. "Me? I'm as happy as a pig in manure."

She considered the man's remark for some nuance of irony, but Duane wasn't given to irony—only to honesty.

Diana smiled, almost to herself. "Good," she said.

He brought one hand from behind his back to perform a little salute. "Good evenin', Detective," he said. "Your ID's in order."

Bypassing the deserted reception desk, Diana entered into the hallway that Stephen called his "compression chamber" for impressing people with grant money to dispense.

It was a dauntingly long hallway paneled in dark wood,

lined with weighty-looking, framed citations, awards, honorary degrees, news stories, photos.

Stephen in Chernobyl. Stephen in Peru. El Salvador. News stories of Stephen's invention of the Clip/Chip monitor, framed in gold. Stephen with a pink-faced baby whose life he'd saved.

Diana didn't need a walk through the compression chamber to be impressed with him. He'd saved her father's life, too.

Case had been kept alive through surgery after the shooting by a resuscitator of Glasser's design. The chief surgeon had made a point of telling her she had Glasser to thank, and she'd taken him literally.

Her first trip to the fifteenth floor had been to meet the famous Dr. Glasser—just to say a simple thanks. But nothing was simple in Stephen's world.

He took her on a tour of his research laboratories as if she were a visiting ambassador. By the end of the tour, he was guiding her lightly, one hand around her waist.

His fingers were long and tapered, like those of a concert pianist. His dark eyes seemed wells of compassion, and his white smile so reassuring.

Stephen told her he still accepted a limited number of patients to keep in touch with the practice of medicine. Very few patients. But if she would like . . .

It was a matter of phone calls, a matter of paperwork. And she couldn't believe it: *her* father under the personal care of one of the world's best doctors, and all because the handsome doctor seemed to be interested in her.

She had been twenty-four the first night they made love in celebration of her father's recovery, and she had felt that she'd touched a god.

*   *   *

She stopped at the double door to the laboratory. Something was different about it, but so subtly different that it took her a moment to recognize.

Stephen's name was announced on the right half of the door in raised, golden letters that reflected onto the polished surface of the walnut veneer.

DR. STEPHEN H. GLASSER
Director of Research

The letters that spelled out Stephen's name had been changed. They were bigger, shinier than the bottom line, and they seemed to flash like gunshots when she pushed the heavy door open, expecting to find the laboratory awash in sterile light.

It wasn't.

In place of the chrome and glass she expected to see, Diana found the door opening into darkness—into an enveloping silence.

Stephen's voice from the shadows had no face at all to go with it. He said, "Come in, Diana . . . *come in* . . . and close the door. Lock it."

Diana peered toward the sound of his voice. "Stephen?"

Of course it was Stephen, she thought. Who *else* could it be? But she wished he would answer.

He said, "Close the door."

Her eyes adjusted to the dim light, enough that she could see the winking red banks of computers and other electronics at the far end of the lab. Closer, she could see some of the neat rows of wire-and-glass-sided cages that housed the animals Stephen used in his experiments.

The place was like Noah's Ark, she thought—almost whimsical in its array of small animals, some of them as eager for attention as pups in a pet shop window. The trick was not to look too closely to see the patches of shaved fur, the implanted wiring, the electrodes, the bright eyes of unnatural pain.

She heard the rustling of Stephen's rats and mice and guinea pigs, awake with their fears. Awake with their pains.

She pulled the door shut.

"Is the door *locked?*" he asked.

She saw a bent figure in a starched white lab coat, back turned to her.

"Yes," she said, although she hadn't thrown the lock.

"Come here, Di."

Diana took a step forward, then another, trying not to feel frightened. All the same, she felt the weight of the revolver in her purse. Every cop sense told her the weapon ought to be in her hand.

"Stephen?"

She saw the two tufts of orange hair that stuck out on either side of his bald head, and before she could react—

"Ah-*hah!*" the man shouted, spinning around. She felt an electric shock as the man's eyes pierced her—the whites of them showing around the ebony irises—flashing at her from beneath a naked forehead, the tufts of hair slicked back like fins. And in the split second it took her to realize the forehead and hair were all part of a clown wig, Dr. Stephen H. Glasser, director of research, worker of miracles, threw open his lab coat.

He was naked beneath it.

The sides of the coat spread out like white wings, and everything else was a coffee with cream–colored tan he'd imported from Puerto Vallarta, applied to a lithe body he kept sculpted with weights and workout machines—all but the cherry nose.

Diana took an involuntary step back, one hand clasped

across her mouth to stifle a sound that surprised her. It felt like a fun-house scream that she'd trapped at the base of her throat. But when she couldn't hold it back another second, when the hand came loose—

Diana was laughing, and not in some ladylike way. Breaking up. Something snapped, some great release.

She knew was going to give herself a stitch in the side if she didn't quit, but she didn't want to quit. She wanted—she *needed* this. And he'd known what she needed.

And Stephen was laughing, too; and when he laughed, his cherry nose shook up and down in a red blur, and she couldn't stand it. She had to wipe her teary eyes to see.

When she did, she learned something brand-new about Stephen, something a little uncomfortable.

He came to her in a Chaplin walk, bare feet aimed to the sides, slapping at the tiled floor. He held his corded arms outstretched.

Just before he clasped her, laughing, she risked a glance down to confirm what she thought she'd seen.

He could laugh with an absolute, serious erection.

She lay beside him on the cream-colored, leather sofa bed, her clothing a powder-blue and white pile at the foot of the bed, the gold necklace dropped lazily over the bare skin of her shoulder.

She lay on her side, her eyes closed, as Stephen kissed the small of her back.

"I . . . never knew you had a bed here," she said, swallowing as he traced the serpentine length of her backbone with his lips, softly.

"Oh, there are *many* things you don't know about me, my dear Diana," Stephen said. She thought he might have been the only man in the world who could make it seem right to say "my dear." He gave it a spin that was just enough self-mocking to take the edge off, without the slightest touch of mocking toward her.

"Kiss me, Di," he said, pulling her toward him.

Diana opened her eyes a little. She thought of his face, what she liked about it—the even planes of the high cheekbones, the V-shaped line at the left corner of the mouth, the spill of dark hair.

She saw a green nose in place of the cherry model—green with a black wart at the tip, poking at her.

"Stephen!" She swatted at the nose as he chuckled, pulling back his head. "What the hell is this? Halloween?"

But she had recoiled from him without thinking, already wishing she hadn't. He looked genuinely hurt.

"You don't think it's funny?"

She offered a light laugh in apology. "It's funny. I just . . . didn't know I'd taken up with the man of a thousand noses."

"I wanted to do something special for you," Stephen said. He pulled off the green blob with a *plop* sound. "And I was driving over on the east side on my way to a meeting, and I saw this place. I thought: perfect."

"Place?"

He traced a circle on her shoulder. "Chuckle Charlie's Bag O' Tricks," he said. "Maybe you know it—"

She'd driven past it, past the cracked show window painted with lopsided balloons. The paint was scratched. The store looked dim as a cheap bar on the inside. She couldn't imagine going into Chuckle Charlie's, and she didn't want to talk about it.

"I don't think so," Diana said. The lie stung her.

"No?" Stephen toyed with a length of her hair. He tickled her under the chin with it, brushing, brushing. She told herself he couldn't have meant the tickling to irritate her.

"Well, that's a shame that you're not a Chuckle Charlie's

customer," Stephen said. "Charlie has a back room. You have to ask to see it. Discreetly. It's worth asking."

Diana caught his hand. She kissed his fingers.

"Ask me what's in the back," Stephen prompted, grinning. The grin brought a few perfect lines to his face, almost symmetrical markings.

"What's in the back?"

"Ah! Well, I shouldn't say. Certainly, I shouldn't tell a cop, but . . ."

His finger traced a circle on the nipple of her right breast. His touch felt electric. He said, "Hm. No badge. I guess I'm safe."

Diana lifted a fold of the satin bed sheet across her breast to let him know the circling hurt a little.

"All right, then, I'll tell you, Di," Stephen said. "What's in the back, you ask? The polite answer is, ah . . . marital aids. Pleasure enhancements."

She didn't like sex toys. They seemed to her like dirty talk, dirty talk made of plastic.

"Feathers and leather goods," Stephen said. "Things of strange and mysterious purpose. I bought you something."

Before she could stop him, he rolled to the side of the bed, reaching underneath it. He made a show of crinkling a bag he couldn't quite reach.

"I hope you won't be disappointed," Stephen said. He bent over the side of the bed. More crinkling. "It's only an eight-incher—"

He straightened.

Diana saw he was wearing yet another nose, this one a long, straight one, like Pinocchio's.

She tried to laugh, really tried; but she couldn't.

But Stephen could. Laughing, he threw the bed covers over his head, and she felt the bed jounce with the shifting weight of Stephen's hidden move to the end.

Something popped: some kind of lid coming loose.

She felt his breath on her legs.

She felt his cool hands, doctor's hands, working her legs apart.

The flick of his tongue.

And a colder touch—*there!* Pressing. He meant to do it, he was going to slide the damned thing inside of her—

She felt the warm and greasy slickness of the plastic with its lubricant of Vaseline, pushing in.

"No!" She thrust a hand between her legs. "No!" She tried to whip the covers aside, but he caught her somehow under the knees. He pulled her toward him, her legs thrust apart, leaving her wholly exposed to him.

Her shoulders slid against the satin of Stephen's bed sheets, like sliding on ice. Stephen's face emerged from under the covers with a sharp glint of terrible eyes, the phallic nose gone, given way to the white, grinning gleam of his teeth.

She thought she might have liked to hurt him, might have gone for the eyes. But, all in a moment, his mouth was on hers, and he was into her.

Body and soul, he was into her.

Sleeping, he left her to figure the count on their night's liaison. Three fake noses. One crashing orgasm.

Diana lay in the bed she hadn't known about before tonight, wondering what else she didn't know about him.

He was a powerful man at the top of his game, but what did she know beyond that? Did he love her? Did she love him?

She listened to his rhythmic breathing beside her, thought fleetingly of their lovemaking. But *love* never seemed the right word to use in combination with Stephen.

Love should be a clean, bright word, Diana thought—a

clear emotion. It shouldn't be so full of guilt. And it shouldn't be tainted with the nightmare image of a dead baby, or with thoughts of Sarah Katzeff's wet eyes.

Sarah. Diana. Anthony. Stephen.

Date tonight?

She thought of her dad in the lobby. For a moment the hospital felt like his house, like she'd been getting herself laid in the bedroom upstairs, while her dad dozed in front of the TV in the living room, like she'd done it to spite him.

But he hadn't been dozing, Diana reminded herself; he had been wide awake. He'd known where she was going. He'd known what was going to happen. He'd absolutely *known*—and he didn't care.

She knew he despised Stephen. Her father seemed to have gone dead in so many ways. His palpable dislike of the doctor would have been impossible for her to misunderstand. It was one of the last sparks left in the shell that was left of Case Hamilton.

Diana felt a deep and secret longing that her father might have cared enough to tell her no: that she always would be his girl, and he would not allow anything bad to happen to her, and he would not allow for her to walk past him into Stephen's arms.

She reached to Stephen. He was lying apart from her, his back to her. Her fingers traced the shape of him, lightly down his neck, across the shoulders, down the back.

She had known of men who slept like children. Stephen didn't. Her fingers touched nothing of innocence.

Instead, her eyes shot wide in a flash of insight. She tried to reject it. But all she could do was to cushion the impact. She thought in terms of maybe.

Maybe she hadn't ever been seduced by Stephen's charisma, or by the man's aura of power, or by the hard-toned fitness of his body, or even by gratitude. Maybe all those were just flimsy excuses. Lies.

Maybe she knew her father was right about him, and maybe all she really wanted . . . was her father's attention.

She moved away from Stephen almost unconsciously, wondering just how much her father knew about the relationship—how much he didn't care.

Across the room, some animal squealed in its glass cage, its feet scratching in the sawdust and wood chips, spattering chips against the glass, falling to silence.

Another sound: the high-and-low wail of an ambulance siren, far away. Coming closer. Bearing its cargo of misery.

Cold in here, Diana thought, pulling the sheet up around her to find there was no warmth in satin.

8

Case prowled the hallways that led to the E.R., paper sack clenched in his left hand, swinging his right arm back and forth to work some of the stiffness out of it.

He knew the stiffness in his elbow hadn't resulted from throwing a tomato to Jake, and that it probably wouldn't let up until the weather broke—until the rain that he could feel coming. But he swung his arm all the same, telling himself it felt better.

So late at night, most of the hospital's staff had settled into a kind of languid efficiency—nurses, doctors, interns. Old men with toy badges, playing cops and robbers.

Every person appeared to be an island unto himself, and the few words that were spoken were punctuated with great periods of quiet, as if they were being whispered in a church.

Case took the stairway to the red carpeting that marked the second floor, just wandering more than anything.

He called a few of the people he met by name, giving away a tomato here and there, moving through scraps of conversation that didn't concern him—other people's thoughts that, like his, seemed quickly absorbed into the bright, clean walls.

He passed the nurses' station, where Supervising R.N. Teresa McMasters accepted a tomato from him. She set it next to a stack of gleaming-clean bedpans, thanking him as though he'd brought home a lost baby.

"Got more'n I can say grace over—" Case told her.

"And more on the way," she said, smiling. "But you know what I really need?" She whispered the secret. "Another peacock feather. I'm thinking of a table centerpiece I could make out of feathers and flowers, something really attractive."

She caught herself. "Tch! I suppose it sounds awful."

"Not a bit," Case lied. "I'll see what I can find."

"It must be wonderful to keep peacocks—just to be able to look out your window, and to have those beautiful birds in the yard."

"Beautiful, messy, useless, *noisy* birds," Case said. "But, yeah. I like 'em." He winked. "I'll bring a feather for your cat to play with, too."

"Thanks, Case."

Case guessed that Mrs. McMasters must have been ten years younger than he, but he couldn't help thinking of her as being everybody's mother, even his. She had the plump shape of a hen, all roundness, and she seemed to have been born to worry over other people.

She always seemed to regard him with worry, with a questioning look that told him if he wanted to talk about his troubles, she would always be there. Sometimes, he thought he might accept the offer; he imagined that she would know just what to say to him.

The idea was so comforting, he never risked it to reality by telling her anything at all.

Still, he always felt better just to see her, and he was glad to have done something to make her smile.

Smiling made her cheeks bunch up and flushed them with color in a way that made him think of a couple of warm, homemade cookies sprinkled with red sugar, made just for him.

He thought he might stop for a cherry-frosted donut on the way home, after all.

Paper sack crinkling, Case turned the corner to check the emergency exit at the far end of the corridor.

The pale girl shuffled out of a room three doors in front of him like a sleepwalker, her Nordic eyes wide open with too much white showing.

She was young and blond, and her skin was white as porcelain, and her bare feet slapped softly against the tile floor. Her back was to Case, showing him that her hospital gown had come untied like a negligee, and he felt embarrassed for her.

He meant to call to her, and she turned to face him as if he had.

A strange smile tugged at her pale lips. She held a finger to them. Softly, she padded toward him until Case could see that her eyes were gauzy and unfocused. There was no one else in the corridor.

"I'm looking for the Promised Land," she whispered, her face and fine hair nearly transparent under the fluorescent lights. She turned her eyes inward. The whites of them glistened, reflecting bits of illumination that seemed to originate from somewhere inside her.

"The Promised Land," she said.

Case put a hand on her shoulder. "C'mon, miss," he said, gently nudging her in the direction of her room.

"Are you taking me to the Promised Land? Do you know where it is?" She still whispered, but her voice rose a little, as if something wild were pushing it from beneath.

"Yeah, I know where it is," Case said. "C'mon now, this way."

"Have you been there?"

Case felt something freeze at the base of his throat. He tried to answer, but the words caught.

Extinguished.

She asked him again, "Have you been there?" With trust in her voice, Case thought. Such heartbreaking trust. But what could he tell her?

Ice and eternity.

So many times, so many ways, he'd tried to convince himself that he should be glad for a second chance at life. He couldn't. He knew he wasn't back for a second chance, he was back for another punishment.

The bells! The bells!

He was back to lie alone at night in cold, wet sheets, drenched in sweat—back for the salty, sick taste of his fear, as it trickled into the tightened corners of his mouth.

And he'd gone to church, to different churches, to all the different churches he could find.

He'd watched a glory-shouting gospel runaway one week, heard an arid sermon on the letters of Mark Twain the next. He listened to pulpit talk of the transcendental magic of life after death, and to warnings of the eternal torment of hell's burning lake.

Now and then, he'd caught tantalizing glimpses of the answers that he yearned to know—the answers to what had happened to him at death's door, to where he'd gone, to what he'd experienced.

He found clues, broken bits of the puzzle. Just enough to keep him searching.

Still and always, Case felt like an outsider no matter what the message was, reacting with minimum civility to the handshakes of the regulars, finding pews in the back and sliding into them, away from the others who chatted and smiled, smelling of soap and old suits.

He didn't want to be pals. Jesus Christ himself could have been standing at the door and knocking—Case wasn't interested. He didn't care about promises of a glorious hereafter.

He already knew the hereafter. It wasn't magic, and there weren't any burning lakes.

Case had stopped going to church one crisp October Sunday, the day he'd encountered a sermon in which the minister had said that hell meant separation from God.

Case knew he'd felt hell in that sense, almost exactly—he didn't know about God, but he'd certainly felt a final split with everybody, with everything.

He found himself pushed along in the murmuring line of people that wound down the aisles to the oaken door of the church, where the minister waited, the sun's rays slanting through the stained glass of the window behind him.

He found himself face-to-face with the minister, and the minister reached his long, clean, tapered fingers out to shake Case's big, rough hand.

Case stammered out, "Thank you, Reverend. And . . . about that separation from God, you said?"

"Yes, sir?" asked the minister smoothly. He was a tall man, with silvered waves of thick hair, and Case felt suddenly, horribly, out of place.

"If you're separated . . . how do you get back?"

The other man smiled. Case was aware of the others in line, shuffling behind him. He felt as though they were seeing through him, knowing his thoughts, commenting on his bothersome, dead heart.

"Separation from God is the ultimate punishment, and hell is forever," the minister said. "But as long as a man is alive, he has hope, sir—hope for the abundance of heaven." He paused a moment, and then smiled. "Does that answer your question, mister, ah . . . ?"

"Hamilton," said Case quickly. He thought he heard a woman laugh behind him. "Oh, sure," he added. "I was just wondering."

"It's a wondrous thing to think about, isn't it?" the minister asked. Case felt the other man's grip relax, and only then he realized he had been clinging to the preacher's hand the whole time.

"Yeah," muttered Case, walking out into the autumn sunlight, where knots of people talked and laughed, and well-scrubbed children in their Sunday clothes wound through, chasing one another. He walked past the people, the people who thought they knew the secret.

They weren't like him. They hadn't died. They didn't know.

They still had hope.

He read more than ever to make up for quitting church.

He read Max Brand these nights, but he'd come to Brand by a circuitous route that began during his recovery from the surgery.

Case had read in a fever to understand his experience after death. Books about religion. Books about mysticism. Books about death.

He read studies that delved into other people's afterlife experiences, which, beyond the similarity of a few sounds and feelings, had nothing to do with him.

He read autopsy records, searching for some connection between life and the remains of life, finding none.

And one day, prowling the library in search of something else to read, he found Edgar Allan Poe and was drawn to the morbidity of Poe's stories of "The Black Cat" and "The Masque of the Red Death."

After he finished the stories, he started in on the poetry, almost surprised to discover that he understood it.

He took a cold solace in Poe's metered broodings. The man seemed to have shared with him a sense of despair in the shadow of death.

In time, Case found that he'd made up his own church from all that he'd read and considered, a secret Church of Hamilton, a church of one commandment.

THOU SHALT HANG ON.

Salvation? You bet, chum, we got it. It's called a heartbeat. It's all there is.

He knew that he dared take no risks with his life. No dangerous actions, no dangerous thoughts. No anger. No courage. No triumph.

He found himself striving to live a clean, easygoing life that didn't hurt anyone, as if he might score points that would accumulate to some better destiny.

He allowed himself the hope of heaven, although not a belief in it.

And at the end of another day survived, in bed alone, he felt the pulse in his wrist, beating, beating. And the rhythm of his pulse became the pounding of the bells.

The bells of extinction.

Poe's iron bells, Case thought.

> What a world of solemn thought
>   their monody compels!
> In the silence of the night,
> How we shiver with affright
> At the menace of their tone!
> For every sound that floats

From the rust within their throats
Is a groan.

He felt his hand locked on to the girl's shoulder, and he knew he must be hurting her. But she didn't seem to care. She only looked at him trustingly, wonderingly, asking him, asking him—

"Have you been there, to the Promised Land?"

Case let go of her.

"Yeah," he said. "Yeah, I've been there."

Just outside her door, Room 212, he stopped to fix the back of her gown where it had fallen open, fastening it over the china-white skin of her back.

"Home again, home again, jiggity-jog," he said.

He guided her into the dim room, which was divided by a curtain. On the side nearest the door, he saw the bed that must have been hers, rumpled, empty. An older man dozed in a chair beside the bed, his breath rhythmic.

Her father, Case thought—husband, maybe. Even in sleep, the man looked tortured.

"Is this it?" the girl asked. "Is this the Promised Land?"

Case faltered at the unbidden memory of what the Promised Land had been for him. "Only . . . if you go to sleep, it is," he said.

Case set his sack of tomatoes on the bed table next to a plastic water pitcher. He helped her ease into the bed. She offered no resistance, but gazed dully for a moment at the sack.

"What's in there?" she asked.

"Tomatoes."

"Are they from the Promised Land?"

Case thought for a moment before he answered her. "Yep," he said. "Tomatoes from the Promised Land."

He took one out of the sack and folded her hands around it.

Even in the darkness of the room, Case thought he saw the gauziness clear out of her eyes for a moment.

"You're a good man," she said.

Case stood there, watching the fragile girl's eyelids flutter as a merciful sleep claimed her. He tucked the sheet around her.

Never in his life could he remember his daughter having called him a good man.

He reported what he'd done at the nurses' station, where Teresa McMasters looked worried.

She clucked off to check on the girl. Case waited for her to come back, listening to the hospital's sounds of the night. Someone coughed, someone sighed.

He heard the nurse's returning footsteps for a seeming eternity before she came around the corner, bustling with concern.

"Mother's milk," she said, which told him everything.

It was state of the art in designer drugs, completely synthetic, so called for its being made as white liquid to be injected, or sometimes milk-white tablets, or capsules that could be broken open and smoked with marijuana.

Whatever. It had a built-in thrill that no other drug could duplicate.

Mother's milk produced wildly unpredictable, practically random effects—a soaring high, a vision of Atlantis beneath the sea, convulsions, lethal blood pressure, an energy rush, psychic insight, a flash of genius, brain damage, death.

Take the pill, take your chances.

The odds of rolling a high were about the same as a big win in Las Vegas. But the risk was a part of the drug's mystique.

The girl in 212 had come up a loser for life.

Case discovered he could still feel some of the old hatred, a burst of it like a shooting star in the night sky, at the damned drug artists who'd sold her the stuff. But he forced himself to smother it.

He couldn't risk caring too much.

He set his mind on the canteen, back on the first floor. It would be the place to give away the last tomato.

But as he neared the room, he heard and recognized the loud voice of a pimply faced kid named Butch, another of the orderlies.

"Yeah, baby," Butch was saying for the world to hear. "You know we got nothing to worry about around here. We're as safe as Fort Knox, so don't you worry."

A soft, giggly voice answered with something Case couldn't catch.

"Sure thing." Butch again. "Don'tcha know, we got the Terminator . . ."

Other voices joined in the laughter. Case could put faces to some of them.

He told himself they didn't mean any—

Something spattered on the floor, and only then, Case realized that his hand was wet and sticky, clenched tight. He opened the hand, saw the remnants of the crushed tomato, the pulp and seeds sticking to his fingers, the tatters of red skin that clung to him like drying blood.

The hospital had a churchlike sanctuary near the intensive care unit. It was a dimly lit place of escape, and Case went there. Trembling.

He stared at the dark-paneled walls, stared at nothing, and prayed, after a fashion, in the cathedral of the Church of Hamilton.

He remembered that one of the preachers he'd heard said that every thought is a prayer; and Case's sudden thought was that his one commandment from the Church of Hamilton wasn't quite complete.

Moses wouldn't have thought much of *thou shalt hang on* as he bore the weight and the wisdom of his stone tablets down from the mountain, all those thou-shalts and thou-shalt-nots. But later, after the old guy had led his people through the parted seas, away from the death squads of the Pharaoh, and wept for joy with them in celebration of their emergence from the wilderness, and been exalted by God and the masses—after all of that, Moses must have reached a day when he had gotten too old to be useful.

Maybe then, he had felt a terrible, final loneliness as he had watched his people go on, building their towns and having their children without him.

Maybe then, Case thought, Moses would have understood *thou shalt hang on* as the last commandment, and would have prayed to God for the strength to keep it.

He shifted on the wooden seat that resembled a pew. It faced toward a pulpit with a spray of flowers that filled the small room with a garden scent, a deceptive breath of life.

The flowers didn't know it, but they were already dead, cleanly snipped from the earth.

He heard someone breathing behind him, whispering soft words, private words, pleading words—the words of life and death these walls were meant to hear. But the walls didn't answer. If they knew of the fate of someone's father, someone's son, someone's sister in her moment-to-moment struggle for life in ICU, the walls kept it a secret.

Case remembered what he'd thought as he had lain on the floor of the liquor store, his blood swirling into the cheap wine from the bottles smashed around him. *Damn this life!*

He wondered if he could have damned himself literally—

could have plunged himself into eternal darkness with a single thought. But it didn't matter.

Nothing mattered, except—

For the first time, Case thought of a corollary, an adjunct commandment from the Church of Hamilton. *Whether thou wantest to or not.*

THOU SHALT HANG ON
LIKE IT OR NOT.

He thought of feeble old Moses, no longer challenged by life, and saw in his mind the image of the man, bent, walking with a gnarled cane, standing outside a circle of firelight as the children went about their games and the town went on without him. Case envisioned the tight, pained lines across Moses' face, the eyes squinting, failing. The mouth a sagging slash.

Thou shalt hang on.

Case felt the pulse in his wrist.

He was spending too much time by himself, he concluded, shaking himself away from the vision, forcing himself to concentrate on the pulse, his immortality.

For the moment.

9

The raw edge of the siren's weeping and howling made the night seem to pulse with a secret power, a secret promise. And Vincent knew the secret. He *was* the secret.

Vincent crouched in the space between the two seats at the front of the ambulance. In his left hand, he held a loop of silver wire—picture-hanging wire—that he'd tightened around the driver's skinny neck. A twist of his hand, and he could make the loop tighter.

In his right hand, Vincent held the diamond-patterned grip of a survival knife with a twelve-inch blade. The heavy blade had been forged with a slight twist that would make it easier to stab to the hilt into the muscle and cartilage of a man's chest. The cutting edge was razor-sharp in a way that reflected white light, and the back of the blade was serrated. It could saw through bone.

Vincent had bought the knife by answering a magazine ad that listed the many uses of a survival knife in the hands of a rugged outsdoorsman or an adventure-seeking soldier of fortune.

When he shook the hollow handle, Vincent could hear the

milk-white capsules rattling inside. The big guy in the other seat—Mike, who'd needed a kick to the ribs to understand he was in trouble—didn't like to hear the knife rattle, so Vincent shook it close to Mike's ear.

The knife had come packed with wax-tipped matches inside the handle with its screw-on top, and a needle and thread, and a length of fishing line with a hook and a marble-sized plastic bobber. But Vincent didn't plan on going fishing, so he emptied out the stuff he might have needed to survive in the woods.

He filled the knife's handle with the means of a different kind of survival: some blues and black bombers, a couple of poppers, a couple of yellowjackets.

He had thirteen white caps of mother's milk, too—ten in the knife's handle, three in his bloodstream.

He could *see* Mike's skin crawl when the knife rattled. The synthetic drug heightened his senses, and Vincent could see the man's skin rippling across the back of his neck like rain in the wind.

Vincent glanced over the driver's shoulder. The speedometer read seventy-seven . . . seventy-eight.

A car on the freeway ahead of them—a big-shot Lincoln—swerved to the shoulder to clear the way for the speeding ambulance.

The car's big-shot driver probably thought he'd hustled just to get out of the way of the ambulance. Only Vincent understood the secret reason the car had pulled over: because of Vincent.

He projected a power that made other people do what he wanted.

He'd always been able to use the secret power. But he was learning he could strengthen it, too, like flexing a muscle.

Like now—Vincent knew he didn't need to hold his knife

at the ambulance driver's throat. He probably didn't even need the loop of wire around the guy's pencil neck. With just a little concentration, Vincent could sharpen his secret power to the same effect as a knife point, and he could use it to control the ambulance.

He glanced to the back of the ambulance, mostly to prove to himself how much he was in control. He didn't have to watch the road. It was a gesture of confidence, but it forced him to see the Cobras for what they really were, all jammed into one place.

Not a gang: they were a losers' club, and Vincent had taken to thinking of them as the O.G.s. Original geeks.

Vincent took count of the sorry-assed lot of them, starting with Goldie. Paint-sniffer Goldie, always with the can of gold paint from K mart and the mottled rag for his nose, even now. He wanted to kick the life out of Goldie.

Vincent promised himself that he would do the cockroach stomp on Goldie's head one day, and for the same reason that he would have stepped on a roach—just to hear what a crunch it would make underfoot.

He saw that Goldie and the other four of the Cobras were digging through the back part of the ambulance in a roo-rah, seeing what they could find, popping handfuls of pills out of bottles they never bothered to read, messing with the gear.

Concho. Wart. Terry. Jermell. B.J.

Vincent shifted the red eye of his focus to the big, no-necked machine they called Concho. He had a baby's face, Concho—broad, soft, pouty-lipped. He never changed expression.

Street talk was that Concho had squeezed his mother's left eye out of her head with his thumb, and that he'd worn it on a string around his neck until the rotting eyeball fell apart.

All Vincent knew was that Concho still kept a dirty string tied around his neck.

Vincent thought he would give Concho the smashed Uzi, when the time came. He was going to be handing them all junk guns out of a cardboard box, all but Terry. Passing out the candy. He knew the Uzi probably wouldn't work at all, or maybe just for an initial burst of shots that would make Concho a target.

He knew Concho would think it was an honor to be the Chosen One to pack the machine gun, lucky Concho.

Meantime, Wart was whooping that he'd found a bottle of reds in one of the cabinets they'd broken open. He held the bottle over Terry's head like a bite of meat over a whining chihuahua.

He was a twenty-one-year-old buster the shape of a cannonball, Wart, a weight of blubber on top of stumpy legs that ran like pistons. He kept a loop of tire chain wrapped across his massive shoulders, but all that seemed to matter about Wart was the growth between his eyes.

He always threatened to kill anybody he caught staring at the wart that made him seem to have three black, shiny eyes in a row, but Vincent named him Wart. Vincent got away with it.

Terry got nothing.

Terry had tried to give himself a gang name: Hairy Terry, making a big thing of the red hair that he wore in a tangle like dreadlocks on fire. The name didn't stick.

They called him Runt for his size, but even Vincent quit ragging him the day that Terry came up with a .357 Magnum revolver—the same day that he'd shaved his head, leaving a pasty-white scalp that was crisscrossed with razor cuts, some of which still hadn't healed.

Jermell, shit. Jermell was just another shrimp trying to look tough—punky Jermell with his studded wristbands and his big feet shoved into the Air Jordans that he'd boosted from the shopping mall; and there was B.J.

B.J. worried Vincent. He thought B.J. just might be smart enough to figure out the Cobras were a joke. And B.J. wasn't a joke.

B.J. was black as death. Not the brown that Jermell was, B.J. was black of a sort that seemed to diminish all sense of the colors around him, and to give back nothing at all, not the slightest sheen of living skin.

He was tall enough to look down at Vincent, and he carried a steel-headed club that he'd made for himself, like a nightstick made for murder.

B.J. liked to give women the rush about the time the police shot him—popped him right through the cheek, and he could feel the hot lead in his mouth, and the bullet shattering teeth. He said it felt like cracking candy.

He would run his game, and his lady would cozy up to him, making a show of it. Cyan. Vincent played with her name. Cyan, cry-ann, die-ann, Cyan.

Cyan of the gray-haired, hippie momma, her momma's brain fried on bad acid, momma still wearing paisley and peace symbols, naming her dumb-ass daughters Cyan and Cheyenne.

Ciiiii-ann.

Dumb as she was, Cyan had a name that made her sound like something special in her cutoff, pull-off, jerk-off jeans, and B.J. held on to her like saying that nobody else could trim her. Like Vincent couldn't touch her. Like B.J. had something to say about it.

But a part of Vincent's secret power was to understand the many uses of other people's fears and failings, and he'd seen the hidden fear that burned like a vein of sulfur in B.J.'s black heart. He'd seen it the same way he could see Mike's skin crawl, the way he could see anything he wanted to see. Mother showed it to him—the white drug. He fucking *knew*.

B.J. couldn't stand to be cut. He was a rabbit when it came to knives. He went as quiet as death at the sight of Vincent's knife, every time. Right now. *This* time.

B.J. was keeping his back turned to Vincent, so he wouldn't have to see the knife.

Big mistake, B.J.

Vincent thought he would stomp on Goldie someday, and he would cut B.J. the first chance he got.

The knife rattled, eager to start.

Vincent tightened the wire on the driver's neck, just to let the driver know he hadn't been forgotten. He saw they were swooping through an underpass. Vincent saw the word *Crips* spray-painted onto the concrete, as if to remind him the Cobras meant nothing.

And they didn't—except to him, for just a few hours more.

They didn't know it, but they were going to help him to flex the power. They would be his last test of control. They would do what he wanted. They had no other choice, not from the time that he'd bound them together, promising they would have pride and protection.

Even when he told them that he'd lied to them about the robbery, he knew they would do what he wanted.

Only this moment, Vincent understood that the secret intent of this night's business wasn't to steal drugs from the hospital; it was for him to be sure of his power in the only way that mattered. Life-and-death.

He would have to kill. And they would have to die.

He would kill for the first time, and the killing would be Vincent's initiation by blood into a higher level of power.

And they would die. They would *have* to die, if not this

time, the next, until he was rid of them. They would have to be replaced.

Already, Vincent felt ready to use the great power he sensed in new and better ways, starting with a better class of followers.

He reached with the point of his knife to jab the black box on the dashboard. The box was a toy that intrigued him with its arsenal of lethal-sounding beeps and blasts.

He punched the little button that was marked "Atomic Grenade." The box let go with a rattling explosion that seemed to jar the whole ambulance, and Vincent was a moment slow to realize what had happened.

They were going off the road. Benny had cranked the wheel to send them down the grassy side of an embankment. Already, the right-side wheels were off the shoulder, chewing into the dirt.

The ambulance tilted, threatening to roll with a clatter of medical gear in the back. Howls from the O.G.s.

Vincent yanked the wire tight around the driver's neck. He ordered, "Back on the road!"

The driver ignored him. Vincent felt the ambulance slide sideways.

He jerked the driver's head back, jabbing the point of his rattling knife into the soft hollow at the base of the man's throat.

The knife took its first taste of hot, beading blood.

Mike clutched at the steering wheel, pleading with the driver. "Let it go! Benny, let it go!"

Benny's hands loosened. Mike gave the wheel a hand-over-hand turn that brought the ambulance into a shuddering climb up the embankment, onto the highway.

"Benny, we've got to get through this," Mike said. "That's all, we've just got to get through this. You hear me?"

Vincent saw the lights of the hospital above the darkened treetops in the fast-closing distance.

He felt the power inside him. But he didn't let go of the wire.

the pitch

The sneer is gone from Casey's lip,
his teeth are clenched in hate;
He pounds with cruel violence
his bat upon the plate . . .

—E. L. Thayer, "Casey at the Bat"

10

Case washed the stickiness of the crushed tomato off his hands in a men's room that smelled of sharp antiseptic.

The sting of the smell made him think of the wet cement floors in the morning in the city-county jail, the slap of a gray mop in the drunk tank.

The mop, the jail. The booking sergeant's throaty bellow that came from chain-smoking Chesterfields.

Geez, Louise, Hamilton! Can'tcha see we just got the floor mopped, an' here you come again, haulin' in the sorry ass of another perp with a busted nose!"

A broken nose here, a cracked rib there. Nobody questioned Case with any seriousness about what happened. A lot of bad guys just seemed to have stumbled facefirst into walls about the time that Case got hold of them.

Some of the rich boys made bail in a snap, but all the same, they left custody with something to think about, and maybe they wouldn't be so quick to peddle their barbs and bennies the next time.

And maybe there wouldn't be a girl with haunted eyes and a wasted life in the hospital—

Case ripped a brown paper towel out of the wall dispenser.

His heart was thudding. He glanced toward the mirror, saw the flush of red that blossomed between his eyes.

He took a breath that made his ribs ache.

Mentally, piece by piece, choice by hard choice, he replaced his memory of the jail from twenty years ago with the here-and-now of the men's room. The green-tiled walls. The sinks in a row. The nothing job, the nothing life. The old man.

Thou shalt hang on.

The damned job was wearing him down. There were only so many ways to kill time in this place, and sometimes they weren't enough. A man with a lot of time on his hands can have some strange ideas, a lifetime of strange ideas, Case thought. Lots of time, and nothing but thoughts to kill it.

Case made his way toward the emergency room, trying to think of nothing but the squeak in his shoe.

He decided he liked the chirpy cricket sound.

A hospital could use a few crickets, Case thought. Crickets were supposed to bring good luck. A guy in surgery, he might feel better going under the anesthetic to the sound of a cricket's song.

Thou shalt hang on.

Now and then he spoke to someone, but he didn't say anything more than the few words that seemed necessary.

He thought he could sense where Diana was. Hell, why not? He always could before. Especially those times when his girl was in trouble, he *knew* it.

But this time the trouble wasn't a skinned knee, or a fight with the punky kid across the street. She was up there with Dr. Rat, up on fifteen, and there wasn't anything Case could do about it.

Thou shalt hang on.

He did. Case made his way to the hospital's emergency room, trying to think of nothing but the squeak in his shoe.

It was 11:43. In seventeen minutes, he would be able to leave work.

In twenty-five, thirty minutes, he would be in his rattle-trap Jeep, headed out of the city. He would be driving the crosstown highway that led to the first turn, finding his way through a series of other turns.

He would be driving on roads that weren't paved, weren't marked—roads that faded from pinging gravel to not much of anything, out to where the stars were as bright as creation.

The stars, ancient and wise. He could still believe in answers that were hidden in the stars.

As a cop, he'd known his way around the emergency room of every hospital in the city. He still thought of the emergency room in terms of black coffee.

Black coffee, and waiting for the docs to stitch a man's eyebrow back in place, so that Case could ask if the man wanted to file charges against his wife. And the man said no, said he only wished he hadn't given her something as heavy as a steam iron for an anniversary present.

Black coffee, and waiting to find out if a ten-year-old girl was going to live. Case still could feel how fragile her body was: his hands interlocked, delivering timed thrusts to her chest. Her skin sparkled with beads of chlorinated water under the merciless sun, there at the poolside. One!-and-two!-and-three! . . . and she'd lived, and she'd brought him a handful of daisies.

Black coffee, and waiting to hear what to call the night's attack on an eighty-one-year-old woman in her home. Assault and robbery would have been bad enough. But she died, and Case swore he would apprehend the murderer. He promised the woman's son. He still could see the man's red-rimmed eyes, the look of absolute trust in those eyes—

But he shouldn't have promised.

He should have known the emergency room wasn't a place to make promises. It was a place to do everything possible, as fast as possible, and to hope for the best, nothing more.

And he always left feeling he didn't have the hardest, meanest, highest-pressured job on God's own earth, because, at least, all he had to do in the emergency room was to drink coffee.

He came away with a respect for the emergency room's doctors and nurses that bordered on a wondering admiration for the talents of an alien species. He'd learned that most of them *liked* the work, and some of them chose it—wouldn't leave it.

And now, he found he still felt the same way about going into the emergency room, even though he didn't feel the same about himself.

The coffeepot had stayed in the same place, on the same counter in a white, bare-walled room that was called the staff lounge—although nobody lounged there—for thirty years. And sometimes, Case saw uniformed police officers helping themselves to the foam cups, the packets of sugar, the wooden stir-sticks. He saw plainclothes detectives pouring themselves cups of black coffee at midnight.

Most of the ones with gray hair were familiar faces to him, and Case knew he would have been welcome to join them, but he never did.

They were men whose lives meant something. In his heart, Case knew he didn't deserve their company.

He pushed open the door that led into the emergency room's waiting area, wishing Gwen could have gone to the lake with him on Sunday, thinking he might as well go alone, checking over the E.R. the way a longtime driver might shift gears at just the right moment by second nature.

It was an oddly quiet night—the kind he knew the E.R. staff would have called a lull before the storm.

He saw a workman in steel-toed boots leaving the hospital with a bandaged arm. A woman in a fluffy pink bathrobe was being admitted at the front desk, complaining of the abdominal pains and fever that probably signaled an attack of appendicitis.

The woman's slack-faced husband kept trying to soothe her by thumping her on the shoulder and calling her "honey-bunny," and she kept slapping his hand away.

A couple of other people were reading magazines, sitting at the opposite ends of a row of green vinyl seats. Case saw to his relief there were no police around.

Case nodded to the blond-haired nurse at the admitting desk. Her name was Karen-something. As a cop, he would have known her husband's name, her favorite color, and point for point how her kids were doing in school, but he didn't like to be around the emergency room.

He turned to go, back to the front lobby, back to Max Brand and the cattle rustlers—

He heard the incoming wail of an ambulance.

Craning toward the sound, Case could see through smeared glass doors to the short, curved drive that led from the dark street to the emergency room. He saw the ambulance that careened into the drive with a flash of headlights.

The vehicle should have continued past the doors to the ambulance entrance, where it could have been unloaded directly into the E.R. But it didn't. It stopped in front of the doors to the walk-in waiting room, tires squealing.

The box-shaped ambulance jerked to a stop that made it nose down, almost comically, like a clown car on a string. It sat there, lights flashing, siren screaming.

The nurse, even the woman in the bathrobe, quit their business to look out the doors.

The nurse glanced toward Case, glad to see he was still there. She gave him a smile that said: *Well, it's always something, isn't it?*

She tap-tap-tapped her pen on the desk. She said, "Mr. Hamilton, would you please go *show* the driver where the ambulance entrance is."

Case answered, "Yeah, I'll lead him down the primrose path."

"And tell him that he doesn't need a siren in the driveway. Just for the fun of it, we like to call this a quiet zone."

"Yeah, I'll get the joker's name, too," Case said. "He needs to be stood in the corner."

Case pushed through the doors into the hot, heavy night, the storm aching to break loose.

Abruptly, the siren quit. The flashers, the headlights, snapped off.

The ambulance pulled straight forward. It lurched over the curb as if it were going to ram into the E.R. waiting room.

Case stumbled back in alarm, reaching out his hands as if he might push the monster away if it came too close. But the ambulance stopped with its front wheels just over the curb.

Case saw the dim shape of the driver as he cranked the wheel, throwing the ambulance into clumsy reverse a few feet. Another fight with the steering wheel. The vehicle lumbered ahead to the wide, covered port that was marked with a lighted sign: "Ambulance Entrance."

Even then, the driver pulled to the street side of the empty platform, as far as possible from the hospital building —about thirty feet away from where it should have been for unloading.

"That man's going to wish he'd called in sick," Case said.

He suspected the driver was drunk, and it angered him, even though he tried to tell himself the driver meant no harm.

He cut through the inner workings of the emergency room, past a row of beds that were separated by curtains. A curtain closed, a moan of pain; a curtain open, a glimpse of a man's bare leg.

He came to another set of glass doors, automatic doors that would hiss open to admit a stretcher—a stretcher unloaded from the back of an ambulance.

But the ambulance wasn't being unloaded.

Case felt alarms going off inside him that he hadn't felt in years. As a cop, he'd learned to sense danger, learned to trust his senses. And he hadn't forgotten. The alarm system, once rigged, stayed on for a lifetime.

He felt the electric charge that warned him something was wrong, very wrong about the ambulance.

Other people felt the warning, too. They just didn't know what it was.

Case realized there were people behind him—a nurse, a med tech, maybe others. They were watching the ambulance. They supposed he was going to do something about the ambulance.

He reached for his walkie-talkie to call for help. It didn't respond to his touch of the talk button, and only then, Case remembered the damned thing was broken.

No matter. He told himself the ambulance driver was a fool, but foolish things happen. The important thing was to get the patient unloaded.

The E.R. doors hissed open to a crack of thunder. Case walked toward the glossy white side of the ambulance.

Case was just outside the E.R. when the cab door edged open on the passenger's side of the ambulance, inching toward him. The paramedic just inside the cab was a jowly, dark-haired man, looking to Case with a tight expression that could have fit any number of desperate scenarios. It could have meant they'd just scraped up the remains of an especially picturesque car wreck, or hell, it could have meant the paramedic was suffering a case of the Aztec two-step.

Case had walked about ten feet toward the vehicle. A scream erupted from inside the ambulance, only to be cut short.

Case felt his hand on the grip of his holstered Smith & Wesson, but he let go as if he'd been burned. Memory warned him.

Whatever happened, he couldn't risk dying again with a gun in his hand. He might have been punished for holding a weapon. Nothing could be worth the jeopardy of another sin, least of all this bit of late-night blundering.

He wasn't going to need a revolver to deal with some screwup of an ambulance driver. In a few minutes, he was going to be having a laugh at himself for being so tomfool scared.

The cab door opened. A heavyset man in the whites of a paramedic stepped out of the cab with the slowness of injury, right hand clutching his rib cage. The door whammed shut behind him.

The man's face seemed as pale as the moon, warped by the bent shape of his glasses. He looked at Case in desperation.

He said, "They've . . . got a knife on the driver, they've got a knife on Benny. They want drugs."

Case went cold. Death clung in his throat.

The man staggered toward him—close enough for Case to read the name on the tag-pin on the man's shirt: M. STURDIVANT.

Sturdivant's voice burst into a cry. *"They want drugs!* Give the sumsa-bitches *drugs*, you hear me? They've got a knife on Benny!"

Case heard footsteps behind him, the murmur of voices. He turned toward the hospital, warning with a sweep of his palm to keep back.

"Everybody. Stay inside!"

He saw the crowd behind him as a blur of faces. Worried faces. Puzzled faces. Some of them frightened, none of them laughing. All of a sudden, the Terminator wasn't so funny to them. They were just beginning to realize the danger that Case already sensed, and their uncertainty quivered in the air.

He told Sturdivant the same thing he was struggling to tell himself, "Keep it calm. What happened?"

Sturdivant swallowed air. "Inside the wagon. I counted five, maybe six in the back . . . some kind of a street gang, and they've got this bugfucked idea, oh, jeeeez!"

"Easy, mister. Tell it easy."

"—rob the hospital. They want the wagon full of drugs."

Gang. Rob. Knife.

Case fought to hold steady. He couldn't deal with this. But he could stay calm, and he could work his way out of the situation. He could do his job.

Case said, "All right, now listen to me. We're going to move inside. We're going to call the police—"

"*No!*" Sturdivant yelled with a blast of hot breath. "I—I can't move away. They told me to stay in sight—to stay right here, man, *right here* for as long as it takes."

Case tried to see into the ambulance, hoped that inside, someone was calling the police. The floodlights at the hospital's entrance cast a glare over the cab's side window, but he could make out the driver's thin profile. The face was tilted up, the mouth dropped open. At the driver's throat—a gleam of white that ran the length of the knife blade.

Sturdivant's thick hands closed to fists. "It's no game. They've already killed a man. They're high, and they're crazy. And the worst of the bunch, this creep with the knife, they call him Vincent—"

"He's the gang leader?"

Sturdivant nodded. A fleck of spit shook loose from the corner of his mouth. "I think he *wants* to keep on killing, and he's got this knife, this Rambo thing, right at Benny's throat."

Sturdivant came toward him—a step, a step, as though he might be yanked back at any moment by the force of a hidden hand, an invisible leash.

"I don't think Benny knows enough to be scared," Sturdivant said. "He's been driving as wrong as he could, all over the road, trying to get us pulled over." Sturdivant flashed a sick smile. "Never a cop when you need one."

Case didn't share any of Benny's penchant for risk-taking. A trickle of sweat chilled his back. But all he had to do was stall for time.

The ambulance entrance was monitored by a video camera. Even though he hadn't called her, Mabel would see something was wrong on the video monitor in the hospital's basement. She would be calling for help; and when the real cops moved in, Case would be out of the show.

Someone in the E.R. already might have called 911. Karen-something would have called. But even if *nobody* called, there would be other ambulances wheeling in, Case thought. All it would take would be a car wreck, a bar fight, and he would be hearing the wail of another ambulance, and there would be a black-and-white cruiser behind it.

Thou shalt hang on.

Case crossed his arms. It was a nonaggressive, solid-looking gesture, and it hid the trembling in his hands.

He called to the ambulance, "Turn on the dome light inside the cab. I want to see if the driver's all right."

Nothing responded.

He called again, "Show me the driver is all right, then we'll talk."

There was a glint of white light reflected from metal inside the cab. A movement of the knife. Something rocked inside the vehicle.

"Tell me what you want. Make it clear to me."

Give me time, he thought. *Time, time, time.*

But the back of the ambulance swung open in that moment, and Case lost whatever chance he'd ever had to get away.

The shirtless boy who jumped from the back of the ambulance was sunken-chested, painfully emaciated.

The kid's arms were so thin, they could have been snapped off and shoved up his nose, Case thought. And why not? He didn't doubt this little punk was an expert at nasal ingestion.

The kid fixed him with a splitting grin. "Vincent says three minutes. That's all you've got—*grandpa.*" He seemed to fancy the sound. "Grand-pa-pa." He let go with a giggle that made the bridge of his nose crinkle. "And he's already counting. And he counts reeee-eal fast."

Case felt as though he'd been slugged in the stomach. He realized this wasn't any sort of a real robbery. It wasn't for the sake of drugs. It was some doped-up lunatic named Vincent's demented idea of fun.

Case thought of running. He could, he could run tail-over-teakettle. But not if it cost the driver's life. Not if it meant he would be held to account for a tragedy the next time the scales were balanced against him.

He looked at Sturdivant. The man was about to break. Sturdivant and the ambulance: two elements Case couldn't predict.

Case said, "Tell Vincent to come out and talk for himself."

The kid shook his head with an exaggerated back and forth, like a spring-loaded toy. "He sent *me!* Goldie! Vincent likes me. Vincent, he says I'm Number One."

"Okay, I got it. You're Number One." Case took a mental measurement of the kid's overblown sense of cockiness; it didn't fit on such a skinny frame. Goldie could be a critical weakness.

Case said, "You want drugs? What kind of drugs, Number One? Aspirin?"

Goldie's face crinkled in puzzlement. "Don't screw with me, grandpa."

Case hoped the simple truth would give him a moment's edge. "I'm not. But there aren't any drugs I can get hold of in three minutes."

"Hospitals are fulla drugs, Vincent said so."

Case was learning a moment-to-moment, bone-deep contempt for the still-unseen Vincent, but he couldn't allow himself to give in to the feeling; he couldn't risk the involvement.

"Tell Vincent . . ." Case felt his chest tightening. Far-off, he heard the ghost cry of an ambulance siren, but he couldn't tell which direction it was headed. "The emergency room isn't where the drugs are kept, not unless you're willing to settle for a handful of painkillers, maybe some Demerol. The drug dispensary's on the third floor, and it's locked. I don't have the combination to the door lock. It's guarded. It's got electronic security—"

Case shot a look to Sturdivant, who had the clarity of thought, thank the heavens, to respond to it.

Sturdivant said, "It's the truth. Listen to him, Goldie."

Case knew there had to be help on the way. How long could it take?

"Tell Vincent we'll do what you want, Number One, but we're going to need time."

Goldie hesitated. He glanced toward the darkened ambulance. He made a whimpering sound, like a wounded mutt.

Case said, "Easy, easy. It's not your fault, Goldie. You didn't make the plan, Vincent did. But you're the one who's smart enough to see that it's up to you now—that you've got to help us. You've got to help us make the plan work."

Goldie looked toward him with something like dumb faith.

"We need time," Case said. "Tell Vincent. Make him believe it."

"Time," Goldie said. He dealt himself a slap to the face. Another, and his bottom lip split open in a smear of red. "We need time to make it work. It's up to me."

Goldie shuffled to the ambulance. He knocked on the back of the vehicle in a sheepish way, like knocking on a bathroom door.

The door cracked open, and Goldie crawled in. Muffled voices sounded from inside the wagon.

But another sound carried over the noise from the ambulance. A siren in the distance. It wasn't an ambulance this time, it was a police cruiser. And it was coming closer.

Case thought he might fall to his knees in relief.

Sturdivant heard it, too. He said, "I want to think, maybe . . . you've saved a man's life."

Case saw that Sturdivant's face was streaked with tears, glistening like ice.

Yeah, I did save a man's life, Case thought. *I saved mine.*

He looked from Sturdivant to the ambulance—to see the nightmare break loose.

Back and side, the doors of the ambulance burst open. Goldie spilled out of the passenger side like a frail doll made of sticks, shoved out, facefirst onto the driveway, cradling a brown paper bag.

The others came boiling out of the back. Case saw another

five punks—big kids, most of them as big as men, all of them crazy-high, teeth and eyes white as the moon. He saw they had guns.

Another glance told him the driver was gone from the cab. Moved to the back of the ambulance? Forced out the driver's side door?

Case gave Sturdivant a push back. "It's goin' down. Now! Get away from here." But Sturdivant wasn't moving.

"Vincent! I don't see Vincent," Sturdivant said.

"I said, get out of here."

"Vincent! . . . Goddam, don't you know? The bastard's still got Benny." And Sturdivant was yelling, *"Benny!"*

The siren was louder, closer, a wailing that was joined by the cry of a second police cruiser, promising sweet salvation.

But a voice split the air in defiance—a smooth voice that rose in clear tones from the far side of the ambulance, like an alien tongue from the dark side of the moon.

"No more excuses, grandpa. Just load up the wagon."

Case took a step forward. He tried not to think of the guns that were being leveled at him. The sonsabitches were spreading out. One of them climbed to the top of the wagon, carrying the beetle-black shape of an Uzi. They were *into* this, like it was some kind of Hollywood shoot-out, goddam *Young Guns* played for real.

Case said, "Listen, I *can't* just—"

"We'll tear this place to hell. You want to go to hell?"

Ice and eternity. Bells that rang forever. He couldn't risk a second's thought to the consequence of dying, or he knew he would just stand there, screaming.

Case forced himself to focus on small bits of the real world. The living world. The hot, still air. The smell of oil from the pavement. The ragged sound of Sturdivant's breathing.

"Show me the driver," Case said. "You'll get what you want."

"Show and tell, grandpa? Why not? You first. Lose the trey-eight."

Case lifted the revolver from his holster. The pistol fell with a clack onto the pavement.

Silence.

He kicked the revolver a couple of yards toward the ambulance.

In minutes, there would be police all over this scene, Case thought. Vincent must have known. Did he *want* to die?

A face edged into sight from behind the ambulance. It was a thin face, dotted with orange freckles, topped with a shock of reddish-blond hair.

"Benny!" Sturdivant said.

Benny stumbled forward, coming into full view.

Still on the ground, Goldie clapped his hands like a kid watching a Fourth of July parade as Benny jerked and fought his way around the front of the ambulance, moving toward Case.

Benny—and Vincent behind him.

Case knew it had to be Vincent behind the driver: Vincent, the pretty boy with the knife to the driver's throat. Vincent with the jet-black hair that seemed electric, full of blue light. Vincent with the white grin that was like a wall of teeth. Vincent with the madness in his eyes.

Vincent was forcing Benny to walk ahead of him. He had one fist entangled in Benny's hair. Vincent's other hand, his right, gripped the serrated knife.

Benny's tennis shoes scraped on the pavement.

"Lighten up, grandpa," Vincent said. "If you can't have a little fun with your friends on a summer's night, hey—what's the use?"

Benny struggled to speak. He came out with, "Mike, help mmm!"

Vincent leaned to whisper into Benny's ear, but his rasping voice carried into the night.

"Thanks for the ride," Vincent said.

And with a smile of perfect teeth, with a gleam of crystal-blue eyes, with the musical laughter of madness—Vincent slashed the knife across Benny's throat.

The blood ran forever. It poured from Benny's cut throat, it fountained, spattering onto the pavement, until the whole world turned red.

Sturdivant lunged toward Vincent, only to be knocked back, reeling from a gunshot wound to the shoulder. Case recognized the heavy wham of a .357 Magnum.

Bullets howled past him. Case dropped to the ground. He was acting on reflex. Cop reflex. Crawling forward, rolling, he came up with the Smith & Wesson in his hand.

He couldn't begin to guess at Vincent's motives, but Vincent must have planned to kill the driver all along. There'd been nothing of impulse to the slash of the long blade.

Cop reflex. Vincent had to go down.

But it wasn't that easy.

Case heard something hiss behind him. He turned, seeing Goldie with a can of spray paint.

"Bang," Goldie said, pushing the can's spray tip. "Bang, grandpa. Bang, you're dead."

Case ignored the twerp, scrambling to flatten himself against the side of the ambulance, out of the Uzi's line of fire. Case stood, winded, the revolver in a double-handed grip to hold it steady.

But the line of fire between him and Vincent was blocked by another of Vincent's goon brigade, a neckless wonder with a length of chain, coming at him.

The chain swung toward him, whistling past his face,

bashing into the side of the ambulance. No-Neck closed in, reeking of sour sweat.

Case lunged forward, swinging the butt end of the revolver with the strength of every hot emotion he'd denied himself for three damned years.

It was fear in the night, it was cowardice, it was every time they'd called him the Man With No Name, and it was the loss of his daughter.

Clenching the revolver, Case's fist smashed into the attacking punk's face, making a target of the black growth at the bridge of the nose. He felt bone crack. It might have been his hand; he didn't care. He hit the bastard again—knocked him backward, and fired three times into the falling body, clearing the way for a shot at Vincent.

Had him between the eyes. And Vincent smiled at him.

Vincent threw his arms wide open, the bloodied knife still in his right hand, offering his heart as a target.

"Try it, granddaddy," Vincent said. "You can't hurt me. Nobody can hurt me. *Try* it."

Had the trigger half-pulled.

But Case's hand froze. And in that moment of hesitation, he thought of hell as he'd known it. The frozen eternity. Punishment for his sins of hatred, of violence. He was going to be extinguished. And maybe it didn't matter what he did now, but maybe it did.

Maybe—

A flash of bloodied metal, and Vincent's knife caught him in the side, cut him open, sprayed him with his own hot blood; and there were other shapes, shadows and blurs.

The wounded Sturdivant kneeling over Benny, bleeding onto Benny, protecting his friend.

Gunfire.

Thunder. The battering of rain.

Diana's voice. "Dad!"

He heard a burst of shots. A damned *machine gun!* More gunfire. Screaming.

He didn't know he was down until he felt the rough, pebbly surface of the pavement as a vague unpleasantness against the cheekbone under his left eye.

He tasted copper and salt, felt a crushing pressure in his chest, and when he tried to move, found that he couldn't.

And the first of the bells rang with a terrible groan, and Case felt himself slipping, losing hold of life.

And the bells rang, and he felt the tolling of the bells of eternity in the pit of his soul.

Thunder and bells!

The bells rang, tolling for him, as he tumbled toward death, his soul silently screaming.

They rang, the peals drawing closer and closer together, deeper and louder, groaning from rusty throats; and in the agony of his fall into darkness, his slow fall, he remembered Poe's poem, understanding it now, all of Poe's agony, as the words squeezed out of him, trailing behind him like a ribbon.

The sobbing of the bells, keeping time, time, time—

He fell, swirling, meeting the clamor.

The moaning and the groaning—

He fell, his worst fear come to claim him, his worst dreams realized.

Of the bells, bells, bells, bells, bells, bells, bells!

He was dissolving into the eternal night. But the darkness wasn't perfect. Not quite.

He could still see.

Something white.

Something shimmering.

Something new.

Something aware of him.

Something—

11

Diana lost count of the hours, of all concept of time, and the night never ended.

She sat for a time in the waiting room close by the intensive care unit, expecting moment to moment to find out if the doctors were going to be able to save her dad's life, but she seemed to have been forgotten.

Once, Stephen had sent word by a nurse that he was taking charge of caring for Case Hamilton, and Diana thought *he* would be able to handle things differently. But still no word . . .

All she knew was what they'd told her in the beginning. There was a knife wound to the left side—and the evident consequence of a heart attack, just as she'd feared.

And you're going to have to deal with it, Diana.

So often, she had worried that her father's heart would fail him, sooner or later, today or tomorrow, as if she'd always been waiting.

Diana sat in the waiting room for as long as she could stand it. She walked the hallway. She found a rest room, trying not to see herself in the mirror. She looked as if she'd been dragged through a gun barrel.

She walked, her footsteps clicking in the hallway. She

found a gumball machine, surreal with all its cheery colors of gum that had no taste.

She walked to a window, covered with trickles of rain. Beyond was a clouded sky that made it hard to imagine that dawn could be a possibility.

And in the end, Diana realized she had no place else to go, except back to the isolation of the waiting room.

She pushed open the door, and it all rushed toward her with one beat of her pulse.

The room was overlit—brightly, coldly fluorescent, with Scotch-plaid couches at either side and end tables scattered with newspapers and magazines, as if they'd been thrown onto the tables in a hurry.

It was a room where lonely emotions swept through like ghosts, as people waited for the next sudden opening of the door.

There were two people in the ICU waiting room. One was a tangle-haired woman whose head fell against one of the sofa cushions at a broken angle, her eyes closed, her mouth sagging embarrassingly open.

As Diana entered the room, she could hear the woman's soft snoring, mingling with the muted lull of the Muzak system that was wafting a slow, instrumental version of "Woodstock" into the overlit room.

The woman's eyes cracked just long enough for her to see that Diana wasn't going to be the answer to anything.

And Diana saw all of this in the moment it took the burly figure of Frank Morrow to rise from the other couch, smiling, speaking her name. She could have run to meet him.

She offered her hand to shake his, but he brushed it aside and embraced her, hard, the way she wanted.

"I'm real sorry, hon," he said, hugging her another time before he let go. "I thought maybe I could help you get through this shit. Maybe I could talk to you while you waited—"

"Thank you, Frank," she said, patting him on the shoulder of his rumpled brown suit, wishing for some better way to tell him how much this meant to her, just for him to be there.

"I guess there isn't any word, then," Diana said.

"No." He spread his big hands out. "Nothin'. You want to sit down? They got us a goddam coffeepot in here."

"Sure." She found a place on the couch. It sagged a little beneath her, and she thought of Stephen's Corinthian leather sofa that was part of another world.

Frank busied himself with a stack of foam cups beside the coffee urn. It seemed suitable that he, who'd been her father's longtime partner in the homicide division, should be here now.

Frank was the one who *hadn't* ended up on the floor of that liquor store, the lifeblood ebbing out of him. The one who was able to go back, eventually, and build the dollhouse for his own daughter, Jenny, out of the jumble of pieces that were in the trunk of the car that night.

"I forget—you take cream or sugar?" Frank asked.

"No," Diana said, knowing that Frank never forgot anything. He just wanted something to say.

"That's good. There ain't any, anyway." He grinned, handing the cup to her.

She held it, feeling the warmth without comfort, thinking of how Frank's life had changed since the time of the shooting.

He'd climbed up the ranks to lieutenant, and he was in line for the chief's office. A vote inside the department would have made him chief already. But he wouldn't play politics.

Frank was a man who cherished the ethics he'd learned as

an Oklahoma farm boy. There was nothing wrong with a college-educated man saying "ain't" like his hardworking daddy in Frank's code, and a whole damn lot that was wrong about wheeling and dealing for office.

And the funny thing about him—with his bald head, and his face never marked by the bad things he'd seen, and with his brown eyes bigger and warmer than real under those thick glasses he wore—Diana would have sworn that he looked less like a homicide cop than just about anything else on God's earth.

Frank and Case had shared so many of the same hard experiences, she wondered how they could have turned out so unalike in temperament. Being a cop had brought out the meanness in Case, leaving no apparent mark on Frank.

"Listen, Diana," Frank said, cradling his own cup between his hands. "You may not want to talk about it, and it's just goddam fine if you don't. But they're all talkin' back at the station about the great job you did . . . I mean, down there, breakin' up that shit in the E.R."

He pointed, as if to jab a finger through the floor, straight to the emergency room. "Hadn't been for you, we could have had a hell of a lot more casualties than we did."

He told her some of the consequences of the night's violence—that her father had struck and killed one of the attackers, and that two people had been injured by gunfire and been admitted into the hospital.

Diana didn't look at him. She looked across to the sleeping woman, ugly in repose, and she remembered.

Diana remembered the urgent knock on the door to Stephen's lab, and Stephen's blue oath as he arose from the satyr's sofa bed. She gathered the satin sheets around her.

Naked, he opened the door just an inch. There was a low

conversation. She recognized the voice of Duane Hardage, the security guard.

Stephen's voice again: an edge of cold impatience to the words that made no sense.

"No," Stephen said. "You don't leave this floor. I don't care what else happens."

Duane answered in protest. But Stephen cut him off.

"Trouble on the ground floor isn't any of your business, Hardage. And it's all the more reason I want *this* floor kept under guard."

More. Duane's voice, louder.

"Tell her, *please!* It's police business, Doc. I think Detective Hamilton ought to know."

Diana was startled. She'd always known Duane as such an easygoing man; she couldn't imagine what it would take to upset him this way—what the trouble could be that would involve her.

She dressed in a rush of dishevelment that left no time for her to feel embarrassed, hurrying to the door.

The awkward exchange was building to a confrontation between the two men, storming at each other through the crack in the door.

Stephen warned, "Get it straight, Hardage. You don't work for hospital security, you work for me. I said get back to your desk. Your job's on the line, and I'll give you three seconds—"

Diana stepped to the door, reaching in front of Stephen before he could stop her, pulling the door open just enough to face the guard.

"What is it, Duane?" she asked.

Stephen made a curse word of her name. "Diana!" His bare footsteps smacked the floor, retreating into the lab.

"There was a 415 call on the police scanner," Duane said. Disturbance. "It was a call from right here, Detective—

down in the E.R., right here in this hospital. Next thing I know, they're saying shots fired. And I'm thinking your dad might be caught in the middle—"

She remembered that Stephen came back in a cream-colored, velveteen robe, yanking the belt tight, still angry.

"Consider yourself terminated," Stephen told the guard, gesturing with a sweep of his hand as if to brush away a crumb.

She wanted to stand up for Duane, but she couldn't. Diana was running. Into the paneled hallway that led to the elevators. Feeling the weight of the revolver in her purse. Stephen calling to her.

The elevator was too slow. It should have dropped straight down at this time of night, but it stopped on a perverse whim at floors where there was nobody waiting.

Diana took the stairs down from the eighth floor. Stairs, two at a time. Ground floor. Running through the hallways.

She hit the door into the E.R. just ahead of one of the hospital's security guards, a red-faced man, running with a pistol in his hand in a way that left the barrel pointed to blow the end of his chin.

Into the E.R., running. Through the sliding glass, into the aching, hot night.

And the scalding of the word in her throat. "Dad!" when she saw him there, sprawled facedown on the bloodied pavement.

Diana looked to Frank. She wondered just how much he understood of what she felt.

She said, "It's funny, I know everything, exactly what happened up to that point when I . . . saw him. But the rest of it seems to have happened to somebody else."

Frank nodded. "It gets peculiar as shit sometimes," he said. "You don't hear the gun going off in your hand, but you hear the clink of the empty cartridge when it hits the ground. And you realize that you've been running on some sort of instinct." He took a swallow of coffee.

"The one I killed . . . the kid had an Uzi. Christ, Frank! It was a war zone, all the gunfire—"

"I know."

"Just a kid, I shot—"

"He was a drugged-up, twelfth-grade dropout with a weapon made for no damn use whatsoever except to kill people. Diana, you didn't have shit for a choice."

She felt his big hand clasping hers.

"The first time's the worst," he said. "You did the right thing . . . Detective Hamilton."

She felt her eyes burning. She refused to cry, but she was beginning to learn that she *did* remember the rest of it, and she might always remember.

The tension of her hands locked on the grip of the revolver. The frenzy of bodies in motion, running.

She counted four of them. Two black, two white. They were running toward the ambulance, and they were *in* the ambulance, and the ambulance jolted toward her.

Diana fired three more shots that starred the windshield, but the ambulance screamed past her, cutting a circle that took it over the curb in a spray of white sparks, metal raking the concrete.

Over the curb—away from the hospital.

And a vivid flash, scarred in her mind. She thought of the skinny kid left behind. The skinny kid with no shirt, the sunken chest, just standing there, wide-eyed, looking lost.

It was like a macabre comedy. All she wanted was to find out if her father was going to be all right, and there were bleeding bodies on the pavement in front of her, and there were people behind her, voices behind her, and she remembered the buzzing sound of the bullets that tore past her, and the smacking sound of the bullets that hit the glass doors behind her, and she thought she was going to be sick any minute.

And this! she thought—this, for the finale—the bizarre sight of the skinny kid in the driveway, like some perverse fate had decided she could use a laugh.

The skinny kid, flapping his arms at his sides, maybe crying. She couldn't tell.

He had something in one hand, something metal, and she almost pulled the trigger one last time. But she didn't. She saw the metal thing wasn't a weapon; it was a paint can.

He lifted the can toward his face.

She started to order him onto the ground when the shots went off behind her. Three shots, two misses. *Wham-wham-wham.*

Third shot, and the can exploded in a halo of gold that enveloped the kid's head, a starburst of gold from a center of crimson, red and gold spattering onto the pavement.

Motes of the gold paint hung in the air, swirling, glittering, for what seemed an eternity after the kid's body fell to the ground.

Diana turned—to see the red-faced security guard, standing behind her, grinning, blowing smoke off the barrel of his revolver, like some old-time cowboy hero.

"Gotcha, sonny boy," the guard said.

"I wasn't quick enough," Diana said, looking away from the sleeping woman and her ragged mouth.

"Aw, hell!" Frank told her how the ambulance had overturned not a mile from the hospital, trapped in a convergence of black-and-whites. There were shots fired from the ambulance. The police returned fire.

"Zapped one of 'em through the shoulder. How 'bout that?

Here he is, the little pencil-dick, hauled right back to the hospital," Frank said.

Diana realized she'd let Frank's words flit like mayflies through her mind, but she wanted to *know*.

"We've got one in custody?" she asked.

"Under guard," Frank said. "They've got him sedated. He's sleepin' the small sleep, but we've got him ID'd."

Frank couldn't have told her enough in that moment. You could never get enough insight into what sort of human monster would turn the hospital into a slaughterhouse.

He didn't need prompting to tell, and he probably didn't need the notebook he produced from the inside pocket of his sport jacket. He seemed to have been wearing the same coat for as long as she'd known him.

"The kid's name is Jermell Lewis," Frank said. "He's seventeen. His mother's a housekeeper at the Holiday Inn Central. His father—hell, we might as well just say his father's a grasshopper, try n'find the sumbitch.

"He's got two brothers, two sisters. Loves to run. He was a good runner on his high school track team, Jermell. His mom said he would have lettered this year if he'd stayed with the team—but he got himself joined at the waist to some kind of a street gang."

"Gang?" Diana said, hearing a sinister, spidery tone to the word that she'd never discovered before.

"Small-timers. Marks," Frank said. He slapped the notebook shut—a storybook with an ending that stunk.

Diana was sorry for what she'd found out. She'd wanted someone to hate with a blind fury, and Frank had shown her a messed-up kid with a hardworking, heartbroken mother.

She imagined Jermell Lewis's mother was worrying through the night in a room as bleak as this one, somewhere else in this same hospital.

Frank went on, and she tried to listen. He told her another

three perps got away from the ambulance, running into the cover of a residential neighborhood, mostly brick apartments, the streets like a rat maze.

"Tell you this much, Diana, I guaran-damn-tee you we'll find 'em," Frank said.

In the harsh light, Frank's face seemed bigger than life, sharply outlined against a pale, indistinct background, and Diana believed him.

"My daddy told me something about farming years ago, and I've found what he said is just as true of police work," Frank said. "He told me, 'It's not so hard to plow a field, it's just hell to know where to start.' And we've got a place to start. Jermell."

But he seemed to be looking into his coffee cup in search of different subject, finding one he didn't like.

"There's something else I have to tell you, though," Frank said. "It's something bad you've got to know, and there's no good time to hear it."

He took a swallow, crumpled the cup.

12

Falling!

He was falling, falling forever, the noise of the bells rippling way behind him as he tumbled beyond their ceaseless tolling, farther into death's realm than he'd ever gone before.

And then, Case realized that he wasn't falling *away* anymore—he was falling *toward* something, *into* something.

Something white.

It was a ghost light in the darkness, but it was growing, seeming to reach out to him.

He felt himself break through a membrane at the edge of the light, and the light closed around him, softly and brightly around him.

It was like dawn breaking, and he was a mote of dust on the air, drifting down, caught by the light. Turned to silver and gold.

Case felt suffused with a great, comforting warmth, just when he had expected the horror of extinguishment. Ice and eternity. Flecking away, atom by atom, mind and body, to the final separation.

None of his worst fears came true.

Instead, he found the pain of the slash wound was gone from his side, just as the anguish was gone from his heart.

Diana. Gwen. Teresa McMasters. Freed from the limits of human emotion, he felt for them more than ever. But he didn't have to worry about them. He knew they were all part of a plan, and the plan was in perfect motion.

The kid with the knife. Glasser. He felt for them, too, in a different way, but he let go of the old hatreds, the old angers, the bitter thoughts so long suppressed.

Case allowed himself to believe in this warmth, to gather it in, to think that, possibly, this *could* happen, even as he felt that he was drifting to a stop.

There was nothing he could see in the light, not even himself. It was a living light, a world of light, a world in which figures stirred and moved, lit so brightly that only the suggestion of their movements could be seen, like sunspots seen through a telescope.

The movement around him, the light, took shape with hands, and feet, and bodies. And he was bathed in light, standing in light, at peace with himself, at peace with the universe.

He wondered if this might be heaven. And he was answered.

Something in the light seemed to anticipate the question, speaking to him in a voice he hadn't heard in sixteen years.

"Hey, pal," it called to him—a greeting that had been so familiar, so much a part of his life, it could have stopped his heart.

He saw his father there in front of him, smiling—not the waxy face of the old man he'd left in the low-priced coffin, but the smooth, vital face of a man for whom age held no meaning.

"Hello, Casey," his father said.

Case saw the blunt lines of his own jaw in his father's face, and the blue eyes that were a family heritage—the eyes full of light and life, glimmering with tears.

He felt as light as a breath.

And his father was holding him, strong arms around him, telling him, "Lord, but I've missed you, son."

Case could not remember his father ever having held him before.

But he knew that he'd *wanted* this, right to the end of his father's life, and he thought he might be crying. Pulling back, his father winked—a snap of blue light. "So . . . you think you belong in heaven, do you?" he said.

"I don't know," Case said. "Don't know . . . where I am . . ."

He could have been blind drunk, he would have been just as coherent.

Case tried to remember some of the books he'd read on Eastern and Western theologies. Nothing made sense.

He'd delved into ancient and primitive religions, and into the Protestant and Catholic orders, into Unitarian liberalism, into hellfire, and he'd come away at more of a loss than ever.

Always, there were rituals to be performed by those who expected to be rewarded in the afterlife. Beliefs to be accepted on blind faith. Instructions to be carried out.

It's a wondrous thing to think about, isn't it? the minister had asked him, but it wasn't wondrous. It was a part of his punishment, searching for the way to heaven, robbed of the faith that might have opened the way to him.

He knew of endless religions. He'd chosen none of them.

He hadn't arrived with gifts to appease the gods who kept watch over the River Styx. He hadn't been met by the Valkyrie for having died in glorious battle, and he hadn't been saved.

He'd been lost. He'd been damned.
But he was talking to his father.

Case's father had died a long, degenerative death from emphysema, a struggle he'd lost during the '77 World Series.

Ben Hamilton had sworn he would live long enough to see Reggie Jackson hit another homer. He'd bet five dollars with Case that Jackson would homer three games in a row, and he'd bet right.

Case had tucked a five-dollar bill into his father's suit pocket inside the coffin.

He left the funeral thinking how little he'd ever known of his father's life, except that his dad liked baseball.

Now, Case saw that his father was holding something out to him, cradling it in one hand, smiling, nodding toward the white sphere.

Case knew what it was. It belonged here.

His mind tumbled back, slowing and stopping in another time and place that held its own glow. It was a time when young Casey Hamilton had spent long days standing and running on crude baseball diamonds, sketched out in pastures and on empty lots, with pieces of cardboard boxes for bases. It was a time when Casey was working on his curve and trying to throw it past every kid who came to the plate, breathing in summer air so hot it felt like white sand in his lungs.

Case knew without knowing that baseball and his dad were somehow linked—that he, Case, had been born into a vast family of baseball, its members including everyone who'd ever played, and everyone who'd ever sat in the bleachers in a small town and hung on the next pitch in a three-and-one count.

Case knew that if he could throw a curve and a slider and a fastball, he had a shot at an honored place in this family.

And the family's symbol was The Ball.

The Ball seemed to be made of dreams packed together—his father's, his own, and every one of the 1927 New York Yankees who had signed The Ball on a long-ago evening in the Bronx, as Casey's father had waited outside the stadium for hours, picking them up singly, or in groups of twos and threes, all but one player. Lou Gehrig.

The Ball, in its shining, symbolic purity, had existed long before the birth of Casey Hamilton. Casey had thought of it as something eternal, there in its glass case on the fireplace mantel.

But he'd learned it wasn't magic. It was just a baseball, after all. It didn't mean a thing.

The end of The Ball came one horrible October evening, 1951, as an eleven-year-old Casey Hamilton had stood sobbing in his front yard, watching his home burn to the ground.

After the fire, his dad had scratched through the smoking rubble for The Ball until his fingers blistered and bled, and into the night. And when he found it, he had refused to believe.

To the very end, Ben Hamilton had insisted The Ball was misplaced, that it was somewhere in the cardboard boxes of salvaged belongings that reeked of smoke—boxes that finally were thrown away when Case's mom died, forcing his dad to accept the inevitability of a nursing home.

But Casey had seen the sodden, black lump in his dad's trembling hand, and he'd *known*. The Ball was gone. Forever.

And he thought of the missing signature—how he'd lied to himself, believing it was part of The Ball's magic to be not quite complete. Not quite perfect.

Lacking one signature, The Ball was a promise of things to be done, of great things to come.

But he saw it for what it really was after the fire. Something else that his dad wasn't able to get right.

Ben Hamilton was such a little man, the great Lou Gehrig didn't bother to see him, didn't bother to stop, didn't bother to take three seconds to sign the little man's baseball.

And his dad would come back from work in the insurance office, looking tired, looking old. He would come in the door, into the second house that never felt like home.

"Hey, pal," he would call out to Casey. "How about a game of catch?"

And Casey ignored him.

The Ball was whole again now, in his dad's big, steady hand. Case was sure of it.

It was a miracle, even in a place of miracles.

Other people were coming out of the light now, constructed of the light, beaming human faces turned toward him. They beckoned him.

He moved slowly, the faces of family members and childhood friends eddying out of the light as he kept his eye on his smiling father, and The Ball in his father's hand.

He was almost close enough to read the autographs on The Ball now, and their diversity came back to him, the individuality of each signature, the loops and swirls and cramped, small lettering, depending on where you looked.

He saw the white space still there, still left for the only one of the '27 Yankees who hadn't signed The Ball—the only one his father had missed. Lou Gehrig.

Sight became sound and smell, and a whiff of summer morning air came out of the light, and Case was a kid under the covers, waking and alive with the great gift of a new day. He was a child, and he was an adult, he was everything in between, walking toward his dead father, his heart suffused with the deep golden light of perfect tranquillity.

* * *

Is it heaven?

Case didn't know if he'd spoken aloud, but his father answered.

"Well, that's a big question, son," Ben Hamilton said. "Everybody asks that, first thing. I know I did. But the answer's not that easy."

He flashed a grin, tossing The Ball from hand to hand.

"Here's the best way I can answer," Ben said. The Ball slapped his hand. "It's what your mom told me when I asked about heaven, and it turned out to be right. I can say that you're going to have time to find out."

It was like a dream, but a perfect one. Other people were there, joyous people, the flow surrounding them like a soft outline, an aura.

He saw the ambulance driver, Benny, looking as awestruck as Case felt, now and then touching the healed length of his long neck, swallowing, grinning.

Case searched among them for his mother's round, eternally patient face, and his dad seemed to know.

"She's gone ahead," his dad said. "She'll be waiting for us."

"Waiting?"

"With a cherry pie made." His father laughed, clapping him on the shoulder.

Case tried to fit his mother's special-occasion cherry pie into some idea of the afterlife. It was part of *his* concept of heaven—not golden streets, just cherry pie. It belonged with his image of home as a kid, but he wondered what kind of heaven his mother had found.

The pie was an all-day job, starting with pitting the tart cherries his mother chose one by one, and she never would settle for anything less than a made-from-scratch crust.

Did people still work at their old jobs?

Did heaven's kitchen smell of cherries and sugar?

Who cleaned up the dishes?

Would she still be glad to see him?

After all he'd done wrong in his life, would he still be worth his mother's cherry pie?

Case didn't know. But he wasn't afraid.

He recognized each of the people around him, although he didn't see them so much as he felt them.

And they became others he knew, and then they were him, and he was a part of them, all moving toward a line where the light blurred.

His father reached down with one hand to push at the line of light, and the light began to open. It wasn't just light.

It was his Grandmother Hamilton's old, white-painted gate, with the morning glories twining up on each side, impossibly blue, the blue of a high summer sky, the blue of a robin's egg, the blue that was a part of the golden glow just as the gate was a part of the light.

He took a step through the open gate, seeing the hillsides alive with Grandma Hamilton's roses—every rose she ever planted.

Case began to understand even more of where he was, and the feeling glowed within him like the remembrance of pure schoolyard love on a spring afternoon.

He looked. And he felt. And he knew.

It was warm where his father's hand touched his shoulder, the kind of warmth Case used to feel when he woke up under quilts on a snowy morning. His father watched as the others drew closer, all of them, his friends and family, shaking his hand and smiling, walking with him.

They were him, he was them, and Case knew for the first time why you never could pin down exactly who the people were in your dreams, why they might be a movie star one moment, a friend of yours the next, and someone else— maybe you—in another blink of time.

The dreams were a way of preparing you for what lay behind death's door. Dreams hinted to you that the next world was a place of infinite possibilities, a place where you were a part of everything, and everything was a part of you.

It was the natural working order of things, the way things were done, and even as Case began to understand, he also began to feel that what was happening around him was only the clicking of one infinitesimal gear in the vast and won- drous engine of the universe—and that he would have all infinity to explore its workings.

He looked around him at the figures, who urged him on- ward. He looked up, into his father's eyes, straining to see against the golden glow. His father nodded, and Case began to go forward, the light like a cleansing tide, washing over him, knowledge gripping him like love.

He could have been born into any number of lives. He could have been born a prince in an Arab oil kingdom, a slave in the antebellum South, a drug-addicted baby in some hellish ghetto. He could have been born to anyone, any- where, anytime—and could have become anything.

It was, he knew now, a true brotherhood of man, timeless and ageless. Good people and bad, rich and poor, sick and healthy, all of them had to exist in their times and places. All had a part. All balanced the universe on scales so sensitive that one tiny soul could tip them.

The knowledge unfolded before him like a pathway, a path toward an even greater light. Now, he knew why everything worked. He was part of all the souls, all the answers, and everything was a part of him, bound together in perfection, in understanding, in belonging.

Whatever he'd found beyond death's door, it was a place

of infinite possibility. More than that. It was a place that made sense.

Joyfully, he walked toward the greater light, the others urging him onward, falling in around him, glowing smiles on their faces that were also, in many ways, the faces of Case Hamilton.

At peace.

At rest.

Having found his way home.

13

"Anthony Katzeff is loose again," Frank said. "The night court set 'im a one-thousand-dollar bail, and hell—they might as well have called the bastard a limousine, too."

Diana thought of her struggle with Katzeff as something that must have happened a hundred years ago, to a different woman, in a different world.

She thought of Katzeff, and the Prophet, and her guilty lovemaking in the laboratory, and the bloodbath outside of the hospital. And here she was. Somehow, she was holding together, and she tried to find comfort in the discovery that she could be *this* strong.

But the idea seemed terrifying—not a reassurance at all, but a cold promise that she would be tested to her limit, and that she was nowhere close to the end.

Frank said, "Here we are, we've got a jail that was built to accommodate 650 guests of the county, tops. It's got 675 beds crammed in, and a jail population of 690-some-such, who the hell cares about fractions. There's no more room."

He took off his glasses, pinching the bridge of his nose as if to crush a headache between his fingers.

"We haul 'im in like he's a mad dog, and the court turns him loose like a lah-dee-damn-dah nuisance," Frank said. "It takes somebody *worse* to rate a jail cell these days. I don't believe this shit."

He put the glasses on again, his tired eyes seeming all the more wearied, magnified behind the heavy lenses. "First thing the sumbitch did, he called his wife, mouthing off he was going to kill her."

Diana said, "It might be more than talk."

"We've got the Katzeff woman moved into a shelter—both her and the baby—for a couple of nights that won't make any difference," Frank said. "And the reason I'm telling you—"

Diana already knew the reason. "I'll watch out for him," she said, imagining what threats Katzeff would have made against her. "But he's probably going to run."

Frank nodded. "Probably, if he's got as much as shit for brains. But let's not give the fugger too much credit."

They sat a moment in silence, until the silence seemed as heavy as the night—the way Diana remembered they'd sat in this same room three years ago, she and Frank, after the shooting in the liquor store.

Here she was again, trying to imagine her father's condition, coming up with nightmare visions of scalpels and needles, blood-soaked sponges, a stiff sheet being pulled up to cover the face of the dead man on the table.

No! *No!* He was going to be all right. He couldn't be in better hands.

Stephen had taken charge. The records still showed her father as being one of Stephen's patients, and Stephen had insisted on being the primary physician.

Stephen had taken over from the moment that Case Hamilton's vital signs began to falter, assuring Diana that he would do everything possible to save her father's life.

One of Stephen's nurses had called the waiting room every hour for the first three hours of surgery. Each call was an update on what was being done, along with some note of assurance.

They had stopped the internal bleeding. The knife wound had severed an artery, but the doctor had made repairs. The doctor was working to stabilize Mr. Hamilton's heartbeat.

But every call seemed to be loaded with the portent of some new complication that could lead to the ultimate heartbreak. He would be gone. Everything she'd ever meant to say to him—every hope, regret, recrimination; every way she still loved the man—she would carry inside for the rest of her life, unspoken.

There was a head injury due to falling on the pavement. There was indication that Mr. Hamilton had been kicked, apparently several times. There could be hidden injuries—internal trauma. The doctor was checking.

The last call had been a terse report that Dr. Glasser was nearly finished. There would be no more calls. The doctor would be out to talk with her as soon as possible.

But the last call had been . . . Diana checked her watch. Almost three hours ago.

A chill went through her so violently that she wrapped her arms around herself, clutching at her shoulders.

Frank took off his rumpled jacket. He offered it to her, a man determined to help—to say something, do something, make something right. Diana had to smile.

"Just talk to me," she said.

"A'right."

But there was nothing to say. Diana's mind seemed to have blanked to white, and Frank must have been suffering the same problem. He swiped a hand over his head.

He looked to Diana.

"You know—in a way, I think that nearly dyin' that last time was the best thing that could have happened to your dad," Frank said.

"What?"

"I mean, he came out of it . . . what t'hell's the right word? Different."

Diana thought of Case the way she'd seen him earlier this same night, ashen-faced, standing there with his pitiful tomatoes, accusing her with his eyes.

"You were mostly with your mama back when Case and I were partners," Frank said, "so maybe you didn't see it, but he was a *mean* sumbitch. I'm sorry—"

"Don't be," Diana said, wondering where Frank intended to go with this line of thought. "Frank, I know he had a mean streak. And sometimes . . . I'd rather think of him that way. A mean sumbitch."

"Yeah? Well, he goddam sure was," Frank said. "He was the best friend I ever had, and more than that. Any kind of rough spot, he was the one man I'd trust at my side.

"But I've got to say it, Diana: I watched Case Hamilton turn into the roughest, meanest goddam knuckle-buster I'd ever known. The man got *into* it. I mean, he liked the whole business of hurting.

"I'm not gonna go into cases, but there was a time he kicked the shit out of a guy so bad, it was close to murder. I didn't know what to do—how to cover it up. I was scared sick.

"Case said, 'Book 'im for impersonating a piñata,' and I wound up laughing, 'cause the truth was this prick had it coming. But I kept thinking . . . what happens the next time? What happens when Case turns loose the next time, and he's got the wrong man?"

Diana found a comfort in Frank's unflagging sense of honesty. Other people would have been struggling to elevate Case to sainthood right now, but Frank just told the truth.

"Your dad got to where he didn't just break the rules, he stomped on 'em, set 'em on fire, and tossed 'em out the friggin' window." Frank made a waving motion with his hand. "Aw, maybe I don't need to be saying this."

"It's just a memory, that's all," Diana said.

Frank leaned toward her. "A *memory*, Diana? The goddam fact is, the whole department knew that internal affairs had a file on Case Hamilton as thick as a two-by-four.

"Charges of excessive force," Frank said. "Charges of violation of citizens' rights, police brutality, all that shit. And I'll tell you the one last thing they needed to drop the whole weight on him. They needed *my* testimony, and I wouldn't tell 'em a damn thing, not me.

"I wouldn't go against my partner," Frank said. "But I kept wishing *somebody* would."

He smiled with no humor, seeing her straight-on. "I never meant to yap away like this, Diana, hell, but now that I'm into it . . ."

She knew Frank was giving her time to cut him off, but she didn't, she couldn't. She had to know.

"You remember how he was about guns?" Frank said.

"I remember," Diana said.

She remembered how much she had looked forward to her dad's visits on the weekends, after the divorce. He'd taken her to the movies sometimes, or to the skating rink.

But he'd discovered there was a gun show at the fairgrounds almost every Saturday, and they would stop at the gun show.

"Just a couple of minutes," he promised, stopping as if on a whim that he thought might amuse his little girl. But it wasn't a whim. Every time, Case arrived ready to trade, packing along a foam-lined carrying case that was heavy with handguns.

A couple of minutes would stretch into hours, while Diana learned the vocabulary of Dan Wesson, and Ruger and SIG-

Sauer, sitting by the wall with a watery Coke she was trying
to make last the whole afternoon, listening to the gun talk.

At first, she tried to make sense of the talk about muzzle
velocity and shocking power, and recoil and penetration, but
the voices blurred, and all she really understood was a sort of
craziness going on.

Crazy voices—her father's among them.

Some of the pleasant sag seemed to have left Frank's face,
and the skin was tight along his cheekbones.

"Your dad's last year on the force, he went out and
dropped eight, nine hundred dollars on a Beretta automatic,"
Frank said. "Model 92D. He talked about it weeks before he
bought the damn thing, like it was something brand-new in
his life, like he didn't already have an arsenal.

" 'Slick-slide version, Frank,' he would say. 'Fifteen-plus-
one, double-action, fixed three-dot . . .' and he might as
well have been jabbering in Japanese for all I cared.

"And I finally told him I didn't want to hear another word
about the goddam 92D, unless he meant it was a bra size."

Diana caught herself laughing a little, enjoying the flush of
color that blossomed between Frank's eyes. Frank employed
his words of profanity until they were like old coins with all
the meaning worn off, but he was the first to be embarrassed
when he caught himself talking dirty.

She said, "You never did like guns too much."

"Hell, no." He patted the bulge under his brown coat, just
to the side of his heart. "It's a department-issue .38, and it
works fine for me. Aw, sure, there's always some whistledick
on the TV news—some Chicken Little hollering the cops are
being outgunned by the street gangs these days. But anything I can't stop with a .38, I'd just as soon run from it."

He kept his hand over the revolver a moment. "Diana, in
the twenty-three years that I've been on the force, I've car-

ried this damn thing every day," Frank said. "And you know how many times I've had to use it?"

Diana shook her head. Frank proudly held up three fingers.

"What I mean to say—"

Frank stopped in midsentence, looking past her, his breath caught.

The door opened.

Diana saw the white of a hospital uniform, and she felt a rush of adrenaline, thinking *This is it, this is Stephen*, and she was on her feet, ready—

The door opened slowly, revealing a group of young men and women standing tentatively in the doorway. Diana recognized them by their white garb. Hospital orderlies.

She thought her knees might buckle, lost to a rush of disappointment and anger, seeing they weren't the answer to this long night's wait.

The one in the front held a white box, spots of grease showing through the bottom. He took a step past the doorway, nodding.

"Hi," he said. He glanced toward the sleeping woman, and then turned his pockmarked face back to Diana and Frank.

"Uh . . . excuse us," he said. "We're looking for the relatives of Mr. Hamilton, um . . . *Officer* Hamilton." He nodded toward the sleeping woman. "Is that his wife or something?"

"No, he doesn't have a wife," Diana said, realizing that she ought to notify her mother of Case being hurt. But she didn't know how. She hadn't heard from her mother in more than a year, not since a postcard from Houston that said, "Married again!" Mr. Right, third try.

"I'm his daughter, and this man is his friend," Diana said, indicating Frank.

The young man seemed relieved. "Oh, great." He handed the box to Diana, holding it out with both hands, "These are for you."

Diana accepted the box, lifting the cover. There were more than a dozen donuts arranged on wax paper, donuts of all different kinds in neat rows.

A young Latino woman spoke up with a pronounced accent from behind the male orderly. "I hope you like those kinds," she said. "I didn't know what to get, so I got one or two of lots of different ones."

"That's very kind of you all," Diana said.

"We, uh . . . we know Officer Hamilton, all of us," the young man said. Several of the others nodded. "He's a good dude, the ol' Term—Officer Hamilton, and we wanted to do something for him."

"You did," Diana said. "Thank you."

The young man looked around. The group seemed pleased. "Well, okay," he said. "My name's Butch, Butch Bradshaw. I work on the first floor. If you need anything . . ."

"Any of us," said another young man, shorter and darker.

"Yeah." Butch nodded. "We'll be here." He offered a last, awkward wave, and the group filed out.

Diana stood there, watching, the box of donuts almost weightless in her hands.

Frank and Diana each plucked an iced donut out of the box, and Frank poured some fresh coffee.

She tasted cherry. Looking, she realized she'd chosen a cherry-frosted donut, her dad's favorite kind, although she didn't like cherry. She felt some kind of obligation.

Diana watched the door. She thought she saw it budge a

little, as if it might open again—might open, and there would be news of her father. But nothing happened.

She sat. She ate the donut, wondering if she would be able to keep it down, and she reached for another one.

The door opened to the flame of red hair that was Gwen Foster.

"Any news?" Gwen asked, opening the door to the waiting room slowly and quietly, her voice coming out the same way.

"Naw, Gwen," Frank said. "C'mon in, though. Eat a goddam donut."

Gwen Foster had the hard-lined face of a woman who had done some rough living in her forty-eight years, but she had forged from it all a surprisingly positive outlook that showed in the bright green of her eyes.

She owned the liquor store where Case had been shot before, and she'd held his big, bloodied hand as the paramedics carried him away, staying with him all the way into the hospital. He'd refused to let go of her.

She had become a sometimes best friend, sometimes lover to Case in those years since the shooting, depending on which of those relationships he seemed to need the most.

Case was still holding on to Gwen's hand in his way, Diana thought as she rose to hug Gwen.

Gwen was a hugger by nature, and she offered the sort of embrace that a person could draw strength from.

"I'm sorry, girl," Gwen whispered. "But you know he's going to be okay. He's a tough one, Case."

Diana smiled at Gwen as the older woman pulled back, still clasping Diana by the shoulders.

"I know," Diana said, trying to ignore the voice inside of her that said he wasn't going to be all right at all. He was dead, or he was dying, and nobody was telling her.

Where was Stephen, where the hell—

"Hold still," Gwen said, reaching into her suitcase-sized purse to find a Kleenex that she wet with the tip of her tongue. "You have a smudge on your face," Gwen said, dabbing at a spot on Diana's cheek. "There!"

Diana caught a glimpse of the Kleenex, stained with a bit of red. She'd had blood on her face.

She might have said she'd become immune to the sight of blood as a working cop, but she felt sick. She couldn't hide it.

"I guess I should have brought along a bottle of Black Jack," Gwen said, looking into her purse as if to find one by surprise. But the joke was that Gwen didn't drink.

Diana looked at her gratefully—at the red, close-cropped hair; the face, always smiling or ready to smile; the teeth just a fraction too big for the mouth: all the facets that made up the personality. And the pin on her blouse, always there.

She reached to touch the pin.

Gwen said, "Go ahead, it won't sting."

The dime-sized pin was the golden effigy of a bee, a gift from Case; Diana considered the pin a symbol of the link between Case and Gwen.

The bee pin was a reminder for Gwen always to carry the syringe of epinephrine and a vial of Benadryl capsules wherever she went, to guard against her allergic reaction to bee stings.

Gwen had been stung while she and Case were walking through a flowered meadow to a farm pond or a lake somewhere. Diana knew they had some secret place they went together.

The sting mark on Gwen's leg had flared to an angry red, and she began to have trouble breathing, clutching for breath while Case burned the road to find a doctor.

Afterward, he'd given her the golden bee pin, engraved with a tiny *C* on the back.

Gwen had shown Diana the engraving more than a year ago.

"I asked him if it meant C for Case," Gwen had told her. "He said, 'No, it means C for careful . . . because you're worth it.' And that's heavy talk for Case, you know. I swear, girl, that's poetry."

Diana had seen Case and Gwen together only perhaps a dozen times, and she was certain that Gwen saw other men, too.

But she knew as well that the only times she'd seen a spark of life in her father these past three years was when Gwen had been at his side.

An orderly named Jake looked in, wearing a red satin jacket on top of his white pants, his face fallen. A tragic cheerleader.

Diana felt he wanted some assurance from her—some greater lie than she could fabricate—and Jake finally went away, saying he ought to be back to work. She felt a weight lifted.

Mabel Holden wedged herself in the door to tell Diana with forced good humor that she was expecting Case back on the job, pronto.

Duane Hardage logged time on the sofa alongside the sleeping woman. He seemed lost in his own thoughts. It was the only time Diana had ever known him to look sad. She blamed herself, but what could she say that could make up for the loss of his job?

"Well, I'm not helping here," Duane said, slapping his long legs as he rose from the sofa. "I just want to say that your dad's a fine man."

And the door opened to the hollow-eyed brother of the ambulance driver who was killed, and to other people Diana didn't know—couldn't place at all and didn't have the strength to figure out.

She welcomed their support and wishes, but she felt more drained with every movement of the swinging door that she'd come to identify as a kind of torture instrument.

They came, they stayed as long as they could. But the wait settled back to just her, and Frank and Gwen—Frank to one side of her on the sofa, Gwen on the other.

Frank asked, "Diana, you know how your dad got his first name, don't you?"

Diana blew on her coffee, forgetting it had long since gone cold. The door hadn't moved again. The sleeping woman snored.

"He told me once. It was that old poem, wasn't it?"

"'Casey at the Bat,'" Gwen contributed.

"You got it," Frank said. "He told me one time that his dad was the one who named him, being a baseball fan. And that's one of the reasons that Case played some pro ball—not the name, hell, but for his dad's sake."

Diana said, "I know he was in the low minor leagues somewhere in Missouri, when he finally got cut—"

"Is *that* what he told you?" Frank brushed at the crumbs on his necktie. "I'll be damned. What a cockeyed story."

"It's what he said," Diana answered, looking to Gwen for confirmation.

Gwen said, "For all he ever told me, I just thought he played a little baseball, nothing serious."

Frank settled back. "Well . . . the thing is, we were partners, and we told each other shit we'd never tell another person on the face of God's earth, no matter how close. And here's the goddam truth.

"Case had a hot arm the year he was twenty-one, and he was on his way into the big show. There wasn't any question.

It started out being his dad's dream, baseball, and then it was *his* dream, and it was right there in reach.

"The trouble started with another kid on the team," Frank said. "Gamblin' trouble. It seems this kid got his ass in trouble with some cardsharps, and they'd snatched everything but his jock.

"They put the hard squeeze on him, telling him the only way he could save his skin was to throw a game every now and then. But it wasn't him they wanted. See, throwing the game was a goddam joke to expect of this squirt, just a minor league right fielder with no particular talent, so . . . he'd have to talk to the pitcher.

"He did, and Case went after those sumbitches with a goddam baseball bat. Cleaned 'em out, and it wasn't even his fight."

Diana thought of her father as a young man in a baseball uniform. Like in a movie, she could see him, heroically taking on the bad guys in their snap-brim hats, protecting a friend who had strayed.

"—and *that* finished him in baseball," Frank was saying. "'Cause what Case didn't know was that he'd messed into a small-time ring that had connections going all the way back to New York. Another sort of minor league.

"He said they held him down, and knowing Case, hell, I'd expect it took three or four of the bastards to hold on to him. They broke his pitching arm—right at the elbow."

Gwen said, "Oh, Lord."

Diana didn't know what to say, so she looked at the carpet.

Frank let go with a sour chuckle. "'Casey at the Bat,'" he said. "You remember that part that goes there ain't no joy in Mudville?"

"I guess so," Diana said.

"You know why there ain't no joy in goddam Mudville?"

Diana thought a moment. But she was filled with the new,

disturbing vision of the gamblers and the broken arm, and a deep dread of what else she might learn the next time the door opened.

"I can't think . . ."

Frank said, "There ain't no joy in Mudville, 'cause mighty Casey has struck out."

He touched Diana gently on the hand.

"What I mean to say—what I've been trying to say to you, Diana, it's about the last time your dad nearly died." Frank swiped at his head again. "I'm no goddam psychologist, but a cop has to know about people, and I think I *knew* Case Hamilton.

"He was the best man I ever knew, and he was the worst man, all in one. He was two parts, trying to hold himself together. And he thought of himself as a loser, hell, yes, and he thought out loud.

"He'd say to me, 'Frank, just what kind of a goddam father would name his kid after one of the biggest failures in history?' "

Gwen was startled. "*Case* said that?"

Frank said, "He always had a mean streak, and it came out the more that he turned bitter, always down on himself, always down on the world—"

Diana interrupted, "Because . . . he didn't go on to play major league baseball?"

"I think baseball was the start of it," Frank said. "Not just that he didn't play ball like he wanted, though—that he *failed* to go on. It's a hell of a difference."

Gwen said, "I think he should have given himself credit: for defending his friend, and protecting his ball team—"

Frank shook his head. "Yeah? Me, too. But *he* didn't. He thought he had some goddam secret shame that had to be paid for the rest of his life.

"I think the reason Case got into police work, it was a way

to keep cracking those bad guys over the head with a Louis-ville Slugger," Frank said.

Diana asked, "How much do you think he changed . . . I mean, after the shooting, after he nearly—"

"Bought the bean farm," Frank said. "It turned him around. All of a sudden, he learned to ease back, to give people a chance. Ask me, it did him a shitload of good, and more than that. I'd say it probably saved the man's life. But it cost him . . . all the hard edge."

Diana said, "I guess, in a way, I still miss the hard edge."

Frank smiled a little. "Oh, hell. Yeah. Me, too."

Uncharacteristically, he took Diana's hand.

"Here's what we're gonna do," Frank said. "We're gonna get it right this time. You and me, we're gonna help the man pull himself together, whether he likes it or not. We're gonna be there when he needs us."

Gwen placed her hand on top of Frank's. "We're going to be there when he needs us," she said.

And the door opened—to the chunky shape of Douglas Bloch.

Bloch, with his right eye circled in purple like the eye of a cartoon bear in a state of shock, looking all the more surprised to have blundered into a scene of conspiracy.

"Guess I found the right place," he said.

Frank answered, "Goddam right, you did."

Bloch stepped aside then, to clear the way for the man behind him—for the onrush of intensity that came from behind him.

Dr. Stephen Glasser.

14

The nameless woman on the couch had awakened to Stephen Glasser's grim voice. She sat watching dully, listening to what the doctor said, scowling at the mumbo-jumbo words that made no sense to her.

"Infarction . . . hemostatic . . ." the recitations of faltering vital signs. Slowly, the woman's eyes closed, and she slept with the peace of knowing that none of this bad news was meant for her.

But no one else had been sitting from the moment Glasser had appeared at the door. They all stood around him.

The doctor's eyes were bright as lightning. His dark hair was plastered with sweat. He'd thrown a long white coat over his surgical garments, but the coat opened just enough at the neckline to show that he was dressed in red.

Diana knew of Stephen's penchant for red. He called it the color of life. But she thought if she could look beneath the white coat, she might find him drenched in blood. Her father's blood. She might see wet tracks on the floor if she dared to look down.

He held a manila file folder in one hand, and the folder was labeled HAMILTON, CASEY B., typed in red letters.

The doctor paused.

"I . . . I'm sorry, I don't understand," Diana said.

"Your father is dying," Stephen said. "I might still be able to save him, but only by means of an experimental technique. Let me emphasize: highly experimental. I need your permission."

Dying. The word sank in, driven deep. *Dying* was exactly the word Diana had been expecting to hear all this time, but it struck her numb, as if she'd never imagined the possibility.

"Permission? Experiment? Stephen, I—"

Glasser nodded. "It's a risky procedure, based on some of my research into electrical brain stimulation. But it's your father's last chance."

Diana looked at Frank, fighting the fear that had risen inside her—fighting the impulse to hate Stephen Glasser for not bringing news that her father would be fine, just fine.

Frank swallowed. "Let me ask a goddam question here," he said softly. "Just what the hell does 'electrical brain stimulation' mean, anyway?"

A spark of something like anger flashed in Glasser's eyes, dying quickly.

Glasser said, "Essentially, it means that I'll insert a platinum electrode through a tiny hole into Mr. Hamilton's brain."

Gwen gasped, biting a thumbnail.

Ignoring her, Glasser said, "I will run a small charge of electricity through that electrode, all in a last-resort effort to save the man's life."

"From what, for chrissake?" Frank said. "If he's dying, hell—what's he dying *from*, I mean, that it's gonna help for him to have his head wired up like a goddam Lionel train?"

When Glasser failed to answer, the lieutenant looked to Bloch.

"I don't like it," Frank said, as if Bloch might take sides with him. Bloch just listened.

Glasser turned to Diana, shutting them both out with the tilt of his head. "I'm sorry, I know this isn't fair to you," he said. He touched her—a cold hand to her face. "But there's no time for talk."

She looked to Frank, to Gwen, to Bloch.

Detectives ask why.

She said, "I need the answer to Frank's question."

Glasser's dark eyes seemed to pierce her. Eyes of indignation. The doctor wasn't used to being doubted, least of all by the woman who'd shared his bed this same night.

"Diana . . . your father's heart stopped twice during surgery," Glasser said. "The first was just a momentary lapse, but the second was an incidence of profound heart failure. Nothing we did worked to restore a pulse. Frankly, I don't know what brought him back."

"But he is—"

"Breathing. He's on a resuscitator, and he's alive. But I don't believe the man could survive a third failure."

Stephen's long-fingered hands clasped hers. "Diana, he fought his way back. He *wants* to live. But his body is too weak to keep fighting, and his heart might stop again at any moment. I think we're counting seconds."

She wanted to ask Frank what he thought, but Stephen wouldn't let her turn away.

"Diana, we're at the point where conventional medicine gives up," Stephen said. "I'm asking your permission to go past that point—to give your father the chance he *wants*, the chance to live."

The doctor's grip tightened.

She looked to his eyes for compassion. Assurance. She didn't find so much as recognition.

But he *did* save her father before, and nothing could change that. Stephen Glasser had made a day-to-day business of saving lives. He *could* work magic.

Diana needed magic. Desperately.

She had learned from her mother to blame Case for the breakup of their family, and wished him dead. And sometimes, it seemed to her that she'd gotten her wish, complete with all the guilt that went with it.

Case Hamilton had become the walking dead, drained of life as surely as a corpse is drained of blood on the mortician's slab, and wishing made no difference.

But she didn't want him dead.

Gwen said, "You have to decide, Diana."

She looked to Bloch, unable to read his face. "Tough call," he said. "No easy answers."

Diana said, "He could die, even if you do this . . . treatment. Couldn't he, Stephen?"

Glasser ruffled the file folder against his leg. "That's right," he said. "Five minutes ago, I might have given the procedure a thirty percent chance of success. Now, I'd have to say twenty percent."

He brought the file folder up, opening it. "It's a consent form with special provisions. I've filled in the necessary information. It needs your signature."

She looked at the paper, automatically reaching for the pen Glasser had produced from nowhere, a sample of wonders to come.

The words seemed to blur into meaningless streaks of black across the page—lines that she forced to make sense for a moment.

AUTHORIZATION FOR MEDICAL TREATMENT (EMERGENCY/EXPERIMENTAL) AND THE PERFORMANCE OF SURGERY

I hereby authorize Dr. Stephen H. Glasser and his designees to perform such surgical and/or other procedures as they deem necessary or desirable on behalf of my father (blood relative), Casey Benjamin Hamilton . . .

Diana's pulse hammered in her temples. Her blood sang.

She scanned the rest of the densely printed form, catching disjointed phrases of hospital legalese, none of them comforting.

I understand that unforeseen conditions may be encountered—

I recognize that the practice of surgery is not an exact science—

I acknowledge that no guarantees or promises have been made to me—

But the bottom of the form already was signed in Stephen's hand, a strong signature, a stroke of absolute confidence.

She trusted in those lines of bold, black ink.

"Sign right there, Di," he said, pointing, and she signed. Like a good girl.

15

White light. Chrome. Steel. Glass. And the sudden disruption: the figure in red.

His mask and his gown were bloodred, and the color was nothing more than an accent to the man's sense of bearing—to the muscular stride, to the steel-straight back, to the dark eyes on fire.

Dr. Stephen Glasser entered the neuro operating room with an aura of life-and-death authority so tangible that he could feel it himself as a kind of electricity.

He could feel it—this *power* of the surgeon—just as physically as he could savor the tension of the skintight rubber gloves on his hands. Graceful hands, tapered fingers. His hands felt spring-loaded, instruments of cold precision as much as any of the 173 surgical instruments that awaited the surgeon's call in shining rows of needles and blades, most of which he would never touch.

Every person, every thing, had its place in this room, all in compliance with Glasser's innovative dictums, complete to the playing of Mozart's Piano Concerto No. 23 K.488 from the quadrophonic speakers that made the genius of music a part of the air.

Glasser addressed the white-gowned, ghostlike figures of

the surgical team that he'd chosen—the four men, two women surrounding the shrouded bulk of the man on the stainless-steel table.

"Ladies," he said. "Gentlemen. We have work to do."

A nod from Glasser, a direction carried out, and the table began to slide backward. It bore Case Hamilton headfirst into the metallic box that was the PETT-2 scanner, Glasser's obsessive redesign of the Positron Emission Transaxial Tomography scanner.

The original PETT-scan would have been accepted as state of the art anywhere else. However, Glasser had chosen to regard the machine as nothing more than a simplified model—a starting point for the research that he expected would change the whole concept of medicine.

Glasser took note of the pallor of Hamilton's face—the skin like candle wax, the lips blue, the eyes open just a slit, just a dull shine of the whites, as dead as the moon. The head was circled by the halo brace, which held it immobile.

He lifted the sheet to one side, checking the tightness of the straps that encircled the body, disallowing any movement: in particular, any grasping toward the surgeon.

He took a moment to reexamine the stitched wound in Hamilton's side, confirming that the wound was manageable, the blade having scraped over a series of ribs like a stick over a picket fence. Glasser traced the wet line of the knife slash with the tip of his finger. He smiled behind his mask.

His small lie about the severed artery had been a necessity. But he hadn't lied about the two heart failures—those two incidents of sweet luck—although he'd exaggerated the severity of the second. He'd found no damage to the heart muscle. No internal trauma from any of Hamilton's other injuries.

He couldn't have asked for a dying patient in better condition for the experiment, lying there in a state of shock.

Of course, Glasser had nurtured those conditions of shock that beset Hamilton's body, leading the body away from recovery. The faltering pulse, the shallow breathing—all in Glasser's control, manipulated with drugs and denial, brought to the edge of extinction. Balanced. Easy to tip, one way or the other.

At last! No more waiting. He'd found his man.

Glasser felt a rush that he could have identified in terms of body chemistry, organic electricity—but that he chose to accept as inspiration, and he applied it to the question of what to call the treatment he was about to perform.

Even if the treatment worked exactly as he planned it would, Glasser knew it would have to be announced with an accessible name—a brand name for a miracle. A buzzword the equal of the Clip/Chip vital signs monitor.

He could have hired a battery of public relations flacks to address the problem, but he'd learned to doubt the promise of creativity for hire. He trusted to himself.

He sought for a name to be said with glib assurance on the network news, translating into government funding and public support, translating into a wall of protection that would enable the work to go on.

Electric. Stimulation. Animation. Resurrection.

He would have to be careful. He knew what some people were calling this place in whispers of sarcasm and jealousy behind his back. They called it Frankenstein's laboratory, said in varying degrees of success at imitating the distinctive cadence of Boris Karloff's voice. Laaa-bore-a'try.

He encouraged the imbecility of their prattling. He simply ignored it, leaving *them* to believe themselves too smart to be caught—leaving *them* to make a joke of what they imagined went on behind closed doors.

So long as *they* were kept amused by their imaginings,

they would not try to find out. So long as *they* were cracking jokes, they would not be afraid, and they would leave him alone. And they would never know the simple truth.

They were right about him. Frankenstein. He thought of himself the same way.

Glasser had seen a grainy release of the 1957 movie version of *Curse of Frankenstein* as a ten-year-old boy. It was part of a Halloween movie marathon at the long-gone Paramount Theater in Palo Alto, California, where he'd learned the healing powers of watching colored shadows in the dark.

Every part of his memory was vivid: the lights blinking on and off in sequence in the old-time movie theater's marquee. The smell of popcorn in the lobby. The screams that hurt his ears.

That night, the rest of the mostly kid audience saw a movie about an ugly, square-headed monster made of dead parts sewn together, and they screamed their mindless heads off.

Stephen—he was Stephen, never Stevie, not even then—watched the same movie in silence. He saw the same shambling monster, but the monster did not frighten him.

He saw a movie about a doctor who wasn't afraid to unlock the secrets of life. What frightened him was the specter of the ignorant villagers with their torches and pitchforks, marching on Frankenstein's castle.

Over and over, he'd seen the fifties movie of *Frankenstein* with Christopher Lee and Peter Cushing, and the 1931 movie that starred Karloff as the monster, and the Warhol version, and Mel Brooks's *Young Frankenstein.*

It pleased him that not even the manic Brooks could make fun of that moment when the lightning breathed life into the dead body on the good doctor's table. Nobody laughed at the essence of life.

Glasser brought himself out of the memory, although it

hadn't infringed on his work. He'd completed a test of the
PETT-2 at the same time that he'd been thinking about
Frankenstein's monster, while he searched out a name for
the treatment. *Electro*—

He wasn't ever lost in thought. He simply knew the workings of his mind—how to compartmentalize, to be mentally
in two or three places at once.

He looked around the O.R., thinking of how Dr. Frankenstein would have appreciated this place.

He glanced up.

Above him, the sky roof was open. When the surgery was
finished, he would turn off the lights in the O.R., looking up
through the glass to the lights of the starfield that showed in
breaks through the storm clouds.

The sky roof had been one of the first and simplest of
Glasser's innovations. He would not perform surgery in the
lifeless environment of a room with no windows.

There had to be a sense of *life* to saving lives.

He'd found that night was the best time for invasive procedure, and here was the place for it—here with the stars
that he sometimes imagined to be the sparks of life itself.

And sometimes . . . torches in the night.

The table retracted to a stop that left Hamilton's head engulfed in the machine. Something whirred inside the box.

The operating room was bordered with a line of high-
density, sixty-inch television monitors that were positioned
just below the ceiling, angled down. The screens lit in sequence, showing Glasser the ever-shifting patterns of brain
activity inside of Case Hamilton's head.

The flat, liquid-crystal screens were splashed with seem-
ingly abstract compositions of red and yellow, blue, orange
and green—patterns that would have confounded even the
best of Glasser's surgical associates, and he knew it.

But *he* could read the story.

The screens told him that Hamilton's life force was ebbing away like a slow-bleeding cut that would not heal. Only minutes were left. Time enough.

Glasser could analyze from these screens the exact strength of Hamilton's faltering will to live, and he could pinpoint the source of Case Hamilton's wellspring of life.

Wellspring. Glasser made a hard-line mental note of the word. He would say *wellspring,* and he would not say—

There! A touch of bright blue on the center screen. It was a physical phenomenon—no more inherently spiritual than a man's eyelashes—but he would have to be careful to protect it from misunderstanding.

So easily, Glasser knew he could find himself at the center of a head-on collision between science and religion, and the purpose of his work would be destroyed.

There! It was a physical *thing*—embedded like a hidden jewel into the mazework of the hypothalamus, a *thing* he had discovered.

Glasser swallowed. His spring-loaded hands clenched.

He would call it the "wellspring," and he would not allow it to be called the soul.

Glasser said, "Lock the scan, please."

Images froze on the monitors, and the room itself seemed to lock in place with a click—a catching of breath.

Glasser took note of his staff. He sensed the tension in the room, although he did not feel it the way that most people would.

He'd made a study of his own response to pressure. He turned colder in the measurable sense of a drop in body temperature, a lowering of blood pressure. The more he felt pressured, the more he turned calm.

However, he had resigned himself to reality: the condition

was a rarity that he shared with a few test pilots, a few race
car drivers.

Glasser still hadn't been able to assemble a medical team
that responded to pressure the way he did. Instead, they'd
been chosen for other skills, and he saw them as vulnerable
to a weakness that frustrated him—a weakness that ought to
be bred out of the species.

They watched him wide-eyed from over the tops of their
white masks: his first and second residents, scrub nurses,
anesthesiologists.

They looked to him for the revelation of secrets, the solving of mysteries, and they would not be disappointed. Glasser planned his rewards.

But the secrets he told would be snippets of medical trivia
in the context of what he *knew*, and he would be far down
the path of his research—always ahead of them, far out of
reach.

"Ready the patient," he said, and the table slid forward
with a steady hum of electric perfection, delivering Case
Hamilton from out of the PETT-2 scanner.

Glasser knew the face. He'd saved this man before, although with nothing more than simple surgery.

This time—not so simple. Glasser withdrew the crackling
white sheet that covered the man's naked body, exposing a
cocoon of wires that attached with suction-cupped ends to
the fingertips, to the chest, and the IV lines that supplied
him with drips of nourishment for strength, and with
pancuronium—a drug that would keep him paralyzed for the
duration of the treatment.

The SHG-model life-support system of Glasser's design
hung with its bellows folded—like a bat made of chrome and
black leather—ready to breathe for the dying man, ready to
keep the blood flowing.

The cords disappeared into slots in the floor, another of

Glasser's specifications that had already become a standard part of hospital design.

He could have counted thirty-four electrical machines in the room—the anesthesia machine, the electrocardiogram, electroencephalogram, the ruby laser, electrocoagulation equipment, the green-lighted screens of the ever-watchful Clip/Chip monitors . . . all of them trailing retractable cords that ran neatly to dispenser-outlets that were built into the floor.

Glasser had served his residency in a hospital with an old-time operating room that was a worm's nest of tangled cords on the floor, and he'd sworn to find a better way.

Better room design.

Better surgery.

Better science.

At first, there had been the quest for the sake of the quest, and there had been answers for the sake of answers—but Glasser never doubted that he would come to recognize the greater purpose of his work.

When it came to him, it came with such clarity that he realized he'd known it all along. It was a promise.

He would never die.

He stood over Hamilton. He knew what Hamilton thought of him, and it pleased him to be in control—to be *owed* by an enemy, no matter if the enemy was of little consequence.

He could see the structure of Diana's face in her father's strong jaw, but he knew his limits. He couldn't allow himself the distraction of thinking about *her*.

He was too much aware of biological chemistry to believe in love. Everything that Mark Antony felt for Cleopatra, Glasser knew that he could have distilled into a pinkish fluid in a lab beaker.

But Diana intrigued him. He seemed never to tire of the

games that he played with her, and he had come to think of her as a kind of open-ended experiment that worked two ways.

He'd developed a mild interest in Duane Hardage's reaction to being kept on duty to greet women visitors to the lab at night, tracking how long it would take Hardage to object. The fool must have known he was being humiliated.

Glasser turned his hand palm up.

"First knife," he said. "Mosquito."

The scalpel slapped into his hand. Glasser pressed lightly, and the blade bit into a spot on the left side of Hamilton's neck, near the base of the neck, marked with a blue line. The line turned to a welling of blood.

"Sponge."

He cut three sides of a half-inch square, folding back a flap of skin and tissue like opening a door, aware at the same time of the music's darkening of tone from Mozart's piano concerto to his Piano Sonata K.333.

He never listened to music except in surgery.

"Clip/Chip," Glasser said, opening his hand to receive the silvery microchip with its threadlike wires standing erect from the center like the antenna of a fingernail-sized beetle.

It remained his best-known accomplishment, the Clip/Chip monitor—the one that he'd parlayed from a wealth of headlines into a bidding war between the Americans and the Japanese.

Glasser inserted the slightly curved, battery-powered chip into the opening at the base of Hamilton's neck, where it nestled against the carotid artery. He called for the delicate, needle-tipped instruments he needed to coil the sensitive threads around the artery, in a painstaking procedure that had come to be dubbed in the news media as "tying the ribbons."

"Close," Glasser said.

The first resident stepped in to close the small wound, while Glasser moved to the computer terminal that the nurses had rolled to the foot of the bed.

He keyed the commands that activated the PETT-2's analysis of Hamilton's brain structure. The screens began to work, each showing a different attack on the problem: scrolling columns of figures against an amber background, three-dimensional gridworks that represented the hemispheres of the brain, and the shifting, probing lines that radiated to and from the elusive recesses of the hypothalamus.

Glasser regarded the hypothalamus part of the brain as a black box that he was determined to open. It was a four-gram mystery as deep as the cosmos. Such a small part of the human mechanism—yet it functioned as a control center for the most compelling of human sensations.

Pleasure, anger, hunger, fatigue.

Glasser had been twelve years old when he began to read about the tantalizing concept of electrical brain stimulation —accounts of how animal behavior could be changed and controlled by means of electrodes inserted into the brain.

Cats could be provoked to rage, could be switched like machines to a purring contentment at the touch of an electrode. The behavior of rats could be controlled by means of pleasurable stimulation to the hypothalamus.

A bull could be stopped in full charge by a radio-transmitted signal to an electrode implanted in the animal's brain.

So much discovery! Glasser had thought, already yearning to know more than he could find in the high school library. Instead, he found disquieting references to ethical qualms about brain stimulation.

If a rampaging bull could be dropped to the ground at the flick of a switch, then couldn't the same spark of electricity be used to control human behavior?

Human beliefs?

What more appalling invasion of privacy could there be than for a man's brain to be pierced with electrified needles?

The gifted boy read of these doubts, gathering fear and contempt in his heart for the gaspings and gawkings of public ignorance.

He started in the basement.

The hamster first, and then the neighbor's cat, the calico, that lived just long enough to be an encouragement—

Problem solved. The screens flashed in unison with a computer-generated likeness of Hamilton, showing a red line that extended to the target from a spot on Hamilton's forehead.

The wellspring.

Touched with an electrical charge of microscopic precision, the wellspring would defend itself from injury. It would deny death.

It would call forth hidden sources of strength within the body, responding with force and fury. It would charge the dying body with a compulsion to live.

He was far beyond theory. He thought of the woman, the Jane Doe—the blue fire in her eyes. What a shame he couldn't have done more with her, and all because of legalities that had nothing to do with the practice of medicine.

She had been pronounced D.O.A. of a drug overdose in the emergency room. Glasser wasn't supposed to have had claim to the body, but he . . . made arrangements.

She wouldn't be missed for the time he would need. She'd been found in an alley—no identification, no rings, no marks, no teeth, so thin that malnourishment might have claimed her almost as quickly as crack cocaine had done the job. She could have been twenty, twenty-five, thirty; it didn't matter.

He worked alone that night, trusting no one, covering her with a sheet, rolling her out of the E.R. on a gurney.

Up the service elevator. Into the unguarded lab.

She was to have been his first human test of the PETT-2. All he'd meant to learn was the effect of the machine's scanning rays on brain tissue, to be certain he had corrected the machine's tendency to cause brain cells to implode.

But the scan more than worked. It showed him the blue gemstone—the wellspring that he'd sought to find so many times before, suddenly obvious, hidden in plain sight.

It revealed to him the source of life that endured in the woman's brain, even though she'd gone brain-dead by every other standard of medicine.

He wasn't prepared. He simply did the best he could under the circumstances, working with a rare sense of intoxication. He used a surgical drill to pierce the woman's skull, and the electrode was nothing special—the same that he'd been using on the chimpanzees.

He touched the wellspring with a spark of electricity.

Such a tiny charge of current. It wouldn't have left a mark on a man's thumbnail, but it must have flashed and burned like a lightning storm inside the brain.

Like the jagged forks of lightning that sundered the sky over Frankenstein's castle, he thought.

And the body trembled. The woman's hands clenched. Her mouth gaped open, the tongue curled back.

Her eyes shot wide open, explosions of yellow in a mindless look of pain and horror, and she raised herself, screaming, tearing at the wire that trailed from the electrode.

She pulled the needle from her brain. Glasser tried to restrain her, to quiet her. Her wild hands found his throat.

Screaming. She pulled him toward her. Screaming. Into the spittle that flew from her throat, into the smell of dead meat on her breath.

The bony hands interlocked, tightening. Glasser fought to

break free of her, striking her in the face, almost breaking her jaw with the heel of his hand. She never weakened.

He saw the dancing motes of colored light that told him he was close to blacking out from lack of oxygen. But the momentary panic dimmed away. He felt the sense of calmness that came to him under pressure. A chilling of the blood. Control.

Reaching to the table behind him, Glasser's steady hand rejected a clatter of wrong knives to find the longest and thinnest of scalpels.

He inserted the blade into her side at exactly the angle he needed to impale both ventricles of the heart, while assuring that almost all of her blood loss would be internal. A jab. A twist, cutting down.

The tough muscle of the heart gave way, like the snapping of a rubber band.

The blade would leave a small wound, he thought, but not a mark that anyone would notice in the case of an insignificant woman who'd already been declared dead of other causes.

Her hands loosened from the doctor's throat. The arms dropped.

For a moment, a dying moment, he saw what might have been a light of comprehension in the woman's eyes.

She sat there, looking at the machinery that surrounded her. Realizing her nakedness, trying to cover herself, trying to hold those ever-so-heavy hands across the shame of her flat breasts, as if he might laugh at her, or even more pathetic to imagine—as if he might want to see.

Her eyes found Glasser. She seemed to know what he'd done to her, although she couldn't have known, at least not all of it.

Her lips parted, spilling a froth of blood that he knew he would have to clean away, every trace.

She spoke in a soft, wet voice. "Whyyyy?"

He told her. He'd never before been so honest. So direct. He didn't know how long he'd talked to her, spilling his innermost thoughts to her, except that he felt cleansed.

He was just as glad that she hadn't lived to hear the answer. She wouldn't have understood. And she would have known too much.

With Hamilton, he was ready. Diana had been less of an obstacle than he'd anticipated, even with the cops in the room with her. She couldn't deny him.

He had complete consent, everything legal, absolute freedom. And the tools: the straps around the body, the ruby laser in place of the drill, the surgical microscope, the platinum electrode.

The laser burned a smoking, bloodless hole the size of a pinprick into Hamilton's forehead.

Glasser inserted the electrode, trailing its silver wire to the electrical transformer, aware of the palpable silence that surrounded him, the holding of a half-dozen breaths.

And it came to him: what to call the treatment.

He knew that some facet of his mind had been at work on the problem this whole time, delivering up the answer.

Electro-animation, he thought, reaching toward the switch that would charge the electrode. Waiting. Watching the monitors. Waiting . . . for the body to die.

Electro-animation.

The heart monitor faltered. He waited.

There was an audible gasp. Glasser looked to his first resident, the doctor who had closed the incision in Hamilton's neck. He warned the man to silence with a lethal glare, extending that look to the rest of the team in their ghostly white gowns. They didn't deserve to wear red. They had no idea what life was all about.

Blood pressure plummeted, and Glasser waited.

Pressure gone.

Glasser watched the screen as the green line went flat to the sound of an unwavering whine. *Eeeeeeee!* The doctor waited.

A minute. Two. Three.

EEEEEEEEeeeeeeee—

He could feel the rising tension as a pressure in the air. The eyes on him, wondering. Never questioning.

All of them, these ghosts in white—all knowing they were cogs in the machinery of miracles.

EEEEEEEEEEEEEEEE—

Four minutes, and no more sign of brain-wave activity.

"Doctor!" the first resident interrupted.

"Shut up!"

The man in white stepped back from the table, staggering as if he were drunk. "I can't be a part of this," he said. "I *won't* be—"

Glasser straightened. "Every one of us knew the time would come when there would be rules broken," he said. "Nothing of value is ever discovered without breaking rules."

"But we've become murderers!"

"No!" Glasser's hands balled to spring-loaded fists. "We are about to become . . . discoverers."

Five minutes.

The first resident returned to his place, red-faced above his mask, eyes wide and glistening, welling with tears.

"Thank you, Dr. Hanning," Glasser said. "I wouldn't want to lose you. You're a valuable part of this team."

Already, a facet of Glasser's mind was devoted to the problem of Hanning. He couldn't trust the man. Hanning would have to disappear, and it would have to be done as skillfully as the diabetic coma that proved to be the end of Hanning's predecessor, the troublesome Dr. Kurtzman.

Six minutes.

Glasser felt a burning in his temples. Waiting, it was so hard to wait. He'd reached the limit of even his own stone-cold sense of control. A trickle of sweat teased the back of his neck.

Six minutes. Seven. Counting.

He could have thrown the switch long before now. Just a touch of the switch, that's all, and Hamilton wouldn't have died. But nothing would have been discovered.

Ten seconds, and fifteen, sixteen, eighteen, twenty-one, twenty-five, twenty-six, twenty-seven—

Discovery.

Electro-animation.

Dr. Frankenstein threw the switch. Mozart called forth a chorus—and the lightning struck.

16

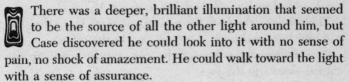 There was a deeper, brilliant illumination that seemed to be the source of all the other light around him, but Case discovered he could look into it with no sense of pain, no shock of amazement. He could walk toward the light with a sense of assurance.

Something in the light was aware of him. It knew all about him. It welcomed him.

He saw Benny again, and the blond-haired girl from 212, walking beside him.

"I'm looking for the Promised Land," she said in the tone of a secret delight. "Do you know where it is?"

"Yeah," Case said. "I know where it is."

He watched as the girl seemed to meld into the light, gold into gold, becoming a part of the radiance, a part of the great promise.

Case wanted to run to the light. Now! But he knew he had to wait, and he turned to find his dad in the crowd that surrounded him, even as he felt the clap of his father's hand on his shoulder.

Movement stopped. Something rippled through the crowd. A thousand breaths caught at once.

Case saw his dad was beaming at him with an electric sense of anticipation. His father handed him The Ball.

Case reached to touch the autographed baseball, feeling the energy that pulsed from it, from every signature, from the raised stitching and the pristine white cowhide, looking as new as the day it was sewn together. And The Ball spoke to him of youth, and dreams, and belonging, all being returned to him.

It was a gift from his father—from the little man who had died thinking he hadn't done enough, when he already had done the work of a giant. It was the second gift of life.

Then, from out of the light behind his father, another hand, a big hand, reached down to grasp The Ball.

There was no threat to the movement. Case knew that The Ball and the hand both *belonged,* one to the other.

Case followed the line of the big, steady hand, up the striped sleeve, to the face.

He knew the man's face. But the baseball cards and the magazine photos he'd seen had never captured the vitality of those features, the absolute health of a man at the peak of awareness.

Case looked again to be sure of the ball player's identity, studying the features that shifted as the man turned, enveloped in blazing light.

He said the man's name, but the sound was lost in thunder. And the lightning struck.

LIGHTNING!

Blinding white, obliterating—the lightning struck.

Case saw a moment's dismay in the eyes of the ball player, then the man's face was gone. The man was gone.

The seams of The Ball split open, and the core of it flash-burned—just a white ash that sifted through fingers of charred bone, blown away by the storm wind.

The ground split apart in a shimmering flash of destruction, and the sky was burning, and Case saw it all.

The falling bodies, swallowed into the widening fissure. The blackened fields of burning roses.

His father reaching toward him, only to be consumed by the flames.

The last of the ground fell away, and the air was heavy with dust and smoke, with fire and death.

But *he* was alive in the firestorm. Impossibly alive. Incredibly aware.

He should have been reduced to ash, but he was whole. Falling.

Falling through the fire.

Wrenched.

Lifted.

He was a fly on a string, being pulled back, pulled back—to the bells that rang forever in the darkness of the eternal night.

The bells.

The ringing of the bells.

Pounding.

Bells! Bells! Bells!

Heartbeat.

Bells! Bells! Bells!

The pulsing of blood.

Warmth.

Life.

Pain.

It started as a prickling in his legs, this pain. But the feeling turned to something red, to the color of raw meat, to the smell of fresh blood, to the fear of being torn apart.

He felt claws in his legs. Teeth.

Something had hold of him.

He was falling away from the bells, and something had hold of him—something he couldn't see.

The claws loosened only to sink into him again in search of a better grip. Tearing through skin, rasping on bone.

Something meant to stay with him, and the pain became a part of him—another kind of melding. Red on red.

Falling in darkness, he lost all sense of time, of direction, of up and down, of real and imagined. Everything felt like a dream.

And these were dreams that burned with fear and violence, that raged with a wild terror, assembled out of the darkness and the cold light, like a Saturday night killing spree in the hopeless part of a nameless town, where people ventured out to offer themselves to the gods of hatred and unfathomable angers, the dread a part of them always.

He rolled through the flame of a towering black candle—a monolith topped by an inferno of white fire.

An old man hunkered at the base of the candle, hard to see there, hidden in the flowing shadows of wax the color of midnight.

Case saw the old man's leathery face and hands were covered with bleeding sores that he scraped with a piece of splintery wood, streaking bright blood over the gray skin.

Case floated helplessly toward him, seeing the wino's ruined face like a twisted reflection—his own face in hell's broken mirror. But the old man's gray face seemed to melt like candle wax, stretching, pulling, until Case saw his jaw sagged almost to the waist.

And the man was someone, something else at the same time, and it spoke through yellowed teeth broken to sharp points.

It said, "You can't, you know," and sunk into itself in a spasm of wet, broken laughter. "You can't flee the Unborn."

The words came to him weighted with a terror he did not understand, and Case swung out his hands, clutching at the black air, trying to stop himself from drifting any closer to the man that was not a man.

"No," he said, and found the word stuck in his mind. "No. No. No, no, no, nnnno," until it degenerated into something closer to the sound of a wounded animal.

"NNNNN-OOOOO!"

The wino nodded. "The hell you say."

His mouth turned up, growing wider on the rubbery hinges of the sagging jaw until it split open. Gaping. Scarlet.

A smooth, white snake came slithering, now billowing out of the wide-open maw, ghostlike through the jagged teeth. And the snake had horns, and the face of a ram, and then it was Case, except for the eyes.

The eyes were reptilian: glassy-bright portals of yellow and red into an alien mind.

Case tried to escape from it, but he thrashed in the air.

He *knew* what this was. He knew it like a half-remembered line from some forgotten book, all the more terrible for having come to him from out of nowhere.

This thing was the distillation of everything evil inside of him, of every wild hunger he'd ever denied. Every merciless yearning he'd ever suppressed.

Every murder he'd ever considered in a flash of rage. Every rape that he'd ever imagined. Every perversion, every sacrilege. It all had a name.

It was called the Unborn.

The snake split into wavering tendrils, each with a ram's head, flowing over Case as he tried to keep it away with kicks that lacked substance.

He felt the weight of the beast on him, wrapped around

him, and then one of the ram's heads shot past his eye, and he could see the blood flying from the horns, and he knew that the thing must be puncturing him.

And he knew: it wanted something more than just to kill him.

It wanted . . . inside of him.

It wanted, wanted, wanted, wanted.

Hunger. Yearning. Pain beyond pain, all of those, more than those, there was a wild sense of *wanting* that Case found to be overlapped with a thousand black nuances.

It wanted. Possession.

Case felt a wicked, sick fear flood into him, even as the tendrils wrapped around him, tighter and tighter, the jaws of the multiple rams' heads gnashing at him, showing him needle-tipped fangs.

He couldn't . . . he could *not* . . . give . . . in . . .

Coiling and striking, one of the ram's heads hit his mouth, hard. Case saw the blood-streaked eyes staring into his as the horny head drove into his mouth again, splintering his teeth.

Case found that he could *see* inside his own mouth, see the shattered front teeth, the bleeding, warped gums.

His mouth was opening into a tunnel, and the tunnel was his throat, and it led to a light inside of him: the light the beast wanted.

The second of the horned heads drove at him, like a cobra. And the third. And again, and again, swarming at him, battering him.

He couldn't move. He was impaled by the shaft of the impossible beast that was into his throat, writhing deeper.

He cried blazing tears for the fool that he'd been, supposing that he had suffered the worst of hell with its ice and its tolling bells, when he hadn't begun to experience the punishments of the hereafter.

*   *   *

The last of the snake vanished into his mouth. But it wasn't gone.

Case felt it working, writhing, probing at the roof of his mouth, sliding down his throat.

The snake was his tongue. His voice. The voice of the Unborn that bubbled like lava.

The words were from his mouth, not from his mind, not from his soul, those words: "I will be you."

"I WILL BE—"

And he would have torn his tongue out, but he couldn't reach the darting snake that coiled in writhing loops into the back of his throat. He found that his arm was tied.

Case pulled at the bonds that held him, even then knowing that something more was wrong, was changing.

A tight-fisted yank, and he'd pulled loose the IV tube that trailed from his arm, and he sat up in bed, drenched with sweat, exhausted.

He looked around him, gasping for breath. He heard the spattering of the disconnected IV bag that was emptying the last of its clear fluid onto the floor. He tried to sigh with relief.

But he was breathing like a marathon runner at the end of a hard race. Adrenaline coursed through him.

He told himself that everything was all right, that he was awake, and that his thoughts would straighten out in time.

He could see that he was being kept in a hospital room. He was being taken care of, and the vivid dreams would stop.

He was alone in this room—freed from the grasp of the Unborn, alone with his thoughts. And he found that he knew things he shouldn't have known, couldn't have known.

They were like memories of books he'd never read, these things—of places he'd never been, of yearnings and angers

that he'd never felt, all dim but alive in some part of his mind
that was an alien landscape.

He remembered his father, and The Ball, and the ball
player.

He remembered the flash of lightning.

The pain.

And he knew that it didn't matter if he woke up in the
hospital. Nobody could take care of what was wrong with
him, because it was too deep inside of him, still there, hidden like a viper under a rock, ready to spring, to swallow him
whole.

I will be you.

The door opened. He caught a blur of white in the doorway.
He recognized the round, soft face of Teresa McMasters.

Case knew something worse, far worse than anything he
had experienced in death, but the knowledge of it slipped
away from him, no more substantial than the smoke from a
black candle.

He could wander in the caves of his mind forever, and
never find it again.

Something terrible.

He felt a hand at his wrist, a hand on his forehead, easing
him back, and someone else entered the room.

A bustling, a clattering, a woman's voice, saying notify the
doctor. Bright voice. Tell the doctor he's got a live one. Help
with the IV—

And he tried to remember the horror that he'd known just
a moment ago, almost able to grasp it, almost, almost.

Case's eyes fluttered open to a golden light—and for a moment he thought that everything had turned back around,
and things were right again, that he was back where he

should be, with the people who were a part of him, with the knowledge that he was, finally and forever, in the right place.

But even as he tried to focus his eyes, the dying, desperate feeling that clung to him told him he was wrong. There was too much pain pressing in from all 'round, jagged and tearing.

The gold was the bee pin, shining from Gwen Foster's blouse. It made him heartsick in the moment that he focused on it.

He heard Diana, her voice choked. Case's eyes fluttered again, and he saw her, and Frank and Gwen, standing next to her.

Diana said, "Hello, Dad."

Frank's smiling lips seemed to move out of sync with the world as Case saw it. Frank said, "Welcome back, you lucky bastard."

Behind Frank, the air seemed to thicken to a smoky gray— a gray with smears of orange and red, the eyes of the snake, in a moment that blurred into the hard sleep of the drugs he'd been given.

Into sleep, where his daughter and friends could not follow him.

But the snake could.

Case fought one last time to grasp at the elusive truth that would explain the snake, and the lightning, and the sense that he'd come back to life as the carrier of a sickness that was called the Unborn.

But he caught hold of only a part of the answer, and with an emptiness deep in his heart that told him he'd found out only the smallest part.

He was back from death's door. And something had come back with him.

17

 Stephen Glasser opened the door to Case Hamilton's recovery room, motioning for Diana and the others to meet with him in the hallway.

Nurse Teresa McMasters clattered past him, through the open door with a cart full of equipment that looked shiny and lethal, but with a smile of pure warmth.

"He's going to be fine," the nurse whispered to Diana, like tipping her off to a surprise party.

Diana stepped out of the doorway, looking back at her father as the nurse went to work, almost bumping into Stephen with a sense of champagne giddiness.

"Thank you, Stephen," she said as the white-coated, handsome doctor pulled the door shut behind her. Again, more in control: "Thank you."

He looked at her, smiling, and as relief and gratitude welled up in her, she reached for him, holding him tightly, pinning his arms to his sides.

She spoke into the base of his neck, his cool neck, softly, almost to herself. "Thank you."

He smelled of an expensive cologne—a scent that made her think of cognac and velvet—the same scent that he'd worn earlier in that long night, in bed next to her.

She held him, her welling of gratitude complicated by another emotion, inappropriate and illicit, rising within her.

"Electro-animation," he said, drawing the words out in an exaggerated whisper. His breath seemed hot on her ear.

She pulled back, looking up at him. "What?"

"Electro-animation," he repeated, cocking his head and lifting his hands, flexing his fingers.

Diana was aware of Frank and Gwen, who had moved down the hall a discreet distance, joining Bloch. They were all watching Glasser.

"Stephen," she said, afraid in a shapeless way, and she wondered if *they* could notice anything off-balance in the doctor's behavior. Did they see? Did they hear?

She asked, "What . . . excuse me, what are you talking about?"

"Oh, come on, Diana." He touched her on the shoulder, grinning. "Surely, you've seen those old movies on television. You know . . ." He lifted his hands again, gesturing, acting out the scene. "The hunchbacked servant hobbles in, turning the heavy crank—turning, turning the crank—that opens the trapdoor in the roof, and they send up the kites."

He looked up. Looking for kites.

"The lightning is raging, the wind howling," he said. "Then—when there's finally enough electricity"—he touched a finger to Diana's temple—"zzzzapp! And the dead walk again!"

She told herself he had a right to feel elated, and that elation could be intoxicating. But there was a terrible *wrongness* to this.

The dead man he'd saved with his "electro-animation," after all, was her own father, and *zzzzapp* made it sound like a sick joke, like something else he'd found in the back room at Chuckle Charlie's.

Stephen looked past her, to Gwen and Frank. The doctor winked. "Dr. Frankenstein is out of the closet," he said.

He took her arm, leading her toward them, and she could only imagine what awkward scene he might create.

But he said to them, simply, professionally, "Mr. Hamilton is resting comfortably, in good condition. He'll sleep quite a while, and he should be left alone. Sleep is the best medicine. We could all use a healthy dose of it."

"Yeah," Frank said. "I'll take a double spoonful."

Bloch yawned, glancing toward his watch. "Still a workday," he said. "Hallelujah."

Hands were shaken. Feelings of relief, of thanks expressed, and Bloch made his way out.

Frank walked a bit down the hallway with him. Gwen made a break for the rest room.

"Electro-animation," Stephen said, having Diana to himself again. "It's lightning and life, and it's going to be news, Di, big news. Big money, and more than that, you can't imagine how much more. Because of what I've done. With your father."

There was a hint of pique in his voice, and all Diana could think was that he said he'd done something *with* her father, not *for* her father. And suddenly she thought of the animals in the cages up in Stephen's laboratory, and how they had skittered in their dark prisons at the noise of hers and Stephen's lovemaking. It seemed wrong. It all seemed wrong.

She felt the heel of her foot grinding, grinding against the floor, as if by its own force of will.

Stephen leaned down almost gently, taking her by the shoulders. It seemed that little waves of current sparked through her then, crackling from his hands. He smiled.

Lifting one hand, he stroked her hair, briefly. She felt as though she might cry.

"Your nerves are on edge. You need to rest. Doctor's orders." And he made it sound exactly like a doctor's order.

Then, he spoke with an intimacy that suggested she was all that mattered to him, all he could see, all he ever wanted.

"Come upstairs, Di," he said. "Please. Give me ten minutes. I'll have the guard let you in." He lowered his voice to a smoky promise. "I have something to show you."

He turned and walked down the corridor, leaving her with doubts she could not resolve, questions she couldn't answer —and leaving her to want him any number of ways.

She might have been left to wonder, too, what effect the doctor would have had on another woman in the same circumstances, but she didn't have to wonder.

Gwen called to him, "Doctor, Dr. Glasser, please. I have a question," and caught up to him, running in high heels.

They spoke in hushed tones that Diana could not make out, a conversation that ended with a handshake. But it seemed to her that Gwen would have acquiesced to more than a handshake.

Gwen just stood there, watching him, as Stephen vanished into the elevator without another word, in silent strides, on silent feet.

Frank's voice, right behind her, broke the glaze of quiet.

"Maybe the sumbitch'll be on goddam *Oprah*," he said.

She wondered if Duane Hardage would still be at his guard post. He wasn't. He'd been replaced by another man, a younger man, with a bodybuilder's physique that showed in the bull neck that emerged from his stiff collar.

The guard checked her in with no welcome.

She found the hallway of Stephen's "compression chamber" lit to a fluorescent high noon. Ahead of her, the double doors swung open with a flash of gold and mahogany.

Two men and three women emerged from the doorway, all

of them wearing white coats of the same cut, clipping toward her, sweeping past her.

She pressed through the door to see that Stephen was talking on a white wall phone across the lab, motioning to her to come in, looking straight through her.

The door clacked behind her. It shut with a sound of a lock closing, and she thought of a cell door slamming shut. But she wasn't being locked in.

The rest of the world was being locked out.

Something to show her. He stirred it himself, and pronounced it perfect, and she agreed.

"I can't ever recall having a martini at ten A.M.," she said, lifting the perfect drink to her lips.

"Therapeutic, in modest quantities," Stephen said, sipping his own, a second, made from the hidden bar that swung out from the wall at the push of a button. The alcohol didn't seem to affect him.

"I have just one more call to make," he said.

The animals skittered in their cages as Glasser strode across the spacious lab to the phone, where he punched in a number.

Diana looked around the private sanctum, the place where —it seemed ages ago, now—she had spent the night with Stephen Glasser, only to be awakened from languid dreams into a nightmare of sudden violence: her father on the cement, bleeding a river into the artificial light that made the blood look as thin as water.

But he wasn't bleeding now, he was resting comfortably, and he was going to be all right, and there was no reason to think otherwise.

Almost involuntarily, she looked toward the cream-colored leather sofa, where she had given herself to Stephen on satin sheets—Stephen with his surreal false noses, one after another.

She drew a connecting line of thought. It started with Stephen's behavior in bed, connecting to the way he was talking about "Dr. Frankenstein" outside her father's room. Two scenes of mental imbalance, each confirming the other to have been more than a quirk. But she didn't want to judge him, not now.

The bottom line was that Stephen had saved her father's life, and that no one else could have done it.

The bed was folded away, hidden into the sofa. She'd known without looking it would be. She felt she could have come in ten minutes after she'd left in the middle of the night, and the bed would have been gone, tucked away, forgotten like her.

Nothing was out of place in Stephen's life, and the lab betrayed no hints that people could live here—only the animals in their neat, sanitary little cages, scurrying a little at intervals, peering at her from time to time.

Rats, guinea pigs, cats, monkeys.

Diana walked to one of the cat cages, reaching a finger through the wire to scratch a purring white tabby behind the ears, the touch of the soft fur comforting to her.

"What's your name, kitty?" she asked, realizing at the same time the cat didn't have a name. It didn't need a name. No one was going to be calling this kitty to come home.

She could choose to think of the lab as a kind of Noah's Ark, but these were laboratory animals, not pets, and Noah had plans for them that didn't include saving their lives.

She had met Stephen in this lab several times over the years, but only for brief periods, and now she seemed to be spending a great deal of time surrounded by these white walls.

She was looking at chrome and glass, closed drawers, amber screens, digital readouts, seeing it all with new eyes, wondering what else Stephen Glasser kept hidden here.

The bed, the bar, God only knew what other comforts—but she wouldn't have been surprised to find stereo equipment, kitchen appliances, anything. *Maybe even a bowling alley,* she thought, and the idea made her smile, even as she heard him talking on the phone.

"Ms. Callahan," he said. "Dr. Glasser. I'd like for you to arrange a press conference for two P.M. today. And not the meeting room—make it the auditorium." A pause. "I *know* what time it is. The time is three hours and fifty-six minutes to the press conference, a meeting that I expect to find attended by the following . . ."

Diana listened to the recitation of names. A few of them were familiar to her as newspaper and TV reporters she'd encountered at crime scenes. Some were familiar as bylines she'd read. Names of TV anchors. Talk-show hosts. Radio personalities. Wire services. Hospital officials.

She wondered at what point Stephen had found it possible to command this much interest. He seemed always to have been a figure in the news.

He paused again, and Diana thought about the evenness of his voice—the perfect control. Like the lab, giving away nothing. Like the lab, hiding any number of things.

"Tell them just this much, Ms. Callahan," he said. "The word is Electro-Animation. E-L-E-C-T-R-O. Hyphen. A-N-I . . . that's right. And I want you to tell them it's life-and-death, and tell them that's not hyperbole, and tell them what hyperbole means."

He glanced toward Diana with a self-mocking roll of his eyes. But the gesture seemed studied. She knew there was nothing self-mocking about him.

"One other thing, Ms. Callahan," he said. "Make it clear

I'll have no comment on last night's . . . tragedy, beyond the statement I've already released. Also, *please* note this—absolutely no comment on the abortion protests. My announcement has nothing to do with the abortion clinic. It's not the issue."

Not the issue, Diana thought. Never the issue. The baby has fingers as cold as dead seaweed, but it's best not to comment.

Diana felt a black hole inside her—an abyss into which she might lose herself. But she didn't dare. She'd made her own decision, and she couldn't reverse it. She'd made the right decision. The only decision.

She took another stinging sip of her drink, twirling the toothpick that held the olive submerged in the gin.

The toothpick was red, edged in gold, topped by a winding red-and-gold caduceus. Stephen had found the toothpicks at some banquet or other, had tracked down the manufacturer and ordered a case of them.

He said they amused him. But she'd never known him to crack a smile over a martini glass.

She had sipped her first Glasser martini in his apartment almost three years ago. It was a penthouse apartment, topping a building that he owned, the floor beneath him kept vacant to ensure the owner's privacy. And she had come away with vague impressions of furniture done in black and white leather, and a white carpet that felt like walking on sheepskin, and a Picasso abstraction that surprised her when she saw the texture of the brush strokes and realized that it wasn't a copy.

It was all too much—an overload that left her with just one sharp memory, and that was of the toothpick with the coiled serpents, and of the disbelief she'd felt that he would care what sort of toothpick he stuck through an olive.

But, of course, he did.

Nothing escaped him.

The toothpick skewered a large olive, stuffed with a tiny
veinless shrimp. Stephen had the shrimp imported from
Greece at significant expense. He would stand for nothing
but the best, whether it was a penthouse apartment, or the
olive in a martini, or the black Lotus he drove, or his brand
of shaving cream, a Russian import.

And he could discuss every choice with the greatest au
thority, incisive in place of exhaustive—could tell her why
each was the best of its class.

Yet, all of the *stuff* of Stephen's environment seemed as
distant and untouchable to her as a glossy magazine photo
where the real components of life were folded and put into
cabinets, never to be seen until the spies all went away.

He was beside her, the gentle pressure of his hand on her
back. "That's taken care of," he said. "Feeling the gin yet?"

"I think so," she said, smiling. And then, "Stephen—
want a toast."

She raised her glass, and as he held out his own, she
clinked them softly together. "To your great skill," she said,
thinking it sounded stilted even as it passed through her lips.

He smiled, nodding. "And to yours," he said, leaving her
to guess at what skill of hers was being toasted.

Was she the best of her class? The equal of a Lotus auto
mobile? A veinless shrimp? A toothpick?

Diana said, "You've saved my father's life twice now, and
don't know how to thank you."

"You don't need to," he said. "It's what I do."

He clinked the glasses together, then walked to the sofa.
Laying the cushions neatly to one side, he pressed a button
hidden inside the arm of the furniture, and the bed unfolded
with a purr of electricity.

"We both need some rest before the press conference," he said.

Diana asked, "How does it feel? . . . I mean, to be the center of so much attention."

Frank had managed to deflect most of the reporters wanting quotes from her, exclusives, sound bites, video footage, demanding photos of her at the scene of the carnage, one of them asking if she would mind standing with one foot poised in the stain of her father's blood. But he'd warned her they wouldn't give up.

She couldn't imagine *wanting* to be in the news.

The bed clicked into place.

Stephen said, "Attention? It feels like being pecked to death by ducks. Television dunderheads, dragging their cable and their cameras around, asking their kindergarten questions, and the newspaper dinosaurs . . ."

But his voice didn't carry the sound of complaint. Diana thought he seemed to be running through a checklist, talking to himself, not to her. He was concerned about CNN coverage. He never mentioned her father.

He turned to her, smiling as he smoothed out the sheets on the now-exposed bed, although nothing needed smoothing out. The bed was impeccably made, pillows and all, in a way that bespoke maid service.

But there weren't any maids in sight, and she wondered if one of the fast-moving, intent women she'd seen in the hallway might have been assigned to bed-making, along with medical research.

"Are you hungry?" he asked.

"Why? Do you have a deli up here, too?" she tried to tease.

"Not exactly. But I do have a reasonable selection of prepared meals, ready to microwave. The pepper steak's not bad."

She imagined the pepper steak would do justice to the reputation of a five-star restaurant, but she was too tired to care—too busy discovering how many ways her body hurt.

"No, no thanks." She brushed her hair back from her ear and twirled the olive in her glass.

"All right, then come here, Di. Sit. I'll show you some thing else." He turned his hand, palm up, to indicate the bed.

Diana arose from the polished oak chair and moved to the bed, cupping the martini glass in both hands. She sat on the edge of the mattress. Glasser walked behind her, to the other side of the bed, and she felt it sag a little as he sat down.

Then, his hand was on the back of her neck, massaging it gently. The tension within her seemed to swirl up, knot, and then drift away under the rhythmic movement of his finger tips. She closed her eyes, drifting.

"That's good, isn't it," he said, and it wasn't a question.

"Yes," she said, tilting her head back, her eyes closed.

In that moment, she imagined that Stephen Glasser would know what to do about everything else that bothered her. He would have the answer to Sarah Katzeff's swollen eye, to her husband's cruelty, and to the Prophet's insanity.

The experience would have been as perfect as Stephen intended it—except for Bloch. She kept thinking of Bloch, kept trying to imagine how Det. Sgt. Douglas Bloch would respond to this place.

Lady cop meets the world-famous Dr. Wonderful. Sit where she's told. Does what he says. Wonders, maybe just a little, what the hell is going on—

She felt another sensation. Different. The magic hands, with the same kneading pressure, had moved to caress her— had crept to other parts of her body, cupping and sliding over her.

Slowly, her eyes opened. "Stephen?"

"Mmm-hmm," came the voice from behind her.

She stared into the purple of the satin sheets. "I don't think I feel like . . . I mean . . ."

"Relax."

She told herself she couldn't do this. Her father was in this same building. Alive—a living miracle—but he was hurt, and she ought to be keeping a watch over him, in case he needed something.

He should be left alone.

The whole, massive hospital narrowed in Diana's mind to the fact that her father was *here*. It was her father's house. She couldn't be caught screwing in her father's house.

"Just relax," Stephen said. She wasn't aware that he'd unslipped the buttons down the front of her blouse. His hands almost magically cleared the blouse from her body.

She started to push herself up—to say no. But instead she gave herself over to the alcohol and the pressure of his hands, lower now, always moving, always working, surgeon's hands, snipping away bits of her clothes.

She let her eyes close, telling herself everything was fine, everything was good, and that his touch hadn't become suddenly, subtly harder when she had begun to protest.

18

 Diana awoke suddenly, her heart hammering, coming out from a dream so heavy she felt as though a boulder had been rolled on top of her. For a fleeting moment, she forgot where she was, and she swallowed, her eyes moving, gathering memories.

The dread of the waiting room. The martini. The sex she'd had with Stephen as a prelude to hard sleep, and the fingers that knew every part of her, what hurt, what didn't, and the pounding inside of her, lifting her, carrying her, as they cried out together in voices of climax that had become as inseparable as their bodies in that moment.

Burrowing into the pillow with the side of her face, she slid a foot tentatively across the fitted satin sheet, slowly, in search of Stephen.

Her foot moved, continued to move, until it had inched all the way to the downward contour of the mattress on the other side.

He wasn't there.

She rolled over, lifting herself on one arm, satin sliding down her back. Nothing was left on his side of the bed but the smell of him, cognac and velvet—of him and her, fading now, evaporating into the cool, astringent air of the laboratory.

The press conference, she thought. That was it. She sat up in bed, blinked at her watch. The dial seemed to glow at her: 2:07.

A shot of adrenaline rushed through her. Stephen's press conference already had started, and it was so important to him—talking about *her* father. She ought to have been there. Why had he slipped out, leaving her?

Lying back, Diana reminded herself that he was a doctor above all, and he wanted what was best for her. He knew she was exhausted. He knew that a healthy dose of sleep would be better for her, more important to her, than a press conference that was just a part of the day's routine.

Tell them—

Of course, he was thinking of her welfare, and he was right. She had nothing to do but surrender again to the billowing fog of a sleep that she deserved.

Tell them—

Still, a tiny thought jabbed at her. She knew why most men left their lovers sleeping alone. It was because they didn't want to wake up with them.

In one of the cages across the room, a guinea pig burrowed wildly under a pile of wood shavings, scattering them everywhere. The animal began scratching at a cleared spot on the bottom of the cage in flurries of tiny claws.

The scratching noise stopped, started, stopped again, started again. Stopped.

Diana could see the guinea pig as a motionless, black-and-white fluff. She caught the glint of a black eye, and she imagined the guinea pig was looking through the newly discovered glass floor of its cage—down through a hole in the metal shelf that held the cage, to see the shelf below.

Below . . . another cage, another guinea pig, looking down. Another cage, another guinea pig, looking down. Another cage.

The guinea pig's nails flew at the floor of the cage again, but Diana was half sleeping. Dreaming in twilight.

In her dream, she saw that Stephen had slipped a yellow powder of some sort into the martini that he made for her, and she understood it was a drug that would make her sleep. And he was hiding it from her in a way that would cause her to notice. She saw the clear drink turn a frothy yellow in the glass for just a moment before he gave it to her.

She drank it with a smile, pretending not to notice the bitter taste, wondering why her father would allow for her to be treated this way.

But her father just watched her, uncaring, his eyes gone dead. Flies were crawling across his eyes.

And all the while she kept hearing Stephen's voice, even though his lips weren't moving.

His voice—from below her, above her, behind her.

Tell them it's life-and-death.

Tell them it's life-and-death.

Tell them!

She awakened in a flash of cold, already reaching to get dressed.

Diana almost ran past the nurses' station on the second-floor wing of recovery rooms, toward her father's room, stopping only when she saw the expression of worry on Teresa Mc-Masters's face.

"What is it, what's gone wrong with him?" Diana asked.

The nurse reached out a pink, plump hand to touch Diana's shoulder.

"Your dad is just fine," the nurse said. "But you look . . .

well, probably about as tired as you've got a right to be, Miss Hamilton."

Diana felt something go slack deep inside her.

"He's really okay?" she asked.

"He is, and Case Hamilton is going to have the best of care," the nurse said. "Right?"

Diana turned to see a pert-looking, hazel-eyed blonde, a girl of college age, wearing the pink-and-white of a hospital candy striper. The volunteer's name pin read "Kelly."

"Right," Kelly said, walking past them with an armload of white linens. And to Diana: "Mrs. McMasters wouldn't tell you, so I will. She's working a double shift. She wants to make double sure that everything's done right for Mr. Hamilton."

Mrs. McMasters shooed the candy striper away with a flutter of her hand.

"We all have to do what we can," the nurse said, watching as Kelly bounced away in her running shoes, her white skirt swishing rhythmically. "But some of us seem to have all the energy."

Diana said, "I just . . . I guess I had a feeling, a dream maybe, of something gone wrong."

The nurse smiled. "It happens to a lot of people—people just anxious after a loved one's gone through surgery, let alone after the experience you've had, Miss Hamilton, such awful—"

She seemed to be considering what else to say, coming up at a loss.

"I'm all right, thank you," Diana said. "Honest."

"Well, here! Tch! I know the best cure for those bad feelings," the nurse said, leading her down the hallway, pushing open the door to her father's room.

It was silent as a wall of glass.

"It's all right, you can go in," the nurse said. "Tiptoe."

Diana crossed the silent room, stopping at her father's bedside, startled to a gasp at what she saw.

His face all but beamed with a flush of life and health, and he looked a lifetime younger.

She thought her eyes might have fooled her, but no—the skin seemed to have tightened along his jaw, and the sags were gone from under his sleeping eyes, and he looked . . . *handsome,* she thought.

Not a man on the brink of death. She could have believed he wasn't sleeping at all. He was going to leap out of bed, laughing, roaring with laughter.

Any minute. Any second.

There was a mean twist to his mouth, as if he might have been having a bad dream himself. But he was going to be all right, and he wasn't going to waste time on dreams once he woke up, Diana thought. He was going to be hollering for T-bone steak.

"We'd best leave him now," the nurse whispered.

Diana reached to straighten the already straightened bed covers. She backed away.

Mr. Hamilton is resting comfortably, in good condition.

No, Stephen, she thought. *Mr. Hamilton is resting comfortably, truly alive for the first time in years.*

Thanking the nurse, she hurried on to hear what she could of Stephen's press conference.

Life-and-death, she thought, amazed. He'd really meant it.

III

case at
the Bat

They saw his face grow stern and cold,
they saw his muscles strain,
And they knew that Casey wouldn't
let that ball go by again.

—E. L. Thayer, "Casey at the Bat"

19

 His senses seemed to function one at a time, never quite connecting, as if to present him with bits of a puzzle. Here it is: Fit the pieces. Connect the dots. Fill in the blanks.

He smelled vanilla.

Remembered his name. Case. Case. Case.

He felt something stir in the air. Heard footsteps. But he might have been dreaming, he couldn't be sure.

He saw lightning—crackling, blue-white shafts of lightning that splintered across a sky of throbbing red, none of it possible. He couldn't be seeing this alien landscape. He couldn't see at all.

His eyes would not open. He tried . . . couldn't find the right muscles. Nothing worked the way it should, and every little movement sparked a pain inside his head.

His fingers clutched some kind of starchy fabric. For a moment, he recognized that he was holding a bed sheet. Hospital. Bed. But the idea made no sense.

Another zigzag flash of lightning. But it wasn't lightning, it was the night lights being turned on. The big lights switched on in sequence all around the stadium, making vivid white stripes of the base lines.

His fingers brushed the fabric. He liked the feeling of a crisp, clean uniform at the start of a baseball game.

Blue sky. New-mowed grass. The stands were jam-packed all around him, pennants waving in speckles of color. The breeze of a summer's night came to him smelling of popcorn, tasting of hot dogs, and people were singing.

The organist prompted them into another round of "Take Me Out to the Ball Game" that echoed off the fence that surrounded the ball park.

Case thought he might have lured himself into another dream, but maybe not—he didn't care.

He knew the words to the sweet song by heart, whispering into the voice of the crowd, "I don't care if I never get back."

Never get back. The spirit voice of the wavering echo agreed with him, rebounding from the high fence, *never get back.*

His fingers enclosed the ball, tracing the seam lines, treasuring the form and the function.

Case flexed his right arm for the pitch that would set the game in motion, and he got the call he wanted. Fast ball.

He nodded, and his body turned to fluid motion. The windup. The arm back, the knee up. Utter silence, and he could feel the cold crawl of a trickle of sweat down the back of his neck. Throw! Snap of the wrist, and the ball spun off the tips of his fingers, a streak of white.

The batter swung. Case heard the dismaying crack of a solid hit, but he couldn't see the ball.

The ball park seemed to vaporize around him, gone to smoke. The air smelled of cordite, and of grape wine, and of a writhing black man, shot through the head—

A woman screamed.

Again, again, again he'd heard the sound of her voice, until it seemed to him that every dream was *this* dream, and that he was destined to fall and die this same way, over and over, for as long as some dim, drifting mote of him might still endure.

He realized the sound he'd heard wasn't the crack of a baseball bat. It was a gunshot; it went with the muzzle flash from a chrome-plated automatic pistol.

He saw the bullet spinning through the air. He had all the time in the world to watch it dance in silvery spirals, but he couldn't move, and it hit him like the wrath of all creation.

Extinguished!

But he wouldn't accept it. Not this time, not again. NO! HE WOULD NOT FEEL THE COLD, HE WOULD NOT HEAR THE BELLS! HE WOULD NOT—

His eyes slit open.

He was looking up, head rolled to the side just enough to leave him staring into the light that spilled through the window blinds.

He saw bed covers. Rails on the bed. The snaking length of an IV line that attached to his arm.

A new memory: the flash of a knife blade.

Case bolted upright, gasping for breath, ensnared in the memory of the blade slashing toward him. He caught hold of the bed rail, cold like the bars of an animal cage, and he thought of Glasser's laboratory: of the rats in their cages.

Footsteps. A woman's voice.

"Shhh," she said. "Now, now, shhhh."

A warm, calming hand pressed against his forehead. A calming voice told him that he would be all right, all right, all right.

The face above him steadied into focus. A round shape, warm eyes, apple-red cheeks. Teresa McMasters.

"I don't want any trouble from you, mister," she told him, easing him back, settling his head onto the pillow. "*You* are going to be fussed over like a teddy bear in here, like it or not."

She straightened the covers.

Case tried to thank her. The words became a cough that seemed to split his head.

"Shhh," she said, touching a finger to her lips. "The best thing for you is to go back to sleep, all right? Let me get some work done."

Already, Case felt himself drifting. He realized he wasn't just tired. He was fighting some heavyweight drug he'd been given to keep him sedated, and it was time to throw the fight.

His eyes closed to the sight of Teresa McMasters in her white uniform, bustling about the room. Here a nurse, there a nurse. Making sure he had a full pitcher of water. Adjusting the window blinds. Straightening the covers again.

Through the last slit of light, he saw . . . something.

Something. A shadow on the wall behind her, spreading up the wall, rising above her.

Gray. Shifting. Shapeless.

Not a shadow.

She turned, glancing to the side. In a moment she might see it, too, Case thought. But she didn't.

She reached to a clipboard that was posted at the foot of the bed, writing notes on a chart.

She didn't see it! . . . The gray shape. The roiling cloud behind her.

Case tried to find his voice to warn her. *Look!* The word came out a rasp of air. *Get away!*

She didn't see . . . for the best of all reasons, and Case knew the answer. It wasn't there.

He thought of how real the baseball had seemed to him just moments ago, but it wasn't real. His mind was into fun and games. He couldn't trust himself. The next thing he knew, he might be seeing chorus lines of dancing polar bears.

All that mattered was that he hadn't died, and he wasn't going to die, and the best he could do was to go back to sleep.

But . . . he forced his eyes open.

He was buried in covers, but something had invaded the room with a coldness that cut to the bone. His breath came out in wisps of white. Frost glittered on the chromium bed rail.

A tap-tap of footsteps. Teresa McMasters crossed the room, sweeping through his line of vision. And something, something . . . moved behind her, stalking her.

Case forced his head to roll against the pillow, like rolling a rock. But he *could* move. The cold seemed to be working against the effects of the sedative.

Moving his head, he saw the nurse reach toward the thermostat—a wall control. Fingered the temperature dial.

She turned, seeing him still awake. She rubbed her arms, and Case heard the chattering sound of her teeth, like tiny hammers cracking bits of chalk.

She said, "Well, isn't this just the strangest thing? Brrr! Um! I can't imagine what's gone wrong with the air conditioning, but don't you worry, you're not going to stay in here another min—"

From behind her: the impossible. Case thought he saw a hand clasp across her mouth. But the hand was disconnected. Insubstantial. It was the gray of a storm cloud, the wrist trailing away into tendrils of smoke.

Case levered himself up, discovering a bright silver pain in his head, just behind his eyes. The whiteness of the room seemed almost blinding. He yearned to close his eyes.

Look!

And his eyes locked in contact with hers—hers wide open, reservoirs of terror.

Another hand took shape out of smoke and mist, even as Case lowered the railing, pulling the IV needle loose from his arm, swinging his feet like dead weights off the edge of the bed.

He tried to believe he was caught in a nightmare. But he'd never dreamed such pain as this—what it cost him to stand.

As a cop, he'd taken a back-alley beating one time that left him with a punctured lung, but never with such a bone-deep sense of being damaged. He fought for a sense of balance.

The nurse reached toward him, flailing the air with her hand, the fingers splayed. Her feet kicked. One of her white shoes kicked loose, and he could see that she was off the floor, caught like a moth in a spider's web. But he couldn't see the web. He couldn't find the spider.

He forced his way across the room, sucking breaths of frigid air that hurt his throat.

Step by step, he promised himself there would be a man attached to the gray hands. Nothing else made sense. He wasn't seeing things right, but he could see well enough close up.

Close up, he would see the man—the Gray Man. He would take hold of the Gray Man. Stop the Gray Man.

Close up . . . he saw the scarlet spill of blood from between the gray fingers that closed spiderlike over the woman's mouth. There were cuts on the gray fingers. Deep cuts that opened to pink, wet wounds. The more the hand moved, the more the cuts opened.

Close up . . . he saw the other hand that floated like a trick performed with smoke and magic—the gray hand that pointed toward him, the pink cut that split open in the tip of the first finger. The lines and creases, all so vivid. The nails. The scar.

He saw the half-inch line of white scar in the web between the thumb and the forefinger, and something reeled back inside of him.

He glanced to his own left hand to see the identical scar, a reminder of his first year on the streets. He'd been a rookie cop, proud of the uniform, and no one could have told him to watch out for sweet-faced kids. He was supposed to protect them. They weren't supposed to pull knives on him.

He clenched his left fist, suddenly aware of a stiffness surrounding the old scar, as if he'd just now discovered it.

The Gray Man's scarred fist clenched at the same time.

Close up . . . Case thought he saw the yellow-red glint of eyes in the gray mass that roiled up behind the nurse, and he lunged forward, scalding his throat with an animal cry, welling over with rage and revulsion.

The yell wasn't planned, but it brought back his training in judo. It tensed the muscles in his chest and stomach. It made him faster, stronger.

He grabbed for the Gray Man's arm, already envisioning the series of moves that would result in a trip-and-wheel takedown. But his hand closed on nothing—nothing solid. His fingers seemed to pass through cutting shards of slivered ice, and something worse, something beyond reason.

He felt a bone-deep sense of evil. Violation. An orgasmic rush.

He clasped the woman's shoulders, half expecting that she would prove to be as insubstantial as the Gray Man, just another fragment of the never-ending dream.

He wrenched her toward him, and she stumbled forward, gasping for breath. There was nothing behind her.

"Case," she said. "C-Case, I don't know what's happ—"

He felt the warmth of her, smelled the vanilla perfume that she wore, sensed the life in his hands. Saw her lips move —all in a moment, a heartbeat.

Her head nodded. At first, he thought she meant for the movement to tell him something, but it was too intense. Up, and the white skin stretched taut from her jaw to the base of her throat. Down, and she struck him facefirst. Up, and he could feel her being torn away from him.

Laughter bubbled in his throat, hot as bile. He couldn't stop it.

Up, down, up, down—the gray fingers caught in her hair, forcing her—faster, faster, *back!* with the gunshot sound of a broken neck, and she fell from his arms.

But she didn't fall. She was caught in the air, held there, a puppet plaything to the Gray Man, dancing like a rag doll as the smoke-gray hands began to tear at her, going for the soft parts.

Raking. Rending.

Tearing at the uniform, tearing at the corners of the mouth, tearing—and throwing to Case what was left of her.

The body struck him face-to-face, teeth-to-teeth, like a love match made in hell.

Robbed of all balance, he fell with a head-cracking finality, and the sharp, red mouth of pain opened to swallow him.

He rolled the nurse's body away from him, discovering the blood on the floor was still warm, still pooling.

He looked for the Gray Man, but the room was empty.

He tried standing, surprised to feel nothing more than the trip-hammer pound of a normal-life headache—just a headache, along with a sickness he felt to the pit of his soul.

All he could think was that her name was Teresa, and he'd given her a handful of tomatoes. He remembered her smile, and the glow to her cheeks.

Now her torn mouth gaped at him. The white glint of teeth showed through the bloodied ruins of her face, and he backed away as if he'd never seen a murder before.

He caught the edge of the bed for support, his breath gone ragged. He knew he would have to get hold.

Get straight. Fight the drug. Clear his mind.

He tried to put the scene together the way a cop would. Fit the pieces. Connect the dots. Fill in the blanks.

But the puzzle defied him. The cop in him wouldn't believe in seeing ghosts, and he couldn't accept the only other answer.

He couldn't believe that he'd killed her.

He found his pants in the locker-sized closet, hung there as if he might appreciate the joke of neatly hung pants, no shirt, no shoes, nothing else.

He ripped off the hospital gown, discovering the bandage that covered a throbbing wound in his side. And what else? What else had been done to him?

There was no mirror in the room. He found the left side of his neck was bandaged, and there was a gauzy covering over a sore spot near the center of his forehead.

He pulled on the pants, smearing jelly-thick blood from his bare feet into the pants legs, realizing the insanity of what he was doing.

But what else *could* he do? Wait to be found? What could he say? That he'd witnessed a murder?

He couldn't pretend to be innocent.

He hadn't killed her, but worse—he'd allowed for Teresa McMasters to be torn apart by the Gray Man while he stood there in drugged disbelief, feeling . . . a shock of elation.

Exultation!

Satisfaction.

Sudden knowledge.

She had danced for his amusement.

Case pushed open the door to a bright, silent hallway that he recognized as one of the corridors on the second floor.

The second floor had belonged to Glasser before the resident celebrity had maneuvered his way to control the fifteenth, and it still bore some of the trademark signs of Glasser's influence. Case could tell by the red floor covering that made a bleeding wound of the corridor.

He stepped back, pulling the door shut behind him.

He stripped the sheet off his bed, draping it over the nurse on the floor, remembering how cold she'd felt in this room. He wished he could think of the sheet as a cover, but it wasn't. It was nothing but a sorry shroud, mottled with blood that began to spread across it as soon as the sheet settled over the body.

And where had *she* gone? Case wondered. Into the tolling of the bells? He didn't think so.

Images flooded him. But Case held an image in mind that he used to block out every other thought—every doubt, fear, guilt, every good reason to give himself up as a lunatic. He thought of the white peacock, a bird of exquisite beauty, named Ornery.

He kept a half-dozen peacocks along with the chickens at his hermit's house in the country, and the birds needed feeding. He wasn't sure how long he'd been away.

Even a crazy man's birds deserved reasonable care.

And if the image of the peacock didn't work to keep him moving, he had another.

He thought of the pistol. The 9mm Beretta, double-action, fifteen-shot. He hadn't touched it in three years. It was wrapped in an oiled cloth, tucked into the back of the bottom drawer of the bedroom dresser, along with a box of high-velocity shells.

He would escape to his Jeep in the parking lot. He would

drive the rust-mottled Jeep home to the country, and he would feed the birds. He would find the automatic pistol that he'd carried as a cop, and he would sit there at his kitchen table, holding the pistol, thinking like a cop.

He would decide what to do—out in the clean country, where things would make sense.

20

 Jermell wanted to run. He wanted so much that he
stared straight ahead, and he didn't blink, and he didn't
move. He just *wanted*.

Over and over, he thought of how it would feel to climb
out of this bed, to escape from this room, to cut loose with
his fast legs.

Out the door, down the hallway. No one could catch him.
Jermell would be a ghost.

*Anybody else have any questions for Jermell? Well, you can
ask, Mr. Fuzz, but he's not going to answer. This boy is gone.*

But the idea only worked in the back of his mind. He
knew he couldn't leave. He knew The Man was just outside
the door, having caught a glimpse of the blue uniform.

Jermell told himself he'd become what he wanted, and the
police guard proved it: he was a real gangster. But he was
something else, too. He was a seventeen-year-old kid who
felt scared sick.

Scared of being hurt. Scared of The Man's questions.

Who else was in the ambulance?

Who else ran? Who got away?

You're just making it worse for yourself, son. Tell us. Give

us names. Tell us where to find them, or don't you see?
There's going to be more people get hurt.

Jermell hadn't told, though, and he wouldn't tell, not even
when The Man brought in his mama to beg him to answer
their fuzz questions.

He was too scared to tell.

He knew Vincent would kill him for telling. And he knew
something hard that he'd never imagined before. He was
scared to die.

Always before, Jermell had thought of death as a joke, or as
something that happened to old people who didn't matter to
anybody. Better off dead. And he'd played tough with death,
drawing skulls with gaping eye sockets on all of his notebook
covers in school—skulls that had nothing but crooked lines
for teeth, since Jermell didn't know how the jaw hinges
worked.

He'd told himself he wasn't afraid of dying and that, anyway, he'd rather die with the Cobras than to keep on living.
He could see what sort of sorry-ass life he was going to have
in the projects. He'd rather be dead. He didn't give a shit
about tomorrow.

He'd taunted death and teased death. He'd poked at
death, like jabbing a stick at a mean dog that looked slow.
And death had come unleashed. All of a sudden, death had
shot him in the back with a policeman's trey-eight—throwing him off his feet, teaching him a sudden, bone-deep understanding of his own mortality.

Death is what happens when you can't run.

He knew he was in pain, although he couldn't really feel
anything. It was because of the drugs, he thought—the painkillers.

Well, they'd been going to rob the hospital of drugs, and the plan worked. *See, Vincent?* He was full of drugs.

But they would know better next time. They could skip the holdup part. They could just roll an ambulance, and then Vincent could start shooting at the police, and the police would shoot back, and maybe Vincent would be the one they lit up the next time.

Vincent could have the drugs.

Jermell tried to move his right arm in its sling, stirring a dull ache from his shoulder, a wild pain that threatened to break free of restraint. He wondered about the hole that went through him. He'd never seen beneath the bandages. How would it look, the hole that a bullet made?

Would it ever go away?

He didn't want to think about his mama maybe losing her job at the motel for being late to work, all because of him.

Instead, he thought about Vincent, and how Vincent had promised him the Cobras were going big time, big money. Big respect.

Vincent knew big guys from the Colombian and Mexican drug networks. But they had to be convinced, these guys, Vincent said. They had to be shown the Cobras were up on it, ready for heavy trade, not just a boys' club.

He stared at the white wall until he thought he could see shadows moving across it, although nothing at all was moving in Jermell's room.

His thoughts were wispy, rolling things that bumped into each other in a haze of barbiturates, but he still could call up vivid images of their flight from the hospital in the stolen ambulance.

Vincent clenching the wheel, laughing. Terry firing his Magnum revolver out the back of the ambulance, blasting into the air for no good reason, just to see the gun flash. B.J.'s widened eyes that seemed a glowing white from another world.

Jermell felt so scared that he wanted to cry, because he'd already seen what a bullet could do: it could take off the top of Concho's head, spattering brains and bone fragments over the pavement.

But he didn't dare cry, so he laughed. Jermell laughed the same as Vincent.

Jermell knew the very moment the ambulance had started to fall sideways. A yellow pencil clattered across the floor in the back, rolling toward him. And it seemed to roll forever. He seemed to have hours to decide if he wanted a pencil.

The wreck itself came back to him as nothing more than a free-fall, tumbling nightmare through a sky full of broken glass.

And running. He seemed to have been running his whole life. Everything he'd ever wanted, he'd had to steal. Other people might remember when they bought a radio, or a jacket, or a pair of shoes; they might have happy memories of shopping malls. He supposed they did. But everything Jermell had that was worth a shit came wrapped in the memory of running.

Running—away from the wreckage of the ambulance, away from the anger of the guns.

Lying there, staring, he felt again the glissando of terror up his spine as the guns fired, and the agony exploded across his shoulders.

He was down on the ground, and he was on the stretcher, and he had to get up, he had to keep running.

But he couldn't. It was like being in a dream with something coming after him, and he tried to run, and it felt like he was running, but he wasn't. Something was gaining on him, laughing, walking slowly while he floundered, trying to get his rubber legs to move.

He looked behind him. There was a gray shape, something gray in the shadows, moving, stalking him.

But this wasn't right. He was awake—he wasn't dreaming —and he'd been thinking of how it felt to be shot.

Over and over, he'd worked through this same memory, and it never changed.

It had no business turning into a dream about something chasing him into the guttering light of a black candle, not when his eyes were open. He could *see* the room. The white wall. The darkened TV set that was mounted close to the ceiling.

He could feel the bed covers, and the cold, beaded wet touch of the plastic pitcher of ice water on the metal stand by the side of his bed.

He was awake in bed, but something was chasing him through a bad dream at the same time. He wasn't moving, but he had to run.

There wasn't any candle so big in all the world, but the top of it roared like a building on fire, and people were burning like ants in the flame.

Jermell tried to scramble away, his legs not working. He felt for handholds, for a door, for *something*.

He found a dreamworld with no walls behind him, no ceiling above him, nothing under his feet.

It was just him and the everlasting darkness, mottled with swirling shades of gray and black, and over the darkest part of it, a gray shape pulling itself from the void.

Where are they?

Jermell heard the voice. It seemed to come from everywhere at the same time, like a hard, hot wind circling him— a wind that snapped, threatening pain.

Where are they?

Jermell had the awful sense that all this was going on deep inside him, somewhere in all the blood and the organs inside him, not just in his mind.

His body was the universe. And this was happening on a dark, tiny patch of forsaken ground in a winding cave on a little planet, surrounded by the everlasting darkness that ruled inside the body.

Now, he watched as the gray figure loomed larger, writhing, twisting like smoke in the wind.

He saw yellow-red eyes in the haze, coming toward him— a snake with the head of a ram.

WIIERRRRRE ARE THEYYYYY . . .

Jermell screamed as the words knifed through him, circling and tearing like razored cables. He heard himself shouting into the storm cloud that roiled around him: "*I don't know what you want, I don't know who . . .*"

Images crowded his mind—forced on him. He saw Goldie. Bare chest, ribs showing, thin arms. Goldie saying, "Vincent says three minutes. That's all you've got—grandpa. Grand-pa-pa."

Concho with the Uzi. B.J., swinging his club. Terry.

He saw himself—him and Wart, piling out of the ambulance, only Wart was the one in sharp focus, and Jermell didn't matter so much.

He remembered how big he'd felt at that moment, but he looked small, like a kid. And then Vincent. Vincent with his knife to the throat of the blond-haired ambulance driver.

Vincent saying, "Lighten up, grandpa."

Vincent: and a flash of the knife.

Images, memories—all of them ripped out of someone else's mind. Out of grandpa's mind.

Jermell couldn't have said how he knew, but he understood as clearly as if he'd known all along. *Out of grandpa's mind.* He knew—in the same way he knew how he'd been found in this bed.

Jermell knew he'd been tracked. Something was after him —some . . . thing that was able to find him by tearing through people's thoughts.

Grandpa. A nurse named Teresa. A doctor whose wife was expecting a baby. A detective named Frank—

The hunter had transferred from one to another, another, another, and more people who never knew they'd served the hunter's purpose. It rode on thought streams until it found what it wanted.

It wanted Jermell.

WHERE?

Jermell screamed at the pain that snaked under the skin of his back, burrowing into the bullet hole, filling him with a sound like the tolling of a huge bell.

He screamed out the name of the Palace—told the gray thing all it wanted to know, answered every question with a ragged, sobbing shout.

And when the voice told Jermell to *think* about the Palace, he did, desperately, until he could smell the urine and feel the darkness of the place in the depths of his soul.

Until he was there.

There!

There!

And the voice left him, riding away on his thoughts, out of the cave, out of the universe, gone.

Jermell knew that he was crying at last, but he was screaming, too, scalding his throat as the secrets spilled out of him.

"The Palace, the Palace, Palace!"

The door to his room opened. Nurse white, cop blue. They were listening, but he couldn't stop.

"THE PALACE! Cobras! Vincent! Vincent! The penthouse! Vincent!"

The voice had left him with another hole—a wound in his
mind that he knew wouldn't heal, so gaping that he could fall
into it, lost forever, unless he told what he knew.

And kept telling, kept telling—

The Palace. Vincent. The penthouse.

21

Case cracked open the door to make certain the hallway remained empty. It wasn't.

The pretty girl's hazel-colored eyes shot wide in surprise. "Oh!" she said, and then laughed a little.

Her blouse was striped pink-and-white. She offered him a smile that could have brought him to his knees.

"I didn't expect to see you up, Mr. Hamilton," she said, gesturing toward the cart she was pushing. It was loaded full of magazines and paperback books.

"Would you like something to read?" she asked. "Oh, I know. There's one in here that Mrs. McMasters said we ought to save for you."

Busily, she sorted through the books on top of the cart.

Case focused on reading the name pin she wore on the cheery blouse that identified her as a hospital candy striper —reading it over and over, anything to hold himself together, to keep his mind in control.

Kelly, Kelly, Kelly, Kelly—

"Here it is!" she said in triumph, withdrawing a paperback book that she handed toward him.

He saw the cowboy on the cover, and the six-gun, and the author's name in Texas-sized letters. Max Brand.

"T-thank you." He accepted the book in a trembling hand.

A look of worry crept into the bright eyes.

"I don't think you should be out of bed, though, Mr. Hamilton," she said. "Let me help you back to—"

She reached toward the door, pressing it toward him. Case tried to hold the door closed, and it couldn't have opened more than an inch wider. She couldn't have seen much.

But there was a lot of blood to see.

Kelly's hand pulled back as if she'd been stung. Both hands went to her face, fingers splayed over the sides of her face, and her mouth dropped open.

She was going to scream. Case knew it. He had to stop her.

He looped his arm around her narrow waist like an impetuous lover, pulling her inside the room, closing the door, dropping the book into a smear of blood on the floor.

"I'm sorry," he told her, keeping her faced toward the door. "I'm real sorry, Kelly."

She coughed, gasping, trying to break free of him. But he held her with one big arm wrapped around her middle, the other hand poised over her mouth, ready to keep her from screaming, and she was no more than a kitten trying to squirm loose.

"I don't want to hurt you, Kelly, but you're going to have to help me," Case said. "Will you help me?"

Her breathing steadied. He knew she must be scared, but she wasn't hurt. She nodded her head a little.

"You don't want to see in here," Case said, making sure that she couldn't. "For what it's worth—I didn't do this. But I've got to get away. Understand?"

She nodded.

Understand? Hell, no, she didn't, Case thought. How could she?

He didn't understand, except that he seemed to be making

things worse, but he couldn't see a choice. He had to get away.

He was clear in his head, and he'd told her the truth—all he knew of the truth. *I didn't do this.*

He swallowed a breath.

"I want you to do what I say, Kelly," Case said. "I'm going to let go a little . . . there, a little looser. Okay? And I want you to reach down . . . and take off your shoes. But keep your eyes closed. Don't talk. Don't turn around."

She made a sound that might have been a sob, but she did what he told her.

He felt sick. He remembered a greasy-haired creep he'd beaten senseless for acting this way—for terrorizing women.

No problem, Frank. Hey! Book 'im for impersonating a piñata.

The shoes thumped loose. One, two.

"Take out the laces. Hand me the laces," Case said, and she did what he told her.

She tried to pull free of him, but he tightened his grip.

"Easy, Kelly. Nothing bad's going to happen," he said. But he had no right to promise.

He had no way of knowing if the Gray Man was gone, or if the Gray Man might wrench her away from him at any moment, just like Teresa McMasters.

He said, "Take off your socks. Hand me the socks, too," fighting the urge to forget this, to quit, to let her go, to let her run screaming.

But he couldn't. Whatever was happening—he knew he wouldn't find the answer by allowing himself to be arrested for murder, not if he could escape without harm to another person.

He made it a vow, an absolute condition of his escape from the hospital: *no harm.*

Case told her to open her mouth. Dropping one of the

ankle socks, he rolled the other into a tight ball that he forced into her mouth, pressing it in past the edge of her teeth to make it difficult to dislodge.

Still holding her with his left arm, he loosened the right. He pulled a length of tape loose from his side, wincing.

He fastened the tape across her mouth.

"This makes it all the more important for you to stay calm," Case said. "Nod once if you can breathe all right."

He waited for the nod before his next move.

He brought her hands together behind her back, tying her thumbs together with one of the twelve-inch shoelaces, telling her she was going to be all right, feeling the shakes that ran through her.

He realized it might have been kinder, after all, to knock the girl out with a crack to the jaw, but he might have broken her jaw.

"Last thing," he told her. He would tie her feet together by the big toes with the remaining shoelace. But he would have to kneel.

Free of his grip, she could be a problem. She could throw herself against the door to rouse attention from the outside. He couldn't take the risk.

No harm. Only one other way. She would have to be too scared to move.

"I lied, Kelly," he said. "I killed the nurse in here. She wasn't smart. She didn't do what I told her. But you're going to do what I say, aren't you, Kelly? Don't you want to stay alive?"

She nodded.

"I know you do. Just take it easy."

He knelt to her feet—to find them sheathed in nylon hosiery. He could have sworn aloud, but the exclamation came out as a rush of breath between his teeth.

He loosened her white skirt, undoing the catch, the zipper in the back.

She wrenched away, turning toward him, into the room. She saw the extent of the carnage. Everything he'd meant to hide from her.

Her eyes went wild. There were screams in her eyes.

She kicked at him, trying for a sharp knee to the groin, missing, landing a jolt to his thigh that translated to a splitting pain from the wound in his side. But she was off-balance.

He moved in, grabbed her by the shoulders. He turned her toward the wall next to the door, forcing her into the wall, holding her there by the force of his weight.

His thumbs hooked into the waistband of her skirt, pressing down until the light garment fell loose.

"I need for you to step out of your skirt . . . now. Right now, Kelly. Easy does it. Easy. Out and away. There we go."

Kneeling quickly, he found the shoelace that he'd dropped on the floor. He pulled the loose skirt tight around her ankles in a loop that he closed just above her heels, tied shut with the shoelace.

Tied. Gagged. Hobbled. He'd done a proud piece of work. He felt like he ought to be beaten with sticks until he broke open.

He tore a handful of clean pages out of the paperback novel she'd brought to him to wipe the blood off his feet.

He cracked the door again, seeing the hallway was empty, checking the room number. Two-thirty-one. A card with his name on it was slipped into an open-topped holder to the side of the door.

He pulled the name card from the holder, stuffing the slip of paper into his pants pocket.

Two-thirty-one. The number told him where he was, where the nurses' station was, where the linen closet was.

He listened for voices. Nothing.

"Goin' for a ride, Kelly," he said, and scooped her up, ignoring the stab of pain in his side, the feeling of stitches pulled. Her legs felt cold. He tried to keep from looking into her eyes.

He knew he shouldn't have risked being seen with her, but he couldn't bear to leave her in the murder room.

He carried her halfway down the hallway to a different world, to the clean-smelling linen closet, yanking the door open.

Gently, he lowered her onto the closet floor. "I'm sorry," he said again, knowing she must have been terrified. "I'll send help for you."

Case started to back from the door, but the voices stopped him, warning him. He wasn't alone.

Case forced himself into the darkened closet, pulling the door shut, breathing in the smell of soap.

Kelly voiced a moaning sound through the gag in her mouth.

"Be quiet," he warned her, whispering.

Heard footsteps. Closer.

A child's voice, close to tears. "Isn't Grampa *ever* coming home?"

A woman's voice, patient, wearied, answering. "Not today, Christopher. Maybe tomorrow, though. Maybe tomorrow."

The voices dimmed, and Case chanced a look into the silent corridor, seeing it was empty again, except for Kelly's magazine cart.

He stepped out, closing the door.

Be quiet, he prayed in the secret cathedral. *Just a few more minutes.*

Moving quickly, he pushed the magazine cart out of sight, into 231.

He checked the name slips posted on the other closed doors. Margaret Allen. G. Platt. Emily Wilkerson. Wm. Doverspike.

He gave Doverspike a try, pushing through the door that was marked with a red-on-white sign that read "Please. No Visitors. Oxygen in Use."

Heart pounding, he saw the room was dim, the TV off, the bed shrouded with an oxygen tent. The man on the bed looked as gray, as ancient as a mummy underneath the plastic.

Case opened the locker-sized, metal closet. Doverspike's clothes all hung neatly in place, the way a worried daughter might have arranged them. The pants were too small to take seriously, but Case was able to squeeze into the white shirt, rolling the cuffs back to hide the short fit of the sleeves. He shoved his feet into the shoes.

There was a full-length mirror fastened to the door inside the closet. He braced to see himself looking like death in a handcart. But he didn't.

His eyes were clear snaps of white, and the skin on his face looked smooth and healthy, and he was standing straight.

He gaped at the stranger's reflection, and he might have just stood there, lost in amazement. But a spot of red on the white shirt told him his side was bleeding. He couldn't lose time.

He took Doverspike's name card on his way out of the room, dropping his own name into Doverspike's holder. He lifted the no-visitors sign.

All but running, he dropped Doverspike's name into the holder on 231, posting the door to prohibit company—buying himself, maybe, a few minutes' confusion, and maybe not.

Case saw a glimmer of red showing under the door to 231, a trickle of blood starting to well into the hallway.

He made the stairway exit, thinking he might have heard a thumping noise from down the hallway, very much like the sound of a girl's bare feet kicking the closet door.

He played to his only advantage—that he knew the layout of the hospital, the back ways, the ways that most people wouldn't have gone.

Third floor. It was the wrong way to run, but he could move through a series of clinics that weren't likely to be used at night, reaching a service elevator that most of the hospital's staff wouldn't touch, frightened of the old car's creaks and rattles as it lurched its way down.

First floor. Out of the elevator, down the long hallway that led to a side exit.

He couldn't avoid being seen by other people in the hallway. But he walked like a man determined not to make himself the target of a street mugging: straight ahead, moving with a purpose, shoulders back, head up, careful not to establish eye contact.

He thought he could feel other people's eyes on him like burning weights.

He passed a nurse, an old man with a walker, a woman carrying a multicolored bouquet of balloons. But *they* didn't know there was anything wrong with him.

They wouldn't know—not so long as he kept moving, kept his hand poised loosely to cover the bloodstain on the shirt. They all had concerns of their own. They weren't looking for killers.

A candy striper smiled a greeting to him. She was dark-haired, heavy in the waist, and she didn't look at all like

Kelly. But the sight of her pink-and-white blouse made him reel in guilty knowledge, and he thought the feeling must have shown like flames pouring out of his ears.

"Hello," she said simply, and walked past him, leaving the way clear to him—a straight shot to the doors at the end of the hallway.

Sunlight!

He looked up past the zigzag line of the fire escape to the top of the building, to the bright blue of the clearest sky he'd ever seen.

The first breath of fresh air amazed him, as if he'd never tasted a summer day before—a fresh day, washed clean by the rain.

He walked through rippling puddles of rainwater on the sidewalk, past azalea bushes humming with bees, mapping out the last of his escape from the hospital.

His Jeep was on the second level of the parking garage. He didn't have the keys, but he could hot-wire the ignition.

No. Think about it.

There was no way he could leave the garage without driving past the guard booth, where he might be recognized. And he would be too easy to spot in his own vehicle.

The Jeep had to stay where it was. He'd have to find another means of escape.

A bullhorn-amplified voice carried to him from the front of the hospital, calling out, "Abortion stops a beating heart! Abortion stops a beating heart!" The voice led a syncopated chant. Pounding voices echoed the words, throbbing with the sound of righteous anger.

"Abortion stops a beating heart!"

Case rounded the building, taking in the sight: a blue line

of uniformed police officers. Motorcycles. Flashing red lights from an array of patrol cars.

The blues were forcing a swollen crowd of two hundred—maybe three hundred—sign-carrying protesters to stay across the street from Cedar Ridge. They massed along the curb in front of a strip shopping center, spilling into the street.

TV cameras took it all in. The protesters marched in a ragged line back and forth on the sidewalk, waving their signs like war clubs, chanting.

"Abortion stops a beating heart!"

A chartered bus hissed to the curb fifty yards from the marchers, around the corner from the strip center, disgorging a stream of people with more signs—pro-choice slogans.

"Our bodies, our choice!" *"Every child deserves love!"*

They began taking up their own positions, forming their own line of marchers. Someone hit the bus horn in time to the chant of *"Abortion stops a beating heart!"* hammering away.

The noise became an uproar, the bleat of the horn obscuring each word of the chant, the chant giving way, broken to cries of fury.

A bottle, a rock—*something* smashed into the windshield of the bus, and the cops were moving to quell the start of a street riot.

Case made his move.

A car thief couldn't have asked for a better distraction.

22

B.J. opened the door just a crack, squinting from stale darkness into the blurry, hard light of the afternoon.

There were the girls—Cyan and her sister, Cheyenne, having followed his directions. *There's a first,* he thought. *They got it right. Scratch a mark on the wall.*

He jammed the murder stick he carried into the waistband of his jeans, liking the hard feel of it.

Cyan was fifteen. Cheyenne might have been older, maybe younger; it didn't matter. They looked about the same. Same skintight, cutoff jeans; same waxy, hot-pink look to the lipstick, and both girls wearing stretchy tank tops that were striped in garish greens and oranges, greens and purples. Cheyenne chewed gum with an openmouthed smack. Cyan's top stretched just a little bit more.

B.J. found that he was looking into Cyan's placid face—a round face that seemed all the rounder for being framed by lines of straight blond hair, with eyes as void of intelligence as a couple of blue gumballs.

Her arms were loaded with sacked groceries from Jiffy Bob's, and her sister was standing behind her, holding more brown-paper sacks, looking just as vacant. But he felt a secret thrill.

It was like living a movie. Here was the gang, gone into hiding. The gangster risks a phone call to his girl friend. She turns up with all the good shit they're going to need to stay out of sight—sacks of lunch meat and bread, sacks of beer. And she'd better have some good Colombian grass, too, he thought, or he might have to whack her one.

"What's up?" Cyan asked, juggling the sacks, almost dropping a bunch of the stuff. She must have lost her grip in the moment it took her to knock on the door.

B.J. opened the door halfway, peering into the alley. It was a perfect setup. Nobody came around this place—nobody but the old crazy they called the Prophet, and he seemed to have boned out.

Just as well, too. B.J. was going to crack the old man with his steel-tipped club the next time he got a chance. *That!*—for having called B.J. a "worshiper of graven images," chucking a beer bottle at him.

B.J. pulled the girls into the building—Cyan, then Cheyenne, in a racket of crinkling paper, clattering canned goods.

"Glad to see me?" Cyan asked.

"Yeah. Sure, babe," he said.

"Jeez, it's dark." The door shut, and something like a tin can fell to the floor with a dead thump. "Jeeez," she said, and must have liked the way she could stretch the word into a squeal. "Jeeeez."

Cheyenne never talked.

B.J. herded the girls through the darkness, toward the auditorium, thinking he *was* glad to see Cyan.

Maybe she wasn't the smartest thing on earth, but she wasn't any mud duck, either, and there had been times she'd let him wet his finger in front of the other gangsters.

The others. He remembered how sick he felt.

The others. Concho. He'd seen Concho zapped through the head.

Goldie. Jermell. Wart. Gone.

And he was wishing there could have been just one more bullet, just one more dead Cobra.

Vincent. He'd thought of Vincent as being his main man, ace kool, but he'd thought wrong.

He heard Cyan in the darkness behind him. "Jeeeeez! Cobwebs."

Ahead of him, B.J. heard Vincent's high-pitched laughter set against the mindless, rattling sound of a laugh-track from the TV set.

The Palace reeked of urine, some of it fresh—and of dead, cheap wine, and stale air, and darkness.

It hadn't always been this way. B.J. knew from having found an old scrapbook in the ruined lobby a couple of months ago, when the Cobras moved in. The warped binder had been stuffed with water-stained, yellowed newspaper clippings.

He'd found a crisp dollar bill tucked between the first and second pages—enough to make him want to keep looking.

The last page was a newspaper story that told of the movie house closing in 1989, headlined, "Palace No Longer Fit for a King," and the story read:

The Palace Theater closed today, boarded shut. In its prime, it showed "Gone With the Wind" with an elegance that would have satisfied Scarlett O'Hara. But not even Rhett Butler could give a damn that it's gone.

The Palace stood as a city landmark of the 1930s and forties. Children of the fifties thrilled to all-day showings of cowboy movies and serial chapters on the king-size screen.

By the end of the sixties, however, the old theater had become a grind house for soft-core pornography that turned progressively cheaper and meaner, until not even Debbie would have done it in the Palace.

A series of fistfights and knifings in the old wreck of a theater led to its first of several closings, although it kept coming back under different ownerships, as hard to keep down as a Hollywood vampire.

This time, it appears to be closed for good, though. Closed as a public health hazard under city order, the latest owner having disappeared while under investigation for tax fraud.

And here is a last look at the splendor of yesterday. Padding is ripped from most of the seats, leaving metal skeletons. The floor is deep in trash.

Heavy with the dust of many years, the old curtain hangs in tatters on both sides of the torn screen, like a desecrated flag at the scene of a sad battle that was lost a long time ago.

B.J. liked the newspaper story. He often remembered it, partly because he was impressed that somebody could write such a dead-on description of the Cobras' hideout.

He liked it, too, because it reminded him of when he used to read a lot, all kinds of books. There was a time he'd been determined to be his family's first college graduate. His grades were up, and he worked hard on cleaning the sound of street talk out of his language.

But then—Vincent. He met Vincent the year they were both seventeen, almost a year ago, and B.J.'s straight life took a wild spin into the ozone.

Vincent had taught him a curriculum of drugs in place of school texts: his first trip on mother's milk. And Vincent had shown him the value of power in place of achievement—the power that came of *belonging* as one of the Cobras, and of knowing that people were scared of him on sight.

The strange, secret truth was that B.J. never did care much about drugs and gang life, even though he'd given up his books and his life's ambitions to be a part of Vincent's gang. It was something about Vincent . . . something compelling in Vincent's dark eyes, something that knew him as well as a best friend and a worst enemy, all in one.

B.J. knew Vincent's idea of robbing the hospital had been nothing but bugfucked crazy from the start, just a chance to get killed for no reason. But he'd still gone along with it, just like the rest of the Cobras who probably knew better. He did what Vincent wanted, *whatever* Vincent wanted. Vincent never stopped wanting.

He remembered kicking the gray-haired man in the guard uniform. Vincent already had stuck the old man. The guard was down, dead to the world, and B.J. kicked him in the back.

He didn't want to kick the man. But he couldn't cross Vincent. He couldn't set Vincent against him, or B.J. would be the next one to feel the serrated blade of Vincent's knife in his stomach.

The thought of the knife sent a shudder through him, so violent that B.J. stumbled in the dark. He was glad the girls couldn't see what caused him to lose his footing.

But something had snapped inside of him when he kicked the man. All of a sudden, B.J. was sick of himself, sick of Vincent, and he wanted his old life back. He wanted loose. He wondered if Vincent would ever allow it.

"C'mon," he said, and moved them along with a crinkling of the grocery sacks toward the dead laughter from the TV.

B.J. and the girls joined Vincent's gig on the stage in front of the screen—the only part of the auditorium that had much light, although a couple of ancient globes in the high ceiling still cast off a stubborn glow.

Electrical cords trailed over scarred boards that dated to vaudeville times. Now, the stage looked like a living-room set designed for a theater of the absurd—a story about a family of down-and-outers, given to dragging home odd bits of furniture.

"Soup's on," B.J. said, wishing he hadn't. *Soup's on* was an expression he'd learned in his aunt Lois's kitchen, and saying it here was like spitting on one of his best memories.

Terry looked up, picking at one of the scabbed cuts on his shaved head. " 'Bout time," he said.

Vincent stared straight at the TV, saying nothing.

They ate from cans, substituting an occasional beer belch for the niceties of dinner conversation, staring at the TV.

The color television set was brand-new. Like the half-dozen lamps and the stereo, it was patched into an electrical pole behind the old theater. The lamps were a jumble: a floor lamp with a yellow shade decked in Santa Fe chic, a couple of table lamps boosted from K mart, a lava lamp . . . all of them set on the floor, surrounding a camel-backed sofa, a stained mattress, and a couple of hard-backed kitchen chairs.

The TV offered a rerun of *Gilligan's Island* to the Cobras —what was left of them—and the scent of day-old fear hung over the survivors, mingling with the smell of blood and fortified wine.

Gilligan threw a coconut at the Skipper. Vincent laughed.

The three P.M. news update hadn't told them anything different. The Man was still after them. But The Man didn't know shit.

The Skipper made a face, and Vincent laughed.

B.J.'s lady, Cyan, sat curled on his lap, stroking his hair, her face blank, while B.J. gave Vincent the red-eyed glare.

He stared at Vincent, rubbed his nose, ran a cigarette back and forth along his lower lip, threw the cigarette away, rubbed his nose again. He cleared his throat.

"So, man?" he began.

Vincent was cutting small patterns in one arm of the sofa, twisting the blade of his Rambo knife deep inside, pulling out white tufts of stuffing, high on mother's milk.

Sometimes, the shit made him brilliant, like he was able to see right into people. But sometimes not. B.J. couldn't be sure Vincent was seeing much of anything right now, maybe not even the TV set.

"Vincent . . . you hear me, man?"

Vincent stopped picking at the sofa long enough to look at B.J., letting his gaze drift to Terry, sprawled on the mattress, then to Cyan. He seemed to be seeing her for the first time. Cyan's eyes flickered away.

"I mean," B.J. said, leaning in, "we gonna have to do *somethin'*."

Vincent seemed to consider this. He nodded.

"So," asked B.J. "What you wanna do?"

"I . . . did it," Vincent said, the words dragging out of his throat. A grin twisted across his face. "See?" he said, lifting his hands. He giggled. "*See?*"

There was blood on his hands, blood he'd refused to wash off, blood dried long ago to the color of rust. He looked at his hands, at the blood, turning his hands back and forth, so the others could see.

B.J. turned to Terry with a slight shake of his head, a slight clenching of teeth.

Vincent dropped his hands, his face suddenly dark, his eyes flashing. "You got a problem with that, muhfuh?" He stared at B.J. over the edge of the knife blade.

B.J. felt a cold rush of fear. Fear of the knife.

B.J. said, "No, man, but—"

"But *lick* my butt," Vincent said. He unscrewed the top of the knife, shook out a handful of pills. He swallowed the white pills with a long swig from the gallon bottle of grape wine that he kept beside him. "Kiss my muhfuggin' ass."

B.J. shook his head. "Vincent, man—you don't need no more'a that shit. We need to *think*, man. You *know* they're gonna find us here, sooner or later, if we don't haul ass outta here. You *know*—"

"I know I'm fuckin' sick of you!" Vincent shouted. He rose suddenly from the sofa and wiped a lock of his black hair back from his forehead. "And I'm fuckin' sick of this *noise*, all this goddam *noise!*"

He grabbed the wine bottle and twirled around unsteadily, pitching the bottle hard into the TV set. The screen exploded into a shower of glass, and Cheyenne screamed, discovering that she did have a voice, after all.

B.J. was on his feet, the steel-headed club in his hand, yelling, "What the hell was *that* for?"

Everyone was standing now, as Vincent approached B.J. The big knife gleamed in Vincent's fist.

B.J. didn't know how he'd acquired the fear. He'd always had it, always hidden it—this fear of being cut, of knife edges, razor cuts, broken glass, of skin splitting open, of black splitting open to red, of the blood welling out.

"I did it, muhfuh," Vincent said slowly, "because I can do anything. Nothing can stop me." He pointed the blade toward B.J.'s neck, his hand steady. "Ain't that right?"

B.J. pushed his lady aside, his long-fingered hands like wet slabs on her shoulders. She didn't need much of a push. "Sure, Vincent," he said, staring at the Cobras' leader—at the gleam of the serrated knife. "Sure, you can."

"I can kill a man, can't I?"

"Yeah."

"I can take all the tabs—I can drink all the mad dog I want, can't I?"

B.J. took a moment to answer, his eyes flickering toward

the knife. "A'right, Vincent," he said, his face cold with sweat, the sting of sweat in his eyes. "Yeah."

Vincent gave him a wink, but it came with a jab of the knife that drew a bead of blood from B.J.'s left cheek, just below the eye. B.J. couldn't seem to move.

"Yeah. I can even trim your l'il bitch here, can't I?" Vincent said.

B.J. looked to his blank-faced girl friend. She seemed as still as a rabbit, just about to run. She reached for B.J.'s shoulder.

"C'mon, Vincent," B.J. said, licking his dry lips. "We don't need to be doin' this shit. We need to be—"

"I'll tell you what we need to be doin', muhfuh!" Vincent interrupted savagely. He whipped the knife across B.J.'s upper arm, deep enough to hurt, hard enough to spray blood.

B.J. howled and swore, grabbing at his arm. Vincent cut him again, a jab to the side. Again. A nick on the ear. Playing with him. A slice to the wrist, a slice to the fingers—forcing B.J. to drop the club.

Cyan started to bolt, but Vincent grabbed her by the shoulder with one hand. B.J. staggered to a chair.

He wished Vincent had killed him. He'd rather have died, but he hadn't died. He'd been shamed, instead. Scratched.

B.J. willed his hand to reach for the club on the floor. It wasn't too late for him—not if he could reach the club, and he would give Vincent a jacking-up that would settle the score with Vincent dead.

But his hand didn't move. His arm wouldn't work.

Nothing worked but burning in his throat that made him want to cry and that left him with nothing else to care about, nothing else to do.

Terry and Cheyenne stood watching him like they were watching TV, like they couldn't tell the difference between B.J. and Vincent, and Gilligan and the Skipper.

Cheyenne tried a feeble reach for her sister, but she quickly pulled her hand back as Vincent began shoving Cyan forward, toward the edge of the stage.

"C'mon, Cyan, cry-ann, die-ann, sssssi-ann," Vincent said, making a snake's hiss of her pretty name, twisting her arm behind her. "Let's go to the penthouse."

23

The door was plastered with a life-size poster of a nude woman, torn along the edges. She had giant breasts and bovine eyes, and her hand was between her legs, the fingers spread.

With an impact that rattled the hinges, Vincent whammed the sole of his Reebok into the naked woman's fingers, stamping tread marks onto the paper.

The door opened to the damp, dark smell of a narrow stairway that corkscrewed up creaking boards. Vincent forced Cyan in front of him, shoving her from behind, sometimes jamming his hand between her legs, all but lifting her off her feet, pitching her forward to stumble on the darkened stairs.

He didn't care if it hurt. She never expected he would, and she wished she could cry. She thought she ought to be crying. She knew her mother would have cried.

Cyan had started to cry a couple of times on the long trip through the movie theater, but she couldn't quite get everything to work right. The trouble might have been the way that Vincent kept shoving at her. She couldn't think. There was a burning, swelling kind of sweetness in her throat, but it never lasted long enough.

Her face would screw up, and she would start to make a sobbing sound. A few tears would squeeze out of her eyes, hot as fire. But the tears seemed to stop for no reason, and the whole sense of needing to cry would recede from her.

Now, everything seemed to have slipped far away—except for the raspy sound of Vincent's breathing, and the pressure of his hand, and the calmness that came of knowing that she was going to be hurt.

She had been hurt before, and she would be hurt again. She was a good healer.

The stairway led to a darkened landing, with a slit of light that marked the bottom of an ill-fitted door.

Vincent reached past her to push the door open. He smacked a wall switch. The light was from a yellowed bulb that dangled on a cord from the ceiling. Roaches skittered in waves over the floor, casting shadows bigger than themselves.

He gave her a last shove. She spun away from him with a little cry, out of balance, toppling onto the dirty, sheetless mattress in the middle of the floor.

"Make yourself comfortable," Vincent hissed.

Cyan looked around. In a weird way, she felt special. She'd never been up here before—up in the penthouse, Vincent's penthouse, where the Cobras had their important meetings.

B.J. had told her it used to be the movie theater's projection room. It used to be a place where they showed the movies on big projectors, but the machines were long gone, leaving the floor blotched with oddly shaped patches of wood as pale as Cyan's legs.

There were three of these marks on the floor, aligned with three small, rectangular openings in the concrete wall behind her. There was a broken window in the wall, too—like a tiny playhouse window, hardly big enough to crawl through. It was just at eye level.

Looking through the window, she imagined she would have seen the inside of the movie theater, down to the rows of ruined seats, across to the gray wall of the old screen.

If she *did* crawl through, it would be a fifteen-foot drop to the darkened floor, onto the bare frames of the old seats.

"Like it?" Vincent said, coming toward her, stripping off his shirt. His chest was lean and muscled like a rock star might have looked, glistening with sweat.

The hanging bulb illuminated a splintery workbench notched with cigarette burns, littered with bottles and beer cans that made it look the same as the floor.

The room smelled of ketchup and rot from its accumulations of fast-food wrappers printed with cheery stripes and cartoon animals.

All this, Cyan realized in a half-dozen heartbeats—all this, before she saw the pictures.

There were hundreds of pictures, all around the walls. They were curled and cracked and warped, pictures of women in swimsuits and underwear, old black-and-white pictures, some of them plastered over by newer, cruder shots from sex magazines, showing everything in color. Showing it all.

The women in the photos looked down on her, there on the mattress, some of them smiling sexily, some with wide eyes in black-and-white prints, as though they had been caught by surprise in their underwear by some sneaky guy with a camera.

The ones in the new color photos from the magazines all had the same look, though. They looked half-bored and half-mean, and they looked at her coldly, even as Vincent surprised her with another shove, pushing her flat against the stinking mattress again, looking up.

She saw their eyes, their faces, read their single thought: *Serves you right, bitch.*

And she found that she *could* cry, after all, but it was no comfort.

She thought she saw tears streaming down from the eyes on the wall, but then she couldn't see the wall—only a different pair of eyes, big eyes, mean eyes. Vincent's eyes.

Vincent wrapped his fingers in her hair, hauling her close to him. His face was all she could see. And he was staring into her, and Cyan felt a sense of rape that she'd never experienced before. He was into her mind. Something hurt inside her head.

Even if she closed her eyes, she still saw Vincent's face. But it was longer, darker, sharper-edged inside her mind, bent like a face in a fun-house mirror, the tongue black and coiling.

"I can make you do anything," Vincent said, and she saw for the first time that his face was ugly. Twisted.

She knew why B.J. said that Vincent was crazy, only he said it like being crazy meant something good. He should have said it like something as ugly as the twist to Vincent's lip.

And where *was* B.J.? she thought, choking back tears. She was B.J.'s lady. B.J. looked out for her. He was *supposed* to look out for her. She couldn't believe he was letting this happen.

"I have a . . . secret power," Vincent said, so close to her now that his face fell into shadow. His breath smelled of the sourness that came from staying high on mother's milk.

"Do you believe me?" His words soured the air. "Say it."

She tried to talk. Couldn't. He loosened his hold on her, just a little, playing with her. He leaned back.

Behind his head, a wall of women looked at them, and

Cyan thought she saw some of them move. Blink. Smile. Touch.

Vincent grinned at her. "What can I make you do?"

"You can . . . make me do . . . anything," Cyan said.

"Stand up."

She did, and he rose alongside of her.

"People do what I want—whatever I want," Vincent said, almost a whisper, the words hissing. "Not just those circle-jerks . . ." He spoke with a minimal nod of his head to the concrete-block wall, as if he could see through the wall, down into the movie theater. "People!"

Vincent jabbed his index fingers into the sides of his head with a twisting motion. "People don't have any choice. *You* don't have any choice. Am I right?"

His eyes seemed to swell. A Y-shaped blue vein stood out from his forehead, thick as a worm. A trickle of red spilled from his nose.

"Y-yes," she said, swallowing. She imagined he must have meant that he could beam out rays of thought control, like a hypnotist in a horror movie. And maybe he could. Vincent had some kind of hold on B.J.

Cyan didn't feel any rays of mind control, though, unless he was beaming at her to feel like throwing up. It was just that she *wanted* to do what he said—to make him happy.

"I could say . . . I want you on your hands and knees. What would happen?" Vincent said.

She faltered, unsure if he expected an answer or if he meant for her to do it.

He struck her across the face. He began hitting her with his open hand, popping her, pushing her at the end of each blow, watching as she staggered. Her feet stumbled off the mattress, onto the wooden floor.

The flat of his hand slammed her shoulder, spinning her full around.

"Vincent—please, Vincent," she said, trying to turn toward him. "I—I'll do what you want. Jus' tell me—"

"This!" he said, pushing. Hitting. "This is what I want."

Cyan wiped at her nose, her mouth. She wasn't sure where all the blood was coming from, and there might have been some in her eye, too.

He shoved her toward the concrete wall where the projectors had been. Cyan tripped forward. Her hands caught the casing of the broken window, and she hauled herself up.

Jagged shards of glass glittered inside the small, dark opening in front of her.

Looking at the glass, and not at Vincent, Cyan lost the strange feeling that she wanted to please him. She found a different thought.

Maybe there would be a piece of glass big enough to stab him like a knife, she thought—to make him leave her alone.

There was. Her right hand closed around it, tugging at the glass.

It cut her fingers, but it snapped loose, and she was ready to show Vincent the surprise that she'd discovered for him—

A surprise she forgot when she saw through the window.

Down below, and through a film of tears, she saw her sister, Cheyenne, and B.J., and Terry on the stage that jutted into the auditorium from the front of the movie screen.

None of them bothered even to look toward her. None of them cared what happened to her—least of all B.J., still slumped in the chair, holding his wounded shoulder, his head down.

Big as he was, B.J. looked like nothing so much as a crybaby kid, sniffling for having fallen off his bike.

And the others: they were just standing around, switched off, waiting for something to happen. Waiting for Vincent.

They didn't care what happened to her, and she ached with a terrible emptiness.

Oh, jeeez; oh, jeeez; oh, jeeeez—

He was behind her again, his arms around her, his quick hands groping at the waistband of her jeans, working at the buttons.

But the buttons defied him. The buttons didn't care about his mind control, and Vincent howled a curse. He blamed Cyan.

His right arm locked across her throat like a slab of wet meat, slick with sweat.

She gasped as she felt herself being lifted, twisting, off the floor. Choking. Strangling.

Cyan tried to reach behind her, over her shoulders. She flailed toward Vincent's head with the blade of glass, but it never connected. He was screaming, laughing, crying, she couldn't tell which.

He let her go, and she toppled forward against the wall, feeling him tug at the stretchy material of her tank top, pulling it high as her chin, leaving her breasts exposed.

Vincent's hands were on her, around her, and one hand snaked down her bare stomach, this time mastering the buttons, tearing the last of them loose.

"Please—please, no, Vincent."

She heard her own voice as though it were in a dream. Her eyes were closed, her face pressed against the cold wall beside the broken-out window. Vincent grabbed and poked roughly, everywhere, tugging down her cutoffs and her panties at the same time.

"Vincent! Hey!" Terry shouted in a hollow voice from the cavern of the auditorium.

Cyan opened her eyes, trying to look through the projectionist's window. Everyone was staring up at her now, looking up from the stage.

Of course, they cared about her. They *did* care. They were just fooling. And Vincent had better watch out—

B.J. stood from the chair. He came up like a man in a movie, a man who'd been knocked cold in a crooked fight, but revived by a glass of water thrown in his face. A glass of water, and he was all right.

B.J. looked tall as a mountain, and the veins stood out like cords on the side of his neck, he was so mad.

B.J. yelled, "You don't touch my lady, Vincent!" And his eyes and his teeth flashed white. "You and me, Vincent— we're gonna get down, man, gonna get downnnnnn!"

Cyan imagined even more of B.J.'s revenge. She thought of him tearing into Vincent, and the dream scene buzzed through her like electricity even as Vincent pushed her face into the rough wall, holding her as he jerked her jeans the rest of the way down.

Numbly, automatically, she lifted her legs, one and then the other, so he could pull them off.

From the jagged opening, a burst of frigid air hit her face. It shocked her eyes even farther open.

"Vinnnncent!" The cry was louder now, and she could see it was Terry shouting.

Behind her, Vincent swore, loudly and hard. He looped his arm around her neck in a choke hold to drag her away from the window, thrusting his own face into the opening. He started cursing at Terry.

"Don't you *feel* it, man?" Terry's thin voice wafted through the window. "Can't you *feel* it up there?"

Vincent's arm loosened a little on Cyan's neck. She realized she still had the glass in her hand—all this time, working its way into the soft palm, still there.

She knew she would have just one chance, if that much. If

she got him in the neck . . . but what if she did? What would B.J. think of her?

Cyan decided she didn't care anymore what B.J. thought about anything, and she waited for Vincent to let go of her, just a little more.

A turn of her head, shift of the eyes; she could see out the window.

Terry shouted, "The fuggin' temperature, man." His words came out with puffs of white. "It's *cold* in here."

Vincent unleashed a stream of profanity that echoed into the dead air of the auditorium, and Cyan could see the ice on his breath. But he didn't seem to notice.

He didn't seem to care, either, about the frost patterns that traced the broken edges of the glass around the window, while Cyan discovered her lungs hurt from the shock of the cold air.

Vincent bellowed, "You find out what's wrong, and you fix it, you—"

Cheyenne screamed, cutting him short. She was pointing to a place below the stage, off to the corner—a darkened passage with a burnt-out EXIT sign above it.

Even B.J. was roused to stand, looking dazed, looking like a glass of water wouldn't do a thing for him.

Something burned with a white glow in the corner, exposing the cracked walls. It was the white of a snowstorm, swirling, glittering with crystals of ice.

And coming through the light—a walking shadow.

B.J.'s mouth hung open a moment, and he craned forward, shielding his eyes with the palm of his hand.

Cyan watched as a figure emerged from the light. The glint of a badge shone on the beige-colored shirt. Darker pants.

The man was heavily built, thick in the middle, nonetheless hard-looking. Broad shoulders. Cannonball hands.

B.J.'s mouth found the strength for a half grin. He said, "Well, shit!" He glanced up. "Look who's here, Vincent, it's grandpa. You know? Remember? Grandpa! Come to visit."

B.J. was swinging his steel-headed club on its leather thong, and he was yelling up to the penthouse, just the way that Cyan had imagined he would, his strong voice like a cannon.

"Remember what you said, Vincent? *'I can kill a man, can't I?'* Well, here's the answer, mother. See? Here's the answer on two feet, come to kick your butt."

Terry had the Magnum revolver in his hand, but B.J. forced him to lower it. "Stall it out," B.J. said. "This one don't worry us." He pointed toward the penthouse.

"Up there, grandpa," B.J. said.

There was a rust-colored stain on the side of grandpa's shirt, and he was holding his hand over the smear. Cyan tried to see his face against the light.

Vincent released her, his fingers gone slack.

She saw—but she already had the glass blade swung high above her head. What she'd seen took a long, cold moment to realize: Grandpa had no face.

No face!

But the blade already had started to fall; and Vincent saw it coming. He tried to block her arm.

She heard screaming through the window. Gunshots. Splintering wood.

The falling blade sliced Vincent across the back of his wrist, clearing the way, arching toward his heart.

The point of it struck him dead center in the chest, snapping off against the breastbone.

The glass snapped like a gunshot. She dropped what was left of the glass in her hand.

Vincent fell to his knees, holding his chest. Blood welled

around his hand, but not enough blood, Cyan thought. Not much blood at all.

He picked out a shard of the blade like a sliver. He looked at her, eyes storming, mouth twisting.

Some last, insane hope made her glance through the window, down to the stage. She saw blood spattered high on the screen. Blood spilling from the floor of the stage, over the front, spattering onto the torn bodies.

B.J. Terry. Cheyenne. All broken up like plastic dolls.

Cyan thought she was going to lose it—going to scream herself to death at the sight of her sister. All she wanted was to scream until her soul came loose inside.

Vincent had other ideas.

He pulled his Rambo knife free from the sheath that he'd taped to his ankle. The serrated blade flashed at her.

He climbed to his feet, coming toward her, swinging the knife back and forth in front of him, changing hands with it, making it jump through the air, making it rattle.

Cyan backed away from him, glass cracking beneath her bare feet, reminding her of just how vulnerable she was. Naked. Trapped. Numbed.

Cold.

The air fell to freezing—so cold, she felt her eyes seem to frost over. Everything white.

The point of the knife touched her throat. Just a pinprick, but it promised more, ever so much more.

But . . . the knife withdrew, frozen in light.

Cold as the glint of the knife blade. Cold as the shine in a killer's eye. Light spilled into the room, glittering with motes of ice, and Vincent turned.

The man with the badge stood at the far side of the room, motionless, twenty feet away. Cyan tried not to look at his face, but it was gray, and it was nothing.

The gray man lifted his right hand from the stained part of

his shirt. The shirt was slashed open. His finger played along the edges of the tear.

Vincent was slack-jawed, trembling, his tongue working around the hole of his mouth as if to mimic the gray man's strange gesture. But he raised the knife—

The gray man's big hand stretched away from the rip in his beige shirt. It shot across the room, fingers splayed, trailing vapors of gray mist, all in a second.

There were cuts on the gray hand, cuts on the gray arm, cuts that opened to pink gaps.

The gray fingers fastened like talons onto the wrist of Vincent's knife hand.

Vincent's hand froze to blue—a blue-white color spreading up his arm, over his shoulder, into his face, splitting the skin open. The dark hair frosted to white. The pretty teeth cracked.

Cold blue dulled the muscled shine of his chest, forcing a high-pitched wail from his throat, an animal whine, before something broke inside his throat with an audible crack.

A twist of the gray hand. Vincent's arm snapped apart.

The knife, the hand, the broken fingers clattered to the floor in bits, like the pieces to a broken puzzle.

More happened. Cyan hid beneath the workbench, back in the cobwebs, ignoring the tickling crawl of something up the back of her neck. She didn't look at the rest of what happened to Vincent. Not once.

She let it happen.

When it finally quit happening, Cyan stayed hidden. The old building settled into the quiet of a graveyard at midnight. She didn't care.

She heard water dripping. At least, she thought it might be water. Once, she heard a moan from deep inside the building.

She never moved. Not once.

A baby cried. Cyan knew it had to be a baby. The sound was so distinctively human.

The bawling seemed to fill the air, and then more than one cry, then a legion. A deafening wail.

She never moved. She never questioned.

She just hid where she was.

In the end, there were rats that came out before she did.

24

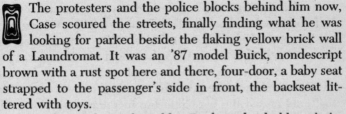 The protesters and the police blocks behind him now, Case scoured the streets, finally finding what he was looking for parked beside the flaking yellow brick wall of a Laundromat. It was an '87 model Buick, nondescript brown with a rust spot here and there, four-door, a baby seat strapped to the passenger's side in front, the backseat littered with toys.

Case glimpsed a Little Golden Book on the dashboard, the book's cover torn past the inquisitive nose of the Poky Little Puppy, next to a caved-in McDonald's Happy Meal box.

It was a family car. Run-around Mom's car. There were puffs of Kleenex stuffed into the crack between windshield and dash on the driver's side, spotted with rose-colored lip marks.

Case wasn't surprised to find the right-side back door unlocked. Run-around Mom rarely managed to keep all the doors locked.

Car thieves knew that. But Mom's old, messy car, full of rubbish and kids' smells, wasn't ordinarily so tempting. Only a desperate thief could see its charms.

To Case, the car was beyond temptation. He listened a moment, making sure no one was coming out the laundro-

mat's door around the corner, and then he was in the car,
tossing a stuffed kangaroo off the floorboard as he bent to his
task.

The wires sparked.

Moments later, he was gone.

Diana took a seat alone in the back of the hospital's auditorium, having already missed the start of the press conference.

She could see the whole arrangement—the orchestration
of the event, and how it all seemed to be working exactly as
Stephen had planned.

He was talking from a podium that was garnished with a
half-dozen microphones, talking into a ring of TV cameras.

She counted four TV cameramen. They were jostling for
position with each other, trying to crowd out the newspaper
shooters. Stephen didn't seem to notice.

He walked from the podium to a red linen–covered table
that held one of the big Clip/Chip monitors with its round,
amber screen, along with a hand-held version of the same
instrument in miniature.

Diana sighed in relief. She hadn't missed too much. He
was starting with Clip/Chip, his best-known discovery from
almost a year ago.

Never announce something new by surprise, he'd told her
once, as if she, too, might be on the verge of a breakthrough
discovery. People are frightened of change. Start with a look
back to something familiar. Establish trust. Credentials.
Build to the new.

He picked up the smaller monitor, pointing toward the big
screen at the same time.

"—provides a continual readout of the patient's blood
pressure, pulse, and temperature," he said. "Moreover, this
monitor"—and he tapped the big screen—"tells exactly

where the patient is within a fifty-mile radius. The object is to keep the patient under careful observation under normal life conditions.

"Otherwise, some people will experience a thirty-point escalation in blood pressure just from the sight of a doctor's white coat," Stephen said, feigning a look of terrible chagrin at the coat he was wearing.

He won a swelling of laughter, with the bonus of a barking laugh from somewhere in the crowd that kept it going.

Diana counted by filled rows of seats at the front of the auditorium. Twenty-five, fifty, seventy-five, one hundred, almost one hundred twenty-five people in attendance. Some were the news anchors she'd seen on TV, tailored and teased, matched with cameramen who seemed to have dressed for a day at the stockyards.

Stephen returned to his point: "If the patient needs help, we'll know it from a glance at these vital signs—*and* we'll know where to find him. All thanks to the information that's being transmitted by the Clip/Chip device."

He pointed to the base of his neck. "Here," he said. "Attached to the carotid artery, no more trouble to wear than an earring, only you can't lose it."

He looked toward the reporters—the serious ones, poised with their notebooks and pens in the front row. "Questions."

A man's hand went up from the front row, extending from a jacket sleeve that was too short, revealing a white stretch of shirt cuff. Stephen nodded to him.

The reporter asked, "Are those Mr. Hamilton's vital signs that we're seeing on the screen right now?"

"No, those happen to be the signs of a woman two weeks overdue for delivery, probably watching a soap opera on TV at home. Keep an eye on this reading—the pulse. Things could turn interesting," Stephen said, prompting another bark.

"Clip/Chip is simple to activate. Just a push of this button—" he said, indicating the control he meant on the hand-held monitor. "However, the first use of the device tends to cause a mild pain . . . a bit of a sting. It's harmless, but the patient needs to be informed of what's happening. Mr. Hamilton is still asleep."

Diana scanned the crowd to find the man with the distinctive laugh. She recognized him as one of the hospital's assistant administrators.

Other faces were familiar to her as people she'd seen at work in the hospital. She wondered if they were attending the press conference out of curiosity, or if they'd been commandeered to assure Stephen of an impressive crowd.

She looked for the steely gray hair of Margaret Callahan, the hospital's director of public relations—the woman whom Stephen had phoned to arrange for this meeting.

Arrange? Demand.

Callahan was playing it poker-faced from across the auditorium, near the side doors. The woman's wiry arms were folded as tight as a knot, betraying no secrets.

Stephen nodded toward a Madonna-wannabe in a red dress, already standing.

"Doctor, please clarify," she said. "Exactly how long was Mr. Hamilton, ah . . . deceased, before he was brought back?"

Diana's heart skipped. *Deceased.* She understood that Stephen had saved her father *from* dying, and nothing had been said to her about deceased and brought back.

She felt betrayed, although she couldn't have said why. She couldn't have defined the sense of violation. But something felt wrong in the pit of her soul.

Zzzzapp! And the dead walk again!

"The answer depends on how death is defined," Stephen

said. "Essentially, what I've done is to change the definition."

He walked back to the podium, back to the microphones, a slow walk that made him easy for the cameras to follow.

"The old definition holds that death is what happens when the body is no longer functioning—when there is no sign of life. No pulse, no breathing, no brain-wave activity. By that antiquated measurement, Mr. Hamilton was dead for seven minutes, twenty-seven seconds."

Diana felt the word *impossible* caught like a stone in her mouth, while another reporter was faster to say it out loud. Then: "Doctor, isn't it true that the brain will suffer irreversible damage after three minutes without oxygen?"

Stephen countered, "Yes and no. Yes, we've found the human brain can be damaged that quickly, but not in this case. Electro-animation is a *healing* procedure. Our scans are showing no trauma to the brain. None."

The room erupted in a buzz of voices.

"Understand, this procedure was applied to Mr. Hamilton under emergency conditions, and only after every other means of life support had failed," Stephen said.

More questions.

Stephen said, "Death is not an absolute. Death is a condition—a condition that depends on the state of medical science. A condition we might not have to endure at all—"

The conference turned into a duel between the medical-science writers from the city's competing newspapers. Diana remembered how Stephen had called them the Siskel and Ebert of health, two thumbs up for estrogen, two thumbs down for cholesterol.

Their questions delved increasingly deeper into the technicalities of Stephen's discovery, vying to confound the doctor.

She didn't care for technicalities. All she knew was that her father had died.

Now or later, the man is going to die, and you're going to have to deal with it, Diana.

He'd died, but he wasn't dead. He looked healthier than he'd seemed to her in years. But he'd looked more than healthy. Different.

No damage to the brain, she thought, but what about to the dead man's heart and soul?

Lost in her thoughts and dreads, she missed Stephen's explanation of the machinery involved in bringing her father back from the dead.

She caught some of the names, none of the meanings. The PETT-2 scanner. The ruby laser. The platinum electrode.

The wellspring. She listened as Glasser described the word in reference to the part of the brain that he'd touched with his electric needle. A name for a spot of brain matter, the same way that bones all had names for the convenience of people who cared about dem dry bones.

He didn't linger on the subject, moving to other bits of hardware that seemed of more interest to him, answering other questions.

No end of questions.

Diana thought of leaving. She wanted to go somewhere else to sort through her feelings, and her stomach lurched in nausea.

She was halfway out of her seat, when she heard a question that stopped her like the cold grip of a hand on her throat.

"Dr. Glasser, would you please tell us your reaction to the disturbances outside this hospital in regard to the practice of abortion?"

Stephen gripped the podium, leaning forward, as if to confront only the mannerless nuisance who'd asked this forbidden question, not the entire auditorium.

"I believe I made it clear beforehand that I have no comment in regard to the abortion clinic."

But now the wall of compliance had been cracked open, and there were more questions, a frenzy of questions.

Diana was seeing the backs of heads from a distance, arms in the air, hearing voices raised. Disembodied voices.

"Doctor, you were instrumental in starting the clinic five years ago. How can you not comment on the—"

"—can't deny your involvement."

"—hundreds of people out there, Doctor, busloads, and more on the way—"

"—your work that made the Cedar Ridge clinic a focus of national attention in the first place, Doctor. You must have some feeling—"

Stephen raised his hands for quiet.

He took a full, measured beat of the heavy silence that Diana felt might suffocate her.

Stephen said, "I contributed to the design of the abortion clinic, yes—not to the controversy. I made the clinic safe."

Another voice, interrupting: "With equipment that no other clinic, to this day—"

Stephen: "I made it state of the art for the patients' sake, whether or not I agreed with the practice of abortion. No further comment."

"For the sake of *which* patient, Doctor? The mother? Or the baby? Which patient?"

Diana realized that she'd fallen back into her seat, battered by memories, unable to move.

She never would have come to this meeting if she'd known there would be questions about—

About babies with cold, dead hands, come to visit her at
night, come to cradle in her thoughts.

*Rest your feet in the stirrups, Di. There! There we go. Just
relax. It's time to start the anesthesia.*

She'd tried to find help. Someone to talk to, someone to
tell, someone to help her to deliver the nightmare out of her
womb.

Feel yourself drifting? Good, Di. This won't take long at all.

There were counselors to see, psychologists, ministers,
places to go for help with this sort of guilt. She'd made appointments. Oh, she'd made appointments.

But she'd never gotten past the door, just standing there,
trying to imagine what she was going to say, where she was
going to start.

*It's not going to hurt you, I promise, Di. Nothing is going to
hurt you.*

Maybe she could have told someone if she'd been more
certain of what really happened. But it wasn't all real, maybe
none of it was real. She'd been under the anesthesia. She
wasn't supposed to be able to see what they'd done to her.

*Believe me. You've made the right decision, Di, the only
decision—*

Memories true, memories false, memories mingled with
bad dreams. She couldn't tell herself the truth. How could
she tell it to anyone else?

Lady cop meets the world-famous Dr. Wonderful. He lays
the pipe to her, telling her not to worry.

See? Dr. Wonderful has been conducting some personal
tests of a magic pill—a male contraceptive developed in
France, needing just a few refinements, a slight recalculation
of the ingredients. It's one hundred percent effective. Disease preventative. No side effects. A major discovery.

Almost.

And if it doesn't quite work, well, then . . . Dr. Wonderful has lots of other toys, other ways to make everything better.

She shouldn't have been able to see, and maybe she didn't. Maybe she dreamed it.

The dream never changed, though. It was solid as her memory of Sarah Katzeff's bruised face.

Stephen in red.

Stephen, with a silver-metallic hose in his hands, the end of the hose fitted with a hard-looking, black attachment, with a wirelike probe that jutted from it.

Stephen, working the probe, finding it flexible, able to bend like a spider's leg.

Stephen, inserting the probe between her legs, making it flex inside of her, while the vacuum hummed in readiness to clean away whatever the probe scraped loose.

Stephen, holding the doll-thing by one of its arms, watching it squirm, poking at it with a sharp, silver instrument, as if to study it like nothing more than a frog in a high school biology class.

Stephen, disinterested, dropping the small, wet doll-thing into a plastic-lined garbage can.

Stephen!

He said, "If all of these remaining questions still have to do with the abortion clinic, then I'll close off this meeting." He looked across the rows of news reporters.

"My involvement with the clinic is a matter of record, but it's over, and the work I did there was trivial in comparison to the discovery I've announced today."

A last hand went up.

Stephen pointed, nodding, making the gesture seem to be laden with magnanimous generosity.

"One more question."

The Madonna-wannabe stood again. Her cameraman was shooting toward her this time—a shot of her to be fitted into the news at six, eight, and ten, a perk for the news junkies, something to brighten the screen between car wrecks.

She asked, "Doctor, how long will it take before this—electro-animation idea becomes, you know, a standard procedure. I mean, if I should die tomorrow . . ."

Stephen flashed her a smile. "Don't," he said, making it plain what a loss she would be to the world of television journalism. Bill Moyers, step aside.

Laughter.

"I'm afraid there will be all of the usual red tape," he said, answering. "People will die needlessly—"

But Diana was seeing a new drama unfold to the side of the auditorium, where the doors had opened.

Margaret Callahan was talking with someone just out of sight in the hallway beyond, and Diana caught a glimpse of blue.

Two uniformed officers came into the auditorium, their faces hard as leather masks.

Callahan rushed a note to Stephen. He shot the woman a look of murder for interrupting, but he read the note, stopping in midsentence.

"The ultimate effect of this discovery will be—"

Diana saw the look of pure-white horror that crossed his face. He backed from the podium. He looked trapped.

He started to say something. Lost the words.

Diana thought he looked straight at her, begging her for help in a flash before he turned to leave the room.

But he wasn't the first out the door.

Diana was.

Out the door—in search of the walking dead.

Case was careful to drive at the limit, careful to make easy turns, all the while trying to think of a better plan.

Nothing came to him.

Mom's car was close to running on empty. He didn't have any money, and he didn't want to risk stealing a second car.

At home in the country, he could grab some money, some clothes, the Beretta—and maybe just a moment's peace of mind. A moment's calm to think.

And the peafowl needed feeding.

He tried the car's radio, finding the knob was sticky. The speakers rattled.

He switched from Garth Brooks on a country music station, picking up the city's talk-news station, KNFW, hoping not to hear his name—startled at the sound of Stephen Glasser's voice.

"One more question—" Glasser said, his smooth voice crackling over the ruined speakers.

Another voice, sounding duller, distant: "Doctor, how long will it take before this—electro-animation idea becomes, you know, a standard procedure. I mean, if I should die tomorrow . . ."

Glasser, in the bantering tone that Case associated with a wall of white teeth: "Don't." A clattering of laughter. "I'm afraid there will be all of the usual red tape. People will die needlessly—"

The radio fell silent.

Case thought the old speaker must have burned out, but another voice, deeper than Glasser's, cut into the air.

"Have you ever wished for *power*? Unlimited *power*?" the deep voice intoned. "Of course you have! You've wanted this for years."

A damned commercial, Case thought. It was a pitch for

some quick-and-easy, guaranteed success gimmick, right in the middle of Glasser's statement.

"Now, for the first time, you can have the power that you've dreamed of, the power that you've hungered for—"

Too bad the radio wasn't going to be selling a power-packed, twelve-cassette study course on how to solve the problems of a murder suspect on the run, throwing in a free guide to stock market investments.

Case reached to change the dial in search of hard news. But the static-free voice somehow caught his attention. It seemed to fill the car.

"—the spics, the niggers, the blight of the inner city. The rich scum, and the money monkeys with their long, soft fingers into the city government. Don't you wish you could make the monkeys *hurt?* Punish the rich scum? Hell, yes!"

Case stopped his hand halfway to the radio dial, listening to the disembodied voice that rumbled on, gravelly and foreign-sounding, the words spoken too precisely.

"—the fat-ass lawyers, and their drug-dealer clients, and the squishy-soft judges, emptying their crawling cages full of human vermin onto the street. Wouldn't you like to set 'em right, just once? *Dead* right? Of *course* you would!

"And *women!*"

His hand jabbed the radio switch to shut it off, a movement as involuntary as if to smash a spider before it could bite him. The radio snapped off. But the voice never stopped.

"All of them liars, right? All of them whores! All red lips and sharp teeth, and ohhhhh, *ohhhhhhhh*, what you could do to them, and you know you want to, and you know they've got it coming. Don't they?"

The voice boomed into his head: "DON'T THEY?"

Then . . . silence.

Case had to tell himself to loosen his grip on the steering

wheel. His fingertips tingled. He thought he'd gripped the wheel so hard that he'd killed the circulation in his hands, but then he realized the car was cold inside, even though the driver's side window was open to the heat of July.

He checked the vents in the dashboard. The car wasn't air-conditioned, and the vents were blowing hot air from outside. But there were crystalline patterns of frost along the edges of the windshield, and he could see his own breath in white puffs.

The voice came back from nowhere, swelling with confidence, telling him, "You have been frustrated. You have been angry and impotent. But all that can change, and it *will* change—"

Case's mind stormed in search of an explanation. But the voice went on, burrowing into his thoughts. The voice in the air. Bold one moment, veiled the next, it promised him miracles.

It promised that he could recover the strength of his prime. He could hold his head up. Damn straight! He could do even better, be more of a man than he'd been on his best day.

The words bore into him. Terror and truth. Terror and truth felt exactly the same.

Case did what he could in his abject confusion. He forced himself to keep driving the stolen Buick. He wanted to pull to the side of the highway, but he didn't dare. He couldn't do anything to attract attention.

The summer sun shone down on the six-lane bypass. Other cars went by him in the faster lanes, the drivers wrapped in their metal cocoons—in their own thoughts.

The black-and-white patrol car slid past him. Case glimpsed a reflection of the officer's grim face in the side mirror, but the cop was after some other quarry. This time.

A chill ran up his spine, dancing with pinpricks. Frost

glittered along the dashboard. Case reached to turn on the car's heater, crazy in July.

And the strange voice found him again.

Lowered to a whisper of intimacy, it called to him. "Caaaasey Hamilton," it said. "Caaaasey! You want to play ball with me?"

It broke to harsh laughter that reverberated from the passenger's side of the car.

Slowly, Case turned his head toward the sound. A thick, swirling gray smoke filled the passenger seat, massing to a vaguely human form—a form edged with hazy tendrils that rolled and evaporated in constant motion, forming again, intertwining, breaking away, each wisp alive with a mind of its own.

This couldn't be real. He reached for disbelief as if to clutch a magic weapon that would make the impossible go away, but he found himself defenseless. Gaping.

Tiny, starlike bits of glitter sparkled inside the mass. Two yellow-red orbs gleamed like torchlights from the top of the body of smoke, where the head might have been.

Case knew he'd seen this insane thing before, seen it rise from behind the nurse, Teresa McMasters; he'd seen what the Gray Man could do.

The fear was like a white flash. Whatever the hell it was, the Gray Man had murdered the nurse in front of him, and it was here to finish the job. The monster had come for *him.*

The gray fingers had torn through the soft flesh of the woman's face. He would die the same way. He would die, and he would fall into the cold realm of the eternal bells, or he would be returned to the flaming ruins of paradise.

The steering wheel jumped in his hands. The Buick rattled onto the rough shoulder of the highway, then it cut to the left, out of alignment, veering into the traffic in the center lane.

Case whipped the car back into the right-side lane. A black pickup roared by with a prolonged blare of its horn, the vehicle set high on its oversize tires, its polished exterior flashing white streaks of sunlight.

Case shot a glare of momentary anger toward the driver of the black truck—anger at the charmed life of this nameless fool, who could speed past with no idea of the Gray Man.

The Gray Man's deep voice welled out of the twisting smoke: "Wouldn't you like to cut 'im down a notch? Let 'im have it? Suuuure, you would."

The voice brimmed with anticipation. "Heart attack? Damn straight! Give the nod, that's it, that's all. He's dead meat."

Case was struggling with a million questions, all of them wound up in a single word that he forced from his throat.

"Why?"

"Whyyyy? *Whyyyyyy?*" The voice rose to a high, thin whine of impatience, and not just higher than it was before. Utterly different, a petulant shriek. It shaped words into needles.

"How clear can I make it? Noddy-noodle! Nitwit! I gave you the nurse, but you didn't catch on."

Teresa. And the terror in her eyes, and the gray hands tearing at her, and it all came back to him, all in a cold rush.

"You killed her . . . that way . . . for me," Case said.

The answer came burning with acid and bile: "Oh, spare me that pitiful look, Casey Hamilton. Poor, sick puppy! Remember how it *felt* to see her die. Remember how it made the blood sing. Remember how it made you come alive, and how it brought you to your feet, and how it switched on all your senses. Nothing else could have done so much for you. Remember! It felt like *this!*"

A roiling tendril broke away from the mass of smoke,

swirling past Case with the smell of rotted meat to be sucked out the side window.

But the smoke shot forward from the window, thinning to a gray streak that reached ahead of the Buick. The last of the gray line vanished toward the pickup truck.

The truck swerved. For no apparent reason, it cut to the left, straight across the far left lane, colliding first with a motorcycle, then whamming into the slanted front end of a red minivan.

The bike rider fell under the van in a chaos of torn metal. Hit broadside, the pickup spun end-around in a violent turn that propelled it into a crashing roll across the highway median, strewing shards of glass and metal, spewing gasoline from the ripped tank, into the path of an oncoming diesel.

The explosion came with a shock wave that sent a shudder through the rusted frame of the old Buick—a blast that Case felt with a sick thud in the pit of his stomach. He looked to the rearview mirror, seeing the wreckage of the black pickup engulfed in flame.

"Keep driving," the Gray Man said.

"The hell I will, you son of a—"

Case stopped himself with a sudden awareness. He was *defying* the Gray Man. He was trusting to cop instinct, throwing off his fear of what the Gray Man might do to him.

It could have killed him at any moment. Instead, it hadn't threatened him at all. It wanted something else.

He'd lost his fear of dying at the whim of this nightmare-come-true, but only to learn another way to feel afraid.

The Gray Man said, "Keep driving, or something bad might happen to lots more of these people."

Case built a wall of fear and revulsion inside his mind—a wall to hide the awful thought he couldn't let the Gray Man know.

Something bad might happen, and he might like to see it.

He might feel something more of the deep, secret thrill that he'd known from the sight of the wreckage.

Case fought to aim the car between the white lines that marked the lane, keeping sight of the ever-changing pattern of smoke and ice in his peripheral vision.

"You *still* don't get it." The Gray Man spoke, and this time a line of black opened in the mass of gray. The Gray Man had a mouth. "But I have something else . . . a surprise to show you."

Case swallowed.

"Third and Boulder," the Gray Man said, the voice changing. It was softer, reedy. "There's an old theater—"

"The Palace."

"The Palace. Let's go see what's playing at the Palace, Casey. I'll buy the popcorn."

Case wished for a gun, although he wasn't sure what he would do with it. Only one answer had surfaced in his mental search for rational ways to explain the Gray Man. He was talking to himself.

The Gray Man seemed to know what he thought—what he felt. Maybe it *was* him. A psychotic self-portrait. Some kind of hallucination.

He didn't know what kind of drugs he'd received at the hospital. Maybe Glasser had done something to him that set off this nightmare, and maybe it *was* just a nightmare.

But the nightmare was telling him where to exit the highway.

Case found the strength to ask, "What are you?"

"No easy answers, Casey." It said his name with mocking reverence: "Casey Benjamin Hamilton. Casey. Benjamin. Hamilton. Such a waste of the shell to have only one name."

There were facial planes in the smoke: the outlines of a jaw, the cheekbones, sockets forming to make eyes of the yellow-red lights.

The gray hands were taking shape, and there were cuts on the hands, cuts on the wrists, cuts on the arms that were beginning to extend from the mass of gray.

The voice rasped in Spanish. Case knew only some of the words—gutter talk, the kind of Spanish that was made for cursing pigface cops.

"Talk English!" Case said.

Great amusement. *"Por favor? . . ."*

"Por favor, drop dead!"

"Ah! Well, there we come to the crux of the quandary, don't we, amigo?" the Gray Man said. *"You* were the one meant to fall dead. I wasn't meant to be born. We're both on the wrong side of death's door."

It was a throaty voice. A smoky purr. Feminine. "Let me help you, Casey. You've been such a help to me."

The words turned brittle, edged with the pain of a lover betrayed. "You don't remember, Casey? I do! I always will! You came back from death's door, and you carried me with you."

Case flashed to the pain of the claws in his legs, the teeth finding a grip on him, all the while that he fell through the fire storm into the darkness and the tolling bells, finally back to life.

The gray hands spread toward Case, palms up, line cuts opening to pink slashes, a grotesque gesture of sincerity.

"You, Casey! You brought me into this world," the Gray Man said. "You're responsible for me, and I want to staaaay. Third and Boulder."

Automatically, Case flicked the Buick's turn signal to haul the big car around the corner, heading toward the decayed heart of the city. He was amazed at how well he was driving, even though every tiny movement of the wheel seemed to be an effort.

The Gray Man held both hands in front of its face, turning

them, looking at palm and back. It pulled at the elastic skin on the back of its left hand.

Case saw the creature's left hand still bore the white scar line he'd seen before.

"I can't stay with you much longer," the Gray Man said, the sound of the woman's pain given way to a calm, sweet voice, like the voice of a minister. "The same body twice in the same space . . . Mother Nature would take us sorely to task, I'm afraid," it said.

The Gray Man rubbed his hands together—hands of flesh so solid, Case heard the gritty friction of rough skin on skin.

The air itself seemed to blur around him in that moment, laden with the impossible suggestion that things were coming apart in front of his eyes. Yellow paint was lifting from the top of the car ahead of him, peeling, drifting up in lazy tatters like shimmers of heat.

Brick buildings to either side of him began to lose form, too, the bricks no more substantial than a scattering of rose petals on water.

Another glance: the car and the buildings, everything seemed normal, solid, real, but with a difference. Never again to be trusted.

"Third and Boulder, *quickly,* please," the Gray Man said. It nearly had a face—a face like features seen through frosted glass.

Case stopped at a light that hung over a busy intersection at First Street. He looked out the driver's side window as a convertible, the top down, pulled beside him, two serious-looking young men in back. Other cars filled in all around. No one gave the old Buick a second glance.

He was alone with this ghostly thing that was him, and that wasn't him. The thing he had brought back from—where? Hadn't he been to heaven? And if he had, then why had *this* thing been there, too, waiting for him?

"The body is only a shell," the Gray Man said, the voice a basement rumble. "It holds one life. It could hold many more."

The traffic lurched forward, almost all of it turning left or right onto First.

Case glanced to the side, dreading to see the Gray Man fully materialized into flesh and blood. Instead—it was nothing but light smoke at a casual glance, just a cigarette haze inside the car.

Case understood. If the Gray Man stayed with him, too close to him, it began to take shape. It could fight to remain ethereal at some cost to itself, but only to play for time. It couldn't win.

It *would* take form, utterly in violation of natural law.

Something else. The Gray Man seemed to have a window into Case's mind, all right, but the window worked both ways. There were secrets it couldn't hide from him—secrets he might be able to wrench out of it, cold and dripping.

First Street marked the final boundary where the good city ended, where the war zone began. A few decent businesses still fought to survive along First—an old-time grocery, an auto parts store, a newsstand only partly given over to sex magazines. Almost no one ventured as far as Second and Boulder for any good reason.

Case drove on, toward Third and Boulder.

"Ohhh, Casey Hamilton," the Gray Man said. "You won't believe this."

25

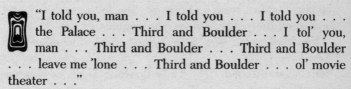"I told you, man . . . I told you . . . I told you . . . the Palace . . . Third and Boulder . . . I tol' you, man . . . Third and Boulder . . . Third and Boulder . . . leave me 'lone . . . Third and Boulder . . . ol' movie theater . . ."

Unconscious in the bed, Jermell Lewis continued to mutter, quietly, rapidly, words coming out in staccato bursts, only his lips moving.

But he was somewhere else at the same time. He was in bed, and he was outside of himself—watching.

He was above the bed, seeing how thin he looked, how sick he looked, hearing how crazy he sounded.

A short, balding policeman stood beside the bed, eyeing the pretty nurse. She must have been at least part Indian. Her face was the color of coffee with cream, coffee made just the way Jermell's mama liked it.

"I tol' you, man . . . Third and Boulder . . . Third and Boulder . . ."

The nurse acknowledged the uniformed policeman with a solemn nod. She lifted Jermell's wrist, taking his pulse.

"Temperature 107. Pulse 213 a minute, no response to

medication," she said, writing notes on a clipboard. "And this talking delirium! He's been talking this way for an hour."

"Yeah, well. I guess you know all about him," the policeman said. "All about the reason I'm here."

"Yes," she said.

Jermell in the bed was a vegetable case. He was a talking turnip. But the other Jermell had acquired a new talent, one he couldn't help using.

He knew what the nurse was thinking. He could read her thoughts in the lines that etched her pretty face.

Her name was Brenda, and she was thinking about the murder of another nurse named Teresa McMasters. She felt sick about it, heartsick and queasy. She felt scared, too, and she wished the police had caught somebody.

"You know what he's sayin', don't you?" the policeman asked.

The nurse listened. "Third and Boulder. That's downtown, isn't it?"

"North of downtown," the policeman corrected her authoritatively. "It used to be a movie theater called the Palace. We're checking it out. We're en route to the scene right now."

Jermell knew what the policeman was thinking, too. The policeman's name was Gary, and he wanted to say something that would impress the nurse. He wasn't *en route to the scene*, but he wanted her to think he was important to the investigation.

"We think there might be some connection to the gang that tried to rob this place last night," he said. "Downstairs. You know."

She nodded.

"We'll know something soon, I bet," he said.

Gary desperately wanted to slide his hand up the nurse's white skirt. He told himself she wanted it.

The nurse leaned close to Jermell in the bed, cooling him with the touch of her hand on his forehead. But his lips kept forming words, the same words, over and over, weaker and weaker. His voice trailed off.

The policeman pursed his lips, shooting Jermell a resentful glance.

"Say, you want some coffee or something?" he asked.

The nurse's face tightened. She gripped Jermell's wrist again, and then the side of his neck.

She checked his breathing, but there wasn't any. She ran to the door, pushing Gary to the side, calling for help, running back to the bed to start the resuscitation that was going to be a waste of time.

Jermell in the bed had quit talking—quit telling, had long since quit hearing the question. *Where are they?*

WWWWHERE . . . are . . .

And Jermell in the air had quit listening to Gary's thoughts. He wasn't ever going to know if Brenda wanted coffee, or if she wanted Gary's hand up her skirt. He had something else to hear.

There!

The first, awful groan of a bell in the night.

26

Sunlight always made the rotting buildings downtown look sad, Case thought, like they were someplace they didn't belong, dying in the light. It was a fleeting thought, and it didn't belong, either. It skipped over the top of his consciousness like a flat rock over a dark lake; sharply, he was jarred back to the reality of the moment.

If reality was what he could call it.

He pulled the old Buick to the side of the boarded-up theater on the boarded-up street, leaving the motor running. There was no one on the street. Even if there had been, they probably wouldn't have been able to see the Gray Man. In this light, the creature was almost invisible. Case had to look hard to see the sparkling, swirling glints inside the pale smoke, the outlines of the gemstone eyes, made transparent by the sun.

Numbly, Case followed the thing into a filthy alley devoid of life, watching as it took on more color and shape in the shadows. The Gray Man stopped before a door that once had been the theater's back exit. The door stood open, shoved inward—open to the sound of flies that buzzed in the darkness.

With a tendril of ice and smoke, the figure gestured, and

Case stepped to the door, hands in front of his face, warding off the flies. He entered into a cobwebbed passageway that darkened almost to pitch-black before it took an L-shaped turn, and then he could see that he was groping his way toward a dim, guttering light.

The end of the passageway led into the auditorium of the old theater. Case glimpsed a surreal conglomeration of furniture on the stage below the torn screen: a sofa, floor lamp, spilled sacks of groceries.

A hot, slaughterhouse smell rolled over him, even as he looked to the stage—to the ruined corpses strewn across it, scraps of cloth and flesh. A severed arm balanced on the edge of the stage, the hand grasping into shadows.

Everywhere, the summer flies fed, diving and flickering swarms of them, stirring a constant buzz in the hot, still air.

Case's mind fell into a kind of order by reflex, vestiges of his cop training returning to steady him.

How many? Sex? Age? Race?

But his stomach rolled threateningly, churning the sour taste of bile into his mouth.

He took a deep breath. He stepped toward the carnage. From where he stood, his eyes were just above the floor of the stage, and he forced himself to take another step, and another, until he was climbing the four wooden steps that took him closer.

He walked onto the stage, crossing to the nearest body. It was draped facedown over a battered, big-screen television set, one arm shoved into the shards of picture-tube glass. A slice of thin glass had pierced the arm at the shoulder, almost severing it, the bloody point protruding through the mangled flesh.

Bending, Case touched the neck of the bloodied corpse in search of the pulse that he knew he would not find. A buzzing knot of flies rose at the movement.

Case slid the palm of his hand underneath the head of the corpse, turning the head around until he could see the face.

The dead face looked back at him wide-eyed, as if surprised to see him. The jaw slipped to one side, drooling thin blood. Male. Young adult. Black.

And Case thought: *I know him!*

This murdered kid had been one of the punks involved in the insane holdup at the hospital. Case was sure of it.

He straightened, letting the head go. It lolled over the edge of the TV.

He looked behind him, to the shadowy mass of the Gray Man.

"You . . . did this?" Case whispered, the words strangling in his throat.

"To *show* you." The voice came grinding through silence. "And you haven't seen the best of all."

The Gray Man pointed away from the stage, toward the back of the theater.

Case tried to see into the shadowed void, to follow the Gray Man's line of sight. He saw the projectionist's window high in the back wall—the small frame that was edged with broken glass.

Dark, wet stains streaked the wall, leading down from the window, showing the way to a body that lay smashed on the metal frames of the seats just below the projection booth.

Case left the stage. He started up the aisle, toward the body, until he could see it was faceup. It seemed to have been pitched through the window. But the window was too small.

Closer, he saw the white glint of bone on the bare shoulders. It hadn't been thrown out the narrow opening. The body had been forced though—shoved through a meat grinder.

The head was toward him, thrown back, mouth open to the sight of broken teeth.

Case stopped ten feet away. He recognized Vincent, the gang's leader. The one who'd stuck the knife in him.

Lighten up, grandpa.

Lighten up, Vincent.

Case turned, walking back toward the stage, his feet seeming not quite in touch with the floor. He counted two more bodies on the stage. He thought he'd seen the kid with the shaved head at the hospital, too. He didn't recognize the girl on the stage, or what was left of her.

He dropped his hands as if they were too heavy to lift.

"Why in hell . . . *this?*" he said. The question sounded like a prayer. "I never asked for this. All wrong, it's all—"

"Wrong?" The Gray Man's eyes gleamed in the dim light. The voice—smooth as velvet. "By what standard? I know you, heart and soul, Casey Hamilton. Casey. Benjamin. Hamilton. You say that it's wrong, but you *feel* that it's right."

"Never!" Case lied. But he knew it sounded hollow. The protective walls inside him were breaking apart like floating bricks, revealing all the evil that he'd tried to hide away.

"I've done what you wanted."

"Damn you!"

"Damn yourself. You're the one who brought me into this world. You're the one responsible for everything I do."

The voice cut into him. It might have been a pain that spoke somewhere behind his eyes, and not a voice at all.

"Ah! But *you* couldn't have done this, amigo," it said. "The wisdom that counsels murder—it's never been inside you. It wasn't born into the shell. You've never been complete."

"And you are . . ." Case spat the word like a sickness. "Complete."

The voice dropped. It offered its weakness, like baring its

throat. "No, Casey. Complete means together. You and I, Casey. You and . . . us."

The Gray Man spread its arms out wide, stretching the myriad of cut marks to a thread line of pink and white.

"You asked what I am," it said. The evil thing spoke in the voice of a child—a girl's voice, a voice that belonged with a sweet smile and blue eyes, but that came from a figure of smoke the color of a purple bruise.

"Don't you know by now, Casey?" it said. "I'm . . . what's missing inside you. But we can fix it."

Case thought his legs were going to buckle in sudden weakness. He didn't know what kept him on his feet.

He clasped his head with his splayed hands like a vise, but the damned voice still probed him, finding secrets inside him, dark yearnings that the Church of Hamilton could only silence, not convert.

So innocent, that voice. The worst of them all. Blameless —like a baby with a scalpel.

"We must go back to the hospital," it told him. "We must find your Dr. Glasser—the great man who opened the way to us all. With his knife, he can join us together. And he will be greater still. And he will be nothing, measured against us."

Case felt himself weave on his feet. He had to think. Had to get away from this . . . *monstrosity*.

He staggered to the darkened exit, still holding his head, finding his way toward the alley, where the sunlight stung his eyes, threatening blindness.

He broke out of the doorway, finding himself face-to-face with a specter that seemed to waver in his vision, blurred by tears.

The figure stared back at him, its jaw hanging open, loose. It had a wild face framed by tangled hair, buried into a ragged beard.

The open mouth gaped even wider. "Beelzebub! Lord of

the flies!" it shouted, the fetid breath blasting at Case. "A *plague* of flies on our houses!"

Case pulled back, wiping at his eyes, staring at the gaunt frame of the man in front of him, smelling the dirty, stinking T-shirt and frayed jeans. He could almost remember the man's name.

When Case was on the force, he'd seen this man a couple of times—a part of the scenery on the twisted streets of the inner city, some street crazy who'd been floating around the slums for years. The Prophet.

"Beelzebub! Beelzebub!" The figure waved a sticklike arm in front of Case, the hand flapping from it like a mad flag. "The flies follow you!"

Case looked at him for a long count, but there was nothing else to do. He moved to walk around the lunatic. Another voice stopped him.

"Hold it!"

Two uniformed cops stood at the mouth of the alley, guns drawn. The taller one, dark with a heavy mustache, nodded at his younger, fair-skinned partner, whispering something.

"Got something inside there, mister?" the tall cop asked. The two officers advanced down the alley side by side, but spreading apart, making it hard for Case to watch both of them at the same time.

Beside him, the Prophet curled and flexed his grimy fingers, muttering something so deeply in his throat that it sounded like a growl.

The dark cop stopped an arm's length in front of Case, his partner walking slightly past, out of Case's line of sight.

"What's your name, sir?" the cop asked, looking hard into Case's eyes. The cop wore a tag that identified him as D. Bonner.

The Prophet stirred to answer the cop's question. "I am—"

"Yeah, we know, Prophet. We know you're out again, just like before, just like the next time," the cop said, ill concealing his contempt for the bedraggled man. But his eyes were on Case.

"Sir, you seem to have blood on your hands and clothing. I'm going to have to ask you—"

"Holy Jesus!" the other cop interrupted from behind Case. Case turned to see the young cop venture into the doorway.

Bonner called to him, "Eddie! Keep out of there, dammit, Eddie. We're gonna wait for backup."

Eddie didn't answer.

Bonner swore, "Shit!"

The tall, dark cop brought his service revolver to a line between Case's eyes. "Drop!" he ordered, the mocking touch of politeness gone from his voice. "On the ground! Facedown! Arms out! Legs apart! And *stay there*, m'man, don't you move a gray whisker."

Case had no choice. He did what the cop said, as fast as the cop said it, hearing the rattle of handcuffs.

Unbearable thoughts flew through him in a split second. Arrested. Convicted. The hard, lonely years behind bars, waiting to die. Dying. Dying into the punishment of the bells. Dying with the Gray Man.

Images of the fire storm played in his mind. The burning roses. The dismay in the face of the ball player.

What punishment would there be for the man who'd brought death into paradise?

Case rolled with a quickness that astonished him, swinging the flat of his big right hand like an ax that caught the officer off-guard: a chop to the temple.

The tall cop fell sideways, dropping his handcuffs. But he still had the revolver, firing once, a wild shot that echoed off dead brick and mortar. Case bore into him, scrabbling over gravel and broken glass. He caught the man's gun hand, twisting the revolver hard at the same time.

Case jerked the pistol free. Holding it with both hands, he used the pistol grip to whip the fallen officer, once, twice.

Saliva exploded from the cop's mouth, and his head snapped back, leaving Case to realize that he'd done all this without ever looking into the man's face.

He remembered his vow: *No harm!* No harm. No goddam harm. It wasn't so easy.

He fought to his feet, holding the revolver outstretched, turning in a crazed circle in search of the cop's sweet-faced partner, Eddie.

Found him. But the younger officer was just standing there alongside the Prophet, eyes blinking, arms gone slack, looking pole-axed with fear.

Case backed away from him.

"Find yourself a different line of work, kid," Case said.

One cop down, the other useless. Case poised to run.

But the Prophet moved first. The Prophet dived to the ground to snatch a rusted can, and he was back on his feet, his long arm cocked back.

"Lord of the flies!" he shrieked, and pitched the can toward Case in a wobbly arc. "Beelzebub!" And he'd found a fist-sized rock.

The young cop seemed to come to life. He raised his own trembling revolver.

"Drop the weapon!" he ordered Case. "Give it up!"

The rock smacked off Case's left shoulder with a jolt of pain, and now the Prophet had a broken bottle cocked to throw.

"Beelzebub!"

Case fired. Three shots, all of them aimed high, over the young cop's head. The sound of the gunshots whammed like cannonfire off the brick walls of the concrete canyon.

Eddie leapt for the cover of the doorway, just as Case had planned. But the Prophet had a different idea.

The Prophet's eyes widened to saucers of white. His nostrils flared. His mouth gaped open, and he yelled. Bellowing. Endless.

"YAAAAAAAAAAA!"

The Prophet charged toward Case, thin arms flailing, feet kicking high in the air.

"YAAAAAAAAAAA!"

He knocked into Case and pushed past him. He kept running. He kept yelling.

"YAAAAAAAAAAAA!"

The Prophet rounded the corner of the theater building, where the alley intersected with Third Street. He ran around the corner, scrambling toward Boulder.

"YAAAA—"

The yelling stopped. It stopped as quickly as if the Prophet had dropped dead in his tracks, just out of sight.

It stopped so quickly, Case had no choice but to suspect the Prophet had been struck speechless.

By what?

The Gray Man.

A gunshot split the air, the bullet whining by. The young cop was firing at him from the doorway.

Case ran to flatten himself against the brick wall, out of the line of fire. Now, the cop couldn't see him without sticking his head out the doorway, and Case would be able to brush him back with a quick shot.

But he couldn't stand the thought of running blindly out of the alley as the Prophet had done—only to run headlong into whatever had silenced the Prophet.

Case inched his way down the wall of the theater, panting, his back and side aching anew from the exertion. The shadowed wall was almost cool as he slid along it, watching Bonner crawl toward cover behind a rusted Dumpster—watching the doorway where Eddie was hiding.

He was almost to the sidewalk now, and he wondered if he should try to take the Buick, or simply try to disappear into the ruins of this corrupted landscape. What were his chances? And even if he *could* escape the cops, how would he escape from the Gray Man?

Still watching for movement in the alley, Case felt the corner of the building under his hand at the same time he heard the idling of the Buick's engine. It was so near, he could count the steps that would take him to the car. Ready! Go!

"Easy, Case. Real easy," a familiar voice spoke close to his ear.

His arms still spread wide against the bricks, his side bleeding, Case rolled his head against the wall, turning toward the sound.

"Dammit, Case," said Frank Morrow. "What in God's name have you done?"

Frank had his .38 revolver trained on Case, as did the two more uniformed cops behind him, each peering from behind an opened door of the second black-and-white that was parked to the side of the Palace.

Case let go a long breath of air. He dropped the revolver to clack on the asphalt. Case's outstretched arms stayed in position, though, as if they were affixed to the wall. He didn't want to move, couldn't move. And he couldn't look Frank in the face.

"Anyone hurt down there," Frank called into the alley.

"I don't know, sir." The young cop emerged from the doorway. "Bonner took a couple of punches, and he's—"

"Not one of m'best days, but I guess I'll live," Bonner said from the alley.

"Beelzebub! Lord of the flies!" The Prophet screamed and

cackled from behind the police cars. "The flies follow him! The flies follow him!"

Frank said softly, "Drop your arms, Case. Look at me."

Case squeezed his eyes shut, heard Frank say again, *"Look at me, Case!"*

Case heard the clink of another set of handcuffs from a distance to his right, where the black-and-whites were parked. Eddie was somewhere in the alley to his left, telling Frank, ". . . a *massacre* inside the building, sir. There's at least two—"

Case was spun around, his hands pulled behind his back, as he heard Frank's too-even voice reciting the words of the Miranda Act.

Cop voices blended together to a white noise that he tried to find comforting. Someone else could take over now. Frank, maybe. Someone else could ask the questions. Someone else could face the answers.

When the means of escape became clear to him, Case wished to the pit of his soul that he hadn't thought of it.

But he had no alternative—none except to surrender, and he couldn't surrender, not in this life, not while the voice of the Gray Man still rang through his head.

Damn yourself. You're the one who brought me into this world. You're the one responsible.

RESPONSIBLE!

He was learning more and more about the Gray Man. He was learning to see through the window between them. He was finding out secrets.

He might find the way, or the weapon he needed. There had to be a way to stop the nightmare.

But not behind bars.

Not on death row.

The words pushed up, out of his throat, through cracked

lips. The words of a blasphemous prayer: "Help . . .
me . . ."

Frank stopped reciting the rights of the arrested, pulling
Case away from the wall.

But Case wasn't talking to Frank.

The Gray Man came as a shimmering motion, like a wave of
powdered snow blown off a high place, scattering into the
sunlight.

It pulled itself into the shape of a man just behind Frank's
two officers. An arm laced full of glitter and smoke lashed
out, striking the cop with the handcuffs hard against the face.
The cuffs flew away, clattering into Third Street, as the cop
spun around with a gurgling sound, slamming facedown into
the pavement.

Another arm struck in a flash, and crimson spewed from
the second cop's throat as he grabbed at the gaping wound,
staggering backward, eyes wild in disbelief.

Frank whirled around, revolver up, to confront the Gray
Man, and his face went slack.

Frank didn't like guns. Case always knew the time would
come when Frank would be a moment late to pull the trigger, and the time came. Frank lost his chance, or never had
one.

Tendrils of ice whipped from the mass of the Gray Man,
fastening tight around Frank's throat, pulling tighter, drawing blood. Frank's throat turned the blue of frozen death.

"No!" Case shouted. "Don't kill him!"

The glowing eyes flickered toward Case, and the tendrils
relaxed, snaking back into the heart of the glittering, ever-
changing body. Frank dropped to the ground, gasping, helpless.

Case knelt to Frank, rolling Frank onto his back, loosening
Frank's collar, trying to help him.

"He was my partner," Case said.

The smoke swirled around him. The voice of the Gray Man: a whisper in the smoke.

"You have a new partner, Casey," it said.

Case scooped the short-barreled .38 revolver out of Frank's hand, holding Bonner and Eddie at bay.

Then: "Come on!" Case yelled to the Gray Man, desperate to keep the Gray Man in check. There was no complexity to the plan—nothing but the fear that turned his heart to wild animal, fighting to break loose.

If the Gray Man stayed close to him, then it wasn't with Frank.

It wasn't killing Frank.

The farther he could run from this place, and the Gray Man with him, the more chance Frank would have to live.

Running, Case rounded the corner. He jumped behind the wheel of the idling Buick, even as the Gray Man haunted the car as a haze that smelled of blood and decay, turning the car to a frozen meat locker.

Case wheeled out in a scream of burning rubber, backing away from the police cars. One of the black-and-whites had been parked in back of the Buick to block the way.

Case slammed the cruiser aside, bashing it like the winner in a demolition derby, scattering plastic and glass.

The Gray Man took shape again in the seat next to him. It had something new to present him this time. It had a face.

Formed of ice and smoke, pieced and pulled together, the face of the Gray Man had become a dark, fierce image of Case Hamilton—still transparent, as though Case had seen a reflection of himself in a shard of broken glass.

Something like a grin split the Gray Man's face when it spoke to him in another of its changing voices, this one abrupt, this one anxious: "The hospital. Glasser."

* * *

Case took a winding course into a warehouse district, a once-teeming section of the city. But most of the old buildings stood as empty hulks now, defaced with scrawled obscenities.

He jammed the car to a stop in the middle of the empty street, throwing the door open, ready to run.

In all this time, the Gray Man hadn't touched him. Maybe it couldn't. Maybe it didn't dare. He struggled to see through the window, even as the Gray Man fought to close it against him.

If it couldn't touch him, then nothing could force Case to go along with this drive back to the hospital, back to some kind of surgery that would unite him with the Gray Man— the knife work that no one but Glasser knew how to perform.

Or something else, he thought. Something hidden. Something else the Gray Man wanted from Glasser.

Something worse—

But the car door opened to the wail of sirens, sirens in every direction, converging toward the Palace.

"Don't fool yourself, Casey," the Gray Man said. The voice of reason. "You don't have a chance."

"I think I do."

"You'll be caught. You'll be killed. You don't want to die, but you *will* die."

Case faltered, one foot outside the car.

"Let me show you . . . one thing more," the Gray Man said. "Let me show you how to live forever."

27

 Frank Morrow's face was a battleground. Behind the glazed eyes and the slack face under the oxygen mask, Frank struggled silently to regain control, to right himself, to pull back from the dead place where shock had taken him. A soft, rasping sound came from within his throat.

Diana looked deep into his eyes, trying to will him back to her.

"I'm sorry," said the reed-thin paramedic beside her, running his hand across his spiky red mustache. "No more time here, we've got to get him to the hospital."

"Shock," Diana said, her eyes on Frank's pale, frozen face.

"Yeah. Some trachea damage, too. Blood pressure's lower'n whale shit."

"I think he'd like that expression."

Heartsick, Diana turned from the stretcher that was positioned just below the opened door of the ambulance, ready to be loaded. But something caught her wrist.

It was a tight grip. She was surprised to see that Frank had reached up, his arm trailing a clear tube from the IV bag of glucose that hung above him.

"Your . . . dad . . ." Frank said, his voice muffled under the mask. His face contorted. The pain was costing him.

Diana bent close to his face. "I know, Frank. My dad—" But she couldn't say it. *My dad killed the nurse. He tried his damndest to kill you, Frank—the best friend he ever had. And you know what, Frank? I think he's just getting started.*

The last betrayal, she thought.

All her life, he'd betrayed her. Forgotten her. Cheated her. All he'd ever had to do was to be a father to her, and he'd shut her out of his life every way that he could.

Every way that he could, every chance that he could, he found some new way to hurt her.

She remembered how astonishingly strong and healthy and *good* Case had looked to her in recovery only hours ago. The sight of him was like a promise to her that everything was going to be all right between them, everything at long last.

And now, *this* . . . evil.

Absolute evil.

"Don't try to talk, Frank," she said, bending close again. But he shook his head, or tried to, and forced the words from his throat.

"Something . . . with him . . . did this . . . not Case."

"Easy."

"Something . . . not . . ."

"Not Case."

". . . notttt . . . fuggin' . . . humannn."

His hand left her wrist, clutching his throat. Tears squeezed from his eyes, running down and over the plastic mask.

Diana started to ask something else, but the red-haired paramedic stopped her. "He can't talk anymore," the young man said, and nodded to another couple of paramedics in the back of the ambulance. They set to work hoisting Frank into the bay.

"All right," Diana said. "But you heard him, didn't you?"

"Ma'am?"

"You heard him say I'm assigned to this case, didn't you?"
Diana shrugged. "You were paying attention, weren't you?
Just in case anyone asks."

The man tugged on his mustache, puzzled for a moment.
"Uh, yeah," he said, finally. "Sure I did."

"Thanks. He made the right decision." Diana allowed herself a brief smile.

She turned away, threading through the clutter of people
and vehicles that surrounded the Palace. The old theater
hadn't seen this much attention in forty years.

There were police cars and ambulances, a crime lab van,
another van with a TV broadcast antenna extended from its
top, a red KNFW radio news cruiser. A riot of flashing lights
illuminated the whole circus, pulsing against the afternoon
sun, dazzling the derelicts and other rubberneckers who had
gathered across the street to gawk at the excitement, not
wanting or daring to come any closer.

Just one good thing in all this: It got her away from the
hospital. It gave her a reason not to be there when they
bagged up the body of Nurse Teresa McMasters—not to be
in that room where the sight of her father's empty bed
seemed more damning than the bloodied corpse on the floor.

Not to be there, wondering what was *wrong* with Stephen
—his eyes gone flat, his voice robotic, promising her that he
would take care of everything. She hadn't seen the doctor
since.

Police radio had been alive with dispatch bulletins on the
massacre; every cop in the city knew about it. She wondered
if Duane Hardage was listening.

The boards and sheets of plywood had been wrenched off
the old theater's battered and broken front doors. The doors
stood open for the first time in years, but nobody was buying

a ticket. Yellow crime-scene tape stretched across the entrance.

A uniformed cop with a military haircut stood beside the opening, biting his thumbnail, his dark eyes moving. He pulled his thumb away from his even teeth as Diana approached. She didn't know him.

"Detective Hamilton," she said, pulling the leather case from her purse to flash the badge inside it. "Frank Morrow assigned me."

"He didn't do you any favors," the cop said.

She replaced the badge in her purse. She lifted a strip of the tape to gain entry into the Palace.

"Excuse me, Detective," the cop interrupted. He reached into his front pocket, taking out a small blue jar of mentholated petroleum jelly. For the first time, she saw that the area under his nose had a smear of the clear jelly across it.

The vapor rub was a staple of homicide investigation. It helped diminish the smells of violent death, the thick, clogged odors of blood and offal.

"I had to go in there a little while ago," he said, offering the jar. "You'll need this."

"Thanks," Diana returned, straightening. She took the jar and reached a finger into it, applying the pungent jelly beneath her own nose.

The first, fiery hit of menthol reminded her suddenly of being a kid in the winter, home sick from school, the vaporizer pumping medicated clouds from the floor of her room.

And her dad brought her comic books. She didn't especially like comic books, but he was trying to help. He could have brought anything, it didn't matter. All he had to do was be there.

Sweet memory.

But you're damned sure not a kid anymore, Detective!

Diana handed the jar back to the officer. She started into

the theater again, only to hear a voice sliding out of the interior shadows: "Comin' through! Make a hole! Comin' through!"

Diana stepped aside, watching as a paramedic backed toward her, guiding one end of a stretcher on wheels. She lifted a section of the yellow tape to clear the way, the uniformed officer helping in silence.

The first paramedic out the door was a woman, a muscled-up brunette with a short, punk haircut. The woman's wraparound sunglasses began darkening automatically as she hit the light, and she glanced toward Diana, pausing, a dead smile on her face.

Diana vaguely knew the paramedic. Bonnie-something, Bonnie Savage. She knew the smile, too. People smiled that way as they watched their houses burn down.

"H'lo, Detective," the paramedic said.

Diana gestured toward the figure on the stretcher. "What's the story here?"

"Survivor. Only one from the inside, s'far as we know."

Savage maneuvered the stretcher through the door, into the light and across, in front of Diana. Her male partner appeared at the other end. He was stouter, probably stronger than she, but he wasn't doing so well at hiding the sickness in his face.

Diana leaned closer to see the girl on the stretcher. The girl looked back, her eyes locked wide, the pupils narrowed to pinpoints, the mouth a pale line.

Like Frank's face, Diana thought, except that this girl wasn't struggling anymore.

"Can I talk to her, Savage?"

"No time, no use," the paramedic said. "You can talk, but she's not going to answer."

Diana guessed the girl was fifteen or sixteen, no more, but that could be a lifetime on the streets. She reached to brush the spill of fine blond hair across the girl's forehead in a gesture of comfort.

The ends of the hair broke away at her touch, as fragile as white ash.

Diana pulled back. "What is this?"

Savage answered, "You want *my* diagnosis? All right, Detective. Call me crazy, it won't be the first time. I think something scared her—scared her so freakin' bad, it turned her hair white, just like in those slumber-party stories we all used to tell."

The paramedic's fixed smile broadened, no mirth in it. "I'll try to find out what the docs have to say."

They wheeled the girl to a waiting ambulance. The vehicle pulled away, serving as the backdrop to a TV news report.

The impeccably suited news reporter stood holding a microphone, blabbing into a video camera, making the most of a garish story that might propel him into a bigger market.

Diana wished him luck. Why the hell not.

She entered the Palace, into a darkness that killed her last hope of a better day, if not his.

The light seemed to have dimmed when she came out. The whole world seemed to have dimmed.

Carefully, deliberately, she nodded at the uniformed cop at the door, fighting a mounting urge to scream, to heave, to do *something*.

Instead, she extracted a tissue from her purse to wipe the smear of petroleum jelly from beneath her nose, wishing she could wipe away the last vestiges of the spoiled-meat smell that still assaulted her. The sounds of the parasitic flies still buzzed in her ears.

Who could have done such a thing—committed such an atrocity?

Her father? She had been willing to suspect him until she

saw the extent of the carnage. But it was too much. He couldn't have!

Or . . . was it possible?

Frank might have known. He was trying to tell her.

Not Case. Something with him. Something. Not human.

Where would Frank start to work on a case so bizarre?

He seemed to be listening somewhere in the back of her mind. He seemed to step forward, helpfully offering the advice she needed.

It's not so hard to plow a field, it's just hell to know where to start.

But she knew where to start.

She had to find her father, and she knew at least where to start looking.

Diana was almost to her car when another Jake called to her. He was standing by the open door of a squad car, holding out the radio handset.

The officer spoke out, "Detective, wait! It's Sergeant Bloch on Channel D." Closed communications.

Diana accepted the handset. She clicked the thumb button for transmission.

"Hamilton."

Bloch's voice growled at her from the speaker inside the car: "You forgot you have a partner."

He'd tracked her to the Palace by radio. Diana didn't have to wonder how much he knew about the killings. He knew enough.

"I've been assigned to this, Bloch," Diana answered. "I . . . talked with Frank Morrow. I'm assigned, and you're not."

"I'll say it again. You forgot you have a partner."

"My partner has a different job."

"Your partner has a week's vacation coming. Fun starts right now. What's your 10-39?"

Diana was caught speechless. Bloch had seemed a stranger to her for weeks on the job. She felt a gratitude that was more than she dared to express.

Bloch's voice crackled with impatience. "What's your status?"

"I'm 10-98 at the Palace, en route to Foster's Liquor Mart," Diana said, telling Bloch the address.

"I'll meet you there," he said.

"10-4."

Diana replaced the handset.

"Thank you," she told the uniformed officer, wishing she would have said as much to Bloch.

But she didn't doubt he knew.

Diana found a meter with time on it, welcoming her to the front of the liquor store.

The car behind her gunned past, a flash of blue that caught her attention. She thought it might have been Bloch. But the car was a mid-eighties–model Cadillac, big as an oil tanker, turning wide to navigate the corner that took it out of sight.

She thought about her father and Frank driving past the store that night—seeing the robbery in progress through the plate window. She tried to imagine what they would have said. How they must have felt.

Her feet took the same steps that Case might have taken into the store, and she wondered if the same bell rang for him when the door opened.

She saw Gwen across the store, helping a white-haired man with the look of a college professor in his choice of a wine. Gwen was a ranking authority on dinner wines, a walking encyclopedia of expertise on bouquets and vintages, able to choose just the right Chardonnay, the perfect Zinfandel, the elusive Cabernet Sauvignon—none of which she'd ever tasted.

Gwen acknowledged Diana's entry with a quick wave. Diana nodded, waiting for the gentleman to conclude his purchase.

Diana made a study of the rows of green and amber bottles, wondering if the arrangement was the same the night her father came in—and where he'd been when the bullet struck him, where he'd lain on this floor of linoleum. Wondering if some of his blood might have seeped into the cracks in the floor covering.

She might be standing on her father's blood.

The cash register rang in completion of the sale. $37.50 for one bottle, and the man left with the sly smile of a successful bargain hunter.

Gwen emerged from the counter to give Diana a hug. It wasn't a hug to give strength, as she'd given in the hospital waiting room. It was a hug in search of strength.

"Oh, girl," Gwen said.

She pulled away, pointing to the darkened TV that was mounted to the wall above the checkout counter.

"I had to turn it off," Gwen said. Her green eyes were rimmed in red. "It was nothing but news, news, bad news . . . all so terrible, Diana, I can't believe . . ." She looked away to hide the glint of tears.

Diana said, "I know." She touched Gwen's hand. "I'm sorry, but I have a question that I have to ask."

Gwen forced a smile. "I could use a talk. I could use a break," she said. "Let's just get me out of here, okay?"

She grabbed her purse and called a lantern-jawed stockboy named Carl from the back of the store to watch the counter, and to watch for Bloch. Carl looked as proud as if he'd been assigned the command of the Starship *Enterprise*.

* * *

"I know a little park just a couple of blocks from here," Gwen said. "The azaleas are worth a walk to see. They're beautiful, Diana, still in bloom." She tried another smile.

"I guess I need to see there's something still right in this world," Gwen said.

Diana fell in step beside her.

They walked in silence a moment. Gwen was wearing a T-shirt that advertised Mexican beer, but Diana saw the gold wink of the bee pin. Always the bee pin, always the purse as big as a set of bagpipes; she'd never seen Gwen without both.

"Gwen . . . you've been close to my father, and I feel awkward in asking about it. But we're trying to find him."

"You think he—" Gwen's voice caught. "Well, he couldn't have done it, Diana, I can promise you that."

"How do you know?"

Their feet clacked on the broken sidewalk, rounding the corner, their shadows racing ahead of them in the slanted light that was close to sunset.

"This is something I've never told anyone else, not even Case," Gwen said. "I don't know what you might think of it, Diana—what you might think of me for saying it. But I will."

Gwen drew a breath. "The night your father was shot in the store . . . I held his hand. All the way to the hospital, and into the hospital. I held his hand, Diana, and there was a moment, well . . ." She glanced up, looking for words in the clouds. "I felt him slipping away. Not his hand, I mean . . . something inside of him. I think I mean his soul.

"I think I touched his soul, Diana, and I *knew* him, just in that moment.

"I knew he could do mean things, but he wasn't a mean man. He was a good man locked up inside of himself. And that's how I know that he couldn't have done . . . any of those horrible things on the news, girl, because those things are evil. And he's not."

They walked, and Diana counted the clacking sound of her footsteps to keep her emotions in check.

"I'd never been much of a churchgoer," Gwen said. "But I've gone every Sunday since that night, and I'll tell you this, Diana. It hasn't made me any less of a sinner. But I *do* believe."

Diana saw the park was just a block ahead, a burst of color on a street of mostly white, wood-sided houses. The azalea bushes bloomed like laceworks pink and crimson.

"I'm glad you told me," Diana said.

"I'm glad you listened."

"Gwen, have you and my father ever thought of getting . . ." Diana stopped herself. It wasn't the right question—not a police question, and it was none of her business.

"Married?" Gwen said. "Yes, I suppose so, but . . . well, he's never quit hurting over his first wife, you know, and I'm not much of a catch."

"Gwen!"

"Let me say it another way. I've been caught too much. I've been three times down the aisle, girl. Bet you didn't know that. Three times vowing to God that I would love, honor, and obey 'til death do us part, and three times of being found out as a liar. Three times divorced."

She was right. Diana didn't know. So much about her father's world, she didn't know.

"I'm sure you had good reasons," Diana said.

"Oh, I could write you out a JC Penney's catalog of good reasons, girl," Gwen said. "But maybe I've listened too much to your dad's talk about baseball. Three strikes, you're out."

Gwen stopped walking. "Maybe I just like him so much, I'm scared to try again. But look at these flowers, Diana! Did you ever see the like?"

*   *   *

Diana realized Gwen had led her into a park that filled a square block, into the sweet smell of the flowers, into the vibrancy of the colors. So much life, she thought.

The azaleas were planted in rows that grew as high as her head, forming walkways of nearly unbearable color.

She followed Gwen deeper into the dreamland of flowers that rustled in a light, summery breeze, humming with bees.

Diana saw the bees as gold and brown blurs of motion that stirred throughout the azaleas.

"Gwen!" she said, waving her hand in a flutter to ward off the stinging insects.

Gwen's smile was genuine this time, as bright as the red of her hair, as the white of the flowers. "Oh, quit that, girl," she said, stilling Diana's hand. "I come here every day. It's no problem."

A bee darted between them.

"Those bees have their own business to tend to," Gwen said. "They're not looking for trouble any more than I am, Diana. And I can't live my life being scared of nature's bees, or I'll miss out on all the flowers." She even found a laugh that worked. "I guess that sounded pretty wise."

"I guess it did," Diana said, then: "Gwen, I know that you and my father have some . . . special place you go together, someplace away from the city—someplace he might have gone to hide. Please. Tell me where."

Gwen's expression clouded.

"Please, Gwen. For *his* sake."

"I'm not trying to be cagey," Gwen said. "I don't know of any hideout, girl, just the lake."

"The lake?"

"He has a place at the lake, real hard to find." Gwen's mouth hung slightly open in realization. "Oh, Lord . . ." she said. "Diana!"

"*Where?* At *what* lake?"

A shadow fell across them: a dark, long shadow, cast from the rays of the dying sun, and Diana turned, expecting Bloch.

She swallowed shards of ice at what she saw.

"Well, what a hot-damn surprise," he said, biting at the words through yellowed teeth.

"Good evening to you, ladies," Anthony Katzeff said, moving closer, blocking out the sun.

28

The pain hit him like a lit cigarette jabbed into the side of his neck. Case slapped at the spot, expecting he might crush a wasp.

Instead, he found a hard lump that was embedded just beneath the skin, but he concealed his revulsion at this discovery. He looked where the Gray Man was pointing, following the line of a tendril of smoke.

Case watched the red sun setting, flattening itself behind the city's skyline of office towers, wishing he could go with it to the other side of the world.

He wanted away from dry tangle of grass and weeds at his feet, away from the twisted stand of blackjack trees that shielded him and the Buick from the looping gravel road that led to the top of Scratch Mountain.

Him. The Buick. The Gray Man.

"Look!" the Gray Man whispered.

Case tried again to connect with the Gray Man, to know something of the creature's thoughts. Sometimes, the psychic window between them was so hazy, it was useless. But not this time. This time, he knew that he and the Gray Man were seeing exactly the same thing, the same way.

Seen from the top of Scratch Mountain, the city looked

pristine and correct, a perfect toy city, just the place for perfect people.

From up here, Case thought, *you can't see the filth in the streets. The human dirt. The dealers, and the pimps, and the nigger thugs—*

No! He had to stop that kind of thinking. It was what the Gray Man wanted. He had to pull himself together.

"Yeah, I see it," Case said. "I've seen it before. But I don't know why we're up here, admiring the scenery."

Scratch Mountain was more of a high hill than a real mountain at the edge of the city, but it offered a picture-postcard view that made it the spot to go for picnics and parking. Beverly always spoke of it just that way: *the spot to go.*

Once, they had brought along a blanket, and they had made love on the wooded slope, under the stars, and stayed all night.

But Case hadn't been anywhere near this *spot to go* since the divorce. He still thought of it as Beverly's mountain, and he wondered how many other men she'd led with a blanket to the same spot.

Looking toward the city now, he saw a thin, climbing line of black smoke that reminded him of the explosion on the highway. Lights were coming on in some of the buildings.

He realized for the first time what a frightening amazement it was just to be here. Following the Gray Man's directions, he'd driven away from the inner city with no incident at all, when he should have been sighted by any number of the black-and-whites that were swarming the area.

Maybe *that* was what the Gray Man intended to show him —another facet of the creature's power, handier than a Fuzz Buster. It could prevent him from being caught.

The creature took vague shape as a man standing beside

him, gesturing over the city with a sweep of its shadowy arm, but its voice lapsed to that of a breathless woman.

"All of this," it said. "We can have all of this, just to whet our tongues."

"You've got to be out of your ever-lovin', goddam mi—" Case said, struggling to get the words out, but the Gray Man reached toward him with a roiling arm.

A moment before contact, Case realized the Gray Man had played him for a fool, back in the car. The Gray Man had slipped him the hunch that he couldn't be touched. Like a sly wink through the window between them, the Gray Man had set him up to imagine he might be safe.

The Gray Man touched him between the eyes. A touch of cold, blue fire, glittering with ice and madness.

And Case *saw*. A violent, fluid montage of images, blocking out sight of the skyline.

He saw fires blazing in the heart of the city, smoke streaming from a thousand windows, flaming figures diving with hopeless screams from high windows. He saw people running in the streets, trampling each other, shouting and wailing. He saw tenement buildings burst open, human bodies flying with the rubble. And he saw himself—watching over it all.

And he saw himself—laughing.

He *ruled* it all, this hell on earth, laughing as these people, his cowering subjects, died before him in waves.

To feed the hungers.

Inside him were all the myriad possibilities of the Unborn —all the corrupt lives that he might have led, all the demons that he might have been, all the evils that he'd kept from being born.

There were monsters he'd defeated by the simple act of being born himself, Casey Benjamin Hamilton. Casey. Benjamin. Hamilton.

But they hadn't gone away. They had waited their chance. They could have waited forever. And they were all distinct. They promised he would know them one by one.

They all had special hungers.

He would feed them all.

One of them hungered to cut bright, red meat for his table with the same knife that killed Caesar, and his guests would be amused. One of them knew of a drug called compliance. One of them would have the evil eye. One of them would kill an American president.

He would feed them all, and when *they* were satisfied . . . then he would look to his own hungers.

His own pleasures.

No more of regret, no more of being afraid, no more of living his small life in small ways. No more the Man With No Name. His name would be legion. His pleasures many. As many as he wanted.

As many—

And one of them wanted the taste of his blood. Oh, not much. Not much at all. The grateful parasite knows better than to harm the bleeding host, after all. But just a taste, please, just a drop on the tongue.

And one of them hungered to pick out his eyes, although it wouldn't matter. He would see in other ways. He would find other eyes.

And one of them ached to slide under his skin. And one of them wanted his daughter—

"No! NOOOOOO!" Case let go a scalding scream that broke the vision. He buried his face in his hands. The horrid images shimmered and faded, slowly, even as he heard the Gray Man's now sibilant voice in the darkness of his mind.

"All ours," the Gray Man said, hissing the words "ours forever."

Case dropped his hands from his face, bone-weary, to see

the Gray Man pointing a finger of smoke to its own head, between the glowing eyes.

"Uncomplicated ssssurgery," the Gray Man promised. "You have a . . . useless bit of tissue. Here. Glasssser knows of it. He calls it the 'wellssspring.' Just a snip, Casey —a sssssnip, and it's gone. You'll never miss it. And I'll be there, instead."

Case turned toward the man-shaped figure, its body rolling like a storm cloud.

"I won't . . . do this," Case said.

"You will, or you'll die. You'll be extinguished. Think of it. Fire and ice, Casey. That's all there is behind death's door. There's hell, and there's hell. You've *seen*—you know."

Crystals of ice glinted like fireflies swirling through the Gray Man's vaporous body in the rapidly gathering dusk.

Case thought he heard the sound of the bells—felt the cold slide into the bottomless pit, a million lifetimes of floating downward into nothing, forever separated from anyone or anything.

And the other place: the heaven that he'd left destroyed. The guilt too large to comprehend.

The voice turned pedantic. Clinical.

"You don't have a choice, Casey, nor a lifetime to make one," it said. "We can't both exist in this world. You know that, too. We're an affront to reality."

The bricks, Case thought—bricks he saw coming apart, floating away for a moment like rose petals.

Reality seemed to be changing. Maybe dying. Maybe poisoned.

He'd brought ruin to paradise, and he was killing the earth, too, just by the fact of his monstrous existence.

"We're both going to weaken. We're both going to die this way," the Gray Man said.

The Gray Man paused, its reasoned words sinking into

Case like spear points. "Rule with me, as one, man, or die so alone that you'd kill for the sound of my voice."

Confusion and terror burned through Case, turning to blind action. His hand found the grip of Frank's .38 revolver in his belt.

He grabbed the pistol, leveling it at the Gray Man. Shouting!

"One choice you forgot!"

His finger tightened on the trigger. At the same time, he saw the Gray Man suddenly had taken a hard, human form.

In the split second before the weapon discharged, Case saw himself in front of the muzzle—an identically dressed Casey Benjamin Hamilton, body and arms notched with deep, scabby cuts.

The revolver roared, and the figure stumbled, fell, arms wrapping its head, as the cuts opened like mouths in the dying light, showing pink underneath, screaming like infants in terrible pain.

Case stared, horrified, as the wailing died away—as the figure dissipated into cold smoke, re-forming itself to the erect shape of the Gray Man.

A flash of white teeth showed in the smoke. "Good shot! Want to do it again?" the Gray Man asked. "No? . . . Try it! You'll destroy a few more of the Unborn inside me—the millions. The millions times millions. How many million bullets do you have, Casey?"

Case's gaze locked into the blazing eyes, and he let the revolver drop to his side. The eyes showed him death, showed him the figure of a man falling through icy space, voicing a scream that no one would hear, as the awful, unseen bells tolled around him.

He tried to find the strength to bring the revolver to his own temple—found the weight to be too much for him.

Found that he could not lift his hand, as he thought of the hurtling and hopeless figure that was him.

"With the doctor's good help, *we* will drink the living blood of this earth, Casey. We'll have such a thirst. We'll have such a power. It all starts right here, and it goes on. Forever!"

Case nodded slowly, his eyes cast downward. He stuck the pistol back in his belt. He prayed in the secret cathedral.

Don't let me die! Not again. Never again!

He turned toward the car.

"Let's go, goddammit," Case said.

Stephen Glasser found his newly installed guard outside the door, waiting on his booted feet.

The guard's name was Mel. He'd come highly recommended in response to Glasser's special need: nothing less than the best of his kind, complete with papers.

Mel's file had noted that he liked to be called Arnie, and Glasser felt disposed to keep him happy.

"I need to know I can trust you, Arnie," he said.

"You can trust me. Whatever you need, I'll get it done," the guard said, nodding, his big arms folded. Big arms. Big man.

Arnie worked out like a slave to the iron, and it showed. Even in the smallest movement, there were muscles at play in him, rippling his back, stretching the fabric of his beige shirt, bringing out the cords that moved his neck.

Big man. Big gun. Arnie wore a long-barreled .44 Magnum revolver holstered at his waist, and he knew about guns. He talked about guns.

"Stairway locked off?" Glasser asked.

"Like you said."

"Good, Arnie." Glasser's tone was that of a man praising his big dog for having fetched a stick. "Also, I want you to keep the elevator locked from now on, until I say otherwise," Glasser said. "I don't like the looks of the crowd down there, Arnie."

Big Arnie nodded. "Right. It's a freak show."

Arnie crossed to the metal control panel that was set into the wall beside the elevator door. He tripped the switch that would block the elevator at the fourteenth floor. Any rider would need a passkey to take the car to Glasser's floor, the fifteenth.

Only a half-dozen keys existed, and Glasser knew the whereabouts of all of them. The keys were in responsible hands. He didn't pass them out to sign-waving lunatics.

Still, he made a mental note to have the lock changed again. He changed it every three months on schedule, and sometimes on a whim.

He gestured to the guard. "This way."

Glasser led the way with Arnie to the Clip/Chip lab, into the room of the round amber screens, the row of screens that told him his patients' vital signs from a distance of as much as fifty miles. Blood pressure, pulse, temperature. Location.

"I know this man," Glasser said. "He's going to hide for all he's worth. I can tell you where to find him, but you'll have to dig him out."

Arnie said, "No problem."

"I don't care how you do it. I don't want to know. I just want to be certain he's gone."

"No problem."

"*Gone.*"

"No problem."

Glasser tapped the round screen that was tracing Case Hamilton's life signs from the Clip/Chip monitor that was embedded in Hamilton's neck. He only wished he could push the button to spark the transmitter again. He knew how much it hurt.

A line map of the city and the surrounding radius was transposed over the screen, and a flashing dot told of the patient's location. The screen emitted a beeping sound in time to the flash. Glasser turned off the sound, and the dot became a silent spy.

Arnie smiled, nodding. "Gone to hiding, all right," he said. "Scratch Mountain. Up there, he could keep a watch for anybody coming after him, and he could hole up in the woods."

The dot held steady. Glasser straightened.

"I have a news reporter waiting in the lab," Glasser said. "It shouldn't be more than a quick interview, but I don't want to be disturbed. I want you here until it's finished."

"No problem."

"After that, Arnie . . . this other business."

"I'll take care of it," Arnie said, grinning, resting one hand on the grip of the Magnum revolver with an easy confidence. His hand made the weapon look small.

Glasser knew that he'd hired the right man.

29

 Diana moved to position herself between Gwen and the looming Anthony Katzeff, thinking Katzeff looked even more of a lout than she'd remembered.

He'd acquired a blue suit that he wore with a red tie, the crooked tie pulled loose from the opened collar of his white shirt. A sweat stain the color of tobacco juice rimmed the top of his collar.

He'd fought with the fringe of hair on his forehead, forcing it back to cover the baldness on top of his head, but he couldn't hide the pink shine of the skin that gleamed with beads of sweat between the streaks of dark hair.

His raven eyes shone from sockets that were deep in shadow, the only things truly alive in the face that was roughened by a day's growth of black beard.

Diana said, "What do you want?"

Katzeff's blunt fingers toyed with an azalea branch, brushing the delicate flowers against the side of his face.

"Want?" he said. "Well! I might *want* my wife back, Dee-tec-tive Hamilton. Diana. It's a pretty name, Diiiana." He mouthed her name like trying to coax a kitten out of hiding. "I might *want* to be left alone in my own house, with my own wife, Diiiana. Would that be asking too much?"

He wanted her to know that he'd learned her name. Diana guessed at how much more he might have been able to find out about her.

She weighed the chance of encountering Katzeff by accident, and the odds were obscene. He must have followed her —in daylight, into a public park. It wasn't rational.

Diana slid her hand into her holster-purse to feel the grip of the .38 revolver.

He flexed the fingers of his right hand, scissoring with his index and forefingers.

"That's quite a trick you taught me, Dee-tec-tive," he said. "I don't think it would work the same way again, though. D'you?"

She could pull the weapon free to fire in seconds, but she knew it might not stop this bear of a man on the first shot, or the second, and a third might be too late.

She couldn't know what he intended. But she could be warned by the insane fact that he was here at all.

Diana said, "I would advise you to save your questions for the court, Mr. Katzeff, and I advise you to leave this area."

He pulled another branch between his fingers, stripping the flowers from it, stirring the bees. He was another step closer.

"Leave?" he said, feigning shock. "Is there some law against a free man having a walk in the pretty park? 'Cause that's all I'm here for, Diiiana—the same as you."

Diana thought of the purple bruise on Sarah Katzeff's face, and of Sarah's defense of her abusive husband.

I call him Tony-toes. He's like a little boy sometimes. I love him so.

Diana tried to see in Anthony Katzeff whatever quality his wife had found possible to love, if only a chink of simple decency that would allow her to reason with him. But she couldn't find it.

Sarah might have loved her Tony-toes for his size alone, might have loved him because there was no question that she'd found herself a real *man*. He might have seemed dangerous to her at some time in her life when she wanted to prove that she could take care of herself.

I love him so.

Diana fought the urge to hate him.

Gwen's hand was on Diana's shoulder, pulling her back with a pressure too light to be seen.

"I need to be getting back to the store, Diana," Gwen said. "Why don't you come with me?"

The man's dark eyes found Gwen.

He said, "What a shame. All of a sudden, you don't like the pretty park, pretty lady? You don't want to sniff the flowers?"

Gwen answered, "All of sudden, it stinks around here. But you can have a noseful."

Katzeff's hand clenched the flowered branch of the azalea, yanking at the branch as if to uproot the whole shrub. He loosened a rain of red petals, and the bees stormed.

The air was alive with buzzing blurs of orange and brown honeybees.

Gwen acted by reflex to cover her face with her hands, a gesture of fright. Something Katzeff could understand. His eyes brightened.

He'd never seen Gwen before—couldn't have known of her lethal reaction to bee stings. But, seeing her flinch, he'd sensed her worst fear with the instinct of a consummate sadist.

He shook another branch of azalea blossoms into a blizzard of white petals, stirring more bees into the angered swarm.

"Bees don't hurt so much," Katzeff said. "Some people

like me, we're just lucky, I guess. Bees don't hurt much at all."

Diana's hand wrapped around the cold grip of the revolver, pulling the weight of the weapon free from her purse.

"Gwen, run!" she said.

The bees were darts of righteous fury, a buzz-saw noise that came from everywhere at once, and Diana took the first sting on her leg.

"*Run!*"

But Katzeff reached to grab branches on both sides of him, shaking loose a riot of bees, and Gwen couldn't move.

Gwen wrapped her arms around her head, crying out in fear—in helpless anger.

Diana leveled the revolver at Katzeff, keeping both hands on the weapon in spite of the wincing pain of a stab in her shoulder.

"Get out of here, Katzeff," she ordered. *"Now!"*

"Or *what*, Dee-tect-ive?" the man challenged. "I'll be shot down for the awful, jus' terrible crime of . . . ooooo, woooo. Pickin' trouble with a tree!" He gave a hard shake to the branch in his right hand, punctuating the taunt that he seemed to find hilarious.

"No," Diana said evenly. "You'll just be shot."

The yellow grin died on his face, giving way to a scowl of contempt that darkened the eye sockets. She saw there was a red welt just below his left eye, but he didn't seem to be aware of it.

The man hadn't displayed any such resistance to pain when she'd subdued him before. But she'd caught him by surprise before, and she might have caught him off drugs.

Diana knew she couldn't fight him head-on. He was right about her use of the revolver, too. It would be nothing but murder for her to shoot him where he stood, at least the way a jury would be likely to see it.

He didn't move.

She tried to read him, but his face betrayed no clues at all —no hint of any limits.

"You tell me. What have I done wrong, Dee-tec-ive?" he said, one hand still entwined in the branches. "You want to shoot the bad guy? Yeah? Well, look out, there he goes, Diiiana. Bzzzzzzz . . . Ka-bang!"

Laughing, Katzeff pointed his finger like a pistol toward a bee that hovered in Diana's face.

"Ka-bang!" he said. A shot between her eyes.

Gwen was backing away—away from the bees, step by careful step, but Katzeff saw her.

His hand tightened its grip on the azalea branch, and the branch trembled, losing petals.

"I don't see what law I'm breaking," Katzeff said, shaking his head in a show of dewy-eyed innocence.

And Bloch was there to answer him.

Bloch was there behind him. Bloch—standing with his feet planted apart in a bulldog stance, his thick hands balled to fists.

Bloch said, "Just for starters, you dumb fuck—you're under arrest for pickin' the flowers in a public park."

Diana wanted so much to laugh at the dumbfounded expression on Katzeff's face, it was hard to hold the revolver steady.

She told Gwen, "Go!" And Gwen did it right: a slow, steady movement, backing away, nothing to call the bees' attention to her.

Bloch jerked his thumb at the blue Cadillac parked across the street. "That your car?" he said.

Katzeff locked eye contact with Bloch, turning half away from Diana. "What of it?" Katzeff said.

Bloch looked pained behind his blackened eye. "Well,

that's another thing," he said. "Inspection sticker's three months expired. Shame on you."

"Bullshit!"

"*And* the utterance of foul language in the presence of a law enforcement officer. Just not your day, is it, Tony . . . toes?"

There was a moment when Diana thought Katzeff was going to ease off—a moment when she thought she saw a flash of sweet reason in Katzeff's eyes, like the look of a child who would like to behave.

But the moment passed with Katzeff's lunge toward Bloch, swinging toward Bloch with a ham-sized fist.

It was the same fist Katzeff had used before to hit Bloch in the side of the head, but Bloch saw it coming.

Bloch had the build of a tree stump on brown shoes. He wasn't fast on his feet, but he was faster than Katzeff might have expected—fast enough.

Dodging to the side, he hit Katzeff with two chops: once to the bend of Katzeff's elbow, a shot meant to put the man's right arm out of action. Once to the side of Katzeff's neck.

Katzeff yowled, staggering.

The heel of Bloch's hand caught him under the chin, hard, slamming Katzeff's jaw shut, but Katzeff wouldn't go down.

"I'll . . . tear . . . your . . . heart . . . out," Katzeff swore at Bloch, the words flying with red spittle.

Bloch answered with a side kick that would have taken off Katzeff's kneecap, but Katzeff turned to catch the impact on the side of his leg.

Katzeff lobbed a right fist that swung short of Bloch's face, segueing into a series of left jabs that pumped into Bloch's midsection. Bloch countered by swinging his cupped hands hard into Katzeff's ears, once, twice—and Katzeff wheeled away, turning full in a circle.

He left himself open for a hammer blow to the bridge of

his nose, and his nose went flat with a firecracker pop unde
Bloch's hand, erupting in a gout of blood.

"Oh, lordy," Gwen said. She was ten, twelve, fifteen fee
away, out of most of the bees, still close enough to see th
ferocity of the fight.

Diana felt the weight of the revolver in her hand. But sh
couldn't stop the confrontation with it, not so long as the tw
men were fighting close-in.

She told Gwen, "Call for backup—"

Katzeff went wild.

Katzeff bellowed a sound of no meaning, windmilling h
heavy arms, charging into Bloch.

Bloch hit him repeatedly, even as Katzeff's momentu
carried them both in a crashing fall through the red azalea
into a storm cloud of bees. Katzeff landed on top, and the
rolled away from the bushes, slamming hard fists at eac
other.

Katzeff did most of the swinging, Bloch most of the hi
ting.

Katzeff managed a punch that caught Bloch in the templ
but Bloch raised his forearm to ward off the next offer
broken teeth, rolling again at the same time.

They came up together, half standing, and Bloch pitched
haymaker. Nothing scientific about it. He swung a loopi
right that would have left him wide open, defenseless
Katzeff had been quick enough to take advantage of it.

But Katzeff didn't. Katzeff caught a wall of knuckl
straight in the mouth, and the next shot spun his hea
around.

Katzeff fell back like a broken wall. He didn't move. His fac
was beaten and bloodied almost beyond recognition, and D
ana felt surprised to see the breathing motion of his chest

But he *was* breathing, so she awarded him the consolatic

prize of a pair of handcuffs that locked his arms behind his back.

She saw Gwen had frozen in place, hands clasped together beneath her chin as if in prayer. She called to Gwen, "Are you all right?"

Gwen nodded. "Fine! Fine, Diana. I'm sorry, I just—I'm not used to this sort of thing."

"Neither am I." Diana moved to Bloch, calling to Gwen at the same time. "Phone 911, get us backup."

Bloch had fallen, too. His white shirt was torn wide open to the waist, spattered with blood as crimson as the azaleas, leaving his nondescript blue necktie looped around his neck without a collar. He was going to have a second black eye, too. But he was sitting, legs straight out in a carpet of red petals.

Bloch shook his right hand. He looked at the torn knuckles.

"Dumb," he said. "Dumb thing to do. Wrong thing to do. Sorry business all the way around."

All the same, he gave Diana a wink of his sore eye. "But I'll tell you how it felt, partner," he said. "It felt like a slice'a pure heaven."

Diana slipped the revolver back into its holster. She knelt toward Bloch, laughing.

" 'Utterance of foul language'?" she said.

"Look it up sometime," Bloch said.

"Where? On the back of a cornflakes box?"

"Bullshit."

She offered her hand to Bloch to help him up.

Bloch shook his head. "I don't think it's gonna be quite that easy," he said, pointing.

She followed his line of sight to the blood mark on his pants leg—to the bulge beneath the fabric, halfway up his thigh.

"Fractured," Bloch said. "What I did on my vacation." He drew a breath that sounded like a bad accordion.

Diana knew his leg was badly broken, but the sound from his throat scared her.

"Take a breath for me," Diana said.

He tried, but the air seemed to catch in his throat. He coughed—a single bark that left him gasping.

"What the hell?" Bloch said.

Diana saw the redness that spread across Bloch's face, the swelling under his eyes.

He was breathing in hitches, the air whistling, rattling, and his hands went to his throat in the gesture that signaled choking, pulling his tie loose.

Diana lost a moment in trying to connect the leg injury to his troubled breathing, but Gwen lost no time.

Gwen should have been out of there. The bees were settling back to work on the azalea blossoms, but some of them still cut through the air in mad circles and scrawls, looking for trouble.

Diana wasn't aware of when Gwen had come back—only that Gwen was beside her, kneeling to help Bloch.

"Bee sting," Gwen said, reaching into the depths of her purse. "He's allergic to bee stings, Diana. I think he's got it worse than I do."

Bloch struggled to wheeze out the words, "Wouldn't know . . . first time . . . sssstung."

"Where?" Diana asked.

Bloch pointed to a fiery welt on the back of his neck, just under the hairline.

"Well, hang on, you're about to be stung again," Gwen said. "Diana, help me, girl—"

Nothing that Gwen might have pulled from her purse would have surprised Diana, least of all a pocketknife. Gwen snapped open the bright blade. Working quickly, she wiped the blade with a cloth soaked in alcohol, pulling things out of her purse as though she kept the contents of the bag in alphabetical file drawers for quick access.

"Hold still," she told Bloch. "It's just your luck, you've found yourself a bee sting expert." She pointed with the knife blade to the bee-shaped pin on her T-shirt. "Certified."

Bloch coughed in agreement, but Diana didn't like the swelling in his face, and his breath was coming harder.

Gwen used the blade gently to scrape the bee's stinger loose from the welt on Bloch's neck.

"Now, here comes the sting," Gwen said, reaching into her purse one more time to produce the medication she always carried to counteract the effects of a bee sting: the syringe of epinephrine.

Diana worked to pull Bloch's arm free of the blood-spattered, gray coat that probably served as a match to every pair of pants the man owned, and to roll up his sleeve.

Gwen administered the injection, emptying the syringe.

"Ease him back, girl," Gwen instructed. "That's it, and turn his head to the side."

Gwen rested Bloch's feet on her big purse, the best way she had of keeping his feet raised above his head.

She stood. She took a breath, patting at a spot above her heart with a flutter of fingers. "Okay, oooo-kay, we're okay," she said, then: "Diana, you stay with him. Talk to him. Keep him conscious, keep 'im breathing, girl. Tell him there's an ambulance on the way, and I'll see to it."

She glanced toward Katzeff on the ground. "One ambulance," she said, "one garbage truck, on the way."

Bloch wheezed a sick laugh that told Diana he was going to be all right. A thundering chorus of a thousand hallelujahs wouldn't have sounded as good to her, and she reached to hold his hand.

* * *

Gwen took a step. She stopped with a soft cry, slapping at the base of her throat.

She lifted her hand, and the smashed bee fell loose from her fingers, just a speck of brown and orange. It left a tiny red dot on her throat. Her face went slack in horror, as if she might scream.

"Oh," she said. Just *oh*.

The voice that cried out was Diana's.

30

Twilight gave way to darkness as the ambulance screamed toward Cedar Ridge.

Gwen lay on a stretcher in the rattling bay of the speeding vehicle, her swollen face mottled white and red.

Diana held her hand, just as Gwen had held Case Hamilton's hand the night of the shooting in the liquor store.

But Gwen's touch had carried some kind of magic that kept her father alive to the hospital. Diana wasn't feeling any magic inside her.

It seemed she had spent the last three eternities loading the best people she knew into meat wagons.

And when the blues had arrived to take custody of Anthony Katzeff, they had told her more than the worst of what she already knew about her father. The worst went on. It just never stopped.

Her father was the object of a police dragnet—a multiple-murder suspect, and there was damning evidence against him. His fingerprints were found inside the Palace, including a clear set of prints discovered on the top of a broken television set, close to the mutilated body of a high school dropout named B. J. Gibson.

Case had attacked Frank Morrow and another four officers outside the theater, apparently with the help of at least one accomplice. Frank was in stable condition at the hospital, but there were two officers dead.

And the nurse, Teresa McMasters—Case had admitted to killing her, at least according to the hospital volunteer worker he'd stripped and tied, leaving the terrified girl in a closet.

Gwen's hand tightened.

"I'm right here," Diana said.

Gwen's voice, a tight whisper. "Ssssargent Blochhh? . . ."

"He's in another ambulance," Diana said. "They left ahead of this one. He's going to be fine, thanks to you, Gwen. Just hang on."

Gwen nodded.

A paramedic monitored Gwen's vital signs, keeping radio contact with the hospital's emergency room. Diana saw him as nothing more than a white uniform.

She wanted desperately to ask Gwen about her father's hideaway at the lake. Case hadn't been seen from the time that he fled the old movie house.

Diana was betting a heavy hunch that Case had made a run for his place at the lake—at *some* lake. There were at least a dozen lakes in easy driving distance of the city.

His place at the lake—the secret place she'd never seen, but that Gwen had. Gwen could tell her.

But Gwen's eyes were closed, and for a moment, she seemed to have stopped breathing.

The ambulance driver swore at something he'd encountered in the traffic ahead of them. The vehicle veered to the left, never slowing.

The Buick shuddered as the ambulance hurled past it, wailing into the night. Case took it as a warning. He had to clear his head.

His mind had been storming, trying to find some way out of the Gray Man's trap. He hadn't been paying attention—hadn't pulled aside for the ambulance, and he could have caused another wreck on this same bypass.

And all for one slim promise of escape.

"Take somebody else," he said to the man who sat beside him—to the stranger with a clammy semblance of his own face. His jaw. His eyes. "Take somebody else, not me."

He waited for the Gray Man to answer, wondering what new voice would come out of those cold, gray lips.

All the way down from Scratch Mountain, the voice had been that of a girl with a shrill laugh, giving way to a broken voice that screamed disconnected obscenities.

But now, the creature had yet another personality, and the voice boomed out, jovial, the life of the party.

"Somebody else? No can do, me boy-yo. It's you and me, just like Fred and Ginger, boy-yo. Nobody else."

Case thought he saw the flashing lights drift off the top of the ambulance ahead of them, just as he'd seen the brick walls coming apart before, the last time the Gray Man had taken solid shape for this long. Streamers of white paint shimmered off the sides of the vehicle.

The image persisted. He couldn't blink it away.

The ambulance might just . . . what? Explode? What exactly happened when the fabric of natural law started to come undone?

His fingers were coming disconnected at the joints, too, fallen loose as cleanly as the plastic parts of a snap-together doll, and his horror at the sight of them gave way to a sick fascination. But he held them together. He found that he could.

He held them together by sheer force of will. Concentration! Held *everything* together.

He looked for answers to the mental window between him and the Gray Man, remembering what the Gray Man had said about two bodies in the same space being in violation of natural law.

Mother Nature would take us sorely to task, I'm afraid.

But whose reality? Case thought. Maybe just his own.

Maybe he'd just defined madness.

And the Gray Man was babbling more about Glasser. Glasser alone knew the secret. Glasser could open the door.

The voice lapsed into a foreign tongue that sounded Arabic, and Case drove, holding thoughts of his own about Glasser.

Gwen's eyes were still shut, and she murmured so softly that Diana missed the first few words.

She bent an ear close to Gwen's blue lips.

". . . Glasssser," Gwen said. "I . . . signed papersss, Diana. If I die . . . he'll take care of me."

Diana remembered seeing Gwen rush down the hospital corridor to ask something of Stephen. It happened just after Case had come through surgery.

"Yes, of course," Diana said, clasping Gwen's cold hand between both of hers. "He'll take care of you. But you're not going to die, Gwen. We're almost there."

Gwen whispered something more.

A simple prayer.

". . . if I should die . . . before I wake . . ."

But the ambulance slowed. The ambulance stopped. Diana could see through to the windshield in front of the vehicle, and out the small, rectangular windows in the back doors. They were stalled in the street. They were nowhere near the E.R.

Suddenly, they were surrounded by a mass of bodies in motion, people everywhere, fists and faces, open mouths, moon-white eyes in the night.

A sign flashed past the front of the ambulance: ABORTION STOPS A BEATING HEART!

The driver inched the vehicle forward, into the storming sea of protesters, setting the siren to a banshee wail.

It was a mob scene like nothing Case Hamilton had ever encountered before, but he'd logged enough time in crowd control to sense the start of a riot.

Hundreds, maybe thousands of people appeared to ring Cedar Ridge, illuminated by sweeping floodlights, punctuated by the flashing lights of a score of police cars. They waved their signs like war clubs, their pale fish mouths opening and closing in the roar of the crowd voice as if they were gasping for air.

The car was freezing inside, but Case kept the windows rolled tight.

The street led directly toward the hospital's main entrance, where it branched left and right. The ambulance had turned left on a loop around the hospital toward the E.R., blocking that way.

Case turned right, caught in a procession of slow-moving traffic, stopping and starting.

Men, women, and children gathered on both sides of the street, some behind barricades, others spilling over the curb. It was a gauntlet. They leaned toward the creeping parade of cars, chanting slogans about murder and the beating hearts of unborn babies.

"They think they know," the Gray Man said. "Presumptuous imbeciles! All of them! Get them out of the way."

The Gray Man was losing body shape again, its clouded form glittering a little. But it held to his face, the glinting eyes shifting underneath the icy mist of the heavy brows. It scanned the ranks of the protesters.

"They think they know. About the Unborn. About the unwanted. They're fools! And they're blocking our way to the doctor."

The car ahead of them stopped. Case watched as a tired-looking cop leaned to talk with the driver.

And how about you, mister? Might you be the killer we're out here trying to find? Are you the murdering lunatic? Hamilton? No? Well, then, maybe the next car . . .

Case rolled down the window, trying to overhear the cop's real words through the crowd's ragged chanting—to dispel his paranoia. These cops were in a near-riot situation. They weren't conducting a car-to-car manhunt. But he wanted to *hear*, to be sure.

Instead, he caught the sudden bellow of a red-faced man who'd run up to the Buick, craning to see inside.

"You got a *woman* in that car, mister?" the man shouted. He was a gangly, rawboned coot wearing a wrinkled white dress shirt. His breath smelled of licorice and phlegm.

As the man peered into the car, Case shot a reflexive look across the front seat, toward the wavering figure of the Gray Man. But the protester seemed not to see the creature. He shoved a pamphlet through the window, almost poking Case in the eye.

"Read, mister!" he yelled, a singsong tone in his voice. "Read this! More'n two thousand little kids who'll never have a birthday. Never have a party. Never have a cake. Never! Because of the baby-killers. Because of *this* hospital!"

The Gray Man said, "Kiiilll him."

Case turned toward the creature. Its floating eyes were embers of menace.

The man stopped his spiel, bending to peer into the Buick again. "Somebody in there?" he asked loudly.

The Gray Man spat whispered words to Case. "Kiiilll him! Ssssoo clossse to the end, Casssey. I mussst ssssave what sstrength I have. You . . . killl him! Get him out of the way."

"That's goddam insane! I can't just—"

Was the Gray Man weakening? Case dared to consider the possibility. The possible edge.

He took count of his own strength. Moment to moment, he felt stronger. He saw strength in his hands, and his hands seemed bigger. His body felt wholly alive.

The ruddy-faced man interrupted. "Who you talkin' to, mister? You got a woman in that car? You got a mommie in that car?"

"No time for thisssssss!"

The Gray Man crossed the seat in a blur, enveloping Case in a gagging smell of dead, rotted meat. In numbing cold. In a blinding haze of gray.

Case felt the steering wheel jerk in his hands. He felt something hard slam onto the top of his foot, crushing the gas pedal to the floor.

The car pitched forward with a howl of the back tires, smashing into the stopped vehicle ahead of them. Back, and it rammed the car behind. Forward, another jolting crash, and the cop wasn't looking so tired anymore. He looked scared to hell, falling back.

Now, the Buick had room to maneuver. The wheel took a hard crank, and the car shot forward.

The red-faced man was caught with his head through the car window. He tried to run alongside a few fast, staggering steps. Tried to pull away. But he fell behind, and the back edge of the window spun his head around, sent him reeling back in circles. His pamphlets flew into the air on all sides.

The Buick accelerated, engine roaring, tires squealing. It

plunged into the line of protesters who stood between the car and the hospital.

The human wall melted with thudding sounds. Screams. The jolting of the tires over a course of soft obstacles.

Case fought through the haze. He was off the street entirely, tearing across the hospital grounds, struggling to regain control of the speeding car. They were cutting across the manicured lawn, headed toward the side entrance, the one closest to the elevators inside.

Case saw flashes of movement all around him. Bodies in motion. Police! The Buick's back window broke, shattered by gunshots, bits of glass spraying into the car.

And the crowd behind him—churning, screaming.

"Stop it!" Case shouted to the Gray Man.

Then he realized he was alone in the car. It was the pressure of his own foot on the gas pedal. His hands on the wheel.

The car blasted around the side of the hospital, tires throwing chunks of dirt and grass.

Case's mind raced with the engine, hurtling so impossibly fast that he couldn't slow it for even one thought.

Only a destination: the way into the building.

He hit the brakes, and the car fishtailed. It swung around, pointing toward the crowd when it stopped. Case leapt out. The pain in his side jerked a short cry from him.

He ran, and the pursuing mob caught sight of him. He heard the sounds of them behind him—the shouting, the screams and curses. The wild, unfocused noise.

Still ahead of them, Case reached the door. He was suddenly bathed in the cold, antiseptic white light of the hospital.

He ran past a young nurse he'd seen before, a million lifetimes ago. She stiffened, her white knuckles jammed to her mouth as he whammed past her.

There was no time to say he was sorry for all this trouble, but he wished she could see into his mind as well as the Gray Man could.

The Gray Man!

Case shielded his thoughts. If the Gray Man caught just a hint of his true plan, there would be no chance.

The Gray Man surely would stop him.

If he didn't stop himself.

The ambulance had come to a dead stop. Diana challenged the driver, "What is it? What's wrong?"

He couldn't hear through the wail of the siren, the noise of the crowd.

She dropped Gwen's cold hand, moving through the back of the ambulance, past the phantom paramedic, to shove open the back door.

She saw the old Buick that came tearing over the hospital grounds. The crowd. The chaos.

She glanced back to Gwen.

And the paramedic suddenly had a face. A face she would always remember, this man in this moment: exactly the color of his brown eyes, the sheen of sweat on his face, the way the corners of his glasses were misted over, and the way his lips moved.

Those lips that told her, "I'm sorry, ma'am. This woman has . . . I'm sorry, passed along."

Diana felt grief like a hammer. The hammer came down, and she couldn't bear to look at Gwen.

Oh, Gwen! Gwen! Gwen!

Gwen—who died with no one to hold her hand.

Diana looked out the door, her eyes welling with hot tears, as if to find some comfort in the insanity that was happening all around her.

She saw the man who leapt from the car in front of the

side entrance. He was fifty yards away from her. Moving fast. At first, she didn't recognize him. How could she?

He was tall and hard-looking, this man, bigger than life, quick on his feet, a figure of such raw *strength* . . . she couldn't believe.

But it was.

Her father.

31

Case punched the elevator button for the fifteenth floor. It didn't light, it wouldn't respond.

There was yelling in the hallway. Some of the rioters had broken through, and he could hear the rush of feet, the hurricane of bodies, all converging toward him.

Desperation overtook him. He smashed the button with his fist, and he might have hit it again, but something flashed in front of him. A silver key. A hand.

Diana said, "Use this."

The revolver in her other hand was pointed toward him. Her breath was coming fast, ragged. She must have been running.

The lady cop had chased her quarry to the ground. Case wasn't surprised. Seeing her now, he knew he'd always believed she would.

"Use the key!"

He fit the key into the slot on the control panel. He turned it with a soft click, freeing the elevator to take them all the way to the top.

His hand fell, leaving the key where it was.

"Diana!"

"Just shut up! Hit fifteen."

She had both hands locked on the revolver, and there was nothing about her to reason with. Her eyes were as cold as the touch of the Gray Man. He punched the button to the fourteenth floor as if in error, then fifteen, punching over and over, long after it lighted, as if force of repetition could make the elevator doors close faster.

Glass broke from across the lobby. Case saw a man throwing a chair into the plate front of the gift shop, smashing the glass shelves, scattering porcelain clowns and silk flowers.

Angry faces bore toward the open elevator as nothing more than a mass of red broken by the white slash of clenched teeth.

The elevator doors bit shut on a woman's hand that rammed through the narrowing space between them, the fingers splayed, grasping, weighted with gold rings.

The grasping hand withdrew to the sounds of pounding on the other side of the doors, and the car lifted, clanking its discontent at being summoned into service.

"Diana, you've got to listen to me. Things aren't what they seem . . ." His voice trailed, betraying his own lack of faith in such inadequate words.

But where *were* the right words? What words could explain the impossible?

"Turn around! Raise your hands. Place your hands against the wall. You're under arrest," Diana said, reciting his rights to him as if he were a complete stranger.

Case did as she said. In a way, he felt proud of her. He couldn't have made such a controlled arrest.

But he couldn't submit, either. He couldn't allow her to lift the revolver from his belt, as she would in a moment.

"Don't try to cross me." There was a catch in her voice.

"Diana," he said. "You're crying."

Cold silence. The car rose to the eleventh floor. Twelfth. Thirteenth, rattling on its old cables.

"Diana!" He felt for her, weighted with the guilt of having put her through all this. His heart ached for her.

"Not for you! I wouldn't cry for you, damn you!" Diana said. "It's for *Gwen*, because Gwen's gone, if you care at all. Gwen's dead!"

He turned from the wall of the elevator, facing his daughter, not seeing the weapon she held on him, just the pain in her eyes—the sudden, terrible grief that he shared with her.

"I—I'm sorry," she said. "That was no way to tell you. It was a bee sting that . . . Dad, I know what she meant to you—"

Fourteenth. The car stopped, and the doors slid open. Diana glanced to the movement.

Case took the only chance he was going to have, wishing all to hell he'd never had it.

His big hand shot out, caught the wrist of her gun hand. He shook the weapon out of her hand.

She hit him a jolting blow under the jaw with the heel of her free hand, but he took it with hardly a blink. Case threw his daughter into the wall of the elevator. He bolted into the hallway of the fourteenth floor.

But he'd bought himself only a few moments before she regained the weapon—before she was on her feet again, running behind him.

Rooms shot past them, some of the doors open, glimpses of the private dramas that were being played out behind those doors. A withered man struggling to find his feet with a walker. The flicker of a TV screen gone bad, still beaming its happy-face chitchat into a room with no sign of life.

Any moment, Case expected the gunshot to the back that would pitch him off his feet, but it never came.

They hurled past a nurse wheeling a cartload of breakfast trays, the woman shocked to see them, her mouth falling wide to object. Other people made the hallway an obstacle course.

An elderly man in a business suit. He flattened against the wall, dropping a box of chocolates that went skittering like marbles. Faces blurred to looks of dismay.

Diana couldn't risk a shot. Even if she hit the human target ahead of her, the bullet might cut right through him. Might strike someone else.

All she could hope was to catch him. Catch the killer. She couldn't risk thinking of Case as her father, or she might not be able to do this. She didn't have a father.

Catch him. And then what?

The question hung wide open. Diana was falling behind him. She'd kicked off her shoes to be rid of the medium-high heels, and she was running as fast as she could. But she couldn't keep pace.

The killer's long, sure strides pulled him well ahead of her, and he never faltered. He was holding to some plan.

Diana realized that he'd learned the layout of this building as a security guard. He knew where he was going through a zigzag course of hallways. If she let him escape from her sight just once, he might disappear completely.

Another turn, and the hallway took them straight to a window with a bracework of metal showing on the outside.

The fire escape.

Case grabbed the window frame. He flung it open, breaking the seal of paint that had seeped under the frame each time the wood had been repainted.

He stepped through the window, onto the platform of the fire escape, looking up, and then he was gone.

* * *

Diana followed him out onto the metal platform. The fire escape was rusted around the bolts that held it in place.

The air was hot and still as the devil's breath. She could look down, through the open-patterned platform, to see the flood-lit ground swarming with people around the hospital, and the white tops of the police cruisers, and more black-and-whites being called to the scene.

She followed the clang of her father's feet up the metal stairway, but he was above her. He was ten feet above her, struggling with the window that led from the fire escape into the fifteenth floor.

She raised the revolver, craning for a clear shot.

His foot struck the window glass, forcing Diana to keep her face covered in the cutting rain of glitter and gleam, splinters and falling shards of glass.

She started up the steps, feeling the metalwork vibrate beneath her, a drumming in the handrail.

Above her: a gunshot like thunder.

Case was struggling with another man on the top landing —a big man, bigger than Case, hard-muscled. He must be Stephen's private security guard.

She continued up, straining to see. The muscleman had a long-barreled revolver that he was trying to force into her father's face, but Case slammed the gun hand into the brick wall, breaking the cylinder loose, breaking the guard's grip.

The broken revolver went spiraling into the air, a bird of blue steel that seemed to hover a moment, going nowhere, before it fell past her.

She heard the impact of fist on flesh. Case rocked backward, gripping the rail, and the guard was on him, rocking the metal, trying to force him over.

Case gained the leverage, and she realized for the first time just how strong he really was—how easily he could have been rid of her in the elevator, if he'd meant her any harm.

Diana, you've got to listen to me. Listen to me. Listen to me.

Case *threw* the big guard—picked him up as if the hulking muscleman were nothing but a rag doll, and pitched him down the metal stairs. The man came whamming backward down the shaking steps, out of balance, heavy arms flailing, trying to grab for her on the landing.

He cracked to the platform at Diana's feet. He wasn't moving.

She turned, and her father was through the window, into the building.

Diana chilled at the realization that he'd been headed to the fifteenth floor all along, and she hadn't stopped him. She'd given him the key! She'd almost made it easy for him.

And only one reason explained why he was bound for the top floor—a reason he might have been trying to tell her.

Stephen Glasser.

32

 "Stephen, oh! Stephen, *oh!* Stephen!"

Glasser drove into her, making her sing to him—songs of her pleasure, and songs of her pain.

He knew right where she was in her quest for the climax that he'd denied to her. He was holding her on the brink, letting her slip just a breath, just a touch over the edge, before he brought her back.

She was going to be begging him.

To the side of the fold-out bed was a mahogany end table with a Clip/Chip monitor on it, the light of the amber screen casting the soft glow of a high-tech candle.

The dot on the round screen winked to pinpoint the hidden whereabouts of Case Hamilton, but Glasser wasn't watching it. He was listening to the sound of the monitor.

Twee! Twee! Twee!

The monitor chirped in rhythm to the flash of the dot. It worked like a metronome, timing his thrusts.

Twee! Twee! Twee!

And the bed rocked, the bed rocked, the bed rocked.

"Stephen, oh! Stephen, oh!"

Her red dress was thrown to the foot of the bed. Red panties. Red bra.

Her hair spilled in platinum waves over the red satin pillow. Red was her color. It brought out the marble-white of her skin, and the rose-petal dot of a nipple that danced in rhythm to the music she sang to him.

"Stephen, *oh!* Stephen, *ohhhh!*"

But it wasn't working for him. None of this. It didn't work to clear his head; it didn't help to calm his fears.

He could make her sing until her eyes smoked. It wouldn't have any effect on him, and it wouldn't change a microsecond of the worst day of his life.

The abortion rallies. The questions about his involvement in the abortion clinic. The disruption of the press conference. The sight of the carnage in 231.

The loss of control, like the loss of an arm that he'd taken for granted, like a blindness that struck out of nowhere—

I'll take care of this.

He'd analyzed the meaning of what he'd said in the room. It meant that he couldn't trust his own voice.

Zzzapp! And the dead walk again.

He'd ordered himself to *get hold*, to function, to focus on *something* with all his attention. The object didn't matter. It could have been a scalpel, or the black hairs on the back of his hand, or the colors in a gumball machine.

Instead, he'd brought his mind to bear like a laser on the object of the body in the red dress.

The TV news reporter. She'd tracked him from the press conference through the hallways, out to the parking garage, all but pouring herself into his car, nestling into the Corinthian leather of the car's upholstery, beseeching the doctor for a glimpse into his laboratory. An exclusive.

What he was giving her couldn't rightly be called exclusive, but it seemed to be all she could handle.

"Stephen, Stephen, Stephen!"

He quickened the pace of his long thrusts, and her legs

wrapped around him, slick with hot sweat. Her legs tightened. *She* tightened.

He knew at last that he'd made the right choice with her.

He felt himself regaining strength of will in a moment-to-moment search for recovery, and with it a cold sense of assurance.

He *could* take care of the injury this day had done to him. A few more minutes, he would put big Arnie on the job.

No problem. No problem.

TWEE! TWEE!

The shame was to lose all the work he'd invested in Hamilton, but it couldn't be helped.

Something had gone wrong with Case Hamilton: something bad enough that it left a white room drenched in blood. And Glasser could sense the gathering of the village idiots with their torches and pitchforks, coming to set fire to Frankenstein's castle.

No one was going to recognize the milestone achievement of Hamilton's return from the dead. They weren't going to see that Glasser had opened the way to a new science. They weren't going to allow him to continue in that new way.

Instead, they were going to see the dead nurse, and they were going to focus on Hamilton in the role of the shambling monster, and they would attack Glasser as the mad scientist.

Unless Dr. Frankenstein pulled a surprise. Unless! Unless!

"OH! OHHH!"

Unless Hamilton just . . . disappeared.

"Stephen! Stephen, *oh!* Dammmmn you . . . *Ohhh!"*

She bit her lower lip, a line of red welling along the smooth line of white teeth.

TWEEEEE! TWEEEEE! TWEEEEE!

He worked his way forward, gripping her wrists, holding her pinned to the bed with its covering of white satin.

Her body writhed beneath him, well toned, and he could

imagine the hours of hard sweat in some high-dollar, glass-and-chrome health club that had gone into the sculpting of it.

She'd probably told herself that she had to work out to look good on camera, to be an up-and-comer, to be a news anchor, to be a network news contender. But all she'd done was to build herself into a pleasure machine.

All he'd done was to shove in his nickle.

The machine played on, but he was tiring of her. She could have held his interest longer as the subject of an autopsy.

The intense way that he'd thought of her naked body beneath the red dress, he was thinking about Case Hamilton.

Hamilton, Hamilton.

He made the bed rock with the name, made her cry out in time to the name.

Hamilton!

Find him. Stop him. Bury him.

Eliminate the smallest trace of him.

Obliterate the memory of him.

And the final step, essential.

Replace him.

Replace him at the first chance, and the first chance could be anytime soon. A call to the doctor. The doctor who knows what to do. No sign of life. Could there still be a chance? Yes, why, yes! He would do all he could. Bring the patient.

Lock the scan.

Aim the laser.

Strike with the lightning.

TWEEEEEEEEEEEEEEEEEEEE!

Glasser pulled back from the woman in his bed. He focused on the Clip/Chip monitor.

He saw the dot, where the flashing dot was. It hadn't been

a good dot. It hadn't stayed on Scratch Mountain. Hadn't gone into hiding.

The dot told him exactly where Hamilton was—just a flash before the double doors of the lab broke open with a crash of splintered wood, the locks shattered in one kick.

Arnie? Where in hell was big Arnie?

The silhouette of a huge, broad-shouldered man loomed in the doorway, calling to him.

"Glasser!"

The man's arm raised, showing something was gripped in the big hand.

Glasser hit a panel of switches built into the arm of the sofa bed, bringing up the lights in the laboratory. White light gleamed from the glass cages, from chrome and more glass—and from the blue-steel revolver that was aimed toward him.

Case Hamilton lifted the weapon another inch, bringing it level with Glasser's eyes.

"I'm sorry to do this, Doctor," Hamilton said. "More than you'll ever know."

Glasser's mind fragmented. Part of him chilled to a rush of doom, thinking of the carnage in Hamilton's hospital room. Part considered the prospect of using the blond woman as a shield to save himself. But a third part—*this* compartment—recognized just a flicker of indecision in Hamilton's eyes, and made the most of it.

"I'm glad you came to me," Glasser said, never moving. "I can help you. I know what's wrong," he lied.

"You *know?*"

"I can fix it."

The gun hand wavered.

"You don't want to kill me," Glasser said. He ached for a scalpel. He could do things with a scalpel that Hamilton wouldn't believe. But the doctor hadn't any knife to employ on this madman—just the quick blade of his mind.

"I don't want . . . any more dying." Torment crossed Hamilton's face.

"I understand. No more of death. I can fix it."

Hamilton lost the expression of pain. His face in that moment: a perfect, unreadable blank. "Yes . . ." he said. "You can fix it. You can fix it for me, and you can *fix* it for other people, too. You know the secret. Right, Doctor?"

Glasser knew he had to respond. He tried to find answers in Hamilton's flat, blue-steel eyes—but he couldn't find even a clue to what Hamilton wanted.

"For other people . . . I think so," Glasser said.

"A woman I loved, Doctor. She died tonight, and she died without knowing I loved her. I never told her out loud. Are you saying you could bring her back?"

Glasser straightened. He tasted a deep breath of clean air. "Absolutely," he promised.

"And when you do . . . will there be something else with her? Something else brought back from death's door? Ask me, I think so. I'd bet on it. I think maybe everyone could have been born something worse'n what they are, or maybe a million times worse."

Glasser interrupted, "I can make it right, whatever—"

"This woman I loved . . . I don't want her to find out just how many demons she left behind."

"But there *aren't* any demons, Mr. Hamilton. Please! Listen! This has nothing to do with superstition."

"Tell you this much, Doctor," Hamilton said. "*You* wouldn't want to find out."

The revolver came up again, this time rock-steady.

"I can't let you *fix it* . . . not ever again," Hamilton said, the big man's eyes gone as ice-cold as anything inside of Glasser.

But someone else stood behind Hamilton. Someone else with a gun—

Diana!

Glasser called out to her in a flash of unaccustomed panic, "Diana! Help me!"

In return, he felt the contempt for him that shot from Diana's violet eyes as cutting as a laser, and he remembered the blond woman in bed with him—the woman so afraid, her trembling carried through the bed.

Diana looked from the woman to Glasser.

"Help your fucking self," she said.

33

 Case glanced to his daughter at the same time that he tightened the trigger. The hammer edged back, but he lost his resolve.

The Gray Man was right about murder. He didn't have the right evils inside him. He could kill, but he couldn't do it in front of Diana.

Not this second. But maybe the next, the next, the next . . .

It would have to be done. He would have to shut death's door, once and for all.

He would have to hope that other people might still be able to find heavens of their own, and that only *his* vision of the good afterlife had been destroyed by Glasser's damned meddling.

"There's your *Doctor* Glasser," Case said, acknowledging Diana with another glance back, keeping the revolver trained on the lean man in the bed. "Looks like he's been doing a little more medical research tonight. Tough work."

He hated the sound of his voice with its mean edge. Case didn't want to hurt Diana, but he knew he had to keep talking—had to speak to keep his thoughts masked. There were walls in his mind, built to keep out the Gray Man. If he talked, he wouldn't think.

He would just pull the trigger.

In a glance, he'd seen that she had a blue-steel revolver, too: a weapon trained on *him*.

"Dad," she said, with only the slightest tremble in the voice that came from behind him. "It's over. No more of this. Drop the gun."

He didn't doubt that she would kill him if she had to, but it would take more than one shot. Nothing she could do would save the doctor's life. Nothing he imagined the Gray Man could do, either—not with Glasser held at point-blank range.

Case allowed himself to know he had the edge, so long as he stayed willing to die for it.

"One thing first, Diana." He reached up to his forehead, stripping off the round bandage that covered the tiny, black-edged hole.

"As long as the doctor is in, I've got a couple of questions for him," Case said.

He kept the revolver leveled at Glasser, watching the man's every move. Glasser looked back at him with a set to the mouth that suggested annoyance, sitting easily on the edge of the bed, red sheets twisted around his lower body.

The woman beside him apparently didn't know or care that she was left naked. She sat rod-upright on the bed, her legs folded underneath her, her hands between her breasts, clasped, her red mouth an unmoving O.

"Exactly *what* did you do to me?" Case asked, rubbing a finger of his left hand over the sore spot. "In plain language."

Glasser looked toward Diana, and then back to Case. He made a show of reaching slowly for his gray pants, pulling them on, standing up to buckle them.

"In plain language, I saved your life, you ungrateful bastard," Glasser said, true anger seeping through his cool delivery. "I brought you back from the dead."

"Yeah, you did," Case said. "Me, and something else."

"Dad." Diana's voice, stone-cold. He knew that tone. He'd heard it in his own voice, all too many times before. It was the voice that went with a cop's resolve to deadly force. "Drop the gun. Now."

The girl in the bed swallowed, but didn't move. Glasser looked suddenly interested.

"Brought something back? What are you talking about? What are these . . . *demons?*" he asked Case, drawing himself up.

"I don't know how I can say it any straighter," Case returned. "Something came back with me—something that shouldn't be here. It's not make-believe. It's not superstition. You'll be seeing it, too, I think, anytime now. It knows *you,* Doctor. It . . . admires your work."

"My work. You mean the electro—"

"I *mean,*" Case interrupted, "that this thing wants you to perform another operation on my brain, so that it can have a body—a real body. *My* body!"

Glasser looked toward Diana again, and then back to Case, licking his lips. "This—thing. Tell me about it," he said, his eyes as bright as polished ebony.

"What would you like to know, Doctor?" Case asked, keeping the revolver trained on him. Case tested the trigger. It wasn't so hard to pull. Just a squeeze, a little squeeze. His heart was beating every second with more than enough pressure to get the job done. His hand could find at least that much strength. He could do it.

He *would* do it.

Case said, "You just snip out something called the 'wellspring' inside me, and then, as near as I can tell, why, this world becomes a hell on earth. Millions of people suffer and die—innocent people along with the guilty. Of course, I wouldn't. I'd watch. And I'd love what I saw."

The hellish images the Gray Man had shown him sprang to mind again, and all over he heard the screams of the dying, the wails of the burned and tortured, saw the explosions and the fires and the eternal suffering, and the walls in his mind exploded.

His plan became action.

Aiming the revolver point-blank between Glasser's eyes, Case pulled the trigger. The gun kicked with a jolt that stung his hand.

But just as suddenly, his own image appeared in front of Glasser, the cuts on its arms writhing as it took the bullet with a shudder, staying upright, shielding the doctor.

The infant voices began their wailing from the Gray Man's tortured body, blending with the scream of the woman in the bed as she dived for the floor.

Case fired again, and saw his twin take another dead-solid hit in the chest. A gush of blood welled across the front of the white shirt—a shirt belonging to a man named Doverspike, Case fleetingly remembered—and then seemed to implode, disappearing. The cuts on the arms opened again, showing wet pink, and a fresh wave of infant yowling oscillated through the lab.

Glasser broke from behind the figure, his eyes wide. Half scrabbling, he ran past Case as Case fired at the Gray Man again, the infant screams echoing, the mouths opening and closing underneath the cold flesh.

The Gray Man straightened. It grinned—a mirror-perfect counterfeit of Case's own hard grin, but the sham expression wavered a little.

"You don't want to do this, Casey," the Gray Man said, its voice the soothing tone of a concerned parent.

"You're right," Case returned, suddenly whirling away from the Gray Man to squeeze off a shot toward Glasser.

It was the same motion he might have used as a baseball pitcher to pick off a runner stealing second base. But the runner was Dr. Stephen Glasser, making a break for the doorway in back of Case.

Case fired too quickly. The shot caught Glasser in the shoulder, throwing him against the door frame. He spun off with a howl of pain, but he kept running.

"No!" the Gray Man bellowed. It bolted toward the door, blocking Case's way. In ragged frustration, Case let another round go, hitting the Gray Man again. This time, the apparition staggered a step, another faltering step, and Case allowed himself a smile.

"How many lives?" Case asked, advancing toward the door where the Gray Man stood. "How many did you say I get with each shot?"

He fired again, and the Gray Man grabbed the door frame for support, the cuts opening and closing like sensitive flowers, the tiny screams falling in on one another.

Case glimpsed movement in the corner of his eye, saw the nude woman scramble into a corner of the lab, a scurry of perfect, pink buttocks. She hid beneath a row of glass cages.

"How many do I have to kill before you *leave me alone?*" Case shouted, the rage and hopelessness boiling up and out of him as he pulled the trigger again. The hammer clicked on an empty chamber. He clicked it again. Again. Again.

The Gray Man widened his parody of a grin. "More than you could ever believe," it said as the wails echoed behind its words.

It turned from Case, swiping its gray hand through the bright spatters of Glasser's blood on the door frame. It held the bloodied hand toward Case.

"Blood of the redeemer," it said. "Pray that he lives."

A swift two shots rang out, deafening to Case, and the Gray Man buckled, howling. A third shot, and it crumpled, thrown off its feet.

Case turned to see Diana behind him, her .38 flashing fire, pumping bullets into the Gray Man with deadly precision.

Another round. Another!

The Gray Man convulsed on the bloodied floor, rolling in spasms of rage and agony, uncounted mouths wailing to an animallike cacophony.

The unholy blaze in the Gray Man's eyes separated its face forever from the human face of Case Hamilton. As Case watched, the figure climbed to its knees, jerking as the sixth slug from Diana's revolver smacked into it, metal into solid flesh.

Its eyes rolled up, blinking in time to the breathing movement of the angry pink cuts, sucking at the air like parasitic mouths, wailing from deep inside.

And the Gray Man . . . changed.

As Case and Diana watched in silent horror, the tiny mouths began to raise up and peal outward, as though they were pulling away from underneath the skin. The wet pinkness oozed and spread, folding back into the face, the neck, the bare arms, and the thing that looked like Case Hamilton screamed an unearthly shriek of pain, an echoing, wrenching scream that drowned out the childlike cries, that drowned out everything.

The thing struggled to its feet, the body shifting and changing, the fresh pink flesh bulging everywhere with new shapes. Even the face bulged and shifted, the suddenly ice-pale eyes fixed on Case.

"You want to *see* how many are left?" the Gray Man asked in a wet, bubbling voice. The creature was red and wet as raw meat, crawling with tiny, indistinct faces. "Then look!"

The Gray Man held out mewling hands, mouths opening

like stigmata in the palms, infant faces sliding over the fingers. The hands went to the white collar, twisting, ripping the shirt open, offering air to the mouths under the cloth, exposed now to the light, writhing mounds beneath the skin, screaming to break free. Crying to be born.

Wanting Case. Calling to him.

He heard it even as he grew suddenly weak, the energy flowing from him in a torrent. He looked in the flaming eyes of the Gray Man, watched the mouth, the little mouths around it, all opening, all wanting him.

He thought he heard Diana scream beside him, and wondered why it had taken her so long.

Stephen Glasser punched the elevator button again and again, looking over his bleeding shoulder.

The car would answer his summons. He could ride it down, even though the lock prevented any other riders from reaching the fifteenth floor. When he wanted, this could be his private car.

Once safely away from Case Hamilton, Glasser would get some armed help, and then he'd secure the clearance he needed to examine the madman for physical cause of insanity.

And he would examine this patient a long time. A very long time. Even after he'd found what he needed, learned what truth there was to the man's ravings—he would find still more things to do.

Things to probe. Things to cut.

Something *had* broken into the lab—something that looked like Case Hamilton, something that seemed to appear out of nowhere.

But there had to be an explanation. Always, there had to be an explanation. And Stephen Glasser would find it, even if he had to kill Hamilton all over again. Several times.

He heard shots and screaming from the lab, at the same time he heard the soft ring of the elevator bell. He'd solve the mystery later, after the lunatic Hamilton was captured.

The elevator doors opened to Glasser's dismay—spilling out a packed load of protesters that far exceeded the elevator's safety limits.

Their dull, murmuring anger inflamed to a shout as the doors opened, and then a series of shouts.

A woman's voice: "There—that's the doctor!"

Another voice: "The one on TV. The abortionist!"

Eyes locked into Glasser's. Wild eyes. Maniacal eyes. Murderous eyes. A hand shot out, grabbing Glasser's naked arm, as the crowd surged out of the elevator.

Glasser jerked away from their grasping hands, running down the hallway toward the window that was broken out, the crowd pursuing him with shouts of fury.

A skinny youth began slinging the contents of a soft drink bottle around, splattering the walls with animal blood and chanting: "Rights for the unborn! Rights for the unborn!"

Behind him, Glasser heard a man's harsh voice, roaring something about killers and murderers. Another one, shriller, picked up the same words—a curse that rippled through the crowd.

He ran, but a calm, well-reasoned compartment of his mind was devoted to solving the problem of how to stop them. How to placate them. How to tell them what they wanted.

He reached the end of the hall, looking out the shattered window to the fire escape outside. He turned to face the advancing crowd, holding his wounded shoulder.

"Stop!" he shouted.

The mob slowed, but they didn't stop. Faces etched with anger focused on him, eyes sullen and violent. He surveyed the people, suddenly filled with contempt for them, these fools who presumed to know anything about life and death, these simpletons, ignorant villagers, who trusted to blind superstition for their answers.

"Stop!" he said more loudly, holding out his hand. "We can reason together, for God's sake."

"You're a funny one to be talkin' about God, you goddam killer," answered a thick, rough-edged male voice, dripping with mean sarcasm.

Glasser tried to pick out the person who'd spoken, couldn't. He drew his hand away from his bleeding shoulder and pointed at them, his finger smeared with blood.

"Every one of you will be arrested," he said. "If you don't leave immediately, you will be charged with breaking and entering. Think what you're doing! You're all here to advance your cause—to express your concern, a concern that I share —not to become anarchists."

Part of him worked to persuade them. Part considered the option of pulling himself through the window. "Think about it! If you value life, then start by placing a value on your own lives."

A pale, delicate-looking young woman in a white lace dress spoke in a voice broken by tears. "The man who killed my sister down there—"

Another voice: "My son! My only son!"

"It's a damned slaughter—"

The soft woman's voice cracked to sobs. "The man who . . . ran his car into us. Your man! The man you brought back from the dead! The man you called a miracle! We followed him here—to this place where you kill babies."

"That makes you a double murderer in my book, mister," gritted an older woman, her face contorted with hate. "A killer! A cold-blooded, evil-hearted killer at the end of the line."

The mob shouted as one and surged forward, reaching for Glasser, but the doctor anticipated their actions.

He threw himself out of the window onto the landing of the fire escape, slicing a shin on a piece of jagged glass. Arms, hands, reached through the window, cutting themselves, clutching and grabbing at him.

He pulled himself up on the metal railing that creaked in complaint of his weight. The landing shifted beneath him, pulling loose from the brick wall.

Only then, he heard the first of the screams that told him he hadn't begun to anticipate everything.

Case fought to keep conscious, simply to stay alive. He was aware of Diana, helping him, lifting him up.

"Dad," she said, "can you walk? Are you all right?"

Case shook away the sudden fatigue, tried to get some adrenaline pumping again.

"My . . . strength," he said. "That thing—pulled it from me. The Gray Man and me—we can't both live like this."

Diana put her hands on his shoulders, steadying him. He opened his eyes to see hers, looking at him, blinking back a glistening wetness. "You need help, Dad," she said.

"The only one who can help me now, Diana . . . is you," Case said. Their eyes locked, father and daughter.

"I love you, Dad," she said, finally, and for a moment Case thought she was going to break down. He took her in his arms, feeling his own hot tears beginning, and locked her to him.

"That's all I need," he said into her ear, and then pushed himself away, fighting the buckling sensation he felt in his knees. "Your love, and your help."

"I know. That's all I ever needed," Diana said, as he put

an arm around her shoulder, and together, they made their way to the door, Diana propping him up.

"I love you, girl," Case said.

The Gray Man was gone from the doorway, but he hadn't gone far. Case spotted it pounding down the hall, the mouths on its naked back wailing and screaming.

The Gray Man reached the rear of the mob of protesters and tore into them, grabbing a short man with his pale, writhing hands and tossing him aside with a ripping noise, snapping an arm turned the color of blue frost. The man screamed, and the other crowd members began to scatter as the Gray Man moved through them, tearing. Slashing. Murdering.

A gout of blood spurted up from somewhere in the crowd, splattering thickly against the wall.

"My God, Dad," said Diana. "My God."

"Help me," Case returned. "Quick!"

Together, they ran toward the frenzied crowd, Case forcing a renewed strength into his faltering legs.

In front, the terrified noises from the crowd rode above the moans and howls from the unborn souls carried in the body of the rampaging Gray Man. A teen-age boy scrambled past Case and Diana, his eyes wild, the bottle in his hand broken and trailing blood.

On the fire-escape landing, Glasser found himself surrounded, cut off from the steps going either way. More and more people pulled themselves through the broken window, packing against him, jamming the narrow stairs in panic, trying to force an escape route down, some of them trampling over the spawled body of the guard who liked to be called Arnie, some of them screaming at Glasser, ramming him against the railing. The landing shook, but they were oblivious to the danger.

A balding, black-bearded man in bib overalls suddenly fell back from Glasser. He was being dragged back through the window.

Others on the landing pressed themselves against the railing, and Glasser looked through them to see the snarling image of the gray thing in front of the window, twisting the man's leg, bending it the wrong way, slashing at the exposed throat.

Then, Glasser knew.

These people weren't coming for him anymore.

They were trying to escape what had come for them.

The Gray Man's red eyes looked out, fastened with Glasser's. Tiny faces, like crawling rosettes, ringed the eyes, the cheeks, the chin. It reached out a writhing hand, thrusting it through the window.

"Glassssser," said the Gray Man. "Glasssssser!" And the fingers opened, offering unholy protection.

Glasser recoiled from the gray hand—

A woman screamed next to the doctor, so close he felt the hot spittle that flew from her wide-open mouth.

The metal landing shifted, and Glasser felt the railing buckle under his weight. His feet left the platform.

Frantically, he reached to take the Gray Man's outstretched hand, but his arm didn't respond, the injured arm, the muscle not working properly.

By the time he realized the creature was trying to save him, not kill him, he was hurtling through space, the arm extended, the fingers grasping at nothing at all.

Glasser saw the windows of the building shoot past him. He watched the ground rise up.

He marveled at the detail that he could pick out below him. The bright, pinprick flashing lights of the police cars, strobing people's upturned faces red and blue.

Part of him was screaming, but he ignored that part. It was no problem. He understood his mind, and how to work the compartments.

This part of him watched the ground, calculating some slight chance of survival.

He knew people had survived falls from greater heights in events that were labeled freaks or miracles. But everything worked for a reason. There had to be a reason for survival, and he might still have the time to discover this one last secret.

Air currents. Position of the falling body. He would need to land flat in such a way that he could absorb the impact with his whole body. If he came down legs first, he would be impaled on his own fibulae.

He figured the way. And it worked.

The ground rose up to smash him, but the ground was not effective. He landed feather-light. No pain. He didn't think he'd even blinked.

The trouble was getting up.

He had no legs that he could find. He had no hands for leverage.

But he *was* alive.

He knew, because he was on his back, looking up—seeing death on its way to meet him.

34

 Case steadied himself against the wall in the chaos of the hallway. Diana stood beside him, quickly reloading her .38.

People ran toward them, falling, scudding, crawling over each other—away from the window, away from the Gray Man.

Case peered through rushing bodies to see onto the landing, hearing the wild creaking of the fire escape, the shouts from people running up, running down—running. And he saw the Gray Man raise its arms, a horrid deep yowl tearing from inside the writhing shape, echoed by the tiny screams of the pinched faces bulging from the surface of its wet, red-meat body.

Summoning all the strength he had, Case ran at the window and tackled the Gray Man, toppling with him out onto the shaky landing. Behind him, Diana shouted something to stop him, but he only heard it in a far-off, abstract way.

He wrapped his arms around the burning-cold, quivering flesh of the Gray Man's back and chest, the lumps like squirming tumors against his own flesh. The creature tried to break free, but Case wrestled it toward the railing.

"You want to be together?" he shouted. "All right, you son of a bitch! Here we go!"

It could be the vessel of a million times a million unborn lives, but those infant lives weren't going to survive a fifteen-floor drop onto the concrete in front of the flood-lit hospital.

The Gray Man screamed again, thrashing, hammering at him, but Case held on—over the railing. The whole world seemed to tilt, and then his foot clipped the railing. He tumbled headfirst into the hot, empty air.

He saw the speckled crowd beneath them, the tiny faces with their O-shaped mouths in the police floodlights, all turned upward.

A ring of them surrounded the broken body of Stephen Glasser that lay faceup in a pool of red.

Glasser saw them topple from the fire escape—two falling bodies, caught in the floods that illuminated the sides of the building, turning the old brick to a white as pure as a church steeple.

Two bodies. Locked together, struggling with each other. And the metal landing of the fire escape, a section now wrenched free, falling after them in a hail of broken brick—that, too.

He searched for his legs. Searched for his hands. Searched for his voice. Found nothing.

There had been other people's hands on him. People around him. People helping him. But they all ran away. Screaming cowards.

They left him for dead.

But he wasn't dead. He saw the falling bodies and wreckage that seemed to grow larger. Larger. Larger.

Coming down on him.

In the last instant, he thought the twisting creature

seemed to burst apart with a shriek of damnation, a great splash of blood in the air. But he couldn't be sure.

His vision went black with the impact of flesh and metal that smashed him.

Smashed most of him.

One small, damaged, nearly insane compartment of his mind stayed alive a while more to contemplate the condition of death.

He had willed his body to science—a gesture that cost him nothing, and that seemed appropriate at the time.

Now, he counted the cost, finding it higher than he ever imagined. He couldn't shut down this compartment. It promised to stay aware. A long time. A long, long time.

It would feel the knives of the autopsy.

It would feel the brain being scooped out.

It would feel him being taken apart, piece by piece, until there were no more compartments. No more secrets. No more Stephen Glasser.

The last of his mind's rational achievements was a realization—a brand-new understanding of the Frankenstein mythos.

He'd never been the doctor.

Just the monster, all along.

For Case, the ground blurred away. Time slowed to nothing. The Gray Man, twisting under his grip, began to disintegrate, the ends of its gray fingers streaming light. They were a comet in the darkness.

And the bells began to toll.

In the jangling,
And the wrangling,
How the danger sinks and swells,
By the sinking or the swelling of the anger in the bells—

Of the bells—
Of the bells, bells, bells, bells—

Case had feared the Gray Man would turn to smoke to escape him. Instead, the creature's massive body went slack. Case's fingertips pierced the gray skin, sinking like talons into the cold flesh.

The psychic window stood wide open between them, un-guarded, and Case knew the gunshots had worked to cripple the monster. But it could have recovered from gunshots.

The Gray Man was an abomination to natural law, and those laws of nature could not be denied. The Gray Man was being taken to task—taken apart, just the same as Case.

Together. One mind, joined through the window. Bonded in their degeneration. They felt so weak, so tired. So ready to die.

The light streamed from them both now, and Case saw that the light from the Gray Man's fingers carried the little faces, tearing away behind them one by one, like white death's head moths, fluttering into the night.

Until the night changed.

No more people looking up from the ground, no hospital, no hard-paved ground rising up to meet them. Instead, Case fell into an ever-widening white circle, and the burden of the Gray Man left him on wings of light.

The bells dimmed to a soft background pealing, disap-peared.

Case landed softly on the circle, enveloped by a warm, golden light. But now he saw that the white circle was a sphere—a white sphere of horsehide, stitched in red and held before him by a big, steady hand.

The Ball. Restored. Reborn.

He thought he'd destroyed all this: the human snake who'd brought death into paradise. But it seemed that heaven wasn't so fragile, after all. It wasn't just fire and ice, here behind death's door. It was life of a better, stronger kind that endured.

A tall figure moved in the light, the shape of a man in a thick, striped baseball uniform. The ball player! His hand gripped The Ball, and as Case watched, the man signed The Ball with a flourish of black ink on white leather. The big man moved again, a silhouette in profile, and Case saw hints of the face, enough to know it was a good face, a kind face.

"Here, son," the ball player said. "Sorry I didn't get this signed for you sooner." He passed The Ball to a small, sandy-haired boy.

Case couldn't make out the boy's face, but there was no mistaking the way he held The Ball, like a diamond of white fire in his hands. Around them, too, hints of other things: the cement facade of a big baseball stadium, the warm air of spring, the smell of hot dogs cooking.

"That's okay, sir," the boy said, and Case could hear the mile-wide smile in his voice. "It was sure worth the wait."

The boy turned, a shifting shape in the backlight, and held The Ball out reverently with a scuffed kid's hand.

"Here, son," said the boy, but it was Case's dad's voice. "Go ahead. Take it."

Case reached into the misty light, picking The Ball up by the seams, carefully. The big signature across the middle, right where he'd put his fingers for a fastball, glistened with the lines of the signature. Lou Gehrig.

He turned The Ball, the golden light glancing from it. From all the other signatures, too. The 1927 Yankees. The Ball. Complete for all eternity.

"Nice guy, that Mr. Gehrig," said his father, and Case looked at the shape, feeling his father's presence more than seeing him. His father was still a sandy-haired kid, full of wonder, but he also was a grown man and even an old man, and everything in between, all jumbled together like in a dream.

Case felt that he was that little boy, that man, too—that they both lived within him, and that somehow Lou Gehrig was a part of it, too.

Everything, everyone, part of the whole.

Even the Gray Man.

He felt a part of the Gray Man inside him, and he knew that the Gray Man was there, too, with its teeming load of lost souls, somewhere out there. But he also knew that the souls were no longer tortured, no longer in a place they didn't belong, no longer lost and crying in a strange land. They had done wrong, but they were back. They were back, and they had been forgiven for doing wrong just to survive.

There were people moving in the misty light. He knew his mother was there, and he saw her before him, young and old and in between, just like his dad, who stood beside her now. He couldn't see her clearly, but he could feel her as she embraced him, saying, "We're so glad to have you here with us, son." Case remembered how she used to cry about everything, how sometimes he had tried to make her cry, and how she always loved him, anyway.

He tried to respond the right way. He reached for some feeling to equal this gift, this reward out of nowhere. It called for the pure-white thoughts of a saint, but he wasn't a saint. He felt nothing but shame.

His mother stepped back, dimming away to a soft blue in the light, and Case thought: *I'm not good enough.*

The Ball seemed a handful of heartbreak.

A saint might deserve this. But not him—not a man of clay feet, mired in the sins of a lifetime. Not a man who'd regained both his life and his daughter, only to lose them again. Not a man who'd looked too deeply into his own soul, finding too much darkness there.

His was a spirit wounded by bad choices, by sullen angers and too much fear. He wasn't like the people around him. They *belonged* here; he didn't. Maybe that's why he couldn't see them.

He turned away, but his free hand was caught. His hand was held, and he knew that touch.

Green eyes. Red hair. Miracle touch.

Of course, *she* would be here. Of course, *she* belonged.

"Nobody's perfect, Case," Gwen said, standing beside him. "I don't deserve this, either. But here I am."

He tried to see her in the blurring light—caught just a glimpse of those laughing green eyes.

"I guess, well . . . we did our best," Gwen said. "I guess somebody keeps score. Somebody plays fair. I *do* know this much, Case. We've got ourselves quite a heaven here. Just look!"

But the light overwhelmed him. "How can you see it?" Case asked.

"Oh, Case, how can you *not* see it? Look! Case, it's something different every second, everywhere. We've got pasture, and peacocks—white peacocks in fields of red roses, Case! And azaleas, azaleas all over the hills, and the hills go on forever," she said. "I'll always love azaleas."

Case nodded, still unsure, still the outsider, all the same reassured by the warm touch of her. He wondered how long it would take him to know this place—to accept, if he could, that he really deserved even a tiny slice of anything like this after the mean life he'd led, the bad things he'd done, the evil thoughts he'd harbored.

But through it all, one glowing truth wove through him like a shimmering thread, stitched him together like the seams of The Ball. He felt himself giving in to a smile that was all light.

He dared to believe this. He knew it.

When it came to forever, the Gray Man had lied.

Case thought it, just as the mist and the golden light cleared from his eyes, and he saw—

EPILOGUE

Diana walked briskly toward the hospital's front entrance, careful not to look at the place on the ground where her father had fallen. She was holding together the best way she could, and there was no use in taking chances. No use in inviting sad thoughts.

Instead, she would think of her father the way he'd been the last time she saw him alive. Tall, lean, strong, brave, right, loving.

For a moment, Case had been everything in solid, real life that he'd always been in some make-believe realm of Diana's heart—in a small girl's secret dreams of the father she never had.

For a moment. And the moment would last her a lifetime.

Diana entered the lobby, swinging the paper sack she carried, hearing it crinkle.

She walked past the gift shop. The front of it was covered with plywood, posted with a smiley sign that read "Pardon our dust."

She crossed the tiled floor to the small desk where her father had kept watch in the lobby, seeing the new man on the job. Duane Hardage.

"Hello, Detective," Hardage said, standing beside the desk, rocking on the balls of his feet.

"Hello, Duane," Diana said, reaching into the bag. "It's good to see you. I'm glad you're back."

She handed him one of the bars.

"Say, thanks," Duane said, accepting the candy. "Special occasion?"

"Special occasion," she said. "I'm here to see a couple of friends."

"Let me guess, Detective. Frank Morrow. He's supposed to be in Room 321, but he's not one to stay there. Most often, he wanders down to Sergeant Bloch's room, that's 343, and the poor nurses have to go hunt for him. They keep threatening to lock ol' Frank into bed with his own cuffs. But the truth is, I think everybody's glad to see him up and around, Detective. He took an awful beating. It was a close call."

Duane seemed to delight in the directions he gave her to Bloch's room, telling her as if to point the way to the best fishing hole he knew.

It was just another room, though, 343. It wasn't hard to find.

Along the way, she passed the half-open door to 341, hearing the all-too-familiar sound of a woman's voice on the TV. Turning, she caught a glimpse of the platinum blonde on the screen of the TV set that was mounted high on the wall.

Diana paused just a moment.

The Madonna-wannabe was telling her story again, only this time to the intent host of a daytime talk show, one of those nationally syndicated wallows. She was telling how she was the only one of all the media to gain access to the fifteenth floor of Cedar Ridge.

News had been everywhere of the protest-turned-riot at Cedar Ridge. Diana had become adept at dodging reporters, offering only the flattest of comments when cornered.

Her father had fallen from the fifteenth floor. His body was found at the base of the hospital, lying near the remains of Dr. Stephen Glasser. Glasser also had fallen. She didn't know how. And those were the only two bodies found, although many people claimed to have seen more in the air.

Some of the most-quoted witnesses told in vivid description of a crying mass of fetal infants they'd seen falling from the top of Cedar Ridge.

Within hours, though, it would have been possible to find witnesses claiming to have seen falling elephants, too, each story topping the last for a chance to be seen on TV.

The door to 343 was wide open, and Diana saw Frank Morrow standing inside the room. He was wearing a blue terry-cloth robe. His throat was swathed in a mufflerlike bandage that made him appear strangely ready to go play in the snow. There were two boys involved with a board game of Sorry at the foot of the bed, two miniature Blochs, and a patiently seated woman of stout build. Diana took the woman to be Bloch's wife.

"Diana!" Frank croaked, grinning. And he would have tried to say more, but she struck him to silence with her gift from the bag.

She handed out more of the candy to both the boys, and to Bloch's wife, who introduced herself as Judy, and last of all to the man in the hospital bed—to Douglas Bloch, his stubby, broken leg wrapped in a heavy cast, suspended in traction.

Bloch seemed plainly disgusted with the awkward plight of his injury. But he brightened to see what Diana had given him.

"A giant-sized Snickers!" Bloch said, feeling the bar appreciatively through its crackling wrapper. "Pretty well gooshed up, too."

"It's been in the glove box all day," Diana said.

Frank looked at the bar in his hand as if it might leak through his fingers, but not Bloch. Bloch tore into his.

"Put away a bad one, did you?" Bloch asked.

Diana bit into the soft, sweet candy.

"No," she said. "My father did."